Don't Look Behind the Fridge

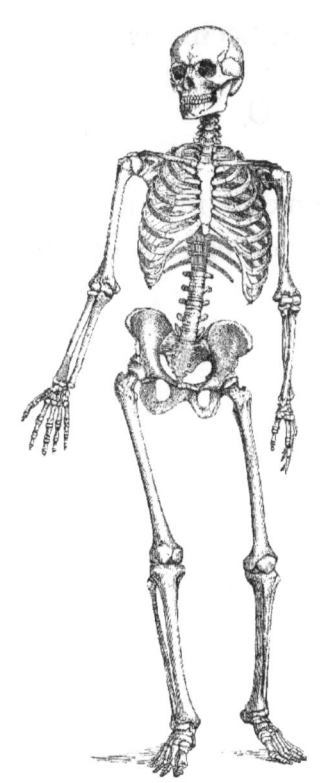

Julian Lechmus

ISBN 9780648821625

Editor Dana McCown

First printing 2023

StoryBridge Press

Brisbane, Queensland, Australia
2023

Cover design Dana McCown

PREFACE

Don't Look Behind the Fridge, is a novel full of adventure and intrique with spies and gangsters. In the setting of Melbourne's familiar places, the plot twists and turns with unusual and interesting characters and a bit of romance. Often the unexpected happens and occasionally acton is modulated with humour.

The influential characters are women, and it's LGBTplus friendly. Much of it is the observations of the main character protagonist called Jules Lemos. Jules is one of those scarred people, a biochemist who refined his father's anti-aging hormone. He returns home after a 10-year hiatus with little memory of his past that he chose to forget for painful reasons. He accidentally bombed an Iranian village that was supposed to be the headquarters of an Islamic terrorist organization, which it wasn't - a fatal mistake. So, what do you do when you're really mentally f..ked up?

Author, Julian Lechmus has written this novel about complex relationships which developed between emotionally scarred persons, some of whom worked for a fictional spy agency (i5), hired incognito by governments to perform politically unsavoury jobs that government agencies wouldn't risk.

The eight other main characters. also have complicated past stories that unravel during the adventure. The many damaged characters uncover their pasts and fears to eventually discover they have much in common, while some still have something to hide. Most of the characters are connected with the i5 agencies and want to get out.

Follow the journey.

Julian Lechmus

Chapter one

"Haven't seen you for ages, Jules, where have you been? You need a shave and some looking after. You look like that unkempt, confused time-traveller who falls out of the sky on that TV series, whatever it's called."

I'm startled and look around in apprehension. I didn't at first notice the elderly, hunched Miss Gribble from townhouse number 2 join me at the row of letterboxes facing the street.

"Hello Miss Gribble, thank you for your concern and directness. To answer your question, I'm not sure where I've been but I'm definitely not a time traveller. I have a problem with my memory, so sometimes forget to shave."

"It happens to all of us dear, sooner or later, but you remembered my name, so it can't be too bad."

I desist from saying that I saw her name on the envelope she is holding.

"You don't say much, do you? If you're not a time-traveller, I bet you're one of those sexy secret agents," she giggles whilst commenting.

"Rest assured, Miss Gribble I'm really no James Bond."

"Come dear, I'll give you a hug; you look like you need a hug."

I stiffen up and look up at the sky. Miss Gribble notices the pamphlet I'm holding in my outstretched hand. Her eyesight must still be intact.

"Jules, is that an offer for a job? I did not receive one of those in my letterbox. This must be your lucky day."

"I got to go, Miss Gribble, thanks for the hug and I will be shaven and presentable next time you see me."

"One last thing, Jules, that lodger of yours, Smithy, is it Smithy? He is a darling, and even though he is more unkempt than you, he always fixes things for us past-our-prime residents. He got my cable TV working again and before that, fixed my jammed bathroom window and he never asked for a cent. He is much appreciated by all the owners of these townhouses."

"You can never judge a book by its cover Miss Gribble. I will pass your sentiment on to him. I'm sure he will appreciate your compliment. Have a nice day."

I close my eyes and give Miss Gribble a hug before rushing to the safety of my townhouse, flopping down inside and leaning against the front door. I wipe the sweat from my brow and re-read the pamphlet.

Finally, notice the hand-written note on the floor. 'Catching up with some buddies, see yah tomorrow', it's signed Smithy.

I scribble on the note, 'Miss Gribble has the hots for you,' and leave it lying by the door.

It's not often you get invited to a job interview, especially when you haven't had a job for a very long time and still have symptoms of disorientation and little recall of how you spent the last ten years of your life. I don't even have a resume. Why would any employer even consider hiring me? Guess it was my lucky day, as Miss Gribble said.

I ring the number on the pamphlet. "St Kilda Library, how can I help you?" I explain to the receptionist about the pamphlet in my letterbox and that I would like to be considered for any employment positions. "Doctor Charmaine can interview you this afternoon at 2 pm. She will be taking a week of leave from tomorrow, so I suggest you accept the 2 pm interview."

So here I am in my bathroom, panicking a little as I try to make myself presentable for the interview. A bit rusty at the ritual of using a razor blade, but finally clean-shaven with not too much blood loss. Briefly, I reflect; when a teen I wished I had some facial hair to shave and had that manly, rugged look, but now I hate shaving and wish I was a non-facial hair teen again. Unsightly nasal hair is then painfully extracted with needle-nose pliers found in the car toolkit. The scalp hair is meticulously self-trimmed using an old pair of rusty scissors and a combination of mirrors to get to the back of the scalp. Cutting one's hair is a cathartic experience. Part of your life you don't need anymore is thrown into a dustbin, followed by a new beginning and growth, plus I always wanted to get into the DIY stuff. Clothing! What can I wear? Eventually, find some clean clothes though they don't colour coordinate too well. I'll say I'm colour-blind if questioned. I then crush a 2mg tablet of diazepam in my mouth before swallowing; it works faster when you crush it. I catch the train and arrive for the 2 pm meeting with time to spare. I also feel reasonably relaxed and tranquilized.

Just spent two hours doing something called a Psychometric Assessment on a computer terminal in the St Kilda Historical and Archives Library in Melbourne. It was my lucky day. I was the only applicant for the job. Thought more people would have applied, especially since it was advertised as a well-paying local government initiative to help the long-term unemployed. Maybe the others didn't check their letterbox or dismissed the flyer as too good to be true.

It's time to go into the office and face the assessor. I tend to avoid one-to-one interactions with strangers. I wipe the beads of sweat from my forehead before going in. The diazepam must be wearing off.

I'm stunned. I rub my eyes. She doesn't belong here, maybe on the set of a comedy TV sitcom but not in this conservative institution. She's dressed in a loose unbuttoned blue medical gown, blue skirt, loose black tie and blue fishnet stockings visible below the knee. Long blond hair with a fringe descending to her eyebrows, about 173cm in height, maybe 35 years old, slim, clear pale skin, big blue eyes, low curved nose and displaying more than a bit of cleavage. She re-adjusts her blue-rimmed glasses and inspects the contents of the blue folder she's holding. A strange association, a name, 'Blue Monkey' briefly flashes past my consciousness as I watch her but cannot make out the meaning, but that would change. Strangely, I start to feel comfortable in her presence and the anxiety eases.

"You're a borderline, goodie, goodie!" the clinical psychologist gleefully announces in a slightly husky voice as she claps her hands in joy.

I'm a bit perplexed and sceptical. It's not the persona I'd expect from someone in her position; it's more of a self-parody. She seems almost childish, and she talks so loud.

"What sort of borderline? What do I border on?"

"Well Jules, according to your psychometric chart - wait, do you want to hear the good news or the bad news first?"

"I'll take the bad news first."

"Correct response according to your chart," she jubilantly exclaims. "You measure high on obsessive compulsiveness, low on emotive cognition, low on self-esteem and high on depressive/anxiety tendencies. You're also on the borderline of the Autism spectrum but have no sociopathic tendencies, so you're definitely not management material and not likely to climb the corporate ladder in any corporate environment."

I lower my head. Justifications rush through my head. Why would I want to work in a library anyway, with all those annoying people?

"I guess I don't get the job?"

"Don't be so serious. I tricked you. That was actually the good news. The bad news is that you have high spatial, analytic and numerical skills. You could be bored in this job. You probably wouldn't last a week."   "Doctor Charmaine, I nee..."
"Just call me Charmaine."

"Charmaine, I need the job. I haven't worked for a very long time. I believe I can be reliable. I like books and can be accommodating to annoying people. I need a chance to prove myself. It would take some major disaster for me to resign from the job."

She looks up from the folder and I notice the hearing aid nested around her ear. Maybe that's why she talks so loudly.

"Well, let's hope that no major disasters happen too soon. There's work to do. Now back to the chart. Wow, you're a bit of a rarity, and I'll have to devise a new classification scheme to accommodate you, but I'll certainly recommend that you be hired. We need someone like you for the library, especially in the archives section."

"What, why?"

"Jules, the archives section is quiet and has hardly any visitors. You'd be scanning historical newspapers and documents and computerizing that section so anyone can access the material over the Internet on their computer or iThingo."

"But why cannot I work in the main library?"

"Jules, you probably could. You'd always put the books, magazines and newspapers in their right place on the shelves, pickup up any rubbish, but you may get perturbed by the occasional angry and troublesome customers who are upset because their pitiful family history documents are currently on loan."

"Does that happen often?"

"You bet it does, Jules. Just last week, we had to hire a security guard because Beatrice, she's a 100% cogni-emotive, suffered from extreme trauma after a disagreement with some of the residents from the local retirement village who visited the library. She went wild, pulling books out of bookshelves and throwing them at those elderly citizens. She had to be restrained. That was definitely not a good publicity scene, especially as it was recorded on a Smartphone camera and appeared on one of those trashy TV current affairs programs. We can't take any chances and besides, the position description on the pamphlet clearly stated the job responsibility as the digitization of historical documents."

My mind wanders. The thought crosses my mind of Beatrice being whacked on the head by a little old lady yielding an umbrella.

"Hope Beatrice is OK, but Charmaine, what is this cogni-emotive stuff?"

"Jules, you weren't supposed to show any concern for Beatrice. I've diagnosed you're worth as a 50% cogni-emotive. If you've learned to feign emotional responses, I can put that down in my report as an abhorrent but an extenuating factor."

I need a job but feel intimidated by this encounter. She makes no sense and talks so fast and loud. The thought crosses my mind again; is this some 'hidden camera' comedy show being filmed that makes fun of interviewees?

"I've learned to be polite and to give the impression of being concerned."

"Whoopee!" exclaims Charmaine.

Momentarily I clasp my ears with the palms of my hands. "Charmaine, how does this work? If I was a normal, suitably qualified guy and applied for this position, would I have a chance of getting the job?"

"Oh Gawd, no! As a 50% cogni-emotive, you just count as half a virtual headcount. That means we can hire another person who is also a 50% cogni-emotive. Local government encourages the employment of cogni-emotive challenged people below the 75% virtual rating."

My head is spinning. What's she talking about?

"And what about your previous jobs? Let's talk about those," she asks.

"Does it matter? You told me I'd be recommended for the position."

"I'm just trying to get a well-rounded impression of you. The psychometric test doesn't tell it all."

I sink back in the chair. "I have little memory of my significant past, well at least the last 14 years. Maybe I hit my head and got some sort of amnesia, but I can't remember much. Fourteen years ago, I believe I may have worked as a Pharmacologist for a Swedish Pharmaceutical company, well that's what a previous old job offer letter implied, along with some other paperwork I still have. The only photo that remains is of me holding an award for 'Individual Excellence' beside a tall bald guy. The photo is low resolution, so I can't make out the name of the company engraved on that bronze trophy. In fact, the 'me' doesn't even look quite like me, well at least not what I look like now."

"Jules, that would be easy to trace on the Internet. Why didn't you? Why did you leave that job? Why didn't you check with the local hospitals if any surgery was performed on you?"

"I can't remember, and I don't really want to find out."

"So, you have a repressed memory disorder as well. Why don't you go back to that line of work?"

She momentarily grimaces and grabs her right shoulder, massages it as if in some sort of pain while still looking at me.

"I had been out of it for too long. The industry has progressed, and I'm out of touch with the new discoveries. For example, out of curiosity, I read a pharmaceutical report on a new anti-depressant drug the other day. It discussed neuron receptors I hadn't heard of before. My understanding of the report was minimal. I can't go back and not sure if I even want to."

"Are you currently taking anti-depressant or anxiety medication?"

"No. Yes, but does it have anything to do with this job application? I lead a reasonably functional life, it's just that there are things in the past that I can't remember, and that's the only thing that worries me a little."

I said too much, but she seems unperturbed.

"Your medication history is of no concern as long you're reliable and turn up to work relatively sober and functional. There's a job to be done. Now, how do you feel working with transgender people? We have a few of those working at the Library."

"I think one may have saved my life a long time ago. I have no prejudice and a debt to repay."

"Do you want to talk about that?"

"No, not now, maybe another time, anyway I don't remember the details; I only get flashes of my past and they don't quite make sense."

"That's OK. It won't affect your job application. You might choose to attend the Mindfulness classes I run once a week on a Friday lunchtime. Unfortunately, Beatrice never attended. Now back to basics, can you remember what you did yesterday and the day before?"

"Sure, I painted a wall in my townhouse. The first job wasn't perfect, so I painted it again and again and again until it was perfect. It took two days to paint that one wall. Charmaine, my memory is getting better."

"Do you keep diaries?"

"Yes, I write down everything, at least for the last 14 years. My memories may be in those diaries. If you asked me what I did on November 22nd, two years ago, I could find the relevant diary entry, but I think I may have encoded it. The entries make no sense to me. I'm just typing all those diary entries into a Word Processing program and storing the transcripts on a USB Flash drive. It's easier to carry than fourteen years' worth of diaries. So far, I've typed the contents of the first 12 years since keeping records. There is a character called 'Blue Monkey' that is mentioned a lot. In fact, those diaries are more like kids' books, almost baby talk. Maybe I'll publish them one day and become a kid's book author."

For a fraction of a second, Charmaine's jaw drops, and her eyes open very wide, but then we're interrupted by a large, rotund, intimidating matronly lady who enters the meeting room. My guess is she has a Bulldog as a pet. I lower my head.

"Any good Charmaine, does he fit the criteria?"

"He's perfect, Ms Valda," Charmaine replies in a quivering voice.

"Good job Charmaine," Ms Valda comments before leaving the meeting room. Charmaine straightens her collar and regains her composure.

"I know your next question, Jules. The answer is that our government funding is based on virtual headcount units, and so is the catering for the Christmas Party and Ms Valda's management ranking and future promotions. We don't care that much about the real headcount though it can be a pain and should probably be factored into the equation. Anyway, congratulations, you've done well."

I'm a bit puzzled. Her sentence constructions when she speaks; they are similar to mine. I also use the word 'anyway' a lot when I speak.

"Charmaine, did you do that psychometric test?"

"Of course, Jules, everyone who works at the library has to do it, even us who are part-timers or on a contract."

I look up at Charmaine. "What was your score?"

"I'm a 100% normal cogni-psycho," she exuberantly announced as if proud of it. "You want to go out on a date?" She asks.

It's all been too much. It seems like a totally inappropriate question from someone in her position. My head starts spinning again and I feel faint due to hyperventilation. "I'm married," I gasp.

"You don't look like a married guy; you're too unkempt despite some failed efforts to look presentable, though likeable because of your lack of a sense of humour. Who is the lucky girl?"

My mind goes blank. I try to think of a female name and finally emit, "Celeste is her name."

"Is Celeste attractive like me?"

"She's a sandy-coloured Labrador dog, my neighbour's pet," I mutter, still dazed and confused.

"So, you married your neighbour's Labrador. You must be good at the doggy position. Whoopee, a dysfunctional animal lover! I'm going to rate you at 25% cogni-emotive, whoopee; this means we can employ another dysfunctional virtual unit to work at the library. Ms Valda will be super pleased!"

Embarrassingly I sink back in the seat, wondering what I have just said and whether it will be published on some Internet Website and get me arrested and put in jail.

"Have I still got the job?"

"You sure have. The paperwork will take a week. There will be a police check, so you have to sign this authority document for the Police check. It doesn't include doggy checks," she giggles.

"I do, well I mean I will, I have nothing to hide."

For a brief moment, she moves her face across the table and stares intensely into my eyes. "Jules, we all have something to hide, something we don't want anyone else to know." She then relaxes back in her chair. "We'll see you next Monday."

"Thanks."

I was halfway down the stairwell exit when feeling the cold, I realised I had left my cardigan in the interview room. It's one of those daggy cardigans that mostly retirees wear, but I like it anyway. I ascend back up but come to a sudden stop at Charmaine's door, which is slightly ajar. I peek in. She has the speakerphone on as she re-adjusts her stockings whilst holding a conversation. I stay motionless and inconspicuous.

"Whoopee! You owe me, Jase. Gawd, he looks like you but not as suave. He's eager to take the job and I've recommended he be hired. He wouldn't do the dating thing, so I'll have to get the info by more devious means. He's storing the contents of most of his diaries onto a USB flash drive. I saw the drive. He fiddles with it when he's anxious. And by the way, is he really married to a Labrador?"

"Charmaine, I'm worried about you and your strange conclusions. He's still legally married to Margaret Milstein, and she's no dog."

"Say hello to Marg for me," Charmaine hesitatingly replies.

"I will, but Charmaine, be subtle. He's fragile, and if you push him too hard everything will be lost."

"Jase, honey, you know Subtle is my middle name. One last thing Jase; is this Jules guy the brain-dead guy that tried to drown himself in his neighbour's pool ten years ago?"

"Enough, Charmaine. He still has something Marg and I want. Just be gentle with him."

"He's weird, but I'll do my best."

"Just try to get that USB drive and find out if backups exist and where he keeps those backups."

"What's on that USB drive that makes it so precious?"

"If you got know, it's the manufacturing process of the peptide that made Marg's therapy so successful. Marg blocked all his memories regarding their past, but if you fail, I'll have to set up a 'situation'. It will be traumatic for him, so suggest you don't fail."

"Who's Marg again?"

"I just said before that she's still his legal wife. Sometimes calls herself Alona. Yes, yes, yes, Charmaine; they are still legally married even after being separated for over ten years."

"Oh f..k. So, Jase honey, you are screwing a married woman?"

"It's not like that, Charmaine, it's a lot more complicated. Trust me for once."

"How low do you want me to go? You know me, Jase. I'm a go-getting type of gal. You should remember the after-hours study sessions we had at university, and you sort of liked the kinky stuff."

"Charmaine, this is also about the potential collapse of e-commerce and Public Key Encryption, not just the peptide. Can you comprehend that? Marg and I are also implicated, as Marg did do some work for the underworld. Now, I've kept your secret and I expect you to keep mine."

"So, I'm the kingpin, oops, queenpin?"

"Shut up and listen or we're all in danger. I just need you to do one thing – get that USB drive and find out if he keeps backups. I want those backups as well. One in two hundred recipients of that peptide produced kids with severe genetic, physical disorders but very high cognitive abilities."

"That's heavy stuff, the genetic disorders. Should be easy though, but what's in for me, Prof? Can I still call you Prof?"

"I'll make sure you get the promotion as quickly as possible, and $50k will be transferred into your bank account. There's a senior vacancy in Community Services. I'll make sure you get the job. I got connections."

"Jase, with your connections, you should enter Parliament maybe as a senator."

Charmaine turns off the speakerphone, muffles the microphone with her hand and mutters a few expletives. "Screw you, Jase, those videos of that big-headed-kid breaking encryption codes were very cleverly faked." She slams the phone down.

My body twinges like some electric shock has been applied then I quietly retreat down the stairs, intrigued by overheard conversation but conveniently try to dismiss it. It must be referring to someone else.

I feel a sense of self-satisfaction; you may call it happiness as I wipe the sweat from my forehead. I pulled it off and got the job. That's all I can think about and the fact that I may have once had a wife, who I can't remember, doesn't seem to concern me at the moment. I'm in the 'here and now'. Sometimes it's good to have no past.

Don't feel like being on a crowded train, so in a pre-occupied state walk back to my townhouse, though take a few wrong turns. I walk past the memorabilia shop and for the first time, notice the 'Blue Monkey' pennant hanging in the window display. It's a small monkey, maybe 3cm long, made of some blue translucent stone and suspended on a heavy silver chain. "How much?" I ask the elderly Chinese shopkeeper whilst pointing at the pennant.

"It is very rare and has a long tragic history. It is not for the faint-hearted."

"How much?"

"For you, $2000."

I examine the pennant with a magnifying glass that lies on the counter. "The monkey has a chip missing from its right shoulder, and its right ear is also damaged."

"OK, for you, $800."

"I have a credit card, but I may have exceeded its limit."

"Give it to me, sir; I'll try to make the transaction. Enter your pin."

"No worries, sir, the transaction was accepted. I will wrap Blue Monkey for you. It will make a very special gift for someone you love or may have loved."

"Thanks, don't wrap it. I'll just hold it."

I'm walking, clutching the Blue Monkey, hoping it will trigger a memory or flashback. Someone is mowing a grass lawn - the smell of freshly mowed grass. Smell is probably the most important memory trigger we possess. It triggers a flashback of my deceased father mowing the lawn and me sitting outside and sniffing that smell. Then that 1970's song, 'Emerson, Lake and Palmer' – 'Lucky Man' emanates from my townhouse at the back of the long driveway. I remember that song. Have to tell Smithy, my tenant, to keep the stereo down low. Have to maintain a low profile in this salubrious neighbourhood. Then again, Smithy has done a good job keeping all the fussy neighbours placated for so many years, and I like his choice of music. I relate to the song at the moment, though not the fateful ending.

I open the front door and notice, for the first time, the clean, spotless lounge. It was probably like that before, but I never paid any attention. I'm now noticing. Smithy's framed his Medal of the Order of Australia, and it affronts me as it hangs above the fireplace. He got that medal after his service in Afghanistan. He is another scarred human being. We haven't talked much since I've been back from wherever. We just smile at each other and luckily have the same taste in TV programs, music and takeaway food, but otherwise, we lead very separate lives.

"Smithy, I'm grateful you looked after the house so well, and Miss Gribble expressed her gratitude for helping her and the other unit owners, but you got to find another house to mind. I need my space. Could you find alternative accommodation and I'll certainly recommend you and write a very positive reference?"

Smithy looks more unkempt than I did before prettying myself up for the interview. He's a big burly guy with long untidy, slightly greying hair, long beard, moustache, and wears a baggy tracksuit and worn-out runners. He could have been that character in a Harry Potter movie, no makeup required. I can't imagine when he showered last as he smells of sweat, but the townhouse is spotless.

"But, but can't I stay here?"

"You want to die prematurely?" I don't know why I said that; maybe it was some premonition.

"What could be worst, you gonna kill me? I died inside ten years ago."

"Smithy, I just need my space and you need your own; plus you're a slob even though you do keep the house perfectly presentable."

"Who are you to comment? The times you've returned from wherever you've been, I've had to put up with your nonsensical ravings, and you stunk as well. I had to bathe you and feed you. Who is she?" Smithy less than subtlety enquires as he grabs my throat. I reciprocate, holding his neck, which I can barely grab a hold of because it's so wide. We both let go and flop on the couch, panting. Smithy gets up and grabs two cans of beer from the fridge and tosses one to me. We sit on the couch and once our panting ceases, we scull the beers.

"There's a thirty-pack of canned beer in the kitchen cupboard. It's warm beer; hasn't been refrigerated yet." Smithy says as he fumbles his way to the kitchen and returns with the carton of beer. "Just pretend we're English. They like warm beer."

We are competing, taking turns to hand each other a can of beer and downing it as quickly as possible.

Awaking next morning was quite a shock. My head is against a snoring Smithy's shoulder on the couch. Have a slight hangover, but it's not too bad. I drastically need a pee.

I recall what I suggested to Smithy; 'move out'. Now I think I may miss him and regret what I said. Smithy wakes up some two hours later, sounding perfectly sober, though makes a dash for the toilet. When guys share a living arrangement, they rarely bother closing the toilet door. You hear it all. Smithy must have the largest bladder in the world. After what seemed like an eternity, he comes out.

"Your bills are filed and paid for as you instructed. And Jules, I have friends who can help if you are in some sort of trouble."

"Smithy, thanks but you got to move on. Smithy, I'm not sure if any of this is real anymore. And Smithy, thanks again, the house looks great, and the neighbours really appreciate you."

Smithy comes over and gives me a hug, something I was unprepared for, and I flinch. I feel uncomfortable hugging, especially with big, burly smelly guys and little old ladies.

"Jules, it's OK, mate, you saved me the job of telling you myself. I thought you'd be upset but here goes; with the money I saved minding your house rent-free for all those years, I accumulated enough to put down a healthy deposit on my own apartment. I've purchased one. Also got an inheritance, so it's all paid off. It's around the corner from your place, and I have just given the tenants a month's notice as they're not on a lease. You're invited to my apartment housewarming party. It's in a month, no actually it's in 2 weeks, the tenants moved out early. I hope you can make it and bring some friends, preferably ladies, as my friends are males, gentle ex-veteran males. And mate, can you help me go furniture and kitchenware shopping?"

"Congratulations on your purchase, Smithy. Of course, I'll help you do some furniture and cutlery shopping." With some reluctance, I hug the guy. We both feel relieved.

Smithy walks away to his bedroom as if a great weight has been lifted off his shoulder, just as mine has. I go to the fridge and grab another beer, except there's none there. Only half the slab of warm beer is laying near the couch alongside about 18 empty cans strewn across the floor. I guess it's been one of those male bonding sessions. I plonk on the couch and ponder – I'll have to learn how to keep a house tidy; the instructions should be on some Internet website.

Smithy and I go shopping to purchase furniture, cookware, towels, toiletries and all those other things you need when starting up a home. We make many car trips over the next few days and deposit the purchases in Smithy's apartment. The large items are delivered by truck, and there's a lot of unpacking and assembling to do in Smithy's new apartment. And so the week passed quickly without any incident, apart from a minor spat about the colour of the couch to buy at the discount furniture store.

When not shopping or assembling furniture, Smithy and I go on long walks along the beach track, drink a lot of beer afterwards and watch crap on TV. He also helps me complete all the job documentation that arrived by post. You know that stuff about superannuation and bank details for your salary payments and who to contact if you accidentally cark it – that was the hard one. I name Smithy as next of kin even though we're not related. Other family members may be deceased, as far as I know. Smithy is the only person I know.

Then Monday finally arrives, the first day of work at the library. I'm slightly panicking. Had set the alarm clock 3 hours early; it's only 6 am. Three hours to get dressed and make the 3km journey to the library. When did I last do the clothes washing? Eventually, find some clothes that don't pong too much. Luckily have a bottle of Cologne and liberally apply the spray on the clothes and all over myself.

I got to the library an hour early and am shivering in the Melbourne spring weather. Finally, the library doors open. The formalities of being a new employee don't take too long, and I'm given one of those plastic keycard passes that looks like a credit card. A tall, skinny lady, grey curly-haired, guides me down the stairs to the library archives. "This is what you have to do, Jules. I will demonstrate. It's a simple process."

"I'm sorry, but what is your name?"

"My name is Doris. I'm the tea lady, we still have those here, thank God, and I run the library cafeteria. Luckily there aren't too many patrons anymore as I do the cooking as well as serving the occasional customers who don't like those automatic food dispenser machines."

"You must indeed be a busy lady," I comment. The thought crosses my mind; why isn't Doris doing the archiving job? It's probably better paid than serving coffee and sandwiches. At the time, I didn't know or remember that 'tea lady' was the code for the most powerful women who worked behind the scenes for a global intelligence agency.

Doris is guiding me through the scanning process. She then watches me as I carry out the process. I can see her partial reflection on the computer screen and feel a bit uneasy by her close proximity.

It doesn't take me long to learn the sequence of tasks as Doris is a humble but good instructor. She is motherly but a watchful figure. I'm a bit suspicious or just plain paranoid. Much later, I would find out who Doris, the tea lady, really was; a perfect cover, almost.

On the third day, I make a wrong turn in the downstairs library archives corridors. My keycard opens a sliding, mirrored door. I take a few steps inside.

I never imagined a library could have so many glass-walled meeting rooms, and all seem occupied, some with what looks like military personnel in uniform. I thought I saw Doris in one of those rooms. I quickly turn around and walk back. My keycard would never open that sliding door again; out of curiosity, I tested it. I dismiss the unexplainable incident. It doesn't fit into my current view of the world.

Another week passes quickly, and I'm furiously scanning old local newspapers and converting them to digital format – PDF files, more accessible since people can view them online on the library Web site. That's life at the library at the moment, and I'm left alone, except for Doris, who brings down coffee for morning and afternoon tea.

I go up to the cafeteria, which coincidentally times with Charmaine's arrival for lunch. Even though she implied that she only works part-time at the library, she seems to be here every day since I started employment. We sit at the same table and talk.

Our conversations have been about trivial stuff, such as do I like the performer Lady Gaga. We discussed what the possible meanings of her songs and videos could be, which she enthusiastically shows me on her Smartphone. She insisted it was not just pop culture but a political statement. In the end, she had me convinced. She also keeps on asking if I remember my past.

Doris comes over to take our lunch order.

"Doris, how's your son doing?" Charmaine hands a carefully rapt gift to Doris.

Doris opens the gift and exclaims, "It's the part of the puzzle I've been missing - the Silver Beetle!" She enthusiastically hugs Charmaine. "Thank you, Doctor Charmaine, this means so much to me. You must have gone to a lot of trouble to get this, thank you. And my son, he's changed a bit but otherwise seems fine. I'm sure he'll get back in line."

Charmaine and Doris both briefly glance at me as if observing my reaction. I remain motionless; besides, their conversation means nothing to me.

"Doris, please just call me Charmaine".

After Doris leaves, Charmaine turns to me. "How's your Labrador friend going?"

"You know that wasn't serious. I mean, there was no Labrador. I was nervous and anxious at the interview. I said things I couldn't live down to. I mean, I never really did that stuff. My neighbour doesn't even have a Labrador."

"So, how are things really going?" She looks up as she stuffs her mouth full of the Burger Special.

"Fine. Making good progress. Will take at least another year to get all those documents scanned."

"You like it down there?" she coughs and sends scraps of burger in my direction. I brush them off my shirt and face.

"It's peaceful and quiet."

"Well, you're making good progress. Ms Valda is happy with your work."

I may not be the brightest spark in the world, but I notice her attention on the little USB flash drive that I fiddle with when socially encountered. I remember the overheard conversation with 'Jase' and the instructions he gave Charmaine.

"Hey, I have a favour to ask."

"Fire away, Jules, I'm here to listen."

"Would you accompany me to a party? I've been asked to bring someone and a few single ladies. You probably know some. It's Smithy's, my previous house tenant and house minder; well, anyway he's having a flat warming party. Smithy is the guy who's been looking after my place for about ten-plus years, and he's finally purchased his own flat. He's a nice guy and has several other ex-veterans attending. I imagine his friends are good guys as well. I don't really particularly want to go, but it would be easier if accompanied. It's on a Saturday starting at 5 pm."

She checks her calendar on her Smartphone. "I'm free. I will speak to the rest of the girls once I finish this burger. Wow, this is a good burger. You should order one."

"Charmaine, for how long did you know?"

"Know what, Jules?"

"What you are."

"What am I, Jules, apart from a human being? And what are you, Jules? Have you worked that out yet? How much time does it take? I'm just a human being who may have made a few mistakes and may not be quite what I seem. Now, order the burger; it's yummy."

I have no conscious idea why I asked Charmaine that question; it just came out of my mouth. I glance around. It's only Charmaine and me at the library cafeteria. I order a Burger Special even though I'm mostly vegetarian. Don't want the place closing down due to a lack of patrons.

Five minutes later, the smiling Doris lays the burger on the table. I thank her and then hone into it, making sure none of it lands on Charmaine's face or attire.

"Charmaine, would you like to come over tonight? Just for some Lentil soup. Nothing else, though there are a few coincidences I would like to discuss with you in private."

"Sure, Jules, give me your address. No, you don't have to, it's in your job application. I can look it up."

That night I copy the USB flash drive to two other flash drives that I purchased on my way home from work.

I have no idea what's so precious on that USB drive that I can't even read because it's encoded, and I have no memory of what coding was used for the plain text or the encryption key for the jargon stuff. I copy the contents of the original USB drive to the ones I had just purchased. Just in case, I do a deep reformat of the original USB drive ten times over, far more than what's required by security standards to erase previous content. There is no way the original content can be recovered. I then copy the digitised versions of my favourite music - Leonard Cohen, Bob Dylan, and Dire Straits albums onto the original USB drive.

Charmaine arrives, and I feel totally left out. Smithy had popped over to collect the last of his belongings and is totally dominating the conversation whilst I cook the Lentil soup. I can't get a word in as he mesmerises Charmaine with his wartime stories in Afghanistan. Smithy has also had a shave, a haircut, dyed his hair to get rid of the grey and is wearing clothing more suitable for a 30-year-old hipster. He must be on a radical diet because he's looking a lot trimmer or is wearing a girdle.

I should have kicked Smithy out of the townhouse earlier. I'm a bit angry and I do feel a sort of envy, a feeling I'm not comfortable with, and that goes against Charmaine's initial diagnosis that I don't feel, and then there is another flash of a 'Blue Monkey' in my mind that probably makes things even worst.

I slam the Lentil soup in front of Smithy, give him a slightly nasty look and gently, with a smile, lay a bowl in front of Charmaine. I also leave the USB flash drive at the kitchen table, the bait, the one with the music.

The night ends at about 11 pm. I never got to have that private conversation with Charmaine. Smithy calls a taxi and escorts Charmaine to the cab. The USB flash drive is gone. Charmaine was quite tipsy, and maybe I could have gotten some information out of her, but Smithy was there.

Smithy and I don't exchange many words before he departs with a couple of bags of clothing. I notice a telephone number scribbled in biro on his left forearm.

Next Monday morning, I'm in the dungeons of the archives section of the library, busily scanning newspaper articles. Charmaine ventures down. She gives me a big slap in the face, and I bow down in pain. She starts going back upstairs while uttering, "I found it in the carpark," and with a disgusted look on her face, she throws the flash drive at me.

The week passes and it's Saturday. Hadn't seen Charmaine in the cafeteria all week, but she arrives at my house ready for Smithy's party, dressed in a skimpy, ostentatious Leopard skin outfit oozing sexuality. She claps her hands and exclaims a loud 'whoopee'. I nervously glance around the front door, wondering if any neighbours had seen her come in.

"Charmaine, you're going to have to wear something a bit more conservative.

I'm driving you back to your place so you can change into a long dress, and could you desist from the whoopees."

Charmaine comes over and kisses me. "You're right, Jules, it's time to move on."

The old VW beetle car miraculously starts, and we drive to her apartment. It's a short drive. She turns the music on as she does numerous costume changes and then parades. I seem to know my pop hits pretty well. A 'T-Rex' track 'Cosmic Dancer' is playing on repeat playback. The music track is sort of sad but hypnotic. I wonder if Charmaine is trying to tell me something; I'm a bit worried about her. The music that enchants us reveals a lot about ourselves. A song I put on repeat playback when at home is a 1970s song – 'Eve of Destruction (Barry McGuire)'. It's not a happy song.

While cracking my knuckles due to boredom between her costume changes, I quietly open the door to her spare bedroom or study, whatever you want to call it.

I glance around and look in astonishment at the affirmations plastered all over the walls, written in bold blue Texta pen on sheets of butcher paper. 'Think positively, don't care what anyone else thinks or says. Love yourself for what you are', and hundreds and hundreds of others plastered on any wall space available. Then another one, 'You have a job to finish'. Below that is a sticker of a blue chimpanzee swinging through a tree about to catch what appears like a wounded silver beetle. I quickly exit and close the door before she comes out again.

"Is this conservative enough, Jules? It's blue or should I wear pink?"

"Blue will be fine. We're running late, and I like your choice in music."

I give Charmaine a monstrous hug. Her story through the affirmations makes my journey seem minuscule.

"Charmaine, have our pasts crossed before?"

"I'll leave that for you to work out," she replies. She doesn't seem to want to talk. I glance at her. She's not her usually talkative, bubbly self. She is unusually reserved and keeps rubbing her left shoulder as if in pain.

The girls are waiting outside the patio entrance as Charmaine and I parade into Smithy's new apartment. Five beings enter Smithy's household. Beatrice, Edwina, Laura, Charmaine, and me. All apart from me, look stunning. Smithy and three well-aged, silver-haired bikies, ex-veterans greet us. It's not unexpected. Three Harleys are parked outside the apartment.

The ladies are served champagne and presented with platters of smoked oysters and other delicacies. I look and observe. These guys are total gentlemen despite their appearance, which on closer observation, appears like they have gone to a lot of trouble to be presentable. Smithy looks trim and also well presented. He must not have eaten for the last two weeks. I look the odd person out.

The conversations are lively and there are smiles on every face. I kind of feel awkward in these party situations, so I sit in the living room, observing the patio and glancing into Smithy's photo album, which lay on the coffee table.

After a brief chat with Smithy, I watch Charmaine, who is socialising with all the guests. By my count, she has downed five glasses of champagne and appears a little bit wobbly on her feet. A confusing thought flashes by - Charl never drank alcohol.

A couple of hours must have passed. All the other guests are still standing and chatting loudly on the patio. It's cooler there—another Melbourne weather anomaly – freezing one hour and stinking hot the next. Charmaine makes a quick journey to the bathroom. She returns wobbly but bubbly and sits next to me in the lounge room. She mutters in my ear, "where's the real flash drive?"

"Don't know what you're talking about, except my USB drive containing my favourite music disappeared after your visit a week ago. Thanks for finding it in the carpark because I don't have backups." In the background, a music track is playing on the sound system. The same song Charmaine was playing in her apartment. She must have converted Smithy.

It's time to stretch the legs and see what the other guests are doing. From the patio, I see the usually high-strung Beatrice laughing and hopping on a Harley motorcycle with Jones, one of Smithy's friends. Edwina is embracing with Edwin and exchanging saliva. Laura seems to be having a lively discussion with Thomas. They all seem pleasantly occupied. Smithy is serving drinks. I return back to the couch where Charmaine is sitting. Her eyes seem barely open. I sit down next to her. Her head limply slumps against my shoulder. She is muttering, but I can't make out what she is saying.

Smithy comes inside and notices the slumped body. "What's wrong with Charmaine?"

"I'm not sure, but I believe she may have mixed a painkiller and champagne. She normally doesn't drink alcohol."

"I'll call an ambulance," Smithy responds in a panicky voice.

"No, Smithy, don't do that just yet. Check the rubbish bin in the bathroom for any medicinal wrappers. I'll check her handbag."

"Nothing in bin," Smithy says.

"Nothing in her handbag either, apart from some aspirins. She has a shoulder injury. Smithy, she normally doesn't drink alcohol, and yet she had at least five glasses of champagne whilst here. She may have no tolerance to alcohol. She is most likely just alcohol intoxicated."

Charmaine suddenly lurches forward and makes a guttural sound. Smithy and I quickly help her to the bathroom. She is expelling the contents of her stomach into Smithy's pristine toilet bowl.

"Smithy, I got to get her out of here quickly, without her work colleagues seeing the condition she's in. Is there another way out without going through the patio?"

"There is the back exit and through the car park. It's not visible from the patio."

"It's time to leave."

"I'm leaving too. I'll walk you home. The guests can lock up. I'll leave them the spare key," Smithy announces.

"Smithy, tell 'em I got it, tell them I had an allergic reaction to oysters, and you and Charmaine will help me get home."

"Not a good idea, the 'oysters' thing. It may cause panic. I'll just say you forgot to take your medication."

I hear Smithy announcing to his guests, "Don't drive. You can stay at my place."

"Smithy, we're all quite sober. Do you need a hand getting him home?" Edwin asks.

"No, it's fine. Charmaine and I will manage. Thanks all for coming and keep partying."

We take turns in propping up the stumbling Charmaine back to my place. Fortunately, Miss Gribble wasn't outside in the driveway.

We arrive hot and sweaty and help Charmaine to the couch. She flops her head down. Smithy fills a water bottle in the kitchen and then gently holds Charmaine's head up as he tries to get her to drink.

"Smithy, thanks. I can handle it from now on."

"I'm not leaving Jules."

"If you stay here, you have to shower; you can also help me shower, Charmaine."

"What? Are you some kind of weirdo?"

"No, and it's my home. There is a practical reason for that. Showering washes off dead skin cells, which all sorts of bed bugs love to feed upon. They're not getting a free meal in my bed. If you want to stay, you will have to help me and shower, but I suggest you leave."

"No, I'm staying!"

"Smithy, Charmaine is not quite what she appears to be. If you say anything offensive …."

"I'm staying I said."

We carefully help Charmaine undress.

"Jules, she has lovely breasts but also a small penis. Is it real?"

"This is our secret. Did you get that? Charmaine is transgender though more of a hermaphrodite. She has some pieces from both genders but is also infertile." How did I know? It just came into my head. Maybe it's another repressed memory or flashback that is surfacing.

Smithy looks but doesn't seem perturbed or even flinch. I'm surprised and perplexed. A macho ex-military guy not flinching at the sight. I thought he would be disgusted, to put it mildly.

"Jules, that scar on her right shoulder; it's the type of scar caused by a high calibre bullet, and there's an exit wound on her back. My mate Jones had one of those injuries, so I know. Her shoulder bones must have disintegrated and required extensive surgery and an artificial joint implant."

More memory flashes follow; Blue Monkey pushes me to the ground, takes the shot at close range, and grabs her ears afterwards. The gun blast was deafening. The person, Blue Monkey, is soaked in blood. I can't make out any faces. It's all blurry. Someone yells out, 'don't just stand there, help your partner, you momma's boy'.

"Jules, wake up," Smithy yells, shaking me out of the daydream.

"Jules, was Charmaine an athlete? My first and only girlfriend had well-defined calves and thighs like that. She was a champion. I loved her, and we went running together though she always beat me. I lost contact with her when I went to Afghanistan. She must have met another guy."

I notice Smithy's eyes are watery.

"Smithy, I believe Charmaine was an amateur athlete, but after winning several 5000-metre race titles, she got disqualified from racing when a fellow competitor saw her in the shower."

Smithy has a look of awe on his face. I'm in shock because Smithy is not in shock. Maybe he somehow associates Charmaine with his first and only girlfriend. Eventually, we get the drowsy Charmaine out of the shower and dry her and ourselves with the towels. I check her hearing aid. Luckily, it's waterproof. We lay her in the middle of the bed.

"You seem to know a lot about Charmaine."

"Smithy, she must have told me. We often had lunch at the library cafeteria and talked. Now, there's a battery-powered blood pressure meter in the bathroom cabinet. Can you get it, Smithy? Also, get the digital thermometer and the torch."

"Her eye pupils constrict to the torchlight; it's a good sign. Blood pressure systolic 180, diastolic 53 and heart rate is 83. Those readings are out of normal range for someone of her fitness level. Her temperature is 39 Celsius. We shall take measurements every hour. If the diastolic falls below 50 or her heart rate or body temperature rises, call triple 0 for an ambulance."

"You've done this stuff before. What's wrong with her, Jules? Hasn't she only had too much alcohol?"

"Smithy, I just Googled. She has a fever as well. She'll probably be fine, but we won't take any chances."

"How long did you know about this transgender or herm thing?"

"I suspected she might be transgender when we first met at the job interview. She tried too hard to be feminine."

"Did it bother you?"

"No, not particularly, though she was rather annoying, spoke too loud and the 'whoopees', but I hope I now see people for what they are, and Charmaine is a very caring person. She really likes you, Smithy. She told me."

I pull out the chequebook from the bed cabinet and write a cheque handing it to Smithy. "It's $20k; should cover the cost of a penis removal."

"F**k your cheque! I'll pay for any gender reassignment surgery if she wants it," Smithy indignantly replies, then tears up the cheque and throws it and pillow at my face.

"Smithy, only you and I know about this. She has an important job, a career."

"You think I'm a blabbermouth?"

"I'm sorry, Smithy; I underestimated you."

"Well, I could call you an arrogant prick."

"It's OK, Smithy. It was an inappropriate assertion on my part. I'm deeply sorry."

"Since when have you started using big words? You hardly talked since you've been back."

"Smithy, I may have scars too. I'm just starting to make sense of them. You know yours, but I don't know all of mine, not just yet and Smithy, do you judge people? I mean, what you're seeing here?"

"Jules, I don't judge unless someone has a machine gun aimed at me."

We look at each other and then at Charmaine. The thought crosses my mind of putting the Blue Monkey pennant around Charmaine's neck, but I desist. It may just be a series of coincidences or my mind playing tricks on me.

My left hand wrapped around Charmaine's shoulders. Smithy's arm is wrapped around Charmaine's right shoulder. She lies between us. Three people with penises, the middle one with breasts, in a double bed. It's not very comfortable and highly likely that either Smithy or I will roll and fall off the bed.

Neither Smithy nor I slept. We monitored Charmaine in turns. Smithy talked all night. Heard his Afghanistan stories; how he's half normal, I don't know. Charmaine's heart rate and blood pressure returned to within normal limits for her age and fitness. In the morning, I watch Smithy holding up the drowsy Charmaine and walking her down the street back to his new apartment. She survived the night.

A week passes with no incident, apart from coffee brought down by Doris a couple of times a day. Sometimes she puts her arm on my shoulder whilst I scan the newspapers, and I feel a bit uncomfortable with that. It would take many more months to find out who the inconspicuous Doris really was and the nature of our relationship and that with Charmaine.

It's another Saturday night and a sense of loneliness pervades me. I wander over to Smithy's apartment, my head down and preoccupied. Charmaine is likely to be there. I have the Blue Monkey pennant with me and was going to give it to Charmaine. I'm about to ring the doorbell but then stop. The song 'My Boy Lollipop' is playing really loud. I step back and carefully peer into the window of the ground-floor apartment. There are Charmaine and Smithy wildly dancing, flinging arms and legs to the loud 1960's music, oblivious to the face looking in through the window. Charmaine looks her usual bubbly self and Smithy seems more alive than I've ever seen before. He's enjoying his newfound life.

Three may be a crowd, so I walk away feeling a bit envious, dejected and empty. Maybe it's a good sign to feel again, even if the emotions are painful. I choose a song on the phone and put the earbuds on. 'You're not alone' by Tinchy Stryder.

Then there's a tinge of something positive. The song reverberates through my head, and I skip back home, probably looking quite deranged, but I don't care. A sort of subconscious glimpse, Blue Monkey is happy. Then another brief thought; why the need for the façade? The library job interview couldn't have been our first meeting.

Back at home, I try to relate the thoughts and memory glimpses of Blue Monkey to the seemingly scatter-brained Charmaine but get nowhere. There is no evidence for my far-fetched delusions. I feel restless. I pace the corridor and finally decide to walk to the local Elwood RSL club for a beer.

No, it wasn't one of those random events that change your life forever. This encounter with the mysterious Alona at the RSL club was carefully orchestrated but not by me. I guess your past eventually catches up.

Chapter two

The Elwood RSL club provides some solace after seeing Charmaine and Smithy doing their erotic dancing. I've just realized that I miss them a lot but then a close encounter of the second kind occurred. No aliens involved. It was brief, a most enchanting, unforgettable moment, except I forgot most of the conversations that occurred in those 10 hours. What I can remember is that she gave me a phone number that I seem to have misplaced and can't find.

I'm at home, sitting on a stool in the kitchen, propping my head up with my hands, just talking to myself and trying to find an answer.

So, did you ever lose someone who might have become the most important person in your life? Someone who made you feel more alive than you ever felt before. Someone who totally entranced you. Someone you felt totally at ease and content, someone so attractive and enchanting and all within knowing her for just 10 hours. If you had asked the right questions, as a surety for losing her phone number, you might be together now. If the number is lost, you could trace her. What would you need? A family name, whom she worked for, the suburb she lived in, where she graduated from high school or University. She must have told you. Two or three bits of information, and you could easily find her. But I can't remember any of those details except her first name - Alona. It's like 10 of the most significant hours of my life are lost and can't be accounted for. These memory lapses aren't supposed to happen anymore, and I only drank 3 beers, so it's not alcohol-induced memory loss. All I remember is that she looked like the model used by the 19th-century artist called Rossetti. He called the painting Proserpine. Google it; you'll then understand why I am so entranced. She was so beautiful.

Maybe had a fall and hit my head and got concussion during the short walk back home, and that's why I can't remember the conversation we had. It's like I lost my memory again, but rather than ten or so years, it's only about the last 10 hours this time. Past and recent memories can't just disappear.

Hardly slept for the next few nights, tossing and turning whilst thinking about her, churning things in my head, trying to remember anything that could be used to trace her whereabouts. That mosquito bite was still itching like hell, which added to the anxiety. Luckily no one checked my performance in the archives section of the library on the following Monday morning because I was like a zombie. Even Doris didn't come down.

Another morning was aimlessly spent pacing around, so I went to the letterbox to get the mail, something to do besides, the last time I went to the letterbox, it got me the job at the library.

The letterbox is full, mostly bills and other advertising pamphlets, even though it has a 'No Junk Mail' sticker. One pamphlet caught my eye. Luckily Miss Gribble isn't there to give me a kindly lecture and hug. The pamphlet read:

"Elsternwick Hypnotherapy Clinic

We can help you remember or help you forget

We can loosen that craving that nature begets

You can choose to allay your fears

Start again, so no more wasted years

An address, landline and a mobile phone number are at the bottom of the page.

It sounds good but probably another one of those New Age treatments, which I'm highly skeptical of, but when you're desperate, you try anything, and it's very close to where I live. I ring the library to say I may be late and make an early appointment at the clinic. I'm lucky. I get the first appointment. I walk to the clinic listening to music on my phone. How appropriate, a song comes on, 'Bird of Paradise' by a vocalist called 'Snowy White'. I relate to it, and it makes the walk less tedious but also more mentally painful. The whining guitar work. I love it and hate it at the same time. So here I am, at the reception room of the clinic. Strangely feel I have been here before; maybe it's the antique red couch and Baroque prints hanging on the walls, Raphael and Rossetti prints; Renaissance painters. One print catches my eye - 'Proserpine'. I sit on the comfortable couch and study the prints. I've definitely seen them, before because I make a connection with them. They entrance me. I can feel tears forming in my eyes as I admire their beauty. I think that newly discovered emotion is called 'awe'. The receptionist disrupts my rapture by handing me a 3-page questionnaire and a pen. "Sir, if you could fill this in, it will help Mr.. Wilson in his diagnosis."

After 15 minutes or so I hand the questionnaire to the receptionist who fumbles with the papers, drops them on the floor and embarrassingly shuffles them to get them back in order, looking up occasionally as if confused. She beckons me back to the couch.

"Sorry I'm new at this job, only my second day. Mr. Wilson resides in suite 3 and he won't be long. By the way, are you and Mr. Wilson related? There is a discount for relatives."

"No, I don't have a brother or any male cousins that I know of. It's highly unlikely that we can be related, and I don't recall ever meeting a Mr.. Wilson before."

A door opens from one of the offices and out steps a figure. He's about my age judging by skin tone, my height though maybe a fraction taller, similar facial features, body build and even hairstyle. Apart from the fact he's more tanned, we share a remarkable resemblance though he's immaculately groomed but has a few small bandage tapes near the nose, eyes and chin.

"I'm Jason Wilson. Pleased to meet you. Sorry about my appearance. I was involved in a minor car accident and sustained a few minor facial injuries. Step into my office."

He greets and shakes my hand as he ushers me into his office and offers a seat. The office is plain, unlike the reception room. There are no paintings on the walls, no bookshelves full of psychology books, no framed credentials hanging on the walls and not even a couch, which you'd expect at any decent psychologist's office, only a desk and two uncomfortable-looking chairs. I look at Jason. Aside from his self-assurance, I feel comfortable in his presence. It's almost like looking at a mirror image.

"Do I know you or is it just a coincidence?"

"Yes, we do look a bit alike, but I assure you that we are not genetically related. With nearly 8 billion people on this planet, it is quite likely anyone will have at least one doppelganger. It is quite common and nothing to worry about unless your doppelganger commits a crime," he grins. "So, what is it you want to remember?" enquires Jason after glancing at the questionnaire that I had laboriously filled out at reception.

"Anything that might help me find her," I frantically reply.

"You better give me some background, tell me from the start."

Maybe he could see the look of displeasure on my face, but he comments, "Yes, I know you wrote it all down on that questionnaire, but I just want to hear it from you. You just parted with $180 so you might at least get it off your chest. I may be able to help you or maybe not. It's all up to you and how honest you want to be. If you are here to doubt, well I can handle that as I still get that one-hour consultancy fee."

Jason Wilson removes himself from behind his desk and drags his chair directly opposite me; a meter away but not before pressing the play button on an aged cassette player. I recognize the song 'Just a Dream'. I start to feel a bit uncomfortable about the proximity. The thought briefly crosses my mind that Jason may be the 'Jase' who Charmaine chatted to after my interview for the library archives job. I start talking.

"Firstly, I had some memory problems before. Not short-term but long-term memory, so it's not likely to be premature Dementia. There's not much I remember about my life, well the last 10 or so years of it, but I was getting better and I'm holding down a job. I remember everything is the last 3 or so months except for what happened that night a few days ago."

"This is what I remember of that night, but firstly, I'm a bit of a loner, I work in the archives section of a library, but I do go to the local RSL club occasionally on Saturday night to have a drink and listen to some music. I like music and occasionally I get on the dance floor mostly just on my own. I don't care if people think it's strange. Going back 4 days ago, a balmy November night at the Elwood RSL a band is doing a great job at playing Rolling Stones music. The dance floor is packed."

"I'm standing near the bar; looking around for anyone I may know. The lighting is dim. Over the last few months, since back from wherever I've been, have made a few acquaintances, but tonight I can't see any of them. It's not the usual crowd. Through a gap, midst the gyrating dancers, I see her just briefly. She has slightly curled long brunette hair and wearing a white loose long, hippy-style dress and a shawl. She looks like the model in the Proserpine print hanging in your reception room "I reposition myself to be closer to where she is standing and watch her. I'm mesmerized. She's standing there alone, drink clutched in one hand, taking the occasional sip and glances around to the venue entrance. Probably the only time

I've appreciated being shoved by someone inebriated. He pushed me closer in her direction, almost into her. I could now see her hands as she occasionally put her drink down by a table to clap the band after another song. No rings on the fingers yet somehow it seemed she was waiting for someone. I hesitated to ask for a dance but finally took the initiative, though expecting a rejection."

"We must have danced for at least 3 hours and even when the band took a break and the Jukebox came on, we still danced. I was oblivious to my surroundings. I can't even remember what music was playing; I was just gazing at her. Occasionally she'd say something in a mesmerizing, soothing voice - not a trace of any slang or accent. It was just totally mesmerizing."

"Afterwards we walked to the boutique Elwood Bar a few hundred meters away. It was Retro night, music from 60s and 70s played on their sound system. I remember the music, it triggered memories. A song came on 'Summer Wine', by Nancy Sinatra. She left for a seemingly long time to purchase drinks. I was about to leave but she eventually came back. Then another song, 'Year of the Cat' came on in the background. I was too enchanted to analyze the song's meaning. After many hours of talking, we walked to Ormond Hill to watch the sunrise across the beach. A comet streaked by and we clapped. We watched the fading stars as the horizon lit up. I know we did much talking, but I can't remember anything that was said, and I definitely wasn't drunk."

Jason interrupted. "Stop there Jules. When in the bar, did you feel a slight sting or bite before she got up to purchase drinks?"

"She pointed to some revellers dressed in clown costumes who entered the bar. I felt a slight sting in my left arm but dismissed it as a mosquito bite, it's mosquito season. I was just surprised as not many women offer to buy a guy a drink."

"And Jules, you keep scratching your left arm. Have you got an injury?"

"No, it's just that mosquito bite, there's a bit of a welt, with a puncture in the middle and it's itchy. Anyway, after the sunrise, I walked her back to her car. Luckily, I did because some redneck in a black SUV car nearly ran us down. I just dragged her to the street curb in time. She then hesitatingly, maybe reluctantly, agreed to catch up that afternoon and I was going to call her at midday. Neither of us had a pen, but she picked up a piece of paper lying in the street, then a twig and some red Pelargonium flowers hanging out from a fence in the street. She crushed the flower with her finger and painstakingly extracted enough pigment and with a bit of saliva she used the twig to write her name, Alona, and her phone number. She then offered me a lift home but stupidly, I politely declined her offer saying I'd ring her at noon. In hindsight, I imagine pleasant things that may have ensued had I accepted."

"Why didn't you Jules? Why didn't you take up her offer?"

"I was scared, an emotional bubble was about to burst, and I wasn't used to emotions. I didn't know what was happening to me, but whatever it was, I couldn't control it. The feelings felt strange, so appreciatively I denied her offer and said I'd walk back home to clear my head. I watched and waived as she drove off and then commenced the short walk home.

Once back at home, as drowsy as I was, I couldn't force myself to have a nap, I just thought about her, then, when I went to ring her around midday, I couldn't find that piece of paper with that precious number - it had just vanished. I sifted through my rubbish wheelie bin, backtracked and examined every piece of paper along the track I had covered when walking back home, but it had rained heavily in the late morning, and it could have washed into the drains. I went back to the RSL venue that night and asked the regular barman, Martin, if he'd seen me dancing with a beautiful woman last night? He replied he was too busy to notice.

It was all starting to feel like a dream, and the funny thing is that I can't remember any details of our conversation. We must have talked for at least 6 hours, from the time we finished dancing at 12 pm, to the time I walked her to her car as the sun was rising. I just can't remember, and my blood alcohol level would have been close to zero. There must have been something she said - maybe her last name, maybe her job or employer, maybe her address - anything that could help finds her. Some clue must be buried in my head. I've already lost over 10 years of my life which I have no memory of. This is like a repeat experience. So here I am. Can you help me remember what happened that Saturday night?"

Strange, Jason's eyes seem a bit watery.

"Hey, is the story so sad that it raised a tear in your eyes too?"

"It's just an episode of conjunctivitis. I'll get you a glass of water, that's how I start the treatment. Closing your eyes may help. Take a sip of the water. Swirl it in your mouth. Feel it touching the sides of your mouth. Concentrate on the feeling. Keep swirling, feel the swirling, now swallow and feel it making its way down your throat, listen to the sounds as the water descends down your esophagus. Feel as it hits your stomach. You are going to go back; back to that Saturday 4 days ago. You arrive at the RSL club and enter the main lounge. Can you visualize it?"

"It's not the usual people; I can't see anyone I know. It's darkish inside; the lights are dim, and the band is playing."

"You are going to the bar, brushing past strangers and finally you see the barman. Do you see him?"

"Hey Martin, the usual, a pot of Vic Bitter beer please."

"You thank Martin and look for a table to rest your drink. It's crowded, but there is one vacant spot at one of the high bar tables; can you see it?"

"I'm walking there now."

"There are two men and a woman at the table. They are younger than you and the rest of the clientele. You ask if you can rest your drink down on the vacant corner, next to the girl. The girl giggles, the men look at you smiling. Can you see them?"

"It's sort of dark, but I think I can."

"You turn to watch the band, but you're a little annoyed because three young people at the table are very noisy, talking very loud; can you hear them?"

"I can't make out what they are saying."

"You pick up the drink and move away from them, somewhere quieter, but Jules, you picked up the wrong glass. You picked up the girl's beer, and it was spiked with a date rape drug called Rohypnol. Can you taste the beer?"

"I'm thirsty I'm drinking it now."

"Jules - you didn't meet anyone at the RSL club. There was no Alona except for that picture of the WW2 bomber plane in the entry hall of the RSL club; it is called Alona. It was all a fantasy induced by the drug. It was a chemical romance, a chemical romance, a chemical romance, ………."

It seems like only 5 minutes had passed, but in fact, I had spent well over an hour with Jason the hypnotist. I feel peaceful even though another 10 hours of my life is unaccountable but explainable. I had drug-induced amnesia and not some kind of dementia. Alona was just a very pleasant phantasy. There is an explanation, and I feel at peace - $180 well spent. The peace, however, would only be temporary as would Jason's life.

Chapter three

Charmaine took up her new position at the Department of Community Services, at least that's what I assumed from the overheard conversation with 'Jase' and then confirmed by Doris, so it's only me at the library cafeteria to munch on the Burger Special which I quite start to enjoy. OK, I'm a vego, but it doesn't look like a steak, so my conscience is clear.

I do miss Charmaine and her zaniness. She added a sparkle to the place, plus someone to talk to as you munch the burger. Wish Charlie was here, sorry slip of the tongue, meant Charmaine. A few times on my way to work, I pass the coffee shop opposite the library. Doris is there with another lady dressed in blue. I only see her back and not her face. I'm tempted to go in and see if it's Charmaine. Why is she avoiding me? I'm so tempted to satisfy my curiosity. No, I'll ring Smithy to see how things are going.

Whilst in the archives, Doris would bring a tasty coffee on 'the house' and asks me for help with a puzzle, one of those phone puzzles that's supposed to help you maintain your cognitive abilities as you age. I felt like telling her that scientific evidence suggests that those brain puzzles aren't effective in enhancing cognitive function, but I desist. As long as it's harmless, let people believe in what they want to believe. I'm afraid I'm little help to Doris even though I try.

Then one day, Doris shows me the Monkey game on her smartphone. "Jules, you just have to press these left and right buttons so the monkey can dodge the bullets from the bounty hunters. Do you want to try?"

I look up at Doris. "No, no, no, Doris; I don't. Please, I have to get back to work. I'm sorry, maybe another time."

Doris seems unperturbed, unlike me. "Sure, Jules, maybe you can help me with a different game."

"I will, Doris. I'm just not feeling that well today. I have to get back to work.

Thanks for the coffee." My head is spinning, and Doris got a reaction this time. My defences were down. Next time I may ask Doris to sip the coffee before I drink it.

The digitizing of the archived newspapers is taking longer than expected, maybe because I read most of the articles and I am probably now an expert in the history of St Kilda and the colourful characters who inhabited this once notorious Melbourne beachside suburb. Besides, there's no pressure; Ms Valda still gives me high appraisals in the weekly performance reviews. I don't know why, as I'm not that efficient—then the shock, a headline from an article 10 years ago.

'Scandalous scientist, Jules Lemos found floating face down in neighbour's swimming pool. Quick action by neighbour saved his life'.

I nervously glance around and don't read the rest of the article. I consider just tearing it up, but information shouldn't be destroyed. I bite on my lips till taste blood and finally scan the article. It's in the digital archives forever. Hope Ms Valda doesn't read it.

A month passes and the impact of that newspaper article sort of fades from my mind, as does Charmaine, but then that fateful day, I was about to go to work and thought I'd drive as the old VW Beetle car needed some mechanical exercise and the car battery some recharge. The top of the fridge was the resting place of the house and car keys. I always put them there. They stand out against the white panels of the fridge, so I don't waste time looking for them. It's an unusually hot morning, and the fridge compressor motor is working overtime, rumbling and straining to keep the fridge's contents cold. The vibrations must have nudged the keys to the back edge of the fridge. Luckily, I heard them drop.

I pull the fridge out from its enclosure, and there are the keys but also a piece of paper. It has ragged edges and is star shaped. I pick it up. It has very faded red, thick writing on it; childlike writing and not done with a pen or biro. I need my glasses and good light. Outside in the sunlight, I could just make out the text. Inscribed is 'Alona' and a phone number, but I can't make out the last digit. I stumble to the couch except miss the seat, ouch. I clutch my forehead and bend down. In the background, the radio is comfortably loud. "4 Non-Blondes - What's Up", a song from the early '90s. Part of the lyrics strikes a chord "What's going on?"

Ten phone calls later, and still no Alona. She must have purchased a new phone SIM card with a new phone number. That feeling of loss and despair is returning as the flashbacks start. Seeing her at the club. Walking her to her car. Hearing her voice, the conversation but not remembering what we talked about. Maybe she's still living in Melbourne. Several times on the train to work, I could almost feel someone looking at me from an opposite train seat. I'd look up from my newspaper, and she would drop her eyes back down to her book. Her hair is short blond, but Alona was a long, haired brunette; that I can remember. One of those times, she dropped her book and uttered to the passenger beside her to move his 'f...king' foot. Her voice was almost a parody of a colloquial Australian accent. She couldn't have been Alona.

Too much to think about, so never made it to work that day, just got off the train, changed platforms at the station and caught the next train back home. I have no idea why I'm so entranced about a possibly amorous chance meeting. It happens to people all the time. Some people get rejected but move on. I haven't. I haven't moved on. That's the explanation. But how do you move on? Why didn't Jason do as I instructed? He was supposed to help me remember, not to implant some other false memory into my head. I ring Jason's office at the clinic, but I'm diverted to an answering machine. I try to take a nap, but my Internet of Things clock radio goes off. I must have mumbled as I churned. Those devices are like spies. I should get rid of it. It plays a 'Pink Floyd' song 'Comfortably Numb'. I listen and relate to it. The device has chosen well, but it's kind of scary that it knows my preferences. My head is spinning again. Got to relax, do some exercise, go to the gym and get my mind off Alona.

It was almost like seeing your reflection in the mirror. We looked so much alike. "Jason!" I yelled across the gym floor. "Didn't know you were a member. I just left a message on your answering machine. What a coincidence that you're here."

"I just joined last week. Sorry, but what is your name again?"

"It's Jules, Jules Lemos. Had a hypno session with you a month ago. I'm the guy who lost a very important phone number and wanted you to help me remember anything that could help find a special lady I had met. You convinced me it was all a drug-induced delusion, and it made me feel better. But guess what? It wasn't a delusion. I found that piece of paper with her name and phone number."

"Oh good," Jason quizzically replies. "Yes, I remember now. You were fairly distraught when you came to see me. Tell me, did the session help?"

"Yes, initially it did. I was able to get her out of mind. I sort of totally forgot about meeting her, but now it's coming back to me. In fact, I think I remember more than I did when I first came to see you. I must have told you something when in that hypnotic trance."

"And how are you coping with that?"

"Not too badly (I lied). Did I remember anything in that session? Did I tell you anything?"

"You did, and I made an executive decision - I helped you forget."

"Can you tell me now? I'm over it but still need to know."

"Do you really want to know Jules?"

"Of course, I do, and I'm not happy that you took it upon yourself to decide on my welfare."

"Yes, I now remember our session, and you'll know why soon. Jules, Margaret Alona Milstein was her real name, she had several aliases, and I think she liked you very much. The reason why you remembered so little was that she may have been protecting you. Her last academic position was as an Associate Professor of Psychiatry at a New York University, and she knew far more about hypnosis than I do."

"You're implying Alona wanted me to forget that magical night together?"

"I believe she did. I believe she did not want you to remember any of it. I was very surprised you remembered even meeting her. I was not expecting to see you in my office. I was quite surprised."

"Well, can you tell me? Was she married or involved with someone and just having a fling whilst on a holiday?"

"Jules, when you get home, Google her name, then try to put it together. I prefer not to talk about it now. I have a client at 12 pm. I have to go. If you want to talk after that, give me a call. I'm still in the same premises, and the phone number hasn't changed, as you know."

"Jason, do you know a Charmaine?"

"Yes, it's the name of a perfume I buy for lady friends."

I don't finish my gym workout. Just want to get on the Internet as quickly as possible. As I'm driving home, I notice a black SUV in the rear vision mirror. Cannot see the driver as the SUV windscreen is heavily tinted. I have no love for black SUVs after one almost ran over Alona and me. The black SUV seems to follow me for a while, and I'm relieved when it gets caught at a red traffic light behind another car. Much later, when washing my beloved little silver-coloured VW beetle car, I notice the tiny device, on one of the rims of one of the wheels, with a little wire hanging from it. I believe it's a tracking device. Why would anyone want to track me? A brief memory flash - Rule 607-Tracking. 'Never destroy a tracking device. Just divert it somewhere else. It will buy you time'. I carefully remove the device and duct tape it to a small piece of plywood. It will float. The tide is receding and so is the plywood, down the Elwood canal and into the bay. I wave it goodbye. It's sort of like expunging something you don't want to remember. It merrily floats away, but sometimes it does come back, depending on the tide.

Chapter four

I read the Wikipedia article on the Internet:

"Margaret Alona Milstein (5 May 1966 - 4 December 2017) was an associate professor at the New York School of Psychiatry. She was renowned for her contribution to neuroscience and psychology, particularly in the field of memory and hypnosis. Her suicidal death, by a fall from a cliff known as Red Bluff, in a bayside suburb of Melbourne, Australia (her hometown), had focused greater government financial support for cervical cancer sufferers.

Margaret Milstein had pioneered the theory and practice of a technique she termed Traumatic Memory Attenuation (TMA).

The goal of this treatment was opposite to regression therapy, whereby the therapist encourages their client to remember traumatic experiences and come to terms with them. She asserted, "The regression therapist can implant false memories of rape and abuse by family members, and the victim walks away satisfied that their suffering is due to an extraneous factor though it doesn't extenuate cases where real physical abuse happens. Domestic and sexual violence, unfortunately, happens all the time." [citation needed]

Margaret claimed her TMA techniques transformed traumatic experiences by subtlety manipulating the context in which they occurred.

"My technique steers a traumatic memory in a more positive direction. As humans, we all want an explanation, we want to make sense of the world and what has happened to us. The victim of a traumatic experience often feels that she/he is in some way responsible. My treatment attenuates the self-blame by providing an alternative explanation for their condition. By doing so, the memory becomes insignificant and buried, and the victim can devote her/his energy to positive outcomes and walk away from the current situation." [8]

Margaret used medications believed to be benzodiazepine drugs and sculptured peptides to accentuate her treatments.

TMA was criticized by rape victims, also by Government and Public Ethics groups. It is also believed that the results of her research were used by military groups to subjugate torture claims by political prisoners and detainees. [citation needed]."

Scrolling down:

"The post-mortem revealed that Margaret Milstein had advanced cervical cancer with probably only weeks to live and self-medicated with painkillers. Traces of morphine and Pethidine was found in her blood."

The more I read, the more my heart sinks. Her death must have been reported in the Melbourne newspapers and on the nightly TV news channels. There was nothing mentioned about her in the archives library; you'd think there would be, but then I'm still only up to the year 2009.

I pay online to view the archives of "The AGE", the major newspaper in my city Melbourne and look for the 4th of November 2018 edition. Nothing there about Alona or Marg. I try the 5th and find it. It made page 3. How could I have missed it? I was back in Melbourne then, well at least in body. I'm horrified; there's a photo of the battered, contorted body lying face down on the rocks. I zoom in and shudder. The left arm is twisted over itself and facing upwards. I notice a tattoo – one of those pirate ones from child book stories – a skull and crossbones. Can't explain how I feel. All I know is that it can't get any worse. Need a drink but no alcohol in my cupboards. I walk down to the Elwood RSL club. I hadn't been back there for over a month.

"Goo'day Martin, it's been a long time."

"Hey, Jules, where have you been? Hey, you look terrible. What's wrong?"

"Martin, do you remember, maybe four or five weeks ago, when I asked you if you'd seen me with a lady at the club?"

"I actually do now remember you asking me that. Later I remembered something else; do you have a twin brother? That night I served a guy who looked very similar to you. I even called him 'Jules'. He said he wasn't a 'Jules', and he gave me his name that I can't recall, only that it started with a 'J' like your name. So, what's on your mind?"

"That lady I was referring to. I just found out she died the next day after I met her from an apparent suicide."

"Oh shit, mate, are you alright? Here's a free beer on the house."

I'm the only patron at the time, so I dump all my despair on Martin, who turns out to be a very sympathetic listener. Six beers go down so easily, and my speech is becoming a bit slurred.

"Martin, Martin, I know the RSL is soon closing this branch and selling the land to some property developers. Do, do you need a job reference [hiccup]?"

"It's okay, Jules, I'm starting a new job next Monday - head barman at the Elsternwick Hotel."

"Con, congratulations, Martin." I shake his hand.

"Look after yourself, Jules; you want me to call a cab?"

"It's OK, Martin. I live very close by. I'll walk."

I shake Martin's hand again, and while a little unsure on my feet, I make the short journey home but stay on the right-hand side of the pathway, a healthy distance away from the canal. You definitely don't want to stumble into the canal whose water always looks in need of a flush. Then, as I turn into my driveway, a burly guy in a spacesuit-type costume nearly knocks me down. He seems to have come from my townhouse. I'm startled.

"Sorry, mate. Are you John Wellington? Been waiting here for half an hour. You're townhouse 8, aren't you?"

"What?"

"I'm from Freedom Pest Control." He points to the label on the suit. "Had a call from a John Wellington. He wanted some rats in his ceiling exterminated, townhouse 8."

"There's no John Wellington living in this townhouse complex. I live here, and I don't have rats in my ceiling," I reply with a slight slur in the voice.

"Sorry, mate must have got the wrong address. You don't know a John Wellington, do you?"

"No."

"Okay, have a nice day."

I watched as he puts a large case and helmet in his van and then drives off. Once inside, I felt very tired, maybe slightly intoxicated, so took a snooze on the couch. An hour later, I wake and ring Jason. I have a plan to draw some more information from him. It's Jason's answering machine again. I would normally hang up, but this time leave a message that is not quite truthful. "Jason, it doesn't make sense. There were no articles about her death in all the major newspapers. There would have been TV coverage. I don't remember any of it. Please call me, here's my number."

An hour later, a call from Jason. "You couldn't comprehend all that commotion about her death, and there was plenty. She didn't want you to know. She programmed your mind to bypass any reference to her. It was for your own good." Jason continues. "She came back to my place, that's where she was staying whilst in Melbourne. She had to have a pethidine shot as she was in great pain. You read about her cervical cancer. She had only weeks to live and self-medicated. She was dying, but she was going to make the last days count no matter what it took, but she didn't want to hurt you and felt very guilty about that night for possibly leading you on." He continues. "I attended a seminar she gave on Post-Traumatic Stress Disorder - new treatments whilst in New York thirteen years ago. We had always kept in touch since then. When I was in New York, I'd stay at her place. I liked her very much, and though we were once briefly romantically involved, we remained the best of friends. She was a very special lady, my Proserpine, and I too liked the way she talked and her voice. Her premature death was a great shock to me, and I'm still very saddened. Do you think I want to be reminded of it? I was in more pain than you were when you came into my office to have your emotional wounds treated. Do you think I wanted to listen to what you had to say? You thought that you were hurting after knowing someone for 10 hours. I knew her for 13 years."

My head is spinning. This is getting weirder and weirder.   "Did she tell you she was going to kill herself?" I enquire.

"No. I do not think she intentionally killed herself though I suspect she contemplated it at times. She was on a cocktail of painkillers but often walked alone along the cliffs, and this time probably just slipped. The coroner's report was 'Death by Misadventure'. Jules, did you want to see her die of cervical cancer? My mother died of it, so I know how horrible it is, and Alona told me about you, the guy she met who didn't call back. It was a relief for her because she didn't want to put you through watching her health deteriorate. She didn't think you could handle it. You were vulnerable and she knew it. Everything she did was for your own good. She tried to make you forget. Somehow, she failed, which is unlike her. She always succeeded at whatever she did, no matter what it took."

"Jason, you let her go out, drive a car whilst high on painkillers, to do a tricky and dangerous cliff walk when it's pouring rain, and the paths are slippery. That's a recipe for disaster. And Jason, were you walking with her when she slipped? Are you going to try to make me forget again? "

"What the sh.t! Jules, stop being so paranoid! There's no conspiracy. Marg was a prolific writer. If she was going to suicide, there'd be a suicide note. No, come to think of it, a suicide book. She just slipped off the cliff walk."

"Jason, who identified the body?"

"I did."

"Jason, were dental records checked or a DNA test performed to confirm the identity? I'm no expert, just heard that line of enquiry on TV crime shows."

Jason's voice is rising. I triggered a soft spot.

"Jules, where's this conversation leading to? What are you implying? Margaret had dental treatment whilst travelling through third-world countries. They do not keep records there, and there were no DNA tests. You watched too much American TV. We were intimately together for two years. I knew every square inch of her body. That was Margaret lying on the rocks."

"Jason, did Marg have a tattoo?"

"What? No, not last time I looked. She was adamant about no bodily art and forget it, Jules. Leave me alone."

Jason slammed the phone down. He should have zoomed in on the "AGE" newspaper photo of the deceased body lying face down on the rocks. Something is not quite right. I'm not a tattoo fan either. I would have noticed a tattoo no matter how drugged or hypnotized I was. Marg or Alona, whichever name you prefer, did not have a tattoo. I remember - she wore an orange Sari-type dress. Her shawl she tied to her handbag. Her arms and shoulders were exposed most of the time. I would have noticed a tattoo.

Back to the online Age newspaper article. I had to see that photo again to just confirm my mind isn't playing some kind of trick. Zooming into the photo, definitely a tattoo on the left shoulder of the shattered body, and yet Jason claimed he's seen every square inch of her body and had identified the body as that of Alona. He lied.

Those feelings of grief and despair are turning into ones of anger and resentment aimed at Jason. I ring Jason again. The answering machine answers. As tempted as I am to abuse him, sanity prevails. "Jason, I'm sorry but can you ring me? My number is ….."

That night a knock on my door and I open it. "Jason, you asshole!" He grabs me in a bear hug with his hand over my mouth. I cannot breathe. I struggle. Then I hear 'Shh'. My body goes limp. Jason eases his grip and with one hand points to the driveway. I try to speak. He keeps his hand over my mouth and again mutters 'Shh'. I relax and comply. Have no choice; he seems stronger than me. He releases his grip and gestures to follow him down the driveway. He whispers, "Your phone might be tapped, and home bugged." He checks the street, looks left and right, then beckons me to follow. I say nothing. We reach the park at the end of the street. "Jules, they tend to drive in black SUVs. Have you seen any lately?"

"Yes, there was a black SUV behind me on the way home from the gym yesterday, but it got caught at some red traffic light, and I lost it. Anyway, everyone drives a black SUV in this suburb. I'm confused. Who are they? Why did you lie? Can I believe anything you say?"

"They could be Israeli or USA Intelligence or worse, far worse 'LaMosa' a crime syndicate based in Chicago. I lied to protect Margaret or Alona as you may know her, to protect her, myself and even you."

"She's alive?" I exclaim.

"Yes"

"Whose was the body on the beach?"

"Her assumed name was Rebecca Mill, Marg's estranged sister. You might have met her once and her estranged brother. Rebecca was a junkie and dying of cervical cancer. I found her in a homeless shelter, and she had a child. She was going to die anyway, and I offered her $400,000 in a trust fund for her kid if she'd wear Marg's engraved ring and take that fatal walk."

"Did you push her Jason?"

"No! I drove her to the Red Bluff cliffs using Marg's hire car. I wore gloves, so no fingerprints were left behind. It was 6 am in the morning. I walked with Rebecca to the edge of the cliff and helped her over the fencing, but I did not push her. She held her end of the bargain. I left the car near the cliffs and walked back home where I logged into my bank account and transferred the agreed payment to the trust fund that was previously set up by my solicitor."

"Jason, that's still manslaughter. What sort of person are you? And you're telling me Marg/Alona is on the run from governments and crime syndicates? Who is she? What did she do?"

My head is spinning again. This is way out of my league; this is not the kind of thing that happens to a librarian. Then it struck me. What did Jason mean when he said I had probably met Rebecca and Alona's brother? I only knew Marg/Alona for less than 10 hours.

"Jules, we got involved in things we could not control. I cannot talk now. I will tell you tomorrow, same place and same time. Just make sure you are not being followed. Ring me tomorrow. Sound convincing because your phone is probably tapped. Mention her tattoo. Say you liked it or hated it, just subtly mention you saw it that Saturday night when you met her. It's really important you do that. After that don't ever use your landline or mobile to call me. If you have to call me, use a payphone or prepaid mobile with a new sim card and be careful; you're probably under surveillance."

An old noisy car pulls up. The sort of battered car most university students tend to drive, well at least in the old days. The window winds down and the internal light goes on. There's a short-haired blond woman in the driver's seat.

"Jules, I got to go. See you tomorrow," Jason says. Then the female voice projects from the car, "Hi Jules, it has been a long time."

I couldn't make out the face, it was too dark, but the voice was a giveaway. It was Alona otherwise known as Marg. Jason opens the car door and jumps inside. The car speeds off. I had no time to say anything to the driver. I start walking home from the park, feeling very confused but hear someone walking behind me. I don't look behind but cross the road and walk on the other side. Paranoia, maybe, but suddenly there's urgency for being cautious, very cautious. One last look around before entering the townhouse's driveway.

My townhouse doesn't seem like home anymore, it may have been violated. Since Smithy moved out, I always put the alarm system on when absent. It has passive infrared sensors both upstairs and downstairs. It would be hard to bypass unless your whole body was covered with a metallic material that prevents infra-red (heat) escaping, but then you'd self-cook after half an hour. I check the alarm control panel. No intrusions have been detected still, I feel uncomfortable. I examine the space around my landline. Has anything been moved? No - it all seems OK. I'm pretty anal about keeping the house clean and orderly after Smithy moved out. Every appliance has its spot. Nothing appears to have been moved. The cordless landline phone seems untouched. I'll check it thoroughly tomorrow, but then again, phone lines are easy to tap.

I try to sleep but my head churning through all the events in the last few days. Flashbacks to conversations and the SUV that briefly seemed to follow me home from the gym two days ago. What is true and what is a lie. So far Jason's record for telling the truth is pretty poor. What's he going to tell me tomorrow? And then seeing or at least hearing Alona; maybe it's all a dream. That's it; I'm dreaming this. It's too far-fetched to be true. I turn on the radio. A Bob Dylan song is playing, 'If You See Her Say Hello'.

The next morning when I arrive at work the same song blasted through the library from the overhead speakers, at full volume as I walked in. It was deafening. All the library staff were running around, hands clasped to their ears, trying to find the sound system and turn it off. Then it went off by itself and all the staff composed themselves before the doors opened to the public. How or why the sound system disorder happened was never solved but I have my theories that it may be the AI music device which has uploaded itself to my smartphone and communicated with the libraries sound system.

Marg/Alona must have connections and influences, but it was the person you'd least suspect who orchestrated the whole show and made the art of manipulation take on a whole new meaning.

Chapter five

I psyche myself up and try not to think about Marg. The psyching up took almost an hour and a few glasses of wine. Finally, dial Jason's number on the landline phone and actually hope my landline phone is tapped. He answers - a first. I always got his answering machine before.

"Jason Wilson speaking."

"Hi Jason, it's Jules. I just can't get that picture of Marg lying on the rocks out of my head. I remember her tattoo now. I asked her about it when we sat at Ormond Hill on that magical night. She said she was very depressed when she had the tattoo done and regretted it. I guess if you're dying of cancer, you can be forgiven for staining your skin."

"You really dislike tattoos, don't you, Jules? It was a small tattoo, and I never really noticed it. Anyway, how are you feeling?"

"I'm very sad and agitated. Jason, can you teach me that relaxation technique you spoke about once and maybe give me some grief counselling?"

"I'm booked out today, Jules. How about 6 pm on Saturday, at the office. I don't party, and I'm always on-call and work late when required."

"OK, I can wait. Thanks, Jason."

I pat myself on the chest. I think I sounded really convincing down to the melancholic voice, which didn't really need any acting. If anyone was tapping my phone, they'd be convinced.

I accidentally find the slip of paper he gave me the first time he visited unannounced and dragged me to the park. It was in the same jacket I always wear. He was departing with Marg when he slipped the paper into my hand. The little piece of paper had written on it – ' If I arrange by phone to meet you, the office is the park at Mitford Street. The time is what I say but add 3 hours and subtract a day. Remember those details and destroy this piece of paper'.

I never destroyed it or read it till now. Subtracting a day must mean it's Friday, not Saturday for the meeting. Have 6 hours to wait.

It's 8:45 pm, it's dark, so surreptitiously, I sneak out of my townhouse and walk to the 'office' in the park. Jason arrives in a white BMW. Marg doesn't appear to be with him. I feel disappointed. Jason jumps out of the car but leaves the engine running. He is talking very fast.

"Jules, I can't stay, but there are two documents and some tapes in this envelope. Everything in them is absolutely honest and true. The first one mostly addresses you. It is the handwritten one - sorry about the jittery writing. The second document I typed three years ago. It details the work Margaret was doing and for whom and speculates why one or more of the three parties I mentioned last night might be pursuing her. After reading the documents, burn them. I'm dropping another copy of the documents to my solicitor with instructions to deliver them to the Federal Police if anything should happen to Margaret or me."

"Jason, are you sure these documents are not full of lies again? You misled me before. Hey, what's happened to your hand and your face?"

Jason's hand was heavily bandaged, and even though the lighting wasn't good, I could make out that the bandages were crusted with blood. His face showed traces of bruising, and his nose seemed a bit bent to one side.

"Another roadside rage incident which I lost. The transcripts are the truth, read them and you will understand. Everything is explained. Now, here are two mobile phones for you. The SIM cards were acquired using false identities. They cannot be traced to your name. I have turned off GPS and hopefully disabled location tracking, but still be cautious. Only turn the phones on when you need to make a call and turn off Wi-Fi on your internet router when you are not using it. And finally, you're going to need some special protection. I have commissioned two guys, and they're good and loyal. They worked for me before. Their names are Henry and Sam. Sam, the Samoan, is the big guy but don't underestimate the little guy called Henry."

Jason runs back to his car before I have time to speak and accelerates off as if in a hurry. I conceal the A4 brown envelope down my shirt. I start to walk, filled with a sort of excitement about the envelope's contents. I only walk about 100 metres before I hear an explosion followed by the streetlights extinguishing. It is dark except for the moonlight. I run in the direction of the crash. From a distance, there is a white car wrapped around a power-line pole. It's not on fire, but there is a smoky, pungent smell in the air. It's not petrol, it's something else, some other chemical substance. A few seconds later, the fuel tank explodes, and the street is briefly illuminated.

Residents are cautiously coming out of their houses, holding torches. I don't want to get too close. Be careful; you don't want to appear in a photo taken by spectators' smartphones or be filmed by one of those TV news crews once they arrive. I turn back home, hoping against hope that it wasn't Jason's car though deep inside, I know it must have been. He seemed highly agitated when he departed and probably just drove too fast but still, that seemed more like a chemical explosion rather than just a car hitting a pole due to bad driving. I try to stop thinking about Jason and what he said but can't, and bodyguards, why do I need bodyguards? The last few days have been a nightmare, and I'm wishing I never looked behind the fridge.

Five minutes later, the sound of police cars, fire brigade and ambulance sirens awaken the rest of my normally quiet neighbourhood. I'm home and switch on the TV while also opening the envelope but not before pouring a large glass of Vodka. The first of Jason's documents, a letter addressed to me, is about four pages of almost illegible handwriting done with a very unsteady, trembling hand. The second document is typed and about 35 pages long. I skim through the hand-written letter whilst waiting for the 11 pm News on TV.

Jules, there are no coincidences. Aspects of your life in the last few months were carefully controlled and orchestrated, but not all went to plan.

Margaret was quite desperate after 3½ years of ceaseless torment and threats from the people she had done clandestine work. She had been disciplined by New York University and resigned, claiming ill health. She came back to Melbourne, where I harboured her at my home whilst she recuperated from injuries suffered in a minor car accident, coincidently with a black SUV. That is when the pethidine dependence started.

We came up with a plan. We would both just disappear and assume new identities in some far-off place.

It may not be coincidental that she chose me to be her next partner; I'm talking about our resemblance accentuated by a bit of cosmetic surgery we arranged that you probably cannot remember.

Jules, I may have been used too by Marg. Like you, I was infatuated with her and blinded by her charm and looks. Unfortunately, I now ponder if there is only one person in Marg's life, and that is Marg. I can see how her upbringing created the person she is. She is so smart yet lacks introspection. She is totally goal-focused at times and lacks a moral focus.

Jules, I'm very sorry, but you were part of that plan, as was Rebecca Mill, who jumped off the cliff and coincidently was Margaret's estranged junky sister. The Milstein family life wasn't great when the daughters were young; extreme expectations of success were placed upon them. One gravitated to ambitious academic achievements, the other to drugs. Another, the eldest, named Henrick, became a hermit and just vanished.

Rest assured, Rebecca's son is being well looked after, being taken care of by a loving family. He is happier than he ever was and hopefully will lead a trauma-free and productive life from now on.

I first noticed you several months before your meeting with Marg or Alona, whatever you want to call her. I occasionally used to go to the Elwood RSL as well though I just played the pokies and rarely went into the main bar as I don't normally drink alcohol. I observed you walking into the main bar for several weeks, 9 pm Saturdays, give or take 5 minutes. Unlike me, you were a creature of habit, but our physical resemblance was compelling, accentuated by some minor cosmetic surgery. You were the perfect candidate for the role that was contemplated for you. At the time, I didn't know that you and Marg had been married.

Some research indicated that you were disconnected and lived the unfortunate life of a homeless person for nearly 11 years even though you had substantial financial assets. Society was not benefiting from your existence. You just took up unproductive space on this planet. You were no different from Rebecca. You were disposable, and your presence or absence on this planet wouldn't make much difference. You were disposable.

Your intended role, should it be required, was to be my replacement, as I was on the hit list due to my involvement with Marg. We were on the run, so to speak, and so changed leaving locations.

You and Rebecca would appear to suicide together, and I would take over your identity and lead a very inconspicuous existence resigning from your library job and eventually relocating to a far-off island. Marg would come with me, but she would assume Rebecca's identity.

One last thing. Marg is still your wife. You are still legally married. There was never a divorce.

Marg, my wife? I'm flabbergasted, so manipulated. Marg's sister's death was nothing but a contemplated murder, and I was next in line. Had Marg been in on the plan? She must have. Also, that line about Jason contemplating if he's just being used? There's a flaw in his logic. It's not a great feeling to know your hypnotherapist was contemplating your death. It's like things can't get any worse. And Charmaine, she somehow fits into this, according to that overheard conversation as I was leaving the job interview at the library. I quickly down some more Vodka. No glass, just straight out of the bottle. The 11 pm news comes on. I immediately stop reading and watch and listen intensely.

'The white BMW was completely engulfed by flames after its fuel tank ruptured from the impact with a power pole in Mitford Street, Elwood. Power lines in the street were brought down as the ageing power pole was snapped by the collision. It is believed the driver died at impact before being partially incinerated. At this stage, the identity of the driver cannot be determined. Residents of Mitford Street are urged to stay indoors till power is restored in the street.'

Video footage accompanied the commentary. A burnt-out twisted wreck surrounded by two fire trucks, numerous police cars and a superfluous ambulance, all with their red and blue strobes flashing.

Some knowledge of science comes flooding back. Cars don't normally explode when their fuel tank is ruptured. That's American TV drama, and from what I remember, there was no petrol burning smells straight after the incident. Yet, there was an initial explosion and the stench of chemicals that I couldn't identify, but definitely not petrol smells. The petrol smells came later when the car burst into flames. Seems to me Jason could have been assassinated, for I don't know. I suppose I could save the authorities a lot of time by identifying the car and driver, but that would be unwise. I don't want to be seen as associated with Jason or be photographed. I try to feel some compassion for Jason but just now, I can't. I feel angry and used. I down some more Vodka.

Jason's original typed document, meant for his lawyers, would have been incinerated in the crash. I have the only copy of the documents. Have to read them and keep them safe till I can forward them to the Federal Police. As much as I feel contempt for Jason, those documents might be protection if I become implicated in this sordid state of affairs. I flicked to the fourth page of the handwritten document and eye scan to the bottom. The last paragraph reads: 'We got our senses back and seek redemption. We may have performed some unethical deeds, but we are not murderers. Your deceased presence on the rocks would not be required.'

Am I meant to feel relief? I wasn't ready to give Jason absolution, not just yet though the reference to my 'deceased presence' brought a slight smile to my face. Jason was a master of understatement.

It's 11:30 pm, but I can't sleep. Have to read the rest of the transcripts but first, a new regime for home security. In the very recent past, since back, I may have been a bit lackadaisical about ensuring all windows and doors were locked before retiring upstairs to bed. Things are about to change. I meticulously check every door lock and window latch. I find the folder with the appliance manuals and instructions. The alarm system divided the house into two zones - upstairs and downstairs. Before, I never bothered with that functionality except when I went to work. The alarm was turned off when I went to bed but won't be anymore. I also re-organise the house. I move my bedding and clothes to the downstairs bedroom. It's close to the driveway and front door, so I could hear if anyone was trying to enter the house. From now I'm going to arm the alarm in the upstairs zone whilst sleeping in a downstairs bedroom but also need some weapons for protection. What is there? That 30cm blade kitchen chopping knife will be a starter though I've never used a knife for self-defence. Maybe something heavy to throw. I go to the garage, turn on the lights and search through the toolbox: a hammer and a 30cm adjustable wrench. Not much good against a bullet, but that's all there is.

Finally, the chilli spray; I grow the hottest chillies in my small garden. I remember I grew one plant many years ago, but it must have seeded and propagated whilst I was wandering wherever. There are now many of those plants and they're bearing fruit. They're called Ghost chillies, one of the hottest species of chillies on earth, and I recently started to supplement my income by selling them to the local Indian restaurants though it's more of a hobby than a money maker. Strangely I remember that incident many years back, the first time I picked a crop from my first and only plant. I didn't wear rubber gloves. After going for a wee and handling the delicate private parts, what followed was sheer burning agony like you couldn't believe. My antics, hopping around, screaming, using ice blocks to relieve the pain would have made a viral YouTube video. I could have been famous. I remember that incident because pain helps you remember.

I go into the garden armed with a torch. I'm wearing disposable rubber gloves and goggles. I carefully pick twelve ripe red Ghost chillies. I take them inside and put on an air filter N95 facemask. Into the blender they go along with half a litre of vinegar. The vinegar will help preserve their potency. The blender churns. After filtered, the mixture is then poured into a 100ml sealed container and put in the fridge. One glass of the chilli mixture is covered in plastic wrap and will be kept close by me at all times.

It's 11.55 pm. The outdoor motion sensor light goes on and then the doorbell rings. I don't have a peephole. I open the front door armed with the open jar of the Ghost chilli, ready to fling in the face of whoever is there. No one is there, and then I look down. There's a short guy, a midget, dressed in a suit with a chiselled face and big grin. "I'm Henry; we're your protectors," the little guy asserts in a squeaky, almost comical voice.

I'm bewildered. Jason must have been on a tight budget. Footsteps follow, then a thundering voice. "I parked the van around the corner." A massive figure, maybe 190cm tall, appears under the light. I tilt my head up 45 degrees. A man mountain probably of Polynesian background. Must be the Samoan. "I'm Sam. We're here to protect you." Henry jumps up and sends an elbow into the side of Sam's chest. "I already told him that you're an idiot as far as these matters are concerned. You got no experience!"

The Samoan gives Henry a benign smile and pats Henry on the head. That seems to relax Henry a bit. I conclude that Henry is very high-strung.

"Well, aren't you going to ask us in?" asks Henry in a squeaky, agitated voice.

"Yes, yes, of course, come in," I hesitatingly reply. A sort of curiosity overtakes caution, and I rest the glass of the chilli concoction on a cabinet near the door. I wonder if the Samoan will fit through my front door. The Samoan angles himself and barely makes it in. He then brings in 4 large duffel bags. I'm worried about my couch; can it handle the weight of the Samoan? It doesn't take long, and what soon follows could have made it into a Comedy Festival act. I can't believe my eyes. What starts off as my protectors bagging each other soon degenerates to a full-blow wrestling match. Henry calls out to Sam. "Your six-pack stomach is a joke. You got to work out more or else I'll tell the boss."

The Samoan seems only slightly insulted, though gives me a wink and yells out a challenge. "OK, Henry, you leap from that kitchen bench onto my six-pack." The Samoan lies on the floor and challengingly points his hands to his stomach. "You do it, Henry, you jump!"

Henry gets a chair and makes the perilous climb up to the kitchen bench, then flings himself and lands on ground zero feet first, but bounces off the Samoan's stomach, and his head collides with an adjacent wall. I put my hand against my mouth, trying hard to refrain from laughing at the comical tragedy. Sam jumps up and grabs Henry. "Are you OK? Are you all right? It's OK, brother." Henry, somewhat groggy and holding his head utters, "I'm all right." The Samoan gives Henry a big hug.

I don't believe what I witnessed. Jason hired a team of two clowns to protect me or maybe to entertain me. I'm tired, too tired to read the rest of the transcripts. I'll let these guys sort out their sleeping arrangements. "There are three spare bedrooms - two spares upstairs and one spare downstairs. I'll leave it to you guys to choose your rooms."

The next day I'd find out just how effective that supposed team of clowns really is.

Chapter six

It's early Sunday morning. I stumble out of bed and brush my teeth for 5 minutes. My dry breath still stinks. I down three big glasses of water to hydrate and get the saliva flowing. I then wander around the house. Sam and Henry are happily snoring away in sleeping bags in the spare downstairs bedroom. I check the fridge. It's empty except for Wasabi paste and my chilli spray. Not even a carton of milk for a coffee. While making a shopping list, I also ponder how much to disclose to these guys. I don't know what info Jason gave them about their assignment. OK, they are probably trained not to ask, they just do the job, no questions. I don't have to tell them anything.

"Get up, guys there's no food in the house, we have to go shopping."

They jump out of their sleeping bags, ready to go. I would have preferred they take a shower first as I can smell body odour. I detect small scents or smells really well. Must have been a sniffer dog in a past life.

We walk down the driveway and into the street to where the duo parked their van.

"It's gone, the van is gone!" yelled Henry whilst almost having a seizure. Posted with duct tape, on the road, on the supposed parking place of the van was a note. The note read, 'You parked across my driveway, and I couldn't get my car out to get to work. Your van got towed away. The details of this tow company are printed on this infringement notice'.

"You moron!" Henry yells out at Sam and furiously starts jumping up and hitting him with open hands." The Samoan just ducks, covering his head.

"It was dark, Henry, and you know that I don't see that well in the dark. You should have told me I'm parking illegally. It wasn't my fault."

The two misfits make up, and we walk back up the driveway to my place. Henry says, "It was a crappy old van. The springs jutted out of the car seats. At least I won't have an itchy arse anymore. Let the tow company keep that piece of trash. We won't claim it."

These guys are definitely on a tight budget. "It's OK, guys, we can take my car. It's not very fast, but the seats are comfortable."

I'm driving to the supermarket in the old silver VW Beetle car. Sam, the Samoan, lost the coin toss. Henry rides in the front passenger seat. The Samoan could barely fit in and is crouched in the back seat of the two-door car. The aged VW car barely manages to stick to the minimum legal speed limit.

"What did you guys do before this line of work?"

Sam, the Samoan replies first. "I was a Prosecution Attorney; it's a long story." Then Henry replied. "I was nothing special, though. I had to learn to be tough, and I got a family to feed. I know I'm short, but I'm tough. I learnt to be tough."

I turn my head and look at Henry and try to think what to say. "You're awesome, mate." That brought a smile to the little guy's face. Sam also reaches over and puts his hand on Henry's shoulder. I think they made up.

"How did you know Jason?" I quizzed.

"We attended his counselling group. That's where we met. We had some personal issues. Jason offered us this job," the Samoan and Henry replied in perfect sync.

"And you, Jules, what's your story?" Henry squeaks.

"My memory is hazy; I don't know. I believe I may have a wife, and we were involved in the production of a substance that affected people's minds."

Henry snaps. "We're out of this, Sam; we're not protecting drug manufacturers or dealers," Henry yells out.

"I'm not a drug dealer. The substance was natural, a combination of things called amino acids. It affected memory but also aided soft-tissue healing. The type of injuries you get in contact sports." That sort of poured out of my mouth automatically; I have no conscious recollection of what I did in the past.

That seemed to partially satisfy Henry, who muttered, "If you're a drug dealer, I'll get you, I will."

"Believe me, I'm not, Henry. I've spent time sleeping under bridges with people whose lives were ruined by drugs, not Cannabis which is harmless but the strongly addictive stuff like 'ice', which leads to irrational behaviour and violence."

Henry relaxes for a minute, but then a car horn starts tooting behind us. Thump, the little Beetle car jolts. I look in the side mirror. A large ute with bull bars hit the back of my precious, old VW Beetle. I swerve into the next side street and park. The ute follows and stops behind us. Out jumps a tall, burly, unshaven, menacing-looking guy in a singlet, shorts and baseball cap worn backwards; oh Gawd, a road-rage moron. I cringe.

He approaches the Beetle with a very large spanner in his hand, ready to wack anyone. Henry opens the door and jumps out from his seat to face the assailant.

"Sam, do something! Get out of the car," I yell.

"It's OK, Jules, Henry can handle himself," Sam calmly replies.

For a moment, there was a face-off between Henry and the ute driver (we'll call him Burly) who lifts the spanner above his head as if ready to strike.

"Move over, you little twerp," Burly yells.

I guess that comment triggered a sensitive spot in Henry. Before you could blink your eye, Henry rushed over to Burly and butted him in the lower groin with his head. Burly drops the spanner and crouches down in pain. Henry starts furiously bashing Burly with his closed little fists. Burly's face is soon bloodied, and he falls to the ground, where Henry starts kicking him. "Sam, get out of the car; stop Henry before he kills that guy."

Eventually, Sam squeezes out of the Beetle and gently grabs Henry. "You made your point," he whispers into Henry's ear. Henry calms down and returns back to the car. I get out of the VW and check the street for CCTV cameras. There aren't any that I can see. I walk over to Burly to check his vital signs. He has a strong pulse, and his eye pupils respond to light when I open and close his eyelids. Then Burly yells out, "I'll kill that little twerp".

"That little twerp would have killed you. Think about that next time before you get into that road rage mode." I then swing my right foot and hit him as hard as I can in the ribs. It was calculated. It may break a few ribs but not cause any permanent damage. He is lying on the road and groaning. Sam and Henry help me move him off the road and onto the grassy nature strip. I go back to the car, pull out rubber gloves, a Texta pen, paper and some sticky tape from the car's glove box. Yeh, I keep all that stuff in the glove box, just in case. I write 'Road-Ragers will get their due' and tape the paper on groaning Burly's ute windscreen. I then examine the damaged bumper bar on my VW. I grab Burly's spanner and start furiously battering his ute's back bumper bar.

"Jules, that's enough. You've made your point." Sam says as he restrains me. I regain some composure and dial 000 for an ambulance. The mobile device has an untraceable SIM card. "Like to report a perpetrator of road rage. He's lying in Shakespeare Street, Elwood. He has superficial wounds but may require an ambulance."

We're back in the VW driving home. The adrenaline is overwhelming, and we're all a bit stunned and agitated because of that road-rage moron. We forget about the food shopping; we'll have to order takeaways.

"Jules, you realize what you did? You called the authorities on your mobile. I know it's a prepaid, but it's still tracked from cell towers. We don't want too much attention at the moment, even though what you did was right. Get rid of the SIM card. Throw it into the Elwood canal. You can use my mobile. It's clean."

"Sam, Jason gave the phone to me. He reassured me it can't be traced."

That night we walked to the bottle shop 800 meters away and bought back two slabs of beer and some takeaway from the Indian restaurant—a triple dose of spice for Sam's portion. The spicy smells distract us for a while. We plop down on the couch in front of the TV set, watching the 6 pm news whilst consuming the contents of the yummy food and downing beers.

'Is it a terrorist group or just people fed up with the road-rage phenomena? A note was found after a road-rage incident backfired for the perpetrator. A spectator reported that the road-rage perpetrator, driving the ute, picked on a small height-impaired guy who is believed to be the driver of the rammed VW vehicle. This is how the ute-driver ended up'.

Video footage showed Burly being taken away by ambulance and swearing his heart out amidst coughs and splatterings of droplets of blood.

"He won't try that again!" Henry exuberantly leaps from his seat and starts hugging Sam and me.

"Jules, are you sure there was no CCTV footage recorded at the scene?"

"Yes, Sam, I checked. If there was CCTV, the police would be here as the car is registered to this address."

"Jules, things may be more complicated than they seem, but I think you're ready to join SnowPea, if you wish," Sam solemnly announced in a slurring voice.

"Sam, I'll give it some more thought." I'm not sure I want to join a vegetable species at the moment. I would be wrong.

If there was video footage of the lounge the next morning, it would reveal three guys sitting on a couch, arranged in order of height, their heads leaning against each other's shoulders and a lot of heavy snoring plus 30 or so empty beer cans strewn on the floor; just another one of those male bonding sessions.

I awake before the others and do a clean-up job, supercharged; recyclables into the recycle bin, plates washed and stacked and a bit of floor mopping. I then shake Sam's body to try to wake him up. "Sam, who or what is SnowPea? Tell me!"

Sam groggily replies. "SnowPea is the nickname of my daughter, who I'm very proud of. It's also the name of something else, a sort of organization, tell you later, got a terrible headache. Got a coffee?"

"It'll have to be black. We forgot to buy milk or anything else. There's only beer, and I don't think any of us need that right now."

Chapter seven

I have to get to work. I frantically rush to Ripponlea train station, and there she is, standing, waiting for the train. I rub my eyes as not sure if seeing correctly. I think it's Marg though she has dyed her hair black and is wearing a conservative dress and blouse, the business-look not at all like Proserpine.

"Pardon me, are you Margaret Milstein?"

She nervously looks around. "Keep your voice down. Jules, you're still blocking from awareness what you don't want to face; maybe your psychologist friend at the library can explain. You're still legally my hubby-dubby, and I'm entitled to half your assets," she cynically whispers.

I'm gesticulating, waving my arms as if having an argument. "Yes, I remember little bits of our past that I prefer to forget. So much of it was a lie, my Proserpine, I hope you succeed in your ambitious career without causing any more damage." I don't mention that I had read documents that Jason had given me before his death. Got to keep my voice down and the emotions under control. Others waiting at the station are looking at us and probably wondering if this is some ABC TV drama being secretly filmed. I turn around and wave at them and smile.

"Jules, we did have a kid, and you're probably his father. Do you want to meet your son?"

I'm stunned. Jason never mentioned a child. I drop my head. Must look like a stunned mullet as I reflect for a few seconds before answering. "Of course, where is he?"

"I'll tell you later. Jules, I'm not safe where I live now. You have two bodyguards where you live. I want to move into your place, just for a while, until things settle down. I'll sleep on the couch. I'll tell you everything. Now move away, there's CCTV recording us. I know your address. See you tonight."

The day's work at the library passes tediously slowly as my mind churns. I don't get much scanning or cataloguing done. Don't even venture to the café to get the Burger Special. Doris wanders down into the archives with a cup of coffee. I'm fumbling with papers. I stupidly expose my emotional self and tell her that I may have a son in a town in South Australia.

"Just take some time off, Jules. The scanning can wait. I'm sure Ms Valda will understand. Oh, I also got a little trinket for you; it's a small gift for supporting the cafeteria."

She hands me the pendant. It's a silver beetle on a chain, a little bulky. She puts it around my neck. "It's also a birthday present; just wear it for me," she announces.

"Doris, is this a GPS tracking device?"

That question triggers something in Doris. She comes dangerously close and stares me in the eyes. Her humble demeanour suddenly vanishes, and she seems threatening and ready for combat.

"Who the f..k are you and stay away from me," I yell out defensively and try to push her away. It's like a Dr Jekyll-Mr Hyde transformation. Her usually soft conciliatory voice changes to a domineering, aggressive tone.

"I run this show and we fix problems, not just local but worldwide. I've also supported you and your sister or brother, whatever you may call it. I risked my career. I gave you jobs. 'It' had the sense to come back into the fold, and you better too and stop being such a weasel. You do as I say."

I lean back from her, "Doris, are you going to tell me that you're my mother who abandoned us? My mother left me and my brother when I was seven years old, and he was 4. Our father sort of looked after us, but he was always busy. We learnt how to open cans of food and use the washing machine as we hardly ever saw him. He was always at work developing some substance that would make us rich. A carer looked after us. Charlie ran off. I should have too."

"Are the memories coming back, Jules? I hope all the other ones do as well. I've gone out of my way to cover your ass. Now find that son of yours. He and his carer are causing us problems and put two and two together. You were never the brightest spark on the block, but I got you a job, and you couldn't even do that without causing a major international incident. You even let 'it' take the fall for you in another situation. Make yourself useful for once. You owe me. That ex-wife of yours and her brother have also caused several embarrassing international incidents, which we are still trying to sort out. She has to go. If you can't do it, there are many other candidates for the job."

I am stunned and forget about Marg. Suddenly my focus shifts. "Who's 'it'?" I ask.

"Work it out and keep your mouth shut. This conversation never happened. Our interactions are to be the same, cordial, as before when in public or being recorded."

I look up at the wiry Doris. For the first time, I notice her arms. They are slim but muscular, and I'm sure she knows how to use that knife lying on the coffee tray. I'm starting to fume and can feel the blood vessels pulsating in my temples.

"Now sir, would you like a coffee?" Doris politely enquires, regaining her professional composure.

I notice the CCTV is back online. It was off when Doris came in. The red lights weren't twinkling when I moved, but now they are again.

"Is it only coffee, nothing in it?"

"Is it a white but no sugar, and would you still like the Burger Special for lunch?"

"The usual," I reply. That was rule 406 – 'Play the Game' but I can't. She triggered too many soft spots. I rush at her, pinning her throat against a wall with my forearm. The hot coffee tray goes flying, spraying its contents on me and the floor. I don't feel it, not yet; too much adrenaline flowing in me.

"Is 'it' Charmaine? Tell me! I got nothing to lose. I'll kill you even if it's being recorded."

She gargles and whispers, "OK". I release her. A few coughs and splutters follow as she regains her composure.

"Congratulations, you're not a total wimp. It was a test, and you actually passed with no nepotism involved and you and the person who calls herself 'Charmaine' are related; she's your brother or sister. I still don't know which, so I refer to it as it, it's briefer than Charmaine or Charlie. It's confusing. That's why the 'it' reference. I'm not prejudiced. Charlie, or Charmaine, is our most successful employee. She or he is rising up the ranks and being groomed to be my successor when I retire. She'll make a good 'Z' and help keep our country safe from terrorists and economic sanctions."

I'm bewildered and must have that stunned look on my face, as I move away from Doris, staring at the floor, but it's starting to make sense, getting back into the 'fold'.

Doris continues. "The CCTV footage timeline will be replaced by something less nocuous. Now show me that you got some 'balls'. The worst is still to come but you can do it," Doris splutters and then leaves without picking up the tray or knife. I get paper towels from the archives bathroom and clean up the mess. I got to find the truth though most of it is staring me in the eye. Just have to confirm it. I ring Smithy. He answers.

"Smithy, how's Charmaine doing? Tell me."

"What do you want me to tell? She said you two may be related, according to that DNA stuff. She took a sample of your hair from the couch at that party I had. Hope it was your hair and not mine."

"Anything else Smithy?"

"Yeh, you did nothing to find her, you let her walk out the door when she was a teenie, you weasel."

"I've already been called a weasel once today. Anything else Smithy? Did she say anything else?"

"Isn't that enough? I'd tear you apart if you were here."

"Thanks, say hello to Char and tell her that I love her and that I'm so, so very sorry. I'll make up for it. I promise. Tell her. Can you hear me, can you hear me?"

"Stop yelling. I'll pass the message on."

"Thanks, and how are you guys doing?"

"We're doing real fine. We go jogging every night, more like running, and I'm starting to catch up but then she does a sprint to the finish. She is fast, maybe still Olympic standard, and she's challenging me, and I love that as well as I love her. I was once, a long time ago, also a 5000m Olympic contender but not quite good enough. The downside is I had to go clothes shopping, assisted by Charm. I've lost 20kg weight and at the rate Charm and I train I'll look soon like an anorexic."

"You look after her, Smithy."

"Who the f..k you think I am? Of course, I'll look after her and she's moving into my place. We're setting up a home."

"You need any help with the moving?"

"No, I think we're right. I'll call you if we do."

"Best wishes to Charmaine and you." I hang up the phone.

A memory flashes by; Charmaine eating the Burger Special and spluttering a mouthful on my shirt. Strangely I feel hungry but won't go upstairs to the cafeteria;

don't want another encounter with Doris. I keep scanning documents and mulling.

I look up. A pretty, young lass is standing in front of me holding a tray. She has dreadlock hair and earrings hanging from her nasal parts and ears.

"Hi, my name is Cedar. I'm at the library on work experience. Doris asked if I could bring the burger down to you."

"Thanks, Cedar."

"You know, you should stop eating that meaty stuff. It's full of chemicals," she says.

"Cedar, I luuv chemicals. Your shampoo is full of chemicals not that you wash your hair that often. Not all chemicals are bad. We're all made of chemicals and a little bit of meat a few times a week doesn't hurt us, OK, maybe it hurts the beef animals, but they wouldn't be here anyway if we didn't eat them because we wouldn't breed them."

"You're so weird. No wonder you're kept in this cellar," the millennial generation Cedar comments.

"Thanks, for the burger that is."

Cedar gives me a disdainful look and marches off.

I'm hungry. I ravenously consume the Burger Special. It's sort of becoming a vampire ritual. Bits of onion hang from the side of my lips and red tomato sauce drips from my mouth. Oh Gawd, I forgot Rule 313.

I run to the toilet, stick my fingers down my throat and eventually vomit the chewed-up Burger Special. I gargle several times afterwards. 'Rule 313 – Collect a Sample and get it analysed before you eat something that could be contaminated'. I didn't do that. Then the thought hits. Why can I remember the Rules for an appropriate situation? They must have been engraved in my mind.

Whilst wiping my mouth and face I reflect. It may have been a Burger Special that's gone to waste down the toilet. Doris still seems to have plans for me so I can still enjoy a Burger Special, at least for a while. I ring the cafeteria and ask for another Burger Special but also request a chain of custody. I don't want that feral Cedar kid spitting on my burger or anyone else spitting on it. Ms Valda brings the burger down to the archives. "Your burger is clean. I watched its manufacture and followed it."

"Thanks, Ms Valda, you have a reassuring use of words which I find comforting."

I scoff down the Burger Special. Don't particularly want to encounter young

Cedar again, and at the time I didn't know that the meat in the Burger Special is actually made from engineered grain and vegetable protein that tastes and looks like meat.

I don't do any more scanning. I just stare at the computer screen. So much has happened; a very unproductive day as far as the job is concerned.

It's 5 pm. Time to leave work. I do a brisk walk home rather than catch the train. Have to unwind and do some more thinking. It's been the biggest day in the life that I remember, and it doesn't quite make sense. 'It' then Doris's comment 'the worst is still to come' and that Doris runs the so-called 'show'. It's like she's engineering something, and she has the perfect cover – a lowly paid tea lady working for what appears to be just a quiet municipal library.

I'm home and a bit sweaty. I open the door. There's no one there. The place is empty then suddenly the stereo goes on full blast and blurts out 'Happy Birthday to you'. Sam and Henry appear from nowhere and start dancing with party hats on. Then Marg appears in a 1920's style skimpy dress carrying a cake with far too many lit candles.

"Jules it's your birthday, we got to celebrate something."

I glance around, a bit startled. The main kitchen shelve is littered with the remains of empty beer cans and nibbles. Looks like the party started some time ago.

Marg seductively hovers over to me, dangerously close, with the cake. "You want to do the blow job Jules or should I?"

I look from side to side then blow all the candles out. It took three huffs and puffs. Henry yells out, "Can I ask my family over? My wife makes a great Lasagne, and she has plenty in the fridge. She'd bring it over."

"Yes, yes of course, Henry, invite your family over, they are welcome," I reply in a daze.

"Can I ask my daughter over, she's at a police conference here in Melbourne?"

"Fine Sam; do it. Guys I just got to have a shower and change my clothing."

I look back, a bit overwhelmed but can hear the stereo or radio playing. It's a song, 'Bob Seger & the Silver Bullets – Still the Same' playing in the lounge. Must have had some emotional connection because I remember it, the song that is.

I'm in the shower; the warm water hits my body. It's sort of a relief. Things you don't want to think about get washed down the drain. Then the bathroom door opens. I crouch, with hands covering the downstairs parts.

"Jules, I've seen it all before," she says before removing her skimpy costume and walking in. She seductively joins me in the shower.

I'm tempted, so, so tempted, she's so gorgeous, every curve right, my still Proserpine. "Marg, I don't know what your game is but I'm not part of it anymore. By the way, do you know a tall, thin, elderly lady known as Doris?"

She puts her hands on my shoulders. "Jules, just enjoy the shower. Enjoy the water hitting your shoulders and bouncing off, feel it. Just focus on the feeling of the droplets hitting your body. Can you feel it? Feel the water and how relaxing it is."

"Stop it, Marg! I know what you're trying to do. I won't let you practise your hypnotic skills."

A strong emotion can trigger memories. Many come flooding back. I regain my composure and address her. "You were so beautiful but being a wife, or more politically correct a partner, wasn't your thing, so preoccupied with your job. Hey, we once used to do things together; cycle, swim, jog, go to the gym. I didn't want that to stop. It kept us sane. You stopped it, not me. Your obsession to achieve in your work destroyed the relationship. We could have been just normal people, and I don't mind the suburban lifestyle."

"Jules, you weren't exactly easy to live with either; obsessed and pedantic about little things like keeping the house spotless and disinfecting anything we made contact with, then you got worse, you even once hit me in the face with a plastic mosquito swatter thinking that the floater you had in your eye was a biting insect. It hurt. You also weren't ambitious and well, kind of boring. You were impossible to live with, so I fled."

"I remember, you chopped up the swatter with a large kitchen knife and that night we were eaten alive by mosquitoes."

"You could have just bought some fly spray. It kills mosquitoes as well."

"Marg, if I ever hit you, I'm so, so very sorry. Please forgive me. That's hopefully not the way I usually behave. I've done lots of thinking since then."

"Jules, you seem better. My situation at the time was also complicated and way out of my control at times. Maybe we could produce a real normal human being unlike what we did when you were self-experimenting with your peptides."

"You should have done the reproduction stuff with Jason or was he on your 'hit' list as well?" She avoids the question.

"Jules, I told you before or hasn't it registered? You have a son."

We get dressed and walk out to the lounge smiling - fake smiles. There are many people. Henry comes over to me dragging a tall, attractive brunette woman by her hand. "This is my wife Bernadette, and these are my three kids." One of the kids grabs Henry and applies a stranglehold on him. Henry laughs and doesn't seem to mind. They have a physical sense of humour. Henry and his tall attractive wife certainly make an incongruous couple.

"Hi Bernadette, thanks for the Lasagne." I give both of them a hug.

A few minutes later Bernadette brushes past. "He is a great father and I love Henry deeply. He is also great in bed."

I try to imagine their bedroom antics. She continues, "You and Sam look after him while he's on the job and it better be a short job. We miss him very much."

I don't have a chance to tell her that Henry doesn't need any looking after when on the job; he needs restraining. Meanwhile, Henry's kids are laughing and fooling around. Sam gently tosses them in the air and catches them. They giggle. "More Sam, play it again Sam!"

I smile but am not sure what to think. Too much stuff coming into my brain, but it looks good.

"I'll be back kids. Don't damage anything." Sam is furiously dialling his phone again.

Henry turned up the stereo volume in the lounge and put on a Rolling Stones CD. He and Bernadette are furiously gyrating. The previously highly-strung Henry operates totally differently when surrounded by his family. He's relaxed and he is the life of the party. He should change careers and become a DJ. My eyes are getting moist just watching them.

Sam is still waiting for a reply from his daughter. He looks distraught and disappointed that she is not here.

Marg comes over to me. "You want to know the truth about your son?"

I turn and look at her cautiously, "Yes but let's go downstairs to the garage. It's private."

We quietly depart.

"It was all a plan, wasn't it? I don't trust you, Marg. You and Jason were going to kill me just as you both were responsible for your sister's death."

"Jules, can we move on for a moment? Your son has Macrocephaly. He's got a large head. You couldn't cope nor could I. He's being looked after by my brother,

Hendrick. Our son is also very smart."

"There's cranial surgery now that can drain and reduce the size of the skull. I read about it in some of those articles I scan and catalogue in the library. Why hasn't he had the surgery?"

"Hendrick has become very protective and possessive and doesn't want to risk anything going wrong. There are multiple surgeries, not just one, and each one has a risk of infection. Hendrick keeps our son inside his cave house, sometimes they go out at night, and he has to wear a hoody. It is for our son's own good. You know what other kids are like. Anyone a bit different gets picked on and bullied."

"What's my son's name?"

"BHK."

I ponder that's a strange name but then again not as strange as the names some TV celebrities give their kids.

"Where are they?"

"Coober Pedy, a little opal mining town in northern South Australia. It's hot and dry. Everyone lives in cave houses there."

"Good, we go there tomorrow. I'll Google how to get there and book online. Oh, and by-the-way, will you try to kill me?"

"No, you're safe for the moment," she replies.

"Are you still medically qualified? Can you write me a Medical Certificate? I need one of those if I take two or more days' leave from work."

"Jules, I've been disbarred from medical practice, but I know someone who can write you a certificate. I'll SMS her. I'm sure she can email a PDF of the certificate."

"It's OK, I remembered that I don't need the certificate; I have compassionate leave according to my boss." We then uncomfortably go back and join the party.

Sam's daughter had finally made it. She is stunning. There are disco lights vibrating to the music in the lounge. Henry, Sam, and his daughter Annabelle and the kids are dancing. Henry comes over. "Hope you don't mind. Bernadette brought the disco lights over. We like the lights." I again give Henry the biggest hug possible and tears flow down my cheeks. If only life could be simple like Henry's.

Marg and I join in. The music, the lights, the dancing people. You become entranced. Time seems to cease. You forget what's bothering you and just lose yourself in the music. "Do you want one of these?" Marg asks. I swallow the tablet she hands me. It seems to accentuate the experience. It's a wild party though there's still a bit of clarity; I hope the neighbours don't complain.

The personal alarm buzzes. Less than one hour sleep. I wake Marg who's lying in a foetal position on the hard, tiled floor next to me.

"Wake up, Marg, we got to go and have a quick shower before we leave. We stink of sweat."

"Jules you've become so assertive not like the weasel you were before."

"Don't call me a weasel; I heard that reference too many times before. Now, move your ass."

She gets up and seductively hovers around me. "Why couldn't you have been like this before?"

Don't know what we drank but there are adults, scattered and sleeping bodies all over the lounge room floor. No Bernadette. She and the kids must have left early. I write a note in bold Texta. "We're OK, Marg and I will be back within two days." The note is left on Sam's chest.

"We got to move, I've booked the airport bus and airline flights to Adelaide and a coach to Coober Pedy."

"I have no clothes to wear?"

I run to my bedroom and shuffle through the wardrobe. "I have no women's clothing but here's a spare tracksuit, tee shirt, socks and runners."

We just make it in time to the airport bus stop. We definitely don't look our best and it is a 45-minute bus trip plus the wait to get past security.

"What's that in your pants, sir?"

Sanity prevailed, and I didn't state the first thing that came to my head. I shuffle around and find them. I pull out my house and car keys and walk through the metal detectors again.

"Next time put all metallic objects in the basket so they get processed. Have a good day sir."

It's only a one-hour flight and we sleep through it, then a coach bus ride to Coober Pedy, that's the long bit. We just make the bus, screaming and waving our arms as it departs. It stops and we get on board. Marg leans her head on my shoulder. "How long Jules, I'm thirsty?"

The bus stops for a refuel after 4 hours. I purchase 4 plastic bottles of that over-priced spring water and 4 packets of potato crisps. I like the number 4, first non-prime number after one.

"We got at least another 8 hours; can you tell me what to expect?"

Marg drinks a litre of that spring water. Luckily there's a toilet in the rear of the bus. Then she speaks. "Back to what we discussed in the bathroom, you were also very involved in your work even though you had no desire to climb the ladder. I loved and hated you at the same time; a contradiction but most couples operate that way. It wasn't me that abandoned BHK, it was you. You couldn't cope with devoting time and energy to a disabled kid that you produced. I couldn't either; I had to travel a lot. Hendrick volunteered to look after BHK."

I don't reply. There's a lot of time to think during an 8-hour bus trip. Who or what am I? Feel a sort of revulsion towards myself; a failed dad just repeating the pattern of his own father who also abandoned his children due to work commitments. It's definitely not a good day.

We've slept very little in the last 48hrs but finally arrive at Coober Pedy where we catch a taxi to Hendrick's cave home. We ring the big brass bell that hangs over the doorway to the cave. The door opens, he looks around and then Hendrick grabs his sister and hugs her. He's a tall, thin guy. Long grey hair, a ponytail and long beard. He is wearing a colourful Kaftan. He looks like a character from some medieval fantasy movie. Then a loud yell in the background and Hendrick rushes into the cave lounge room; we follow. "I've solved the puzzle; I broke the code!" yells someone in the shadows. He then comes out into the light, head bowed. I look at the kid, Marg looks at him as well. He is so thin, almost alien looking. He must be BHK. His head is disproportionate to his very skinny body.

"Should I put on the hoody?" BHK asks Hendrick.

"No BHK, it is not necessary. Now my dear ambitious sister, what is the purpose of this extraordinary visit?" Hendrick asks.

"This guy is Jules. He is probably BHK's biological father. He wants to see him and have his cranial condition treated so he can lead a normal life."

"So you see him, what do you see Julia or Jules whatever your name is? Is this what you expected?"

"I see a beautiful boy." I'm gut-wrenching and tears are flowing down my face as I get those words out.

Suddenly, Hendrick goes into a coughing fit. I don't think he is well. "Get out, get out, all of you get out!" yells Hendrick then sinks into the couch grasping his chest.

BHK rushes over to him. "Dad, dad, are you all right? Dad, dad, dad!" He lowers his head to Hendrick's chest.

"Marg, what's going on? Check his vital signs."

Marg carefully moves the crying BHK to the side and checks Hendrick's pulse. Then, in a fury, she starts applying CPR to Hendrick.

"Help Jules!" she yells.

"Jules, you do the chest compressions, 100 times a minute and I'll do the mouth-to-mouth, you got that? BHK, is there a defibrillator in the house?"

"No, I don't think so. I wouldn't even know what to look for," BHK replies whilst in a panic and walking from side to side clutching his enlarged head.

Thirty minutes later we're exhausted, and Hendrick hasn't shown any vital signs.

"He's dead Jules, we did everything we could. I don't have to tell you the diagnosis," she tearfully comments. "Call 000 and get the ambulance here. I can't sign a death certificate. I'm not registered anymore as you know."

BHK comes running over. He shakes the lifeless Hendrick furiously yelling "Don't go, don't go, dad, please don't go".

We grab the weeping BHK, both Marg and I. "It's OK, people pass on from our lives. We love you. Do you want to come back with us?"

"I want to stay here; Hendrick was the greatest father ever."

I look at the kid's distress. I refrain from telling BHK again that Hendrick wasn't his biological father.

"BHK, where did Hendrick keep his paperwork, his files? Is there a filing cabinet?"

"Why do you want to know?"

"BHK and Marg, we got to leave. We can't revive a guy who has had a massive heart attack, but BHK we need to find your passport and birth certificate else you can't go to school or go anywhere."

BHK takes me to Hendrick's so-called office. It's messy. There's a folder labelled 'BHK' in Hendrick's filing cabinet. I briefly look inside. The documents are there. He must have been more organised than my first impression indicated. I put the folder in my backpack. Meanwhile, Marg calls the ambulance again not that they can be of any use. They finally arrive. It was less than 10 minutes, but time seems to stand still when you're distressed and waiting. They examine the deceased Hendrick and do the paperwork which must have taken over 30 minutes even though it was death by natural causes. The ambulance officers then take Hendrick's body away. BHK sprints as best as he can, following the ambulance. He comes back crying. Both Marg and I grab him and do our best to comfort him.

We catch a taxi, the three of us, to the Coober Pedy airport. The Cessna flight is stretching the budget but it's faster than the bus. BHK is sobbing and resting his head on Marg's shoulder. We make it to Adelaide Airport. "Do you want me to put the hoody on?" the tearful BHK enquires.

"No, be proud of who you are. No hoodies".

There were a few hurtful comments about BHK on the flight back to Melbourne. Both Marg and I psychologically verbally decimated the perpetrators. Deservedly they walked out of the airport looking like zombies and probably in need of future psychological counselling.

"This is it, kid. That's where we live. There's a spare bedroom upstairs, well study room with a mattress. It's yours."

Sam and Henry come over. "We're your dad's friends; we're just staying here for a short while."

"Hendrick was my dad. He, he isn't." BHK points at me tearfully.

Henry grabs the kid and gives him a hug. "Jules is your real dad, and you have to forgive him."

BHK looks at me, "It's not like home, and I miss Hendrick."

I grab and hug him as well. "It's complicated BHK but just hang in and Henry, go home, be with your family. Come back tomorrow or the next day."

Henry looks up. "Sure boss."

It's only BHK, Marg, Sam and me who are left. I carry the drowsy BHK upstairs and tuck him in the bed in the study room. "It's OK, you had a big day. It will all work out."

"Are we going to Hendrick's funeral? Are you really my dad?" he asks.

"I can't answer either question at the moment. There's a lot I can't remember about the past." I kiss him on that big forehead. "Sleep tight and don't let the bed bugs bite."

"I remember that rhyme. It wasn't Hendrick's, it might have been yours."

I turn the light off and wearingly walk back downstairs. It's been another long, long and very draining day.

"Can I share your bed, or do I sleep on the couch?" Marg asks.

"We can share the bed."

Sam retires to the spare room glancing back. "I'll leave you two lovebirds together, goodnight."

We don't get undressed. Just flop on the bed. I grab Marg's hand and we fade into a very much needed sleep.

A few uneventful days pass. Sam and Henry look after BHK as I go back to work at the library. Marg leaves the house too though foolishly I never asked her what her work is. There is too much going on, and we are too stunned, so we do little talking.

Then one night the phone rings and I stumble to the kitchen to pick it up.

"We can negotiate," says a voice with a thick accent on the phone line. "Bring the flash drive. We will not bother you or the whore anymore if you follow the instructions."

I stumble towards Sam's room and wake him. "We have a meeting to attend. It may all soon be over; a negotiation. We'll be left alone, and you and Henry can go back to whatever other things you guys do. Sam, call Henry. Tell him to come over as quick as possible. We need all hands on deck."

Sam wipes his eyes. "Jules, it's 3 am in the morning, and I can hear thunder, can't it wait?"

"The guys we're meeting are on a tight schedule. This fiasco has to be settled. Sam, I'm giving them what they want, a USB flash drive. I don't even know what's on it and I don't care. I just want it all to end."

Sam calls Henry while I check the sleeping BHK and then wake Marg. We then all get dressed for the occasion that would end up a disaster. People would die.

Chapter eight

It was supposed to be a conciliatory meeting with the LaMosa guys. All that peptide stuff, I just want to leave it behind. They can have the USB flash drive. Marg said she'd join us but would be a few minutes behind. I didn't want her to come along, but she insists. She puts on a tracksuit and a beanie on her head. "I got a sore foot Jules and don't like thunderstorms. Can I have the keys to the VW? I'll drive and meet you there."

"Park the car at least 400m from the rendezvous and stay away from any street cameras." I throw her the keys, hoping the temperamental VW wouldn't start. I don't know why Marg even wants to be there.

Sam complains again. "Why this time of night, Jules? Couldn't they wait till the morning? I'm tired and not feeling 100%."

"Sam, they're just following an old formula. They're stealthy; they do the meeting stuff very early in the morning when few people are around to witness any transaction. We don't have a choice at the moment. We got to meet them near the entrance to Luna Park."

"But Jules, there are CCTV cameras all around; why do they want to meet here?"

"My only guess is that they are unaware of the CCTV monitoring as they are 'old school' and don't know the technology."

"Who are you, Jules? You've changed. It's almost like I'm hearing a different person. Is there something you're not telling me?"

"Sam, we all have pasts, and I'm not sure of mine, but at the moment, I got this gut feeling that you and Henry have to be very careful. These guys are likely to be highly temperamental. Don't, don't do anything rash."

Henry arrives and throws his keys on the couch. "Bernadette drove and caught a taxi back home. She wasn't too happy. There's a storm coming, and there were lightning flashes everywhere. She hardly needed the car-head lights to drive, but boss, I don't like your timing. Bernadette and I were trying to break our record for the amorous stuff when ..."

"Henry, I'm sorry, but the timing wasn't my choice."

The house is flooded by light from the windows, and then a few seconds later, an ear-shattering crack of sound makes the house vibrate. We all look up, a little bit shaken.

"We're walking to the rendezvous. It's only 1.5 km away. Henry and Sam, grab these cans of beer but don't sip too much. We have to appear as revellers but also to be alert."

"Jules, don't tell me you want us to walk in this weather. We could be struck by lightning."

"Sam, Marg is taking the car, and besides, we have more chance of dying when travelling in a car than being hit by a lightning bolt according to the statistics; we're safe."

"Dodging lightning strikes is fun; Sam, get a sense of humour," Henry comments in an excited voice.

We start walking, heads down, to the meeting spot with hoodies covering our heads, pretending to be slightly intoxicated revellers waiving our cans of beer.

Close to the meeting spot, I call a halt. "Henry, you come with me and Sam, you turn right and then take the next side street."

"Why do I have to go the long way?" Sam complains.

"You've got the longest legs, plus there are CTTV cameras on the way. We don't want all to be seen together."

Sam reluctantly agrees and starts marching. Apart from the lightning and thunder, it's a still, cold night, and the real revellers have long gone home, except for a few sitting on the concrete footpaths, leaning against brick walls, heads hung low and fast asleep. It's also starting to drizzle rain as we arrive at the meeting spot.

They introduce themselves as Paolo and Vince. No handshakes. I look at them - both a bit taller than me, thin, greying hair, dishevelled looking despite their black suits and loose ties. I can't see their eyes or faces as they're wearing those clown masks you can buy at the $2 shop. They also appear highly agitated. Not a good sign. Sam and Henry are standing behind me.

"Did you kill Jason?" I ask them.

"Nuw, we just roughed him up a little to get information. We had plans to get more information later, but someone blew him up before we got to him again," Paolo replies in a USA-Italian accent. "Now give us the USB stick or USB drive, whatever you call it. We got a flight to catch in 4 hours."

I hand the flash drive to Paolo and step back. Both Paolo and Vince fiddle with their laptop to start it up. "That plastic thing goes in this socket," Vince points out to Paolo.

"Give it to me, I'll show you how it's done." They hand me the laptop, and I start up Window explorer. "Here, you click on this file, it's an MS Word document, and you appear to have that word-processing software on the laptop."

Paolo and Vince stand behind me, looking over my shoulder. I click on the document that contains the peptide manufacturing process, but only random alphabetical and numeric characters appear on the laptop screen. The screen is semi-down, protecting the keyboard from the drizzling rain, so it cannot be an electrical malfunction. It didn't please the two guys who pull out their pistols. "This USB is garbled crap. If it is encrypted, what is the password?" Paolo yells out. I'm slightly surprised they even know what encryption is.

"I can't remember any password, besides it may be a hardware error in your laptop caused by the rain."

"Mr Jules, this pistol is the only hardware you have to worry about, and it works in the heaviest rain. Your plastic drive is encrypted. You have documents in your house, don't you? Jason said you have boxes of documents. You must have the password written down somewhere." In disgust, Paolo throws the USB stick at my face. It's light, so doesn't hurt much. I picked it up and put it back in my pocket. Both Paolo and Vince aim their pistols at my chest. "You have 24 hours to bring an unencrypted copy of that USB thing and $5000 for new plane tickets for our journey back to Chicago. You cost us money." Vince throws the not to be used plane tickets at me in disgust while still aiming his pistol at my chest. Then the sky lights up again and a thunderous boom follows. Maybe Henry mistook the thunder for gunfire and rushes at Paolo. Sam momentarily looks incredulous but follows Henry. It all happens so quickly. Five more booms follow, and finally, a sixth, but these aren't thunder.

The CCTV footage would have shown five bodies lying in a sort of pentangle formation in the car park between Luna Park and the Grape Wine bar in the Melbourne beach suburb of St. Kilda. No one will ever see that footage, as it was supposedly deleted. Even though it's 4 am, the surroundings are well illuminated, and there's a cloud of acrid gunfire smoke floating in the air amongst the raindrops.

Steam also rises from the pools of warm blood that surround the bodies. I raise my head and look around.

One has his head in an unnatural position, like it was almost ripped off by some powerful force. It's the Vince guy; Sam must have snapped his neck. Next to him lies the accomplice, the other rogue operative, Paolo. He is motionless and has a bullet hole through the upper left of his chest. He's soaked in blood, but in the chaos, I'm not sure who brought him down as neither Henry, Sam, nor I were armed. And there's Henry, poor Henry. He is motionless with a clean bullet hole through the middle of his forehead. His eyes are still wide open, almost with a look of surprise. There is little blood. He was the victim of Paolo. I turn my head towards him, put my hand on his eyes, and gently close them.

On the other side of me is Sam, that massive body twitching. "Sam, wake up, wake up, please, wake up." He is still alive though blood is flowing from underneath his jacket. Then heavy rain starts. I'm propped up on my elbows, observing the surrealistic scene whilst raindrops stream down my face. The rain mixes with the blood flowing all around me. Time seems to have slowed down, perception accentuated. I feel no pain and am strangely aware, more aware than ever before, just the throbbing below my groin, it feels so warm, and I can see a lump in the jeans gently pulsating and feel the warmth running down the lower side of my left leg. I try to lift my chest higher to get a better view, but then a stinging pain. I cough and add a stream to the surrounding pool of blood and rainwater. I turn my head slightly. There's a figure above me, impeccably dressed in a black suit with black tie; it must be Victor – otherwise known as the Doctor or Fixer. He seems impervious to the rain. He looks like a James Bond, the first one, Sean Connery. He is furiously dialling numbers on his phone. He swipes the raindrops flowing down his face exposing slightly bloodshot eyes and a look of disbelief. He regains his composure. I've never seen him in the flesh, just read the description in Jason's notes that he's the right-hand man and hitman of LaMosa, very effective and dangerous. His right arm is lowered but still clenching a pistol. I can see moisture condensing on the barrel and a faint whisper of smoke rising as raindrops drip from the barrel. Strangely I have no fear but think about what will happen to BHK. I look up at Victor expecting the arm to be raised and a bullet through my head just like Paolo must have got, but unexpectedly, he kneels down and examines everyone in the pentangle of carnage.

Marg finally arrives. Victor turns to Marg, who has just run over and is panting. "You are late. You know what to do."

"No, you're late. It wasn't supposed to happen this way."

Victor continues his inspection but gives Marg an icy look. "The islander has abdominal wounds and possibly some minor peripheral nerve damage. Nothing our medical staff cannot fix. Trust me, like you, I have medical training, and I have the best connections, even in Melbourne. I'm sorry about Jason and Henry. Henry's family will be well looked after financially. You have to wear it on your conscience. Hopefully, this carnage has ended, and no more lives need be lost. Now, look after Jules. As you probably diagnosed, he has a punctured lung – clean wound. But there's also probably a small calibre hollow-point bullet lodged below his severed left femoral artery, and he's losing blood rapidly. I can't get my team here in time to save him. It's up to us. Now show him how to put his little finger in the artery to stop the haemorrhage."

Above me is Marg. Her hair is soaked, lying limply down her neck, and rain is dripping from her face. I can feel her unbuttoning and pulling down my jeans. If it were any other circumstance, I'd frolic in anticipation. She digs and inserts her left index finger in the severed left femoral artery. The warm trickle ceases.

"We have to clear this carnage as quickly as possible, you have to help me, Marg, and after that, we fix the injured." It seems like second nature to Victor to make these announcements. His coolness is unnerving.

"Jules, I'll be back soon." Marg removes her finger from my femoral, and there is a gush of blood, then she guides my little finger into the femoral. The blood ceases again. "I'll be back soon," she reassures in a distressed voice.

The rain is thick, but I can see Victor dragging the dead bodies away from street sight and concealing them behind some bushes. With the help of Marg, he drags Sam and then me behind the toilet block opposite the Grape Vine bar. I grab Sam's shoulder; I can think of better places to be than behind a St Kilda toilet block at 4 am in the morning. Then I can see Victor making more calls on his phone. He's yelling, but I can't hear what he's saying.

The rain-soaked Victor rushes over to Sam and inspects him.

"Your wounds are superficial, and you will recover. Your name is Sam, right? Sam, we have to collaborate. Please do as I say, as it's important for your daughter's career. This is our secret. This event never happened. Some medical people will be here very soon to treat you and to remove the deceased bodies."

Then BHK walks onto the scene. Rain drips from his face. He looks horrified and gasps. "What happened to you, dad?"

I tilt my head and look up at him.

"You called me dad. You shouldn't be here."

"I followed you guys; you know I don't sleep much." He kneels down and hugs me. It hurt but was worth every ounce of pain. His tears drip on me and mix with the raindrops. Better than any peptide supplement. He looks me in the eyes. "You won't die, will you? I can't handle another dad dying."

I grab him. "No way, I got the best reason to live. Son, go back home now. I'll keep in touch. You can't be seen here. Please go. I love you. Go. Go now; now. Move, put some dry clothes on and turn on the alarm system when you get home."

Through the drizzling rain, I can see the kid wandering away but looking back with a frightened look on his face. This is not what a kid his age should be seeing. Oh, f..k, the kid will be on his own.

"Marg, give me a phone, hold it and cover it from the rain." I dial Charmaine's number. It takes at least five efforts of wrong numbers before an answering service answers. "Blue Monkey, you got to help my son, you and Smithy. Get to my place as quick as possible. Smithy still has keys and knows the alarm code. Please just look after him till I get back. He may be in danger."

Marg and Victor are there looking at me and each other, rain dripping down their hair and faces. I drop the phone and start fading into unconsciousness. You can still hear when you're fading. The sight goes first, things turn purple, but the hearing goes last, so you got to be careful what you say when someone is dying around you.

Victor is still talking; maybe he's unaware that I can still hear.

"She goes by the name of Charmaine Provist, and his phone call to her might complicate things even more. Now we have to start moving. Most of the mess will be cleaned up quickly but help me move him to the vehicle. You did bring the car, didn't you? And stop him hyper-ventilating. He's going into shock. Put your hand across his mouth and nose. Twenty breaths per minute, and make sure a finger is in that femoral. Yours or his, it doesn't matter and stay off the Peth; we'll save it for him."

Marg whispers to me, "I didn't blow up Jason. I think your mummy did. She was probably hoping I'd be in the car as well. I was the main target; Jason was just caught in the crossfire." I can't respond to her comment. Just hope I'll remember it if I recover, as it sort of makes sense.

I open my eyes. The vision is still purple, then grey and then the bright light at the end of a tunnel; that genetically inbuilt mechanism to make death less ominous and almost palatable: Optical nerves firing away randomly as they become depleted of oxygen. Then there's a replay of your life in super-fast motion, all significant events. In my case, there weren't too many, so it only lasts 15 seconds. Loss of consciousness soon follows.

I wake up on a kitchen table and feel cold. Not the best place; home for more bacteria than your average toilet seat, computer keyboard or mobile phone. I'm also naked, and there's annoying periodic, clashing noise like things dropping on a metal plate. Victor has a towel wrapped around him, as does Marg.

"Our clothes are in Jason's dryer; please excuse our less-than-professional appearance," Victor coolly announces, "I have inserted an expansion tube into your femoral artery. It is a new concept. The tubes have plastic hairs that allow easy insertion into severed blood vessels but don't pop out; like fishhooks, they hold till the blood vessel repairs. They disintegrate after about four weeks. Your other wounds have been stitched up. You will live. Try not to move your left arm too much, as your left arm has an improvised saline drip. I will get the antibiotics soon, and I assure you that the table was scrubbed with bleach. I did hear you ranting about germs and toilet seats."

I look up at the blood-covered Victor, who continues speaking, "I did my research. If you had any history of intravenous drug use or were promiscuous, I would be seriously concerned about contracting Hepatitis C or HIV. You definitely don't fit the profile for being involved in any risky activities."

Strangely I feel insulted. It re-enforces what I had suspected about my sheltered life. Every year blended into another. Nothing ever changed, and I just complacently went along with it. Victor read my mind.

"It is all right, Jules. You stepped well outside your comfort zone today. It is something I never had to do, as there were always very reliable and competent resources I could call on when things got tough. You have done well. I respect you," Victor announces.

I can see Victor removing his disposable plastic gloves.

"Jules, can you hold these gloves for a minute? I have to make a phone call." He also places a small vial and syringe in my hand and applies some pressure so that my fingers wrap around them. He then puts on a fresh pair of disposable plastic gloves. He must also be a hygiene fanatic. Victor shortly returns. "On second thought, you probably have had enough Pethidine in you." He carefully removes the vial and syringe from my hand and dumps them into the kitchen rubbish bin. He then starts furiously scrubbing and putting any items from the table in a big black plastic bag. The smell of that bleach is obnoxious. His phone rings, and he briefly disappears into another room. I fade into sleep, maybe only briefly, then awake startled. A 'grim reaper' like figure, dressed in black, is standing crouched in front of Marg. The face is covered, but its arms are exposed. They are thin but muscular. The reaper soon disappears. It must be just a bad dream.

A minute, who knows later, I can see Marg slumped on a chair, her towel unwrapped, exposing her naked body. Victor emerges and is back in the kitchen. He doesn't seem surprised as he looks at the naked body. I can see Victor checking her neck for a pulse, then he rushes to the clothes dryer, pulls out his clothing and grabs the car keys from the pocket of Marg's dried pants. He wraps a bedsheet around me and then puts his shirt and suit back on. He brushes the wrinkles in the suit.

"She is dead. There is a syringe track mark on her left forearm and a syringe and vial lying on the floor beside her. She probably bought her drugs from dubious sources. I suspect it was Fentanyl in that syringe, hundreds of times more potent than Pethidine. There are 15 vials of codeine-like substances in the 2nd bathroom, which I assume was for her use at Jason's house. She must have shot up before injecting you. She chose the wrong or right vial, depending on which way you want to look at it."

"What about Marg? What shall we do with her body? We cannot just leave her here?"

"I'll make sure she is picked up by my team and that she has a dignified cremation."

"Victor, did you see someone leaving the house a few minutes ago? There was another person in here."

"Jules, you are delusional. I was only gone for a few minutes, and I heard nothing. Just stay calm. It will be all right."

"Jules, you have tears flowing down your face. Believe me, it will all be taken care of, and you will soon see your son. Focus your thinking on your son, not on Marg."

I start drifting in and out of consciousness. For a moment, I wonder if Victor's idea of cremation is to set the house on fire. I look behind at the slumbering Marg as Victor drags me to the VW and then runs back to get the saline drip.

I don't feel that much sorrow for Marg at the moment but do hope she can cheat death again. On second thought, I do feel grief for her, great rushes of grief, but not for long as sleep intervenes, and thoughts cease.

Chapter nine

"Where am I?"

Victor is there and grabs my hand. "It is all right. You are on a yacht on your Victorian Westernport Bay. You were in an induced coma for two weeks in a clinic. My initial assessment of your condition was over-optimistic. We then brought you and your son to the yacht. I kept you sedated so you would not move too much as the expansion tubes are still only experimental and possibly fragile. The good news is the pneumonia and urinary infection you had contracted whilst in the clinic are cured, and your wounds are healing exceptionally fast. Here, drink some water."

It's not the news you want to hear after coming out of a coma. I try to get up but am very disorientated, and there's still a drip in my left arm.

"Stay down, Jules. In a few more days I'll remove the drip, and you'll be able to walk, and now I will give you some water to drink, but please try to use the toilet from now on as our supply of laundry powder is running low."

"Where's BHK and Marg and Sam?"

"BHK is here. BHK, hold your father's hand."

"Love you, dad. Sam is fine and back at your townhouse, but mum had an accident," BHK says. I notice tears in his eyes.

"Good to see you, son," I mutter, then fall back to sleep.

Three weeks have passed sailing on Victor's yacht, well, Nino's yacht, his brother's, as I would later find out. Victor's wife Melissa, and their two kids Peter and Lizzy are also onboard.

I'm able to walk a bit without assistance and can make it to the bathroom, so no more soiled bedsheets. Starting to feel physically fine though my mind is still troubled.

Victor visits me in my cabin. "You are still grieving for Marg. She had injected herself after helping you, and she passed away. She bought 'junk' off the streets. You would be dead as well, if that dose of Fentanyl was injected into you. The coroner's initial report was 'Death by Misadventure' but Jules, I f..ked up and I'm sorry. I may have been able to prevent her shooting up."

"I remember Victor. You handed me the syringe and vial before you tossed them in the bin."

"Jules, that was my mistake. A lot was going on. I was stitching you up and making phone calls to arrange our escape and cleanup of the place. It was a very stressful situation unlike any I have ever encountered before."

"Victor, my fingerprints were all over that vial and syringe. If they do another more thorough coroner's inquiry I'm stuffed." I turn my head away from Victor. Recent images of Marg rush through my mind. Emotions are surfacing. I cringe trying to hold back the sadness.

"She was my wife!"

"Calm down Jules. I am very sorry that she has passed away, but you are only remembering the good aspects of your relationship. We all do that when someone we have known passes away. We turn a blind eye to the less-than-good parts. Jules, Marg was not the person you believe she was. She manipulated many people for prestige and financial gain."

"Who are you to judge my wife?"

"Jules, it is all intertwined. It is a web. One day when your memory returns you may understand. I will give you doses of information at a time, information in digestible doses. I cannot fully understand it all myself, as I do not have all the pieces. Only one person has all the pieces. Have patience, we will work it out eventually."

"What on earth do you mean? You're making it sound like some conspiracy or spy movie. I think I want to get out of here and take BHK with me."

"Jules, calm down, the way that organization works, which also involves you, Marg and me, had dealings with far more sophisticated people than LaMosa. It's on a need-to-know basis. You do your job and don't question because you won't get any replies and unpleasant things may happen to you if you question too much."

"Victor this is ridiculous; this stuff doesn't happen in OZ, you're more delusional than me."

Victor moves closer and wraps his arms around me. He repeats again. "Marg fooled a lot of people, not just you and Jason. I am surprised you were not a tiny bit suspicious. I do not think you and Marg did much communicating. Jules, you turned a blind eye as there were several conflicts of interest not just about that injectable peptide that many governments and individuals would like to have access to."

I'm trying to comprehend what Victor just said. "Did you turn a blind eye too, Victor? She was giving up her habit and was getting alternative pain treatment."

"Jules, it's highly probable she injected herself. I played no part and I do not think you were in a capable state to inject her. Don't worry about any inquest. Marg had a huge stash of codeine like substances, including Fentanyl, in Jason's bathroom. It was concealed but the Police found it. I'm sure the coroner came to the correct conclusion."

I'm in two states of mind. I think it's called cognitive dissonance. Is Victor, the guy who helped me, also guilty of my wife's death? Then that ghostly image of the grim reaper-like figure leaning over Marg. I don't know what to think.

"Victor, why were you there at Luna Park? No one apart from me, Marg, Sam, Henry and LaMosa rogues knew about that meeting. Why did you miraculously turn up?"

"Small digestible doses of information at a time, Jules. You've had your dose for the day."

Our conversation seems to be going in circles, both of us being defensive and elusive. I need time to process it all. Something concrete, think of something concrete. Think of BHK, Henry and Sam.

"Victor, how's Sam and how is Henry's wife coping?"

Victor seems relieved that the subject was changed. "Sam is fully recovered and living in your townhouse in Melbourne as your son already told you. Henry's wife and kids are still in deep mourning. You mumbled on the kitchen operating table when I was stitching you up. You repeatedly said what a great little guy he was. Nino and I have made sure his family has a very comfortable financial future."

Tears are forming in my eyes. It's a sensation I'm getting used to it. "Can I ring Bernadette, his wife, and offer my condolences?"

"You should desist. She is still in deep mourning and has the local Catholic community comforting her 24/7."

"I want to ring her!"

Victor hesitates then hands me a phone. I still remember Henry's landline phone number. I ring. It was definitely a mistake to ring little Henry's family. I got a lot of verbal abuse, profanities, which I prefer not to publish. I didn't think Catholics were capable of vocalizing that sort of language. I sink back on the chair, staring at the ceiling, I hand the phone back to Victor.

"People die, Jules, some sooner than they should. You are not to blame for Henry's departure. Let us go up and eat. You should be able to walk up the stairs, and in time you will stop feeling sorry for yourself. You never know when your last supper will be so make the best of it." Victor seems to be just as good as me at turning off and diverting from painful topics.

Meals are delivered by motorboat from surrounding towns, well only one town to be exact. The peripheral warning system always sounds an alarm as the boat arrives. Victor is crouched down, grabbing the polystyrene boxes handed to him by the boat driver. He then hands back the boxes from the previous delivery. I look up and notice Melissa for the first time, Victor's wife or partner as you call relationships these days. She is tall, jet black hair, prominent eyebrows, long thin face, attractive, on the thin side, but well-endowed in the upper body; also very organized and business-like. I'd say she's genetically a mixture of Italian and middle eastern, judging by her golden skin colour and appearance. She doesn't smile much, and I think she runs the household.

We're on the deck sitting at the table. Melissa serves the food with Victor and me helping as best as we can. The kids, even BHK, ravenously rush for the healthy delights. I've never eaten so well; seafood, baby spinach, tomatoes, feta cheese, avocados, pickled eggplant all sprinkled with olive oil and balsamic vinegar, the list goes on. Seconds, thirds, we all go for it, stuffing our faces in delight. Mutters of 'yummy' resonate. There is much gesticulation and joyous yelling, especially when Victor brings out the hot chilli paste. There is a competition, who can eat a teaspoon, and even BHK joins in. I don't participate but watch. I remember my Ghost chilli concoction. I wish I had it here instead of that puny commercial stuff.

Victor survives the longest and grabs the trophy raising it up high and smiling. Imprinted on the trophy is 'World's Hottest Guy'. Melissa briefly looks at me as if to say, 'are you up to it'. Tomorrow I will challenge Victor. I wish I had my Ghost chillies with me. Victor would have to do the first tasting, of course, after which I'm sure he'd concede defeat. Victor comes over and rests his trophy on the table. He has beads of sweat on his face. "Jules, do you miss ice cream, cakes and biscuits?"

"I haven't really thought about it, but I can taste sweetness in all this food. This is the best food I've ever eaten."

"You are the biochemist or pharmacist, so you must know. That is why my beautiful wife and kids are slim and glowing in health. You are what you eat, my stepfather said, probably the only wise thing he ever said. I also saw your glance. Are you attracted to my beautiful wife?"

"Are you baiting me, why did you even ask?"

"It's highly likely she will be your partner in the future. If that happens, look after my kids."

"You're off the planet, Victor. Have you been smoking something? I'm not sure where this conversation is leading to. Are you bating me in some strange sort of game? If you are, I'm not into it."

"It's OK, Jules, just relax. It may make sense in the future."

I give him a sardonic look. I feel like I want to grab his neck and block his carotid arteries. I evaluate, that would be risky to do, especially since he's probably far stronger than me. I put that notion to rest.

We all lay on the deck of the yacht, covered in sunscreen lotion. Victor is obsessive about not getting wrinkles and liberally squirts blobs of the stuff at us which we all rub in before dosing off on the deck. I glance at Melissa again. Luckily I'm lying on my stomach reflecting. This is paradise. It must be a dream, but the problem with pleasant dreams is that you eventually wake up, and Victor's seemingly inappropriate comments have started the process.

When we moor at one of the mainland piers, they go jogging. Victor, Melissa and the kids, though BHK finds it hard with that big head. I finally joined them, as I think the injuries have healed. I'm not exactly sure how much time has passed as every pleasant day blends into another. It's like time has stood still, and you don't want the current experience to end. Victor and I sprint back to the yacht. He wins by quite a margin. He has longer legs. Melissa and the kids soon follow.

Victor is crouching and puffing. "Jules, there is corrective surgery, extensive surgery, many cranial operations that can correct your son's condition. It is a long process, and there is always a risk of infection, as in any surgical procedure. He would need multiple procedures, so the risk is cumulative. Then you can look at the alternative. He will probably have no more intra-cranial bleeding or spinal fluid leaking in. His head is unlikely to expand. It cannot at his age. If he puts on more weight, he'll pass as a normal kid. He is still very thin; that is what makes him stand out. He needs to eat lots of pasta and veggies. Hendrick must have rarely fed him."

I heard the same diagnosis before from Marg. "You mentioned Hendrick. How do you know about Hendrick? Why did you mention that name?"

Victor is startled for a moment, knowing he had made a blunder and disclosed too much. His head turns sideways several times as if trying to think of an answer. He finally replies. "Your mind is curious about all the coincidences. As I said before, I will explain small fractions at a time, and I do not have all the answers. Would you like to hear part of my story? Do you want to listen?" He's distracting me, but I let him. I nod my head even though I'm sure Marg had explained the surgery BHK could have. Their explanations sounded so similar. I suspend questioning Victor about that coincidence. We sit back on the sand. Melissa is some distance away, looking for crabs with the kids. I can hear excited voices in the background.

"Jules, my stepbrother Nino and I were diversifying far away from Chicago. We set up a type of meat works in rural Victoria. Not exactly meat, but I'll explain about the insect-protein industry later. It is the future and sustainable. Insect protein will eventually save humanity from starvation. Initially, there were some problems, but we natured government contacts. A slim, tall, elderly lady was there at the governmental hearing we had to attend. Her name started with 'D', maybe Doreen. She somehow managed to expedite our applications, but there was a conditional clause. We owed her, and she called me and gave me the location where I was supposed to meet you. My hire car didn't start, flat battery, so I had to call a taxi and so I got there too late to save Henry or you and Sam from getting shot. Jules, it was one fateful incident that changed our lives, a flat battery. Sometimes a simple incident changes many lives."

I don't ask if he opened the hood to check if the battery wires were still connected. 'Rule 451 – quickest way to disable a vehicle is to disconnect the battery. The engine hood on most models can be opened without a key, and it is not connected to the car alarm system.' I let him talk, as it's slowly starting to make sense, the jigsaw puzzle., I refrain from mentioning that a simple incident like looking behind the fridge can also change lives. None of this would probably not have happened if for a struggling, noisy fridge motor.

"Jules, my stepfather was a simple man, a builder who worked his way up before he got involved in all the illegal dealings. Nino, his biological son, and I just want to get out and do something that might feed the world without the current wastage, and yes, we may have taken a few shortcuts. We also encountered many people, some of whom did their best to sabotage us, but we were not deterred, and we won in the end. NV Burgers are available at many health food stores. They're high in digestible, high-grade protein, and no animals were slaughtered to produce the burgers."

"Wait, Victor, you are breeding insects?"

"Yes, Jules, they only require one-thousandth of the resources to produce the equivalent of your beloved beef protein. Our scientists even made it taste the same as a meat burger and to have the same texture. You've been eating them here and never complained."

"A wonderful concept, but Victor, how are Marg, you and me connected to insects?"

Victor takes out his phone, fiddles with it for a while and finds a song a Dire Straits song, 'Private Investigations'. "Do you relate to it, Jules, you have moisture forming in your eyes again?" We look at the ocean as we listen to the song. Victor puts his hand on my shoulder. "It is OK, brother, just recuperate."

"Victor, I don't know if I can trust you even though you did save my life, but some of the things you say and do are quite weird, contradictory and don't make sense to me. The context changes a lot, and that comment about me being with Melissa is highly presumptuous."

"Jules, you're starting to use big words. That is good. Indicates there was no significant brain damage due to hypoxia," Victor laughs and pats me on the shoulder. "My comment regarding my wife was just a test to determine if your cognitive functions have returned."

I can't draw the connection diagram in my head. I need a very big whiteboard. I think I may have been trained to draw those types of diagrams. They consist of names of either people or organizations, which are depicted as circles. It's a bit like Venn diagrams that we all learnt in junior maths, but arrows are also used. There can be circles within circles if it's an organization or family, and the thickness of the arrows between them is a visual representation, a guess based on some evidence of how strongly the connections may be related. It's far more sophisticated than what we see on TV crime shows. I think Victor may be subtly implying that Marg and I were somehow connected in his life prior to that fateful encounter at Luna Park, but he shouldn't have known that, how he could have known that and then there's 'D'? Victor owed 'D' a favour. I suspect the 'D' is Doris. What a perfect disguise, a tea lady.

Time to shift attention again; I look up at Victor, who follows my gaze. I watch BHK play with Victor and Melissa's kids. They come running back, each holding a big red crab and showing off their catches to Victor and me. The crabs would end up on the menu for lunch though Melissa, Victor and I had to peel them. The peeling part is definitely not as much fun for kids as catching the crabs, but while my head is down and thumbling, trying to remove the shells of the crabs, I notice from the corner of my eye, Melissa occasionally looking at me as she peels and cuts with that big knife - if looks could kill she definitely knows how to express that look.

Another great lunch followed by a few bottles of red. Melissa, Victor and I keep a watchful eye from the yacht as the kids descend back to the foreshore. Then Victor takes control of the music system with his phone, gets on YouTube and streams the music up loud; a song by a group called MGMT and the song is appropriately called 'Kids'. It may be just the wine, but the three of us are emotionally moved. We wrap our arms around each other's shoulders whilst glancing at the kids. The song strikes chords in all of us. It finishes. Victor puts it on again. Finally, Victor turns off his phone. We wipe tears from our faces and regain our composure. I look at her. Melissa displayed vulnerability for the first time. She is moved. Why the f..k do I really care. I would care in the end, very much so, but I'm not going to give away the rest of the story, not just yet.

"I hope they find more crabs, darling, maybe they could be crab divers when they grow up," Victor comments with a smile. Melissa turns around at us both and gives a tinker of a smile. The first time Victor made an attempt at a joke. We drink more summer wine whilst watching the kids enjoying life. They seem to get on so fine, and Victor's kids don't care that BHK has a big head and skinny build. BHK has also taken a guardian role, looking after Victor's kids. On one occasion, little Peter climbed over the yacht's railings and fell into the bay. BHK saw the incident, and before we had a chance, he jumped in to save little Peter, even though BHK can hardly swim. Victor and I soon followed, pulling Peter and BHK back onto the yacht. Victor hugged BHK, as did Melissa. "You are a hero, BHK, we have to celebrate!" BHK had the biggest grin whilst Victor and Melissa both snapped photos of him with his arm on the shoulder of little Peter. Lizzy also joins in the photo shoot.

And so more time very pleasantly passes. I have no idea how I can repay Victor's family for their generosity. BHK is also ravenously eating and expanding. He doesn't look like a malnourished kid anymore, all thanks to Victor and his family.

Victor and I seem to have developed a trust and what seems like a sincere friendship. His generosity is overwhelming, though I do remember the mention of a favour to pay back. The only way I can make sense of this friendship is that Victor is paradoxically into Astrology, and we were born two days apart; he's two days older. Victor adopted me as his brother. He even sometimes calls me 'brother', which Melissa, his wife, thinks is a bit strange. So, I feel I got a friend. I feel I got almost everything, except Marg, well maybe just an idealized memory of Marg; I got BHK, Victor, Melissa and their kids, who I'm fond of and chase around the yacht. I occasionally think about Charmaine as well and hope she is as happy as I am.

Everyone is asleep. It's just Victor and I who stay up, sipping glasses of wine and looking at the stars as the yacht gently sways. It's become a nightly ritual. I wonder if Melissa misses him. Victor Then starts one of his many lectures.

"Sometimes I wonder if we think and perceive the world differently because of our cultural genetic makeup. You have a Polish background. The Polish genes seem to accentuate paranoia and depression. Maybe that's not that unusual, as the country has been invaded so many times in the last 1000 years. My Italian genes seem to give me a predilection to indulgences and love of family life."

I interject. "Victor, you've also shot people. How can you reconcile that?"

"They were all bad people – well, actually, I only shot Vince, or was it Paolo, in Melbourne, but I'll come back to that point later. Just let me continue for the moment."

"Oh, and didn't you shoot someone when you were working part-time as a security guard whilst studying medicine? Melissa told me that when we were jogging."

"Jules, it was dark. I had encountered a person attempting a break into a premises I was doing a security check on, and I saw a gun pointed at me. I didn't know it was one of those replica guns with fake bullets. He shot at me, and I shot and shot until the cartridge was empty. I faced the court system. I was acquitted though I still financially help that guy's family as best I can." A tear runs down Victor's face. "Jules, I'm not a killer."

Victor continues. "Jules, when an embryo develops, it goes through the stages of evolution. I once worked in a hospital that catered for abnormal births where the product didn't resemble anything human because genes failed to turn off or on at the appropriate time. They resembled fish-like creatures and actually had gills. We all go through that stage in the womb, but then other genes usually kick in, and we develop lungs and other human organs. You have a hospital for that in Melbourne, where I did part of my internship but back to the story. We could not treat them medically. My job was to humanely terminate them by turning off their life support systems. There was not a choice. Otherwise, they would die a painful death as they tried to breathe outside of an aqueous environment. It brought tears to my eyes having to terminate them but not when terminating that LaMosa guy. He was the scum of the earth."

Victor's eyes are watery again. He is hurting.

"Jules, I did some more preliminary research on your supplement. At first, I thought that some of its apparent actions were just a placebo effect, but after further investigation, I concluded that it accentuates muscle and neural cell growth and new connections between neurons – previously thought as impossible - but it is not selective. It may also activate those primitive genes that are meant to stay dormant after an embryo develops successfully. Most of the genes we possess are leftovers from thousands of generations in our evolution. Turning those genes on would be very risky to the future of humanity. The peptide may have also had some side effects that affect reproduction. Jules, Marg did some work for my stepfather. She was freelancing. She was successful; she made certain people forget so they did not have to be dealt with by means that are more physical. The peptide seemed to affect the Hippocampus and affect memory formation. It also made the brain highly malleable and very susceptible to hypnotic suggestion. There were some transactions that certain parties, who my stepfather dealt with, would not like to be made public. She had access to my stepfather's dealings and may have scanned the transaction documents. Marg was also promoting your peptide on the Dark Web as an undetectable performance-boosting substance. She made a double hit. She could blackmail our family and sell your drug, but I didn't kill her. The tricky manufacturing process for the peptide is on that USB drive that you carry. Don't worry, you still have your USB drive and a record of those transactions. I trust they'll be our little secret."

I go to my bedroom feeling more than a little perturbed. Marg involved with the LaMosa clan? What more surprises can there be? Got to think about something else rather than dwell on Marg. There is Wi-Fi on the yacht, maybe via satellite. Victor has given me the Wi-Fi router password. I turn the Android tablet on and resume the reading. I got this incredible thirst for knowledge. There's a cranium that has been left largely dormant, hardly used for the last ten years. I'm on the Internet and into Wikipedia. I search Epigenetics. The articles are technical, but I understand them. Wow, things have progressed. Then it hits me, must have been involved in this stuff before. It's 5 am, and I turn off the PC tablet, check on BHK, retire to my bunk and fall into a deep sleep, but then BHK shakes my arm and wakes me. "I'm having the best time ever; I wish this would never end." I was about to respond that all good things come to an end but refrain. Instead, I hug BHK and remind him that it is 6 am in the morning and he should still be sleeping.

So, it's another fabulous day of swimming in the sea, playing with the kids, frolicking and enjoying lobsters and all sorts of molluscs, perfectly presented by Melissa. After dinner, Victor and I resume our conversation. Melissa and the kids retire downstairs. I glance at Melissa before she retires. She glances back. Victor notices.

"Jules, have you got sexual fantasies of screwing my wife?" Victor calmly asks. "Or are you gay?"

"What, no! You suggested that before. Yes, she's attractive, but the thought hasn't crossed my mind. I was married to Marg, and I don't see the connection. What you're saying is a confusing statement, two different contradictory questions. It doesn't make sense. You've had too many wines," I reply.

"It's OK, Jules, the main point of dissent between my brother Nino and I is that I support Gay rights and Gay marriage, which is abhorrent to him. He still has that Italian Catholic provincial mentality. Originally there were three of us brothers, Nino, myself, and Mark, the youngest. Mark was not my biological brother, but I loved him."

It looks like another intense story. I pour another glass of wine and swig it down.

"Mark was abandoned by the family because he preferred the physical company of men rather than women. The family pressure was too much. Mark purposefully took an overdose and died. He was never a drug user. He premeditated his death by buying a lot of junk off the streets. He left a long suicide letter that explained his motives. Our father and Nino totally dismissed that letter. I fear for my son, Peter, who may also be gay. I believe it may be genetic. He will need looking after, if anything happens to me. Nino can't do it."

Tears are appearing in Victor's eyes, yet again. It's another tearful night.

"I'm not gay, Victor. I just never met the right woman after Marg. Well, I thought I had, but I believe she may be my long-lost brother; it's a long, complicated story. Now I do promise I will help look after Peter and Lizzy if anything happens to you, and I don't have fantasies about Melissa. I told you that before."

I sort of lied. I'm quite fascinated by the enigmatic Melissa. Victor must have picked that up when I glance at her – maybe for far too long. Got to be more careful. Rule 507 flashes into my mind, 'Be discrete, never stare. Absorb the information in a single brief glance and process it afterwards when alone'.

"Brother, I would appreciate it if you will look after my kids and Melissa, if anything happens to me. I will ask you later to tell me your complicated story," Victor says and pats me on the back. He has repeated his request, maybe too much wine.

"Victor, do you know you have a twin brother? It's not like me and Jason who happened to just look alike but not genetically related. I did a lot of research on Google whilst laying there in the bunk. You had a twin brother and after your real parents died, you were both adopted but by different couples. You were separated from your brother."

For a moment, well more than a moment Victor looks down. "Sounds very much like your story Jules. We have a lot in common."

Before we retire, Victor clasps his hands on my head. His face is very close to mine. I close my eyes and freeze.

"Goodnight, my brother," Victor finally announces. I slowly descend the stairs to the lower deck and check the sleeping BHK. He is fine and roll into bunk. I'm very confused. I don't start the tablet PC. I stare at the ceiling, thinking about Marg and the commitment I made to Victor. Somehow, I still miss Marg, despite the revelations about her motives. I wonder how BHK is coping with the death of his mother. He seems to be still in denial and doesn't mention her, but I'm glad he's having such a good time. Also, thoughts of Melissa intrude into my night-time thinking, though they are not of a sexual nature, not yet anyway.

It's a bit strange that Victor, with his medical training, could be so into a discipline like astrology that has no basis in science. His wife, Melissa thought it strange as well. When Victor was spearfishing, we discussed his obsession – and I only briefly glance at her. We concluded that astrology was Victor's outlet. It provided some explanation for the violent events he had witnessed or maybe participated in. I guess I can only be grateful for being born two days within my 'brother'.

Victor is always generous and doesn't seem to understand the concept of greed. Despite his competence and coolness in handling critical emergencies, there is a sort of naivety about him. His wife loves that aspect of Victor, and we are both enchanted by him, but he also has a vice. It would shock me and be totally contradictory to the rest of his philosophy.

BHK climbs into the bed with me.

"You have to bulk up some more."

"I am, dad. There's a gym set at the bottom of the yacht. I'm pumping iron and eating lots. Dad, stop thinking about mum. Let it go."

I put my arm around BHK and fall into a deep sleep and have many dreams. Some of the dreams included Melissa dressed as a dominatrix, whipping me and I'm actually enjoying it. Others are sad and involve Marg. I wake several times in the night in a sweat, though reflect on the dream before it fades. BHK is still asleep. I kiss his forehead. I don't want to dream anymore, but hope his dreams are pleasant, unlike mine. I stop churning and fall asleep again.

Victor knocks on the door. "You've been gone for 14 hours. There is still breakfast left on the deck, but hurry. These birds you call seagulls are swooping in."

Chapter ten

"Jules, can Melissa and the kids stay at your Elwood place? I have to return to Chicago to discuss some matters with Nino."

"Yes, of course, as long as they don't mind sharing the spare bedrooms. I have self-inflating mattresses and sleeping bags, but the food won't be anywhere near as good as what I've eaten on the yacht. Maybe they can help me clean out the other spare bedrooms. They are full of boxes at the moment."

The logistics of the living arrangement are racing in my mind. BHK may have to share a bedroom with me or use the small study room upstairs.

"Jules, I have given Melissa one of my credit cards. Just buy any bedding you need and any extra food you need. Now please go. I have to do my morning meditation." Victor ushers me out and returns to his cabin. I can hear Melissa and the kids are frolicking upstairs on the deck. I was about to go up but had a question to ask Victor. How long will he be away? I quietly open Victor and Melissa's cabin door. Victor is sniffing some white powder. He turns around with a fiery look.

"Victor, what's going on?"

"Keep Melissa and the kids entertained for the next 15 minutes. I'll be out soon," he says with an icy stare.

I shut the door to the cabin and slowly make my way upstairs. It's not the Victor I've become to know who is a health fanatic. It is contradictory behaviour. Thoughts are rushing, and I probably have a very worried look on my face. Does Melissa know what Victor's meditation ritual involves? Why does he travel so much? Melissa told me recently that the yacht sojourn is the longest he's ever been home in a single stint. Back on the deck, everyone is happy and playful. I observe whilst in deep thought. Victor eventually comes up dressed in a swimsuit and immediately dives off the deck into the bay. I dive in as well, but I should have tightened the shorts before the dive. They slipped towards my ankles, and Melissa and the kids are laughing, as I struggle to pull them up and cover my butt. Eventually, I regain my composure and the shorts adjusted where they should be. I swim out to Victor and catch up. He is not a good swimmer, so we're treading water about 100m from the yacht.

"What's going on, Victor, tell me?"

"I saved your life and possibly gave you the best moments of life you'll ever experience. Now let me swim and never, ever mention what you saw to Melissa or anyone."

"I'm concerned, brother," I replied.

"Don't be. It's all under control, and you should have put the water-proof bandages on your wounds before you jumped into the water. I have no antibiotics left, so you better douse the wounds with methylated spirits when you get back on board. There's a bottle in the kitchen."

He gives me that icy look again and continues his version of a swim. I wade back to the yacht and climb aboard. BHK comes rushing over and asks if he can dive into the water. I say no. "Just climb down the ladder into the water. No diving. I'll watch you." The kids all climb down the ladder and tread water in the bay. Both Melissa and I are monitoring the happily frolicking kids. Parenting rule number something or other: 'Never take your eyes off your kids when they are in water'. Melissa seems to know that. We vigilantly watch whilst I rub the almost healed wounds with cotton wool soaked in metho that I found under the kitchen sink. It stings a little, and I give Melissa a painful smile. She gives a tortured smile back. I glance at Melissa again and feel like asking her if she knows about some of Victor's behaviour. Sanity prevails, and I don't. Maybe 20 minutes or so later, a jovial Victor climbs back onto the yacht. He gives Melissa and the kids, and me a big hug. It's like nothing had ever happened. He's back to his usual self though he avoids eye contact with me. Seems like Charmaine isn't the only complex person that I can't work out. It was an early night for all of us. Victor and I didn't talk, so no more small doses of answers to the big questions,

The next morning, a motorboat arrives and parks next to the yacht. Victor seems highly agitated. Maybe he didn't do his morning ritual. He hugs Melissa and the kids and comes to give me a hug, and whispers in my ear. "Look after them and never mention what you saw about what you call the ritual." The whispers continue. I lift my head and stare Victor in the eyes. "Are you coming back?"

"I don't know. You have a simple task. Look after my family just as I have looked after you."

"Victor, one last thing, you never quite answered the question I asked weeks ago. How did you happen to be so conveniently around at the Luna Park incident?"

"I told you before. If you want to know more, ask your mother, she sent me there part of a deal for her helping Nino and me getting our insect farm proposals being approved. We had a debt to repay to her, and it was."

"Victor, was my recuperation on the yacht part of the deal as well?"

"No, it was my decision to have you here. I'm sure it was more pleasant than recovering in the Alfred hospital."

"I will do my best to repay the favour and thanks."

He carries a duffle bag and descends the ladder to the waiting motorboat.

I'm baffled. Doris is like an octopus, tendrils reaching all the people I know. So much for Victor's astrology theory of why Victor and I may be connected. But how did Doris know about the meeting at Luna Park? My phone couldn't be traced. Marg must have notified Doris, but why? The only other explanation is that my home has been bugged, but I was very careful and never used the landline.

Everyone is waving as the motorboat departs at a furious pace. I turn my head and look at Melissa. "Did he tell you where you'll be living when we get off this yacht?"

"He did, and you owe him. Pull up the masts when I tell you to. We're going to dock soon." She seems to know what she's doing, but definitely doesn't sound happy, more like distressed., I refrain from putting my arm around her to comfort her. I regret that in hindsight.

The yacht is moored, and a security guard comes over. "It's OK. We'll look after the yacht. Have a nice day." There is a taxi van waiting for us. We all get in. BHK is sitting next to me. "What's going on, dad?"

"I'm not sure, but we're going back home."

"What is home, dad?"

"It's where you feel safe."

"Dad, I may not be safe." BHK hands me another flash drive. "Hendrick used Artificial Intelligence algorithms and software to remove the time gaps in the videos. They are called spikes, and Hendrick removed them from the videos. All those videos of me decrypting information in real-time on YouTube were fakes. He was playing a game against big bitcoin corporations. He liked playing games. It was fun."

"BHK, you know what you and Hendrick did? Share prices of companies severely plummeted. There was panic amongst small investors who weren't technically savvy and used online trading. Tonight, you'll make a video and post it on YouTube stating it was all a hoax and describing how the hoax was performed. If you don't do that, then you may indeed be a target."

"Dad, it was a joke."

"I know that, but those videos appeared on morning news TV programs. It would take thousands of years with our current technology to break an encrypted message, but some technically naïve people don't know that. Jokes can sometimes be harmful, and it was probably the 'mum and dad' investors who sold off their shares at rock-bottom prices. Hendrick's joke to punish big enterprises totally misfired."

BHK is tearful. "I'll post a confession tonight."

"Can you be traced?"

"I don't think so. We used pseudonyms, fake names and jumped through many routers. We used the TOR software. We can't be traced. Those video posts probably appeared to be coming from Sweden."

I put my arm around BHK's shoulders and do a cautionary glance back at Melissa, Lizzy and Peter. They seem OK and dozing.

We get out of the taxi with our duffle bags. Sam answers the doorbell. He seems fully recovered from his injury. We're home. Sam looks incredulously as we come marching in. "Anymore to come, Jules?"

"Sam, whisper when talking; my place may be bugged, and I think I may know where the main transmitter could be. Grab the torches; we're going outside," I whisper.

"Jules, why would anyone want to bug you?"

"It's a long story, Sam."

"Guys, Sam and I are just going outside to chase away some possums. Sam told me they have been causing a lot of noise at night and making it hard to sleep. We won't be long. Just wander around the house and have a look around. You'll be sleeping upstairs. There are pillows, linen and blankets in the wardrobes. Choose your sleeping arrangements and make your beds, as I'm hopeless at making beds."

Sam and I go into the courtyard and then follow the pathway that winds around the outside of the townhouse. "Sam, any listening device inside will be short-ranged as to preserve battery life. It would relay to a more powerful device that is probably connected to mains electricity power. There are two power points in the garage and two weather-protected power points jutting from the outside walls."

The most obvious concealed spot was behind the air-conditioning unit. The unit sits slightly mounted off the ground, unlike those that are mounted on walls. Sam and I shift the ground-mounted unit to expose the power point. Lucky first time, a black box the size of a cigarette packet with a thin antenna poking a few centimetres above the unit. It's connected through a thin double adapter to the power socket. That supposed pest exterminator must have been in a hurry as it was easy to find. I extract the black box, and we go back inside.

"It's OK; we can talk now, Sam."

"What about any hidden microphones inside the house?"

"Sam, they couldn't transmit over any significant distance, else their batteries would drain. But that's a good point. We'll also check all the other power points, inside and outside, just in case there is a long-range backup transmitter."

"Jules, how do you know about this bugging stuff?"

"I saw it on TV; how it's done."

"You think I believe you?"

"It doesn't matter what you believe at the moment. We just got to search for any long-range transmitters that look like this one."

It doesn't take long. We shift boxes in the garage to reveal the power-points and furniture inside the townhouse, meticulously examining every power-point. Melissa and the kids wonder what we're doing, crawling around, examining the skirting boards for power-points. Sam tells them we're just checking that the place is clean. It was vacant for several weeks when I was in hospital. Melissa gives a cynical look. We find nothing except a few dead roaches and go back to the lounge. "It seems all clean, Sam. We can look for ear-bud size microphones another day."

"Jules, are you going to introduce me to your guests?"

"Oops, sorry, I almost forgot." Sam and Melissa shake hands, and Sam bends down to shake the hands of the kids. There is some small talk and cordial smiles. I can hear Lissy whisper, "He's even bigger than dad."

We all go upstairs and help Melissa and the kids to make the beds. We're two beds short, but I got these supposedly self-inflating camping mattresses. I run down to the garage and get them. Self-inflating, my foot; both Sam and I huff and puff and eventually get them up till we fall back from hyperventilating. Melissa, her kids and Fabian help with laying out the linen. It's an adventure for the kids though Melissa doesn't look that happy. When no one else is looking, I poke my tongue out at Melissa, and she does the same in reply without uttering a word. She definitely has a longer tongue than I do though. As much as I'd like to get the tape measure out to confirm that, I don't. I may be delusional and imagining it, but I think she may actually like me, despite her behaviour is to the contrary.

Melissa, Peter and Lizzy decide to sleep in the same bedroom. Sam helps them unpack. No one is hungry, just tired. Sam and I go back downstairs after the job is complete.

"Jules, there's a couple of things I have to say or ask; I wasn't prepared that you'd all be back today, and SnowPea is going to visit tonight. She is my daughter. She is here in Melbourne on a Federal Police conference and may want a place to stay. She's coming over soon. Is that OK?" He asks. "The second thing is, what is all this bugging all about? You didn't explain the first time I asked."

"Sam, I don't know, but we had a big, long day. We're all very tired. Sleep in one of the bedrooms upstairs or the couch and give your SnowPea your bed for the night. I don't have any more mattresses."

I look around. The place is spotless, and the fridge is well stocked. Sam is just as house-trained as Smithy was. BHK wanders into my bedroom and flops on the double bed. "Dad, the mattress went flat; it burst at the seams even though I don't weigh that much," he says. After ten or so minutes, there is no sound from upstairs, and BHK is fast asleep on my bed. I log into the tablet PC and again watch the YouTube video of BHK breaking encryption then the doorbell rings. It's 10 pm. I spring up and dash to the kitchen to get the Ghost chilli pepper concoction and the big kitchen knife. Sam is dozing on the couch.

"Is Sam here?" A voice asks as I cautiously open the door. It's a police officer dressed in all the police attire. I cringe.

"He's on the couch. Tell me this is not an official police visit."

"I'm Annabelle, his daughter, now can you please move out of the way and put that knife back in the kitchen, else I'll have to disarm you, and that would hurt."

"I was expecting a SnowPea."

"That's what dad calls me, it's a nickname. You can call me Annabelle," she replies. From the official tone of her voice and manner, she probably takes her job very seriously. I move aside and let her in, along with her two suitcases in tow. I briefly stare at her. She looks like that TV movie character called 'Lara Croft'. I'm besotted. She towers quite a few centimetres over me. Where's she going to sleep, I wonder?

Sam jumps up from the couch and gives me a deadly look that implies, 'Don't even think of it'. I owe Sam, but I was too overwhelmed by other things when I said it's OK that SnowPea can stay the night. A federal police officer staying here could be a mistake, and it cannot be retracted. Got to work around it. Annabelle and Sam embrace and sit back on the couch. As I go to the fridge to get some beers and snacks, I overhear, "Dad, I have been transferred to Melbourne and working with the local police for a while, can I stay at your place until I rent an apartment? I don't like staying at the motel. It's really noisy, as I told you on the phone. I can't sleep there." They are too involved in conversation to notice that I'm still in the kitchen. I listen on.

"Dear SnowPea, this is not my place. I'm just house-minding for the guy who answered the door. His name is Jules. Darling, there are also four other people staying here. It is crowded. Can't the Feds book you into another motel?"

I come out of the kitchen with a tray of cheese and crackers and some tinnies of beer. "Annabelle, you can stay here a few nights till your accommodation is arranged."

"Thanks," Annabelle replies and then grabs the tray. She ravenously devours the cheese and crackers and quickly cleans the plate dry. If there was a devouring event at the Olympic Games, she'd definitely bring Gold for OZ.

"SnowPea, we're just going to prepare a few more snacks," Sam says.

Sam gets up from the couch and beckons me back into the kitchen, and whispers, "Jules, I made an error of judgement in asking if SnowPea can stay. It's just that I hadn't seen her for such a long time. It may compromise her job with the Feds if she stays here for more than a night. If the deaths of Paolo, Vince and Henry should ever become public, then SnowPea's career is ruined. The legal term is guilt by association, and I have done my research. Melissa is Victor's wife, and Victor is a 'person of interest'. Is that correct?"

"You're sounding like a lawyer, and Sam, how do you know about Victor's wife?"

"Jules, Victor had a public Facebook account with photos of his family. He was naïve; you do not make a FB account public. I did a search based on your name, and Victor's page came up. Lousy photo of you crouched down and picking your nose on a yacht, but he had a public page that exposes personal stuff to the world. He was either dumb or had no idea what 'public exposure' means."

"Yes, he was naïve, but I think he is a good guy. At one time, I considered him a friend. Sam, can that FB page be taken down?"

"Only if you know his Facebook password."

I rush into the bedroom and grab the tablet PC. Sam follows. It would not be hard to log into Victor's FB account. Passwords to websites of many adult accounts are a combination of names of your children or your wife or maybe a pet animal. It took 15 tries to get in. The account is cancelled or at least invisible. Victor was naïve.

"SnowPea has a meeting early in the morning, and when she's back will visit the local real estate agents to find an apartment to rent. Can I borrow your VW Beetle to take SnowPea apartment hunting tomorrow?"

"Sure, you can borrow the car but fill her up with petrol. It's been a long time since the VW was used. You might have to push-start it as the battery may be flat."

Sam has a serious look on his face and is whispering fast. "OK, Jules. I will help her find an apartment tomorrow. Her transfer is a month away, and she flies back to Brisbane tomorrow at 8 pm to organize a few last-minute things. Her transfer was unexpected. She has house packing to do in Brisbane and has to organize a removalist. She also has an early work meeting tomorrow, so she will depart early in the morning. Try to keep Melissa and all the kids in their bedrooms in the morning while SnowPea is in your house. It may only be a few hours, and SnowPea may be briefly back after her meeting to collect her belongings."

"Sam, I'll speak with Melissa and the kids in the morning just in case they run into Annabelle in the afternoon. I'll ask them all not to mention Victor, and I'll tell them you are her father."

"Jules, pretend you are all relatives and Melissa, a widow, is your cousin visiting from a country town, Albury. SnowPea wouldn't know that town, so she wouldn't probe. Get them to follow that line."

"Sam, you've really examined every contingency and worst-case scenario. I'm learning from you, Bro." The big Samoan gives me a hug. We walk back to the lounge room. Annabelle is fast asleep on the couch, the empty plate resting on her knees, and her chin flopped down to her chest. She is making slight snoring noises. Sam takes off Annabelle's shoes and jacket and carries her to his bed in the spare downstairs bedroom. He comes out and flops back on the couch. "Got a spare pillow and blankets, Jules?"

"No, all pillows are now in use, but I got plenty of towels which can sort of be turned into a pillow or the log of wood in the courtyard if you want to do the Buddhist thing."

"I'll take the towels," he replies with a grin.

Sam makes himself a pillow from all the towels I find in my bathroom storage cabinet and also a couple of spare blankets, but it's a warm night, and he probably won't need them. I flop down on the double bed next to BHK but can't sleep. The mind-churning has it all started again. Doris and her relationship with Victor. BHK, who may be a target due to those YouTube videos created by Hendrick, Victor's ritual and travel, Melissa and her kids, and now Annabelle, whom we have to keep everything a secret from. Then I notice a note pinned next to the bed. 'I posted the confession on YouTube that the decryption was all just a joke. I can't be traced, so no revenge killing expected'. I give BHK a kiss on his forehead. One less thing to worry about, but then I remember the bugged phone line. No, that should be OK. Sam and I disabled the landline bug transmitter, and BHK probably disguised the IP address when he posted his confession. I didn't give him my computer password. I'll ask him tomorrow how he managed to log in to my PC. I log back into the PC in my downstairs bedroom, bring up YouTube and do a search. Eventually, I find the video. BHK must have learnt to use that camera built into the PC. The video contains the confession. How the scam was done, in detail. Luckily, he was wearing a towel across his head and face, just as he did when the previous videos were recorded at Hendrick's place. I ponder about how people are so reactive in the financial sector. The panic of the 1930s was totally unwarranted. Spread a rumour, and you could make a fortune at other people's expense though that wasn't Hendrick's intention. The impression I get is that Hendrick was just totally naïve - just a big geek kid at heart.

Stock exchange shares prices would rise tomorrow, and a potential global economic meltdown would be averted. OK, that's a bit of an exaggeration. Big companies with savvy cybersecurity teams would have worked that out that it was just a scam. I should place orders for some of those security-savvy company stock right now, but I'm feeling tired and not really into that stuff. I turn off the computer and quietly hop onto the bed. I toss and turn and have the best vivid dreams ever that night; I co-star in a Lara Croft movie. The next morning would also be challenging when Annabelle and I collide in the bathroom.

Chapter eleven

Slightly dozy and rubbing my eyes, I stagger into my ensuite bathroom. She is there looking in the mirror but turns around. She is naked. I'm startled. It's Annabelle, and she doesn't seem perturbed at the accidental intrusion. "Your other guests are using the upstairs bathroom. I'm in a hurry so have to use yours. You can join me in the shower if you are in a hurry. In my culture, we don't view nudity the same way as your culture does."

Suddenly my troubled mind diverts. She is so beautiful. I glance outside the bathroom door. BHK is asleep, Sam is snoring on the couch, and there's not much noise from upstairs. It is like a nerdy guy's fantasy. I must have cracked and become delusional.

I take off my shorts and jump into the shower with Annabelle. She grabs me by the head, then gives me a peck on the face. Can't explain what that felt like and can only just prevent a part of my anatomy from rising. Those few classes of Mindfulness, run by Charmaine, that I attended helped. 'Breathe deeply and focus on your breath, not what is downstairs'.

"Look after my dad."

"Annabelle, it's the other way around. Sam is looking after me and our guests."

"It's not that simple. Dad got shot once already. You did too. You think we don't know? There's another, possibly a government agency, probing into your affairs. We can't trace them as they are always two steps ahead. They are very secretive and have access to far more resources than we do. Now look after my dad and your guests."

She steps out of the shower and leaves me perturbed. Another complication, what does she know? Seems like far more than Sam thinks she knows. I follow Annabelle to Sam's bedroom and watch her dress into her police uniform.

"Annabelle, it's starting to sound like some sort of conspiracy. What do you know?"

"Jules, I believe there is some connection with the library where you work. Somehow it may be connected to this mess. You seem well enough now to go back to work, and you should and when you do, be observant. I will keep in touch." She walks past and gives another peck on my face. I rush into the kitchen and pretend to be washing dishes. She wakes Sam, who's still snoring on the couch. She shakes his shoulders. "Dad, I have to go and attend that meeting. The cab should be here any minute. See you in about 3 hours. Can you get on the Internet and look for apartments close to here?"

"Sure, SnowPea," Sam replies whilst rubbing his eyes.

I give Annabelle a nod as she rushes out the door dragging one of her suitcases with her.

"Sam, we got lots of breakfasts to cook. Can you give me a hand?" Sam staggers over. He's wearing that daggy type of underwear that looks like board shorts. I look down. I'm wearing nothing, so grab a long tea towel and wrap it around the waist before rushing back into the bedroom to put on some clothing.

Sam is tossing omelettes and bacon. He seems a master of the frypan. I put the toaster on as Melissa, her kids, and BHK come wandering in. Must have been the Rolling Stones CD that Sam put in the stereo player at nearly full blast that got them moving. It only took 5 seconds, and then Sam turns the stereo off.

It's initially a bit awkward as all five of us squeeze into the kitchen bench, but Sam does an excellent job making everyone feel at ease with his small talk as he serves breakfast. I stand up and announce. "Guys, you to go to do some food shopping, a lot, so everyone needs to help to carry the goods. Here's $300 and some green bags. I got some phone calls to make, so will stay at home."

Melissa refuses to take the money and throws the six $50 notes in my face. "Melissa, you and Victor fed and housed me on the yacht for over six weeks, now please take the money. It's the least I can do." I stare at Melissa, and she finally accepts the cash.

"Jules, we can't all fit in your VW," Sam says.

"Guys, walk, the supermarket is only 2km away." Everyone glances at each other with startled and astonished looks as if 'walking' has suddenly become a dirty word. I refrain from explaining the cardiovascular benefits of a fast walk, as Victor would have lectured them on that. They get dressed and armed with cloth shopping bags; they reluctantly march out the door. It's 9:30 am. I ring Ms Valda.

"Ms Valda, I think I can come back to work. I've almost recovered; maybe just 20 or 25 hours a week to begin with."

There is a long pause on the phone line. Maybe an outage, then she finally replies,

"Heard about your accident and recovery. Stay away from high-rise balconies in the future; we don't want you falling off one again. We still have work to do, so I expect to see you here tomorrow. We're behind schedule."

"Ms Valda, have you heard from Charmaine?"

"Yes, we keep in touch. She's doing fine in her new role." Ms Valda hangs up.

At times you may doubt your own sanity, but the twisted web of intrigue seems to be increasing. Is Ms Valda somehow involved? My mind is racing, looking at possible scenarios. It's wild speculation, but Melissa must also be involved, or I'm just becoming more paranoid. I hear fiddling at the front door lock. Someone is trying to open it. I rush back to the fridge, grab the ghost chilli concoction, and arm myself with the large kitchen knife before cautiously opening the door. It's Sam, Melissa, BHK, Peter and Lizzy. I conceal the glass of chilli and the knife and let them in.

"Jules, there's a small supermarket around the corner. It's not cheap, but Melissa and I contributed."

They come marching in with numerous bags of food shopping. I grab Melissa by the forearm and whisper, "How much do you know about this whole mess."

She whispers back. "What mess? There is no mess. Now let go, or I will have you up for assault charges."

I let go of her arm and retire to my bedroom. I need a nap. All this conspiracy stuff is taking more of a mental toll than the still-healing physical wounds. Before I go under, I can hear Sam and Melissa arguing about what spices to use for the lunchtime meal. The scent wafts into my bedroom. Whatever they're cooking smells good. A few hours later, the doorbell rings again. I jump up, but Sam opens the door.

Annabelle returns. She's dressed in conservative civilian clothing, not the police uniform. Sam looks up at me quizzically. Melissa and the kids are upstairs but come down. This would be their first contact with Annabelle. I cringe, not for the reason you may be thinking, but will they exchange intel?

"Hi, I'm Annabelle. Sam is my father. He's going to take me apartment hunting. I've been relocated to the Department of Transport in Melbourne." She shakes Melissa's hand, bends down and distributes boxes of chocolates to each of the kids. She is an instant hit.

Sam must have checked rentals on the web with his smartphone. He drew up a list of rentals and arranged inspection times with the agents. I'm standing and observing in nothing but my shorts, as it's still summer in Melbourne. Sam and Annabelle give a wave as they depart. The kids go back to playing computer games and stuffing their mouths with chocolates. I glance at Melissa, who is preparing the final touches to the meals and chopping an onion for the salad. Her face is scrunched up. I dare not try to communicate. I go back to my bedroom but leave the door ajar. No idea how many hours have passed in slumberland again. I check my watch, 7:10 pm. Then the doorbell rings again, and Sam enters, followed by Annabelle. I jump up again. "She can't make the flight to Brisbane to finalise her re-location. We were caught in heavy traffic. The other flights are full." Sam looks down as if to wish to offer an apology.

Melissa comes over and shakes Annabelle's hand. "I'm sure Jules won't mind if you spend a night here. Thanks for the chocolates, and how did the apartment hunting go?" Melissa asks.

No one feels tense except me. Then I look at Melissa. She and Annabelle are fairly evenly matched, except Annabelle is a bit taller. Two equally matched strong females with an ego. An image briefly flashes in my mind—the two of them in one of those caged UFC martial arts fights. I try to dismiss the thought, but it lingers.

It's a late dinner, and no space left at the kitchen table, so I go to the lounge and sit back on the couch whilst savouring the goodies Annabelle brought and Melissa cooked. The conversation is quite vibrant from the kitchen, and I can't hear the late-night news. I start going back to the bedroom. Sam jokingly calls out. "It's your turn to be on the couch."

Annabelle brushes by when getting a glass of water from the kitchen. She whispers. "Are you going back to the library job?"

"I'm starting back tomorrow."

"Good, find out what you can about a person called Charmaine, a supposed psychologist. She doesn't work there anymore, but any info would be helpful." She gives me another exciting peck on the cheek.

I whisper back. "I would never do that. Charmaine helped me through a difficult time in my life and got me that job in the library. I'm not a traitor."

Annabelle gives another gentle slap on my face. "Jules, sometimes people are not what they seem to be, and I'm not talking about the transgender stuff."

Annabelle seems to know more than I first imagined. Enough thinking - time to check that all outside doors and windows are locked and that lights are off. I check the bedrooms, Sam and BHK are sharing my double bed. Melissa and her kids are back upstairs in dreamland. The door is ajar to Annabelle's bedroom, well Sam's bedroom. "Are you OK, Annabelle?"

"Just sending some work-related SMS messages. Come in."

I do.

"This single bed may be more comfortable than the couch but don't even think about sex."

The couch would definitely have been more comfortable than trying to get some sleep with an Amazon-built woman on a narrow double bed which she thought was a single bed. She talked, kicked and flung her arms in her dreams. That's not supposed to happen in REM sleep. Still, it's nice being cuddled up next to the sleeping Annabelle, even though you wake up with quite a few bruises and end up on the floor. Her mobile alarm sounds. "Jules, get back on the couch. I got to get ready for work," she whispers.

I scuffle out and fall on the couch and cover myself with a bedsheet. Perfect timing because 30 seconds later, Sam wanders out, gives me a shake on the shoulders and enters Annabelle's current bedroom. I move close to the door, out of sight, but can hear the conversation.

"Dad, we're dealing with a complex situation at work. I have to continue to stay in Melbourne. I know I said a month for relocation, but things at work are speeding up. Can you convince Jules to let me stay for a little while longer, till we get that rental flat?"

"Dear SnowPea, is this about probing Jules for information? Are you using this situation for some promotional gain with the Feds?"

"It's not like that, dad. Trust me."

"I'll ask the others, especially Jules."

"Sam, I don't think it's a good idea. There must be a vacant apartment close by ready to have new tenants, but OK, for a few more days," I whisper to Sam and shuffle off into my bedroom. BHK is still asleep. I find some clean clothing. Looks like I'm going to be late for the first day back at work. "Sam, can you tell BHK that I've gone back to work in the library? I'll be back by 4 pm."

"Sure, Jules, and congratulations. Can you ask around if they got any work for me?"

"I will, Sam."

I'm rushing to the front door and bang into Annabelle, who is also exiting. A taxi is waiting outside. "Hop in the taxi, Jules. The driver will drop you off at the library. It's on my way."

"Thanks, Annabelle."

We don't talk during the taxi ride. I just wave goodbye when deposited at the library. I knock on Ms Valda's door. "Good, you're here. Now get down to the archives."

I don't know what it was, but something about Ms Valda's manner was a bit different. It's like she knew I hadn't really fallen from a balcony or maybe I was just primed up to be suspicious by Annabelle. So back in the dungeon and no time to read the old local newspaper articles. I'm furiously scanning and converting them to PDF files. At 12:30 pm, I cautiously go up to the cafeteria, where I wave my hand. Little red LED lights on the CCTV cameras flicker. I'm not sure if they collect sound footage as well, so I have to be cautious about what I say.

Doris comes over to take my order. "You're back! We heard about your accident. You know my brother-in-law also fell from a balcony. It was a sixth-floor balcony. The cleaners never managed to scrub all the blood away. I lay some flowers on that spot every month." I'm not sure if Doris was giving me some kind of warning.

"Doris, I'm sorry to hear about your brother-in-law, but I just fell from the first floor and landed in some bushes. Only a few broken ribs, cuts and abrasions, that's all. I'll have the usual Burger Special."

I'm the only one in the cafeteria, and 10 minutes later, Doris brings the plate with a chargrilled burger special. It smells good. "Doris, before you go, have you heard from Charmaine?"

"Why yes, Jules. Charmaine just popped in here yesterday. She gave me this marzipan. I haven't eaten it yet. I'll keep it as a souvenir. She had a long chat with Ms Valda. I couldn't hear what they talked about. Maybe she wants her job back at the library. That would be so good. She was so popular. We all miss her."

"It would be good to have her back," I cautiously reply and get stuck into the burger.

It's 3:30 pm. I've done over six very productive hours of work in the library. The bottom right-hand corner of the computer shows the date. 21st of January. Oh, Gawd, the kids have to be enrolled in school. I rush out and catch the train back home.

I grab Melissa by the shoulders whilst she's preparing a meal. She flinches and is about to wack me. "Melissa, you have to enrol Peter and Lizzy at the primary school. School starts in a week. Just say you've always lived here because entry into local public schools in Melbourne is based on where you live; you got to be a local resident. I've been a resident of Elwood for longer than I can remember. Say you're my partner. I'll find evidence that we reside here – council rate payments and other bills. I'll confirm that at the school interview. The interviews are after-hours so I can be there."

Melissa drops her defensive stance. "Thanks, I'll do that tomorrow, but what about your son? Do you want him to go to school?"

"Melissa, he'd be bullied the way he looks even though he's put on weight and filled up a bit. I have booked a clinical assessment for his cranial condition at the Royal Children's Hospital, but I'm back at work and way behind schedule. I don't think I can take any more time off work at the moment. Could you take him to the hospital?"

She ponders for a short while and then actually gives me a warm look. "Yes, I can do that."

Then Sam wonders in. "I heard the conversation. I'll help out. You got to purchase uniforms and textbooks. I'll look after that. I've done that before. I also had a single bed and linen delivered, and I cleaned up the mess in the upstairs study. BHK can have his own room now."

I grab my wallet, which sits on top of the fridge.

"No, Jules, my turn to pay."

"Sam, you probably didn't receive an income after your former employer,

Jason died."

"Jules, like you, I saved cash when I was working. There's plenty to go around, and you have to spend it for ethical things; it keeps our ethical economy going." We stare at Sam then there's one of those High Five things where everyone bangs each other open hand and smiles.

Annabelle returns at about 9:30 pm. She looks weary, and her white dress may need a wash as there are red wine stains on it. The kids are asleep. I'm in the kitchen, cautiously listening. She leans to Sam and hugs him. "Dad, this is way beyond me."

"SnowPea, are you still using your mother's maiden name as your last name?"

"Yes, does that bother you?"

"Not at all; your mother was a good woman. Now hold in there. It is complex, but you can do it."

"How do you know, dad?"

"I observe and listen but still haven't got it all worked out."

"Will you tell me?"

"Not enough evidence yet, but don't let it drag you down. Hang in there."

Melissa must have come downstairs and heard the conversation from the kitchen. She comes over to Annabelle and gives her a hug.

"This is weird," Annabelle asserts and pulls away.

"No, it is not. We are sisters. We will sort this out."

Melissa whispers something to Annabelle, extends her hand and pulls Annabelle towards her. They exchange a long hug and some whispering.

The kids have eaten and seem to be asleep. I eat the yummy leftovers. Melissa and Annabelle walk upstairs together. Briefly, my imagination deviously wonders. Should I try to join in? Sam must have read my mind. He is very perceptive. He jokingly comments, "You wouldn't last one minute. Let them go, Jules. At least there will be no more babies. Melissa will just be probing, interrogating for information, so will SnowPea. They are both wary and good at probing. I'm sure my daughter already tried to probe you." I lower my head and don't reply as the shower and bed scenes flash by into my mind. I step outside the front door to look at the stars and relax after a sigh of relief. There aren't many stars to see, but I hear Melissa and Annabelle are arguing on the second-floor balcony. I just hope one of them doesn't come crashing down and squash my Ghost chillies.

"Sam, there's a verbal battle going on, on my balcony. Can you intervene and stop it?"

"Jules, they won't do anything stupid. My daughter is well trained, and I'm sure Melissa is as well."

I have a shot of Vodka and offer the bottle to Sam, who declines.

"Jules, you're drinking too much. I learnt other ways to cope with distressful situations. I can tell you those ways."

"No, Sam, not just now, maybe later." I down another Vodka as we silently watch the late-night news on TV. After an hour, Annabelle comes back downstairs. I go into the kitchen and start washing dishes but overhear some of the conversations.

"Dad, it's like talking to a brick wall. She is so defensive, and none of the techniques I was taught worked. I got almost nothing. I think she's connected with them, that organization I mentioned before, and I think Jules is as well."

"It's OK, SnowPea. I'm sure you did your best. Now have a rest."

That Internet of Things listening device that Smithy must have purchased suddenly comes alive and starts playing a song, I heard it before. That 'Dire Straits' song 'Brothers in Arms'. It's just as disturbing as the first time I heard it. I cover my ears with my hands. Annabelle and Sam look up and come over.

"Are you OK, brother?" Sam asks.

"Yes, but could you turn off that song? I like the song but not just now."

"Sure, Jules," he says as he turns off the speaker. My mind is racing again.

"Jules, you never asked what I did before this circumstance. I wasn't just a bodyguard. Set your alarm clock for 5 am. We'll talk before anyone else awakes, and Jules, it's a complex web, a jigsaw puzzle, but no one has all the pieces yet." Sam flops on the couch and is soon in dreamland.

It's late, 12 pm, everyone else seems asleep. Annabelle is rubbing her head as she walks into my bedroom. She just flops on the bed, fully clothed. I remove her shoes and move as far as possible to avoid any sleep kicks. It's easier on a Queen size bed. I look at her, how beautiful she is but then a thought of Melissa flashes by. It's total irony. I'm probably one of the least attractive guys on the planet and yet surrounded by two very beautiful, intelligent women. I give the sleeping Annabelle a kiss on her forehead and then roll away to the edge of the bed, a safety zone, so I thought. She kicked, waved her arms and mumbled in her sleep again. Yeh, I ended up on the carpeted floor a few times that night. A quadruple-size bed with a safety net might have solved the problem.

Luckily, I set the bedroom alarm clock for 5 am. I get up, a little bit dazed. Sam is snoring on the couch. We'll have to have our talk another time. "Jules, I got to get ready and don't wake the others. Did I hit you? You have a black eye. Jules, you have to probe Melissa as well as Charmaine, maybe in the bedroom. It's for National Security, a civic duty."

Oh, gawd and I thought I was crazy. I ponder before answering. "Annabelle, what do you dream about? Your sleep seems to be highly disturbed."

"I'll tell you another time. No, I'll tell you now. It's about that incident when I was a rooky cop. I'm sure dad told you about it. It still haunts me. I got to go. I have a very early morning meeting to attend."

I reach out and give the Amazon a hug and a peck on the cheek, then stumble back to the bathroom. She gets her suitcase from Sam's bedroom. I watch her as she puts on the police uniform. She didn't shower, so I couldn't join her. I better buy more laundry powder and deodorant.

"Jules, can you soak my white dress in a bucket with water, bi-carb and vinegar?"

"Yes, I can do that."

I waive and watch her depart to a waiting taxi before anyone else is awake; well, I spoke too soon. Sam wakes up. "You didn't wake me for our talk, and what happened to your eye?"

"I'm not quite sure, Sam. May have rolled around and hit the bedpost."

"Was SnowPea probing?" Sam replied with a sort of deadly smile.

"No, not at all, Sam. It was just my incompetence. I had a nightmare and hit my head on the bedpost."

I can see in Sam's eyes that he doesn't believe me.

"Did you use a condom? She's engaged to my future son-in-law, who's currently serving in Somalia."

"Sam, I swear there was no sexual contact between me and Annabelle, not ever."

"Come over here, Jules."

Reluctantly I do, expecting a stranglehold. "I know how they work, Jules; a long time ago, for a short while, I was your mother Doris's long-distance toy boy, yes, your mother, the supposed tea lady in the library. I know a lot because your mother talked in her sleep, too and furiously waved her arms. I had black eyes as well."

Sam hugs me. "Stay strong," he says.

"This is weirdness beyond imagination. Are you having me on, Sam? What else do you know?"

"It doesn't matter, Jules, but please stay away from my daughter, no matter how much she probes you. I would like some normal grandchildren. Focus your attention on Melissa; she is also enchanting, if I may say so."

I walk away, gain highly troubled. Who's running the show? There are so many contenders, and now I have to monitor Melissa, an unsurmountable task, but in the long term, it would be fruitful. You know, the 'spy story' stuff about how you fall in love with the person you're supposed to be surveilling, and she's also surveilling you. It's almost a repeat of my relationship with Marg. It would make a good movie, 'Spies in Love', but it was not about to happen for a while.

I stop daydreaming and get dressed but not before a short shower, and then reapply the eye-makeup to hide the facial bruises. As any guy knows the procedure, I also liberally spray the bed and linen with fly spray. Kills any bugs that someone who shared your bed may be carrying and saves you from having to prematurely use the washing machine.

I'm at the archives at 7 am—the first person at the library. I descend the stairs and start scanning. I try to multi-task and think about the last 24hrs, but I'm making mistakes due to a disturbed night's sleep. I can't multitask, so I just focus on the job, papers in, papers out; so simple.

Chapter twelve

It's 4 pm, and I'm back from work at the library. It's only Sam and me sitting by the kitchen table.

"Sam, where are BHK and Melissa's kids?"

Then I hear some giggles from upstairs.

"Jules, we went early to complete the enrolment of Melissa's kids in the local primary school as there would probably be a last-minute rush. We took all the paperwork you left to prove local residency. We also purchased uniforms and textbooks at the school. They may be trying out those uniforms now. Later, Melissa took BHK to the Elwood medical clinic as BHK seemed disorientated and he was mumbling. They're not back yet, and Melissa hasn't rung."

I reflect for a while. Melissa is very competent. There is nothing to worry about; it must be something minor.

"Sam, I know I hadn't asked about your past before, but please tell me about you and SnowPea. It's not just your daughter's nickname. I read some of Jason's notes that he left me."

"I thought you'd never ask Jules. SnowPea is a vine with pods used in Asian cuisine."

"Don't screw with me, Sam. What is SnowPea, and who are you?"

Sam holds down his head and rubs his eyes. "Who am I? You really want to know? Just a lost soul like you. I was once a prosecution attorney, I told you before, but you may not remember, one of few legal staff in my community up in the north. 'SnowPea' was the nickname for my daughter, as you know. Her words when she was young, I'll always remember her words of wisdom, 'Be Kind'. We were living in a small town near Darwin at the time. She got severely bashed by an older man she was sort of involved with, well, I believe, investigating. She was a rooky cop, inexperienced, doing undercover. Through a legal loophole and QC defence barrister, the defendant got bail and then only served a 3-day prison sentence. There were photos of him laughing as he exited the facility. The legal system sucks. If you got the money, you can get away with anything. That bastard was a rich drug baron, so he could afford the best legal defence professionals who debated on what was admissible evidence, and they won. The system sucks."

Sam's whole persona has changed. I just thought of him as just a bodyguard, but now a whole other side emerges. He has been lying dormant since I first met him. His eyes are also becoming watery.

"When he exited the penal system, I was there and watched his every move. It's when he was alone, fishing for Barramundi in a local river, that I pounced. I made sure he suffered. I tore his right arm off, took a lot of twisting and a bit of cutting, and tossed it to the crocodiles. He pleaded. That terrified look on his face – well, it was probably what my SnowPea experienced when he bashed her. Then I tossed the rest of him into the river. I couldn't comply with the 'Be Kind' tenant. It was a bloodbath as several crocodiles swooped in and ripped apart the remaining body. I felt some justice had been done, but I wasn't alone; there was a witness. I looked up, and there was a retired, highly ranked Darwin police officer, we'll call him Mich, fishing for Barramundi as well.

Mich witnessed the carnage but was sympathetic. He too, as most of the town, had seen a quiet community decimated by the drug baron who always got away unscathed by hiring the best defence barristers. Mich's hands were bound by an outdated legal system, and he also wanted reform and maybe revenge.

So here is me, a six-foot-four Samoan, looking down at an old guy in a wheelchair armed with a fishing rod. That's where SnowPea, the group, was born. It's not just the nickname of my daughter. Mich and I wrote down the principles. Mich spread the word through his contacts, and its membership spread exponentially. Eventually, the police found a mangled arm with a cracked analog watch indicating the time of the incident. The mongrel's name was inscribed on the back of the watch, and I was the prime person of interest, but 30 people in the town testified that I was drinking in the local pub at the time. Mich had many contacts, as I mentioned before. SnowPea is now a very significant organization. I don't know exactly how many, but the numbers are growing. We only targeted rapists, domestic violence perpetrators, paedophiles, drug importers and drug manufacturers. We helped the police by supplying sources of information that would convict the scumbags. Some of our members are cops, ethical lawyers, a few politicians, some security guards and computer hackers who can remove audit trails from computer logs when member cops do a search on one of our suspects. Justice has got to be done, and the legal system has failed abysmally. SnowPea is also a democratic organization; neither Mich nor I run it anymore. It's run by a committee. After that incident, I didn't see my daughter 'SnowPea' for four years; she avoided me until now and please don't ever mention the SnowPea organization to my daughter. She doesn't know about it, and it's better that it stays that way. I don't want to jeopardise her job again."

"Sam, I'm glad you have reunited with your daughter and she and you can stay here as long you like, but Sam, the organization 'SnowPea' seems like a vigilante group." I move over to Sam and give him a hug: Not a good idea. He embraces me. I can almost hear the crackle from my ribs being crushed. He wipes his eyes with the sleeve of his shirt. Suddenly we hear the radio that has been quietly playing in the background, 'Learning to Fly' by 'Tom Petty'. I turn up the volume, and we listen.

"You have passed the test. Will you join SnowPea?" enquires the Samoan.

"Not sure, Sam, and by the way, I'm not a lost soul anymore. I think I may have found a purpose."

Sam continues spilling his soul. "After killing the scumbag, I sort of died inside; my daughter wouldn't talk to me. She was a rooky cop, and I placed her in a very compromising position when I stupidly mentioned that I had disposed of the scumbag. She kept it silent. She is a straight-down-the-line cop, and it must have tormented her about where her loyalty lay; the police force or her father, so I gave up my job as an attorney. I wandered about the country with just a swag for about a year. I slept under trees but eventually got work as a security guard. Ever see that movie called Avatar?" Sam asks. His mind is wandering. Maybe the release of facts and emotions is getting to him.

"I have, my favourite movie," I quizzically reply.

"'SnowPea' is a distributed network like the trees and wildlife in the Avatar movie. No single person is in control, and it claims no credit for its successes."

Again, I'm flabbergasted, though, wondering a bit about Sam's sanity. Who is this guy? I so so underestimated him. "Sam, the last 12 months seemed like a series of unfortunate coincidences. It makes little sense to me. What binds them all together? Why do we all seem contacted in our pasts? There are significant gaps in my memory of my past, but it's slowly coming back, but we are similar in a way. We might have done things differently if we had another chance." Before Sam has a chance to reply, the doorbell rings. Sam and I jump up.

It's BHK and Melissa. Melissa comes marching in, followed by BHK. "He needs surgery immediately. His cranial pressure is building up. Spinal fluid is leaking into his brain. The surgery is arranged; just drive him to the Royal Children's Hospital or call the ambulance. Where are my kids? It's OK. I can hear them. Now drive."

I nod to Melissa and Sam and grab the disorientated BHK and steer him to the VW; he is stumbling. The VW starts. Sam comes rushing out the door. "Do you want me to come too for moral support?"

I grab his hand. "Sam, stay here. That will be another worry off my head if Melissa and her kids are being looked after."

We arrive and get ushered to the private section of the hospital. "Your wife Melissa has looked after all the financial arrangements. Now the young fellow has to hop onto the trolley."

I help BHK mount the hospital trolley and follow the nurse who wheels him away. I'm not allowed into surgery. I grab his hand. "I love you, BHK; please make it through."

"I will, dad. Believe me, I will and dad, I have had several dads; now I may have several mums," he winks as he's trolleyed away.

Hours of waiting and finally the head surgeon comes out, pulling off his bloodstained gloves. "He's stable, no more pressure on the brain, and we can fix his skull. Much of his head anomaly was due to accumulation of cerebral fluid in his brain. It wasn't draining away properly when he was young. It's an unusual condition, and I'm surprised you didn't notice it. It would have been simple to fix when he was a toddler. Now it may take several months and several more surgeries till he's completely fixed. We'll keep him here for a while and keep you informed of his progress."

"Can I see him?"

"He's still unconscious. This one was just microsurgery, a drain to relieve the pressure on his brain. He will need more extensive, intrusive surgeries in the near future. My best advice is that you go back home. We'll look after this but check your health insurance coverage. His medical treatment won't be cheap, but your wife implied that was not a concern."

I walk into the recovery ward and kiss BHK on his forehead. "I love you, son." He doesn't respond. I arrive back home, distraught and agitated. Melissa comes over and gives me the first hug. "He'll be all right, Jules. The best surgeons are looking after him." For a moment, the thought flashes by of what BHK said about having another mother. No, no, it's only a fantasy.

I start work early at the library and home in time to pick up Melissa's kids from primary school. Sam often accompanies me. No kid would ever even consider bullying the effeminate Peter when Sam turns up and grabs the youngster. Lizzy is enjoying school and seems very popular.

Annabelle is still with us but rarely comes home at night. Her boyfriend must be back. Sam says she still rings every day, and she's doing fine. When she does come over, she uses BHK's study as a bedroom. She doesn't wander down to my more comfortable double bed. I keep my distance as she does as well, but she discretely gives the peck on the cheek and whispers reassuring words, 'he'll make it'. I look up and try to kiss her. She pushes me away. "I'm engaged, Jules. Dorian is back from duty in Somalia but has to travel to Canberra once a week, and I don't like being alone. I like the company of you people."

"Annabelle, have the nightmares stopped?"

"I think so. Dorian hasn't got any more black eyes," she laughs and gives me a peck on the cheek before departing. She looks back, "I've observed how you and Melissa look at each other but be cautious. When people get together because of mutually tragic circumstances in their lives, it doesn't often last, and those tragic circumstances get repeated in future relationships. I got that info from a sociology course I did as part of advanced police training. I'll try to find the course notes, and I'll give them to you."

"How are you and Draconian doing? I'm sure you both have experienced plenty of trauma."

"His name is Dorian," she laughs as she goes to the study room to sleep. I don't follow.

Meanwhile, every day, when the traffic dies down, Melissa and I drive to the hospital to visit BHK. Sometimes he is conscious other times not if he's just come out of surgery. His head is wrapped in bandages. During the tenth visit, tears flow down my face. Melissa notices and puts her arm around me. "He'll make it," she reassures me again and gives me what could be called a kiss. The visits continue. Sometimes Melissa can't make it, at other times I can't, but ring BHK several times a day. He can't always speak, but I get a report from the nurses. Sam spends much time studying. His room is littered with books. His goal is to sit for the 'Bar' exam again (a legal thing, nothing to do with alcohol), and he did and passed. He got motivated to join the legal profession again as a prosecution barrister with the state government. It took time, but he proved his credentials. He returns home very late and weary. We hug. I still want him to stay here because I need his moral support when things get tough, plus I like him as a friend. He's part of the furniture.

The next six months would pass smoothly, except Sam and Annabelle eventually find a nice apartment very close by. Everyone helped with the move, not that there was much to move. It's a furnished apartment, and neither Annabelle nor Sam had many belongings to pack and move. I'll miss them. Sam still calls us on the phone every night to check on us, and they live only 800 metres away, so if there was a problem, my ex-bodyguard could get here quickly. We'll be safe though I would have thought Annabelle would have moved in with her boyfriend rather than back with her dad.

Doris keeps her distance, and I don't hear from Charmaine except for some SMS messages 'Hope your son is doing well, my thoughts are with him. We'll catch up soon'.

I SMS back. 'Sis or Bro, things here are getting a bit scary.'

'Don't worry, I'm keeping an eye on things' is the SMS reply. It's not much reassurance, though; then again, the likely successor of Doris would carry a lot of clout.

A package is delivered by express post. I open it. It's the latest in the line of laptop computers and a note. 'Get well soon, BHK'. It's signed, Char. I SMS back. 'Thanks, Char, he'll be thrilled. I'd love to talk to you. Ring me when you can'.|

On Friday nights after the hospital visits, we catch up with Sam and Annabelle if she's not on duty. It's Melissa, me and her kids. We all have dinner at the Elsternwick Hotel, but the conversation is sometimes a bit sombre. Sam often intervenes to keep it flowing and tells funny stories. "Hey, I just had this case. No idea how it got to court, but this guy claimed that his neighbour's white rat came in through an open window in his household and stole his money from his wallet - a thieving rat! Its name is Chloe, according to the tattoo on her belly. It was in custody at the St Kilda police station; would you believe that, a rat in prison? The cops really liked the rat, and it was allowed to roam the police station and was fed well and kept all the cops entertained by her antics. Apparently, the rat could even use a computer keyboard and type, but no one at the station could understand rat language. The rat finally got sent to an animal shelter and was adopted by this foreign ex-military guy called Greuger. He apparently donated $10k to the animal shelter after he took the rat." We all laugh but strangely, we felt a little bit uneasy, "An expensive white rat, any other stories that you can legally divulge?"

"No, Jules, there are plenty that could bring a laugh, but there are also non-disclosure issues."

Next day Melissa and I have an appointment with BHK's surgeon to discuss his progress. "BHK is recovering very quickly," the surgeon says. "We haven't seen such a speedy recovery and healing before. Your son is doing exceptionally well, and he also loves the laptop computer. We can't keep him off it when he's awake."

Meanwhile, Melissa and I are forming a cautious but close friendship. Her behaviour has changed. She is cordial and, amazingly, gives me a brief hug when I come home from work. I'm a bit suspicious. I was supposed to gather intel about Melissa, but maybe she's developing this relationship to gather intel about me, but I don't care. It feels good to have her around, so whatever the motives and suspicions, I don't care, but I'm developing strong feelings for her, but then a flashback, 'Rule666 – Never jeopardize an assignment because of any personal involvement, stay objective'. I smash my head against the table, go outside and yell, 'f..k rule 666 and Doris, if you have my home bugged and can hear me, I'm out'. Melissa must have heard and comes out to the balcony and puts her arm around my shoulders. I look up at her and put my arm around her.

Meanwhile, a chaotic song plays. 'Nick Cave & the Bad Seeds – Lie Down Here & be my Girl'. Sam never took that Godzilla speaker device with him, and it appears to self-actuate and is listening again to our conversations. I take it down to the garage. Then our first lip kiss, Melissa and I; it was like being teenagers again, 16yr olds. It feels so good. I hope Annabelle is wrong with her predicted future outcomes.

Finally, BHK is back home. His head is average size, and the scars won't be visible once his hair grows back. I put his protective head helmet back on. He still has to wear that until his head bones fuse. He's not the Big-Headed Kid anymore.

"Dad, I want to be called Fabian, not BHK."

"Fabian it is, high five!" We clap our hands together. Melissa walks in and gives Fabian a hug. "You have my bed for the night alongside Peter and Lizzy. They'll be glad to see you again but don't stay up too late; school tomorrow."

I take BHK, sorry Fabian, upstairs. Peter and Lizzy are overjoyed, rush over and hug Fabian. I go back downstairs and approach Melissa.

"You can have my bed. I'll sleep on the couch."

"We can share your bed; if it is big enough to fit you and Annabelle, it can fit me."

How did Melissa even know about Annabelle sharing my bed, and does she know it was a purely platonic bed-sharing and no hanky-panky involved? I guess she must have calculated the probability, 1 in 10,000,000, of anything happening between Annabelle and me. Melissa's attitude towards me has changed so much, but in a good, positive way. I won't ask if she's going through menopause or she's just gathering information. We cuddle up together and sleep through the alarm clock going off. Nothing more than a cuddle, but it felt so nice, and for as long as I remember, I had no 'night terrors', no nightmares and no waking up sweaty and screaming or being kicked or hit in the eye. Melissa is better than any sleeping pill.

"Mum, what are you doing?" Lizzy yells out, "We got to get to school, and what are you doing in the same bed as Jules?"

Melissa calmly answers. "We are just making use of limited natural resources. You and Peter are old enough to walk on your own. Move your asses. My wallet is in the kitchen. Just grab some lunch money but do not buy any salty or sugary things."

"You're too old for that; you're disgusting, both of you," Lizzy yells out as she marches off.

Melissa turns around and looks at me. "Lizzy is a teenager. It is not going to get any better for quite a few years."

I look at the clock and rush into the shower.

"Melissa, I'm late for work. I'll have to make up time. Can you pick the kids up today?"

"It is only a 600m walk. They will manage. They are becoming independent and learning to walk on their own. You are being overprotective."

I run upstairs and give Fabian a kiss on his forehead, and back downstairs, I give Melissa a peck on the cheek and rush off. I'm feeling better, better than I ever felt that I remember. Thoughts of Melissa intertwine, in the metaphorical sense, with those of Fabian as I walk to the railway station. Also, thoughts of what Annabelle said sort of amounted to 'get close to the enemy'. I don't think Melissa is the enemy, and I'm so enjoying life at the moment and so hope that good things don't come to an end.

It's an uneventful night. The kids are asleep. I did the dinner cooking, and yes, there were comments that my culinary skills weren't that good, but Melissa stood over them and made sure they ate it. No one vomited or suffered severe diarrhoea. Maybe it's some weird feeling, but I think I'm really forming a very strong attachment to Melissa like I did with Marg. Maybe I'm a masochist. I think I may love her, and it has nothing to do with me doing my 'civic duty' as Annabelle suggested I do. On reflection, we often bond with people who share a crisis or sorrowful situation. This may be one of those situations and whether it lasts is another thing. I so hope it does last.

We retire into my bedroom. I kiss Melissa on her forehead and caress her naked body before she drifts into her dreams. A slight sigh emerges from Melissa. It doesn't go any further that night, but I spend several hours stroking her forehead and thinking how much I'm now enjoying life. That ten years spent in limbo and in a deranged mental state is now just a memory, but if it was a prerequisite to what I have now, I wouldn't change a thing. I put my arm around her and fall into a deep sleep, only to wake an hour or so later after a disturbing dream; the dream was that I'm just dreaming. None of this is true, it's just a dream that I'm having whilst sleeping under a bridge. My torso jolts up. I look around and shake the shoulder of the person in my bed.

"What, what is it, Jules?"

"Tell me you're real, and this is not all a dream, tell me and confirm your name."

Melissa grabs her hairbrush from the bedside table and wacks my head. "Did you feel that, Jules?"

I rub my head. "Melissa, I felt that, but couldn't you have found another way to prove that I'm not just dreaming."

Chapter thirteen

Lizzy and Peter arrive back from school. I started work early, so I'm home. I grab Peter, who has a black eye. "Peter, what happened?

"They have started teasing me again. I got in a fight and lost. Now leave me alone." Peter marches up the stairs to the bedroom. He doesn't come down for dinner. Lizzy tries to persuade him to come down. Melissa and I can still hear the sobbing from upstairs. Melissa goes upstairs and tries to console Peter. I wonder what I can do to help.

Eventually, he does come down for dinner, something I cooked, a spicy lentil dish with lots of vegies. No one is impressed, but they eat it. The kids wipe their mouths in disgust as if they ingested some toxic substance and then go back upstairs. My hearing is acute, and no one is vomiting. Plus, they will have healthy bowel movements in the morning.

"I don't want to be around the kids tonight. Can I stay in your bedroom again?" Melissa asks.

"Melissa, maybe we could call it our bedroom, bugger what the kids think about us oldies sleeping in the same bed naked."

"Jules, 40 years of age is the new youngies and I'm 43. They will be babies till they hit 40."

"Melissa, I found what appears like my birth certificate the other day, I may be 55 years old or older and I'm not rich or wealthy and don't fit into the category of the new youngies."

"Jules, don't worry. Victor was two days older than you. Many younger women like me like well-aged, older men. They are much more experienced and have money though neither applies in your case." Melissa gives a smile as she taps me on the face.

"Melissa, enough of this slapping or tapping me on the face. I'm going to slap your butt tonight."

"That would be kinky. I never had any kinkiness with Victor; he was the only person I had an intimate relationship with, but only a few times. We could explore."

Who's spying on whom, I wonder. Melissa and I retreat to my bedroom and fall on the bed staring at some mythical stars as we stare at the ceiling. I think we're both troubled by some of my revelations. I give her a kiss.

"Why are teenagers such a pain," she mumbles.

I put my arm around her, and again we fall into a deep, deep sleep. There was no slapping of butts that night, just sleep.

The doorbell rings. It's 8 am. I put on some shorts but forget to grab the knife and chilli spray. I open the door with a towel wrapped around me. It's Sam.

"The kids have to go to school on time. I'll help," Sam says. Sam goes upstairs and gives a thunderous roar, "Kids, get up and get dressed in those school uniforms."

I can hear scuffling noises from upstairs. Melissa rushes into the bathroom and turns the shower on.

"Jules, I brought some sandwich packs for the kids. You do not have to make the lunches. I can take them to school as I have a rostered day off."

"Thanks, Sam, but we got to go to the school and discuss an issue concerning Peter with the principal; we'll take the kids this time. The alarm clock didn't go off, so thanks for waking us, and thanks for the lunches."

Sam whispers, "You mean Peter's black eye. I noticed it when I briefly dropped in yesterday. Peter said a tennis ball hit him when they were practising tennis against that brick wall at the school."

I whisper, "Sam, I think there was more to it, nothing sinister, but I think the bullying may have started again. I'll explain tonight if we get a chance to chat. I'll ring you."

"Jules, you know you can trust me," Sam says with a concerned look on his face.

"Sam, you're the only person I trust 100%, apart from the kids, even though one of them hates me. We'll be fine. How's Annabelle doing?"

"Jules, she's spending more and more time at the apartment at night and not with Dorian, who's back from Somalia and lives close by. She doesn't want to discuss their relationship, and she doesn't seem happy, so something is not working between the two of them."

"I'm sorry to hear that, Sam, but I have to get dressed for that meeting at Peter's school and then go to the library job. Stay as long as you like and help yourself to the fridge. Here's the TV remote control."

"Thanks, Jules."

Sam seems a little troubled, but I haven't got time to probe his woes. Maybe he's concerned about Annabelle. I ring the library and leave a phone message, "I'm sorry I may be a little bit late to work," whilst Melissa is getting dressed.

Melissa's kids march downstairs, impeccably dressed in their school uniforms. Fabian calls out from upstairs, "When can I go to school?"

"Soon, Fabian, for now, just do those homework assignments that were given by the school."

"Dad, Melissa is really good at Maths. She found mistakes in my last Maths assignments and helped me correct them. I got an 'A+', but she's not that good at geography. She got Austria mixed up with Australia, but dad, could you marry Melissa? I'd like her to be my second mother."

"Fabian, when you are 40 yrs old, you'll realise that marrying someone has to be a mutual decision based on love. You can't just marry anyone."

"Dad, Lizzy told me that you and Melissa are spending time in your bedroom and not wearing any clothing. I Googled to find out what that means."

"Fabian, nothing is going on between Melissa and me, well not yet. When you are 40 plus yrs old, you take things slowly."

"Dad, that's the second time you mentioned 40. Is it some magic number because it's not a prime number."

"OK, I meant 41, that's a prime number, and when you're over that many years of age, you possibly become mature."

"Dad, you have some weird beliefs, but I do like prime numbers."

I didn't know at the time that Melissa was doing some home tutoring of Fabian amongst her many other jobs. She must be good and certainly has Fabian on her side. Now time to attend the appointment with the school principal. Sam stays at my or our place and minds Fabian. Melissa and I march Peter and Lizzy to the primary school. When the kids disperse, we walk into the principal's office.

"My little boy Peter has got a black eye because someone punched him, but he won't say who. What are you going to do about that?" Melissa announces in a loud and more than slightly angry manner. Well, that's actually an understatement. She is furious. That Italian/Iranian blood is boiling. I've never seen her lose her cool before. I put my arm around Melissa to try to calm her down.

The principal diplomatically answers, "Melissa, there are many ethnic groups attending this school. Some are homophobic. We do try our best to educate about diversity, but my suggestion for the moment is that Peter stops drawing attention to himself. Peter insisted on playing the role of a girl in the school play auditions. He was very good, to the dismay of the lasses who wanted the part. We will check the CCTV footage and will find the person responsible and reprimand him or her. Please, I have a meeting to go to, but I'll keep you informed and will make sure there is an extra teacher assigned to yard duty who will exclusively keep a watch on Peter."

The principal was reassuring. Melissa has become relaxed. We walk home, my hand on her shoulder. "Melissa, we should follow the principal's advice and tell Peter to tone down a little. He's starting to wear makeup, your makeup, in case your wondering where your lipstick and blush have disappeared. I got to rush to work, speak tonight."

When I return from the library, Melissa is already upstairs. Lizzy and Fabian warn me that I shouldn't go upstairs, but I do and knock on the door but not before giving Fabian a hug. Lizzy shrugs, so she misses out on a hug. Melissa calls out to come in and I do. She is kneeling and clutching Peter's hands as if pleading. I put my hand on Peter's shoulder. "Peter, listen to your mum."

"Where's my dad? He understood. Where is he?" tearful Peter screams out.

"Peter, you're not alone. All of us understand you in this household, and we're not going to try to change you, but we want you to make it easy on yourself. Do you know what being subtle means? It means you try not to draw attention to yourself, be like the other kids until you finish school."

"So I should be like you, you don't think you draw any attention, but we know something is going on."

I don't know what kids talk about in private, but Melissa and I look cautiously at each other. "Jules, go downstairs and start the cooking. The vegetables have been chopped up. There's also fish and Calamari to fry and a salad to be made. No more lentils for now, as I spent half an hour cleaning the upstairs toilet and bathroom after your body-purging lentil dish. Teenagers never clean after themselves and a mild constipation will not kill them."

I walk past Fabian and Lizzy, who are now exuberant, playing some computer game, and go downstairs to my bedroom, well, our bedroom. As I'm changing into the tracksuit, I notice my desktop PC light is on. I hit a keyboard key and the screen lights up. An MS Word document appears, and it's not something I've written. The title, 'Origin of Cultural Diversity and the Influence of Religion'. The author's name and credentials are below, 'Dr Melissa Mosa'. I'm entranced. She had never once mentioned her academic qualifications. I read the abstract, which is the summary section of an academic article, and continue reading until hearing calls from upstairs, "When's dinner? We're starving."

I come out of the bedroom and go upstairs, "The recipe is on the kitchen table, and most of the work has been done. Move your asses, come downstairs and for once start cooking. It could be fun and a game like who can make the best meal." Fabian and Lizzy look at each as if in a deep state of shock and panic. They pause their game, jump up, and come down to the kitchen. I never yelled at them before, so they are in a bit of a state of shock.

Meanwhile, Melissa is still upstairs with Peter, and I'm back at the desktop computer and reading. There is a hypothesis, evidence from scientific studies, supported by references to other peer-reviewed papers and then a conclusion. The article, called a paper, is brilliant. The logic is impeccable. I must have done this before – reviewing research papers.

Now I know what Melissa did in her spare time apart from chopping vegetables and tutoring Fabian. I didn't yet know that she did other more secretive things as well because I didn't believe Annabelle. I also suspect Melissa wanted me to see that article she wrote else she would have used her laptop computer and not my desktop computer. She's trying to communicate. It's like having some alien living in your house that uses clues to learn about it instead of stating things explicitly. I press the SAVE button from the menu screen, log off, and turn the computer off, but not before making a copy on a thumb drive as backup. Then I finally go to the kitchen where Fabian and Lizzy are having a great time cooking, giggling, smiling at each other as they toss the stir-fried vegetables in the frypan. I'm not impressed. A piece of cheese is hanging from my kitchen ceiling, but I do not comment. It can be easily cleaned up.

Melissa and Peter come down the stairs. Melissa hugs Lizzy and Fabian and gives me a look. "Smell's good and the table is set. Let's start eating." At 8 pm, after we all finished dinner, Melissa announces, "It's bedtime and Fabian, you've been enrolled in grade 11 at the senior school. The uniform, school bag and books are by your bedside. Now all of you go upstairs and sleep. Jules and I will clean up and wash the dishes."

"But, but, but," Fabian exclaims. I nod to Fabian to follow Melissa's orders.

"There are no buts, now get to bed." Melissa has taken over; she is running this household. I sort of don't mind as long as it works. I don't think I was any good at handling responsibility, so it's a relief when someone else takes over.

We're lying next to each other, Melissa and me in my bedroom. I should have quizzed Melissa before, about her past. We hadn't really talked except for survival strategies because, so far, it has all been about survival and no time for deep communication. "Melissa, why didn't you tell me about your doctorate, the research you did and the papers you wrote?"

"Jules, I just thought you were a just dumb-arsy."

"Well, you know I wasn't. I had papers published as well. I just got caught up with other things way beyond my science education, and I'm no expert at the art of manipulation."

Melissa looks a bit distraught. "Melissa, do you miss Victor?" She curls up into a ball and starts sobbing. I wrap my arm around her shoulder. "I hardly ever saw Victor. He was always travelling. The few times we made love produced Lizzy and Peter." Victor and his deceased brother Mark may have had the same preferences, and genetically, it was passed down to Peter. Images come flooding back when Victor and I were on the yacht. He was getting too close. I again wrap myself around Melissa.

"Melissa, as far as I know, and I have recently read some current research studies, is that there is no evidence as yet of a genetic basis to sexual preference. It's still a total mystery, and then again, it may be an ingenious response to world overpopulation."

"Jules, you made a very cold, scientific explanation. There could be sociological factors which your mind cannot grasp."

"Melissa, I'm willing to listen. My ideas are not set in concrete." I then hesitatingly ask, "Are you on the contraceptive pill?"

"Didn't need one when I was with Victor. Have you got a condom?"

"Yes, but they're over ten years past the expiry date."

"Forget it." She turns away but then turns back. A very long pash (kissing) follows, stuff teenagers do, and then we fall asleep, happy. We may be old, but we're both only beginners. The night passes and I keep my arm around her shoulders as we enter our dreams. If there was a CCTV camera above the bed, it would record many REM eye movements, the dreaming state that happens when you got a lot of information or conflicts to process. Luckily Melissa doesn't kick or punch in her sleep. The next morning Lizzy barges into my bedroom again without knocking. Melissa rises.

"Mum, you're naked again, don't you have pyjamas? What are you doing?"

"Lizzy, just go up and get dressed. Jules and I will prepare breakfast and lunch."

"You suck," Lizzy replies and slams the door. It's becoming a regular scenario. I got to ask Melissa to have a talk with Lizzy. I don't mind attitude as long as it's not misdirected, and I don't want to wait till Lizzy turns 40 years old.

"Melissa, can you talk to Lizzy? I know she still thinks of Victor as her dad but can you somehow explain that relationships change and that most adults sleep naked together, especially when closet storage space for pyjamas is limited and it is hot."

"I will later, Jules," then suddenly Melissa grabs me in an arm lock and then a chokehold. It's a full-blown wrestling match that lasts at least 5 minutes till we both roll off the bed onto the floor with a thud. She whispers whilst pressing her fingers on my carotid arteries, "Buy some fresh condoms". Just before almost passing out, I roll her around and pin her hands to the floor whilst she kicks and then Lizzy walks in again, "What are you doing, Mum? This is so weird. I'm going to call 000 and get the Police over here."

"Lizzy, we are just practising the sport called wrestling, and I think I have the upper hand," Melissa says.

"You old people are disgusting," Lizzy comments as she slams the bedroom door shut. I'm distracted, and Melissa takes advantage. She knees me in the lower region; I grunt and roll over in pain. She then jumps on top of me gleefully, raising her hands in triumph. Unfortunately, Lizzy comes back into our bedroom. I'll definitely have to install door locks.　　　"Mum, this is really sick. You're behaving like young teenagers super-charged on hormones, and I don't like seeing old naked people making groaning noises and rolling around. Grow up, why don't you."

"Darling, we're practising to compete in professional nude wrestling at the next Olympic Games. It's all fake. I told you that before darling, so don't worry. We will be out as soon as I practise the 'Claw Hold' on Jules. He may yell, but it is all fake, as I said before, so do not worry if you hear him scream very loud."

Lizzy walks away again, shaking her head. I hear her mutter, "And I thought I had a crazy childhood."

It wasn't faked. I'm still rolling around in agony. Luckily Melissa didn't apply her 'claw hold'. "Don't do that again, Melissa. It's not allowed in wrestling. I would have won. You set up a distraction, so you got the upper hand, or should I say upper knee. I will probably be infertile from now on, so we won't need any condoms." I would end up being very wrong.

"We can have a rematch," she says as she gives me a passionate kiss. And to think I was the only psycho. She has recently started to have extreme mood swings, which make her behaviour unpredictable when she's with me. She used to be predictable, rarely smiled or laughed and very serious but now a child side is starting to emerge. Maybe, due to circumstances, that child side never had a chance to emerge when she was young, and she's just catching up. I go to the bathroom and take a few aspirins. This is definitely taking a physical relationship to a new extreme, and I might have to start watching the wrestling on TV to get ideas. Then Sam's Godzilla music player starts up. The kids must have brought it back from the garage and plugged it in; 'Emerson, Lake and Palmer - Lucky man'. I desisted from throwing the device into the rubbish bin. I like the song, not the part when he dies but the parts when the tuber musical instruments are playing that wheezing sound.

We finally get organised and march to school, the two adjoining schools. I'm sort of worrying about how Fabian will be accepted into the Secondary School. Will he get bullied? He shouldn't. He looks like all the other kids, apart from the thin helmet he has to wear for the next few months, and he luvs computer games as do most other kids. He might just 'fit in'.

There are many parents. One lady speaks to Melissa. "We'd like it if you and your husband could join the school council." Melissa shakes her hand and diplomatically replies, "We shall certainly consider that. Thank you, but not just at the moment." We then walk Fabian to the secondary school. We inform the principal of Fabian's fragile condition and the need for the helmet. She seems understanding. I wave goodbye to Fabian.

"Melissa, I got to go back to my job in the library. Your article is saved. "
"You read it?"
"I did. It was brilliant. I couldn't spot a flaw in the logic from the initial assumptions to the conclusion."
"Who are you, Jules?"
"I could ask you the same question. Who are you, Melissa? We'll talk tonight."

Melissa appears slightly startled. I peck her on the cheek and rush off, waving and looking back at her. That was definitely a mistake, as I wasn't looking where treading and slipped on a banana skin. Schools are definitely a physical danger hazard zone, like a minefield of dangerous banana skins and apple cores.

Melissa rushes over and helps me up. "Watch where you are going, Jules."

I scrub the grit from myself. "Thanks, but is that supposed to mean something else? Do you think I haven't picked up? I'm just putting together all the pieces. I'm catching up."

Melissa doesn't reply but gives a smile and a short kiss. She also gives a brief stare at the CCTV cameras that surround the school.

It's a peaceful night when I get home. The kids have eaten and are upstairs doing homework and laughing. Sam's Godzilla device comes on again. There's a chaotic song called 'We Care a Lot' by some group called 'Faith No More'. We listen to the song whilst lying in bed, 'It's a dirty job, but someone has to do it,' a lyric from the song that resonates. The device must be listening to our conversations and using artificial intelligence up in the Internet Cloud to play the appropriate song. I jump out of bed and turn off the Internet router. There are screams from upstairs.

"We were just about to win!" I go upstairs. "You go to sleep right now, right now, no buts. The router gets turned off at 10 pm from now on, and don't even think of sneaking back downstairs and turning it on. I've put a motion sensor near it, and it will sound a very loud alarm if you do." The kids have horrified looks on their faces, but all put the consoles away and lay in their beds.

"Jules, I heard what happened. You actually displayed some authority."

"Melissa, don't judge me right now unless your goal is to break me."

"Stop being so suspicious, Jules. We both have a common goal, and that is to give these kids a good and happy life, hopefully happier than ours has been, and also to enjoy life ourselves."

A memory flashes by. My bro/sis sharing the same bed when our father drank too much, and we locked ourselves in my bedroom, hugging each other. He never actually hit us but threatened he would. It's strange; I'm reliving that security feeling. It's funny how a new relationship can open repressed memories and feelings. I put my arms around her. "Melissa, you're right. You know I feel so good and so secure when lying next to you. I also think you are very attractive, but please don't kill me yet." A long pillow fight ensued. Luckily the kids were asleep, so they didn't hear. We fall asleep exhausted, our faces close together, rapt around each other, but she mutters, 'young kids should share the same bedroom until they are 14 years old. They could end up more psychologically adjusted and aware of the needs and emotions of their brothers and sisters." I'm not sure what she means except that maybe the kids end up talking to each other about what's going on in their lives.

Morning comes too soon. I give Melissa a peck on her cheek. She wakes up and has a startled look again. No wrestling match. Some subconscious part of my mind takes over. "I love you, Melissa. I could even marry you."

"I think I could love you too."

We part and I rush to the train station, keeping my eyes focused on the ground ahead. Don't want any more slip-ups. I also ponder: If only life could only be like a yummy banana smoothy instead of a slippery banana skin.

Chapter fourteen

It wasn't long before Fabian became the president of the Geeks Club at the local secondary school. Even the school bullies joined the club. They spend their lunchtimes in one of the school computer labs playing games and, surprisingly, doing math challenges against other schools. Their competitiveness seems to have channelled from the physical to the more cerebral. Somewhere there must be a balance. I'm happy but also concerned that Fabian may not develop social skills; still, who am I to talk?

On Friday nights, sometimes as many as 10 of the Geeks would be in the townhouse, and when they are here, the house is a danger zone with those blue LAN cables crisscrossing rooms across the floor and multiple routers and port-sharing devices. Wireless is apparently too slow for them, so they're back to using old fast wire technology. You have to watch where you step so as not to trip on a wire or slip on a piece of pizza lying on the floor. Still, I guess any sort of interaction is good, plus they also allow Lizzy and Peter to join in. My one observation is that the geeks work co-operatively to solve a particular game problem or scenario. There seems to be no centralized control of power. They draw diagrams and arrows on a whiteboard, I supplied and plan a course of action. They interject, present their arguments and add to the diagrams. It's like watching an OZ government parliament session, and even the ex-bullies participate and cooperate; it's almost like the SnowPea organization. All contribute, and newbies are shown the basics and instructed on how to contribute. Lizzy and Peter are learning fast and are just as absorbed in the action as all the other participants. There is so much noise and excited yelling that Melissa and I usually go to the cinema, and there are usually a lot of sleeping scattered bodies and pizza boxes lying around in the lounge room when we come back.

Luckily, we had purchased many blankets and pillows and make sure they are comfortable and then turn off the main router and the myriad of other devices connected to it. On one computer screen is displayed along with lots of graphics, 'Your team has been entered into the Hall of Disdain; the world championships are on the 25th of this month, but this is not an online event, it's in the USA, so just follow the arrows on the WEB page and deposit $1000USD (excluding travel) per participant in the account listed in what will be for them a life-changing event and monetarily fruitful event; they will become rich', definitely a scam. We get lots of those, and the school and Melissa and I have taught the kids how to be wary of the scams. So it's another Friday night, the third Friday of the month, a non-video game night. It's a Family Friday which starts with a jog. The most hated day, according to the kids. Their feigned skeletal and muscle injuries don't work with Melissa. She's adamant, "We go jogging around the streets. Only 15 minutes to start with."

"Mum, you've watched too many of those Jane Fonda fitness videos. Get off YouTube!" Lizzy calls out.

Melissa gives Lizzy the icy stare, and soon we're all jogging. We pass Smithy's apartment, and I try to inconspicuously peer into the windows, hoping to see Charmaine. We also pass Annabelle's and Sam's apartment, but no lights are on. We arrive home hot and sweaty, crouching down and panting after that final sprint up the driveway. Then the doorbell rings. I grab the jar of ghost chilli concoction and the kitchen knife. It's Sam and Annabelle, and they brought plenty of steamy groceries and wine. They dropped in for an unexpected but welcome visit. The kids wrap their sweaty arms around the visitors. Annabelle and Melissa exchange awkward glances. There's no room for all of us at the kitchen table, so Sam joins me on the couch.

"How's the job going, Sam?"

"Well, it's more complicated than up North, but I'm getting there and learning how to cope with the defence barristers and how to keep my cool. Actually, I rescind that comment. So far, I've only been assigned trivial cases that probably shouldn't have made it to court. I'm learning to compromise with the defence. Yeh, you see that on TV crime shows all the time, but it's actually a bit more complicated. I'm glad I did that online 'Negotiation Skills' course."

"Congratulations, Sam." I shake his hand.

The doorbell rings yet again. Sam and I jump up. "I'll handle this, Jules.

Just relax." Sam also nods to everyone in the kitchen. I follow Sam to the doorway. He opens it. "Mogan, how are you, brother? I thought you were still in Afghanistan. What are you doing here?" Sam gives Mogan a big hug, and Mogan's duffle bag falls to the ground. I stare at Mogan. He looks like that boxer, Mike Tyson but a younger version. He's about 6 foot tall, has very short, cropped hair, mixed blood and is covered in tattoos, especially on his face and forehead. He is an intimidating-looking figure. I take an instant dislike to him, but that would soon change.

"Sam, can I stay at your place only for a short while till I find accommodation to rent?"

"Mogan, this is not my home; we are just visiting. You have to ask Jules who is standing behind me; it's his place."

Mogan comes over close to me. He's definitely not the type of person you'd want to meet in a dark alley. "Please, can I stay a night, just one night? I will clean up after myself and as well clean all the plates and cooking utensils in your kitchen?"

Annabelle comes rushing over and gives Mogan a big hug. "We all missed you, and we were so worried about you."

Melissa comes over to join the pack. She whispers in my ear, "Let him stay, Jules, there is the study, and it has a bed. He may be useful." I must have looked puzzled by her pragmatic comment. It would take a while to find out, but Melissa was doing a lot more in her spare time than just writing academic papers.

"One condition: you accompany the kids to school and pick them up afterwards. We've had some bullying issues," I say, pointing at Mogan.

"I'll be glad to do that, dude. I was bullied, too, when I was young. I know how it is. I'm tired now. You mind if I just go to sleep?" Mogan asks.

"You can have Sam's old bedroom. It's on the left."

Mogan goes off to the bedroom. He doesn't come out for dinner.

"He's traumatised, Jules, be kind. He's a good guy despite his appearance."

"Sam, who is he, and how do you know him?"

"We grew up together in the far North. He was known as 'Mogan the Bogan'. His parents were alcoholics and neglected him, so he never had a proper childhood but spent a lot of time at my parents' place. He lived with us until he joined the military as soon as he reached qualifying age. He's a good guy." Sam pats me on the shoulder. We finish dinner. Sam and Annabelle depart back to their apartment. The kids go upstairs to sleep, and there is no murmur from Mogan's room. I quietly open his door. He is asleep, not on Sam's bed but curled up on the floor in a foetal position, another damaged person. I lay a blanket over him, then quietly shut the door and go to my bedroom. I stroke Melissa's hair. "Who are you, Melissa? There's so much going on, I can't make sense of it all."

The clock radio comes on, and not that wretched Godzilla device. That device and my clock radio must have something going on together. A song called 'Fall' by a group called the 'Presets.' We listen for a while. At least this song was relatively harmless.

"You're not the only one, Jules. I'm struggling to make sense of it as well. Now just let me sleep, and I'm not falling all the way to hell. Can you pull the plug out of that tumultuous clock radio of yours? I think it's bugged." She turns around and gives me a peck on the cheek.

"Do you want to do some wrestling or bedroom gymnastics?"

"Did you buy the condoms?"

"Oh, sh.t, I forgot. No, I didn't. I walked past the pharmacy, but I'm still sort of embarrassed buying them."

"Grow up, Jules. People do that all the time." She gives me a gentle knee kick where it hurts and turns away.

The next day I rush to work. Melissa is doing research on the computer. Mogan keeps his end of the bargain and accompanies the kids to school, and walks them back home afterwards.

Back from work. The kids are laughing upstairs, but Peter comes to the stairwell and yells out, "Mogan is awesome!" Mogan has done the food shopping and is slicing vegetables and meat in the kitchen. He's like a replacement for Sam. I come over to him.

"You can stay for as long as you want."

"Jules, I got offered a desk job at the Department of Defence. I accepted. I start in a week. I can still take the kids to school but won't be able to accompany them back."

Melissa walks out, "It's alright, Mogan. Do what you have to." She glances at me as if for approval though I don't think she needs approval.

That night we're staring at the ceiling, Melissa and I. The others are in bed. "Melissa, can we talk about our pasts?"

She turns her head, "Jules, did you ever ask me what I did before I met

Victor? Sure, you read the academic papers that I submitted. All those days when you were recovering, spending late nights with Victor on the yacht, I was doing many things, not just being a housewife. I had an academic career and did quite a bit more."

I put my hand on her forehead. Her face is moist, maybe due to tears. "It's OK. I think I'm ready to listen now."

"I'll tell you tomorrow," she replies and turns her head. She is sobbing again. She is just human like all of us, no matter how invulnerable we appear, and Melissa certainly kept up a good, stoic appearance, but there is a limit after which we get overwhelmed.

"Leave me alone," she mutters again. I put my hand around her shoulder and gently kiss her on her ear. "I know it's wrong, but I think I may love you," I whisper. She doesn't respond. I wrap closer to her, but not intrusively. She seems asleep. I stare back at the ceiling.

The next day I follow Mogan and the kids as they walk to school. I'm inconspicuous, a hundred metres behind and wearing dark sunglasses and a hat. I'm flabbergasted. At the school gate, other kids were eagerly jumping around the previously morose Mogan, trying to pat his head. He is smiling and laughing. He is a 'hit'. Maybe he's catching up on the childhood he was deprived of. Needless to say, Peter was never, ever bullied again.

I walk to the railway station, but my mind is churning. So much to decipher. Mogan and Sam are easy though Sam is highly observant and may know things he hasn't told me yet, but unlikely. He usually spills his soul, especially after a few beers. The two guys are transparent. Victor is a mystery. The four powerful women, Doris, Melissa, Charmaine and Annabelle; well they have secrets. Somehow, they are interconnected. I just can't make the connection, not just yet. A memory gushes by, and yes, I do talk to myself. I don't think it's psychosis anymore, maybe it's just a memory that rises back to the conscious mind. Often, it's better just to forget. It's yourself talking to you again. 'You were an 'X' once, third-highest rank. Get it together. Ten years you spent feeling sorry for yourself. You can work it out'. The self-talk is not very reassuring. That night everyone seems asleep. I did the security checks. It's only Melissa and me who are awake. I lie next to Melissa and put my arm around her shoulders. "I'm not an 'X' anymore. I'm sure you know the hierarchy."

"What are you talking about? You think you are a movie X-man. You are delusional, Jules, now let me sleep."

"No, I won't. You were an 'X' too, an international 'X'. You juggled your academic, family life and other activities very well. Congratulations."

She turns around with an angry look on her face. She explodes. "Jules, you f..ked up badly. That Moroccan incident, I was brought in to fix things up and I did. There was another incident where your judgement was very poor. Your friend, the supposed psychologist, got shot because of your carelessness. Now don't tell me you cannot remember because I don't buy into that bullshit. We can move out tomorrow."

"No, stay, please stay, please don't go." My arm is still wrapped around Marg's shoulders. No, it's Melissa's. I'm losing it, getting mixed up. It's Melissa, Melissa, Melissa. 'Keep calm,' I tell myself. 'It will all make sense in the end.' Melissa settles down and drifts into sleep. My arm is still around her. I lay awake pondering, churning all the facts of recent memories and trying to recall more past ones. What do I usually remember? They seem things linked with a strong emotional content. Eventually, I drift into dreamland. The dreams are not pleasant, only very confronting, and Doris features in many of them. She is chasing us. Charlie and I run to my dad, who is deeply absorbed in a book and pays no attention to us, so we scuttle off. Doris chases us, but we hide in the bushes. I wake up in a sweat and huddle next to Melissa.

When it became clear later, our humble, low-profile tea lady was probably one of the most powerful persons on the planet. She is the top 'Z.' Highest you can get in the hierarchy. She could bring down a third-world government with a single phone call. In hindsight, there are a few other current leaders I'd wish she focus her energy on that 'Tr..p' guy, though that may take more phone calls and tweets, and that's hard to juggle whilst brewing coffee and cooking Burger Specials.

Chapter fifteen

The weekend is quiet. Mogan must have purchased a basketball and takes the kids to the basketball courts at Elwood Secondary College. They are gone for hours and come back sweaty and exhausted but smiling. Mogan is doing such a good job at taking over my role as a parent, which I sort of don't mind as I don't think I ever knew how to be a parent, and Mogan is acting like the parent he wished he had so it works for us both ways. The kids have very quickly grown attached to him, and he seems to relish that. Meantime Melissa is in our bedroom, reading glasses on, and staring at the computer screen, finishing her academic papers. I feel neglected, so marched down to the garage. The boxes are labelled, and I must have done the labelling. It's time to face the boxes. I bring up box-01 to the lounge and start going through the documents. Melissa comes out of the bedroom. "Want a coffee? I'm putting the kettle on."

"Yes, sure, Melissa."

"What are you doing, Jules? The floor is littered with papers and diaries."

"Melissa, this is my past. I still don't fully remember ten years of my past. There may be answers here." She comes over and sits beside me. She gives me a peck on my face and goes back to the kitchen. A sixth peck on the cheek in a week from Melissa; she must be going through some psychotic meltdown or identity crisis. Still, it feels good, whatever the reason. Mogan must have also purchased some more Xbox controllers and games, and he and the three kids are playing games and laughing. I had cleaned up the lounge room, and now all the documents and diaries are scattered in our bedroom. Melissa doesn't seem to care about the mess.

I go out into the lounge. They have stopped playing computer games. Mogan is now playing wrestling with the kids. They jump from the couch onto his supine body.

It reminds me of the Sam and Henry incident. Peter, Melissa's son, tried to bring in the short stepladder and do a high-flying body slam. I restrained him. Mogan yells out, "Have some fun in your heart, Jules, it's all under control." Young Peter grabs Mogan by the neck, and the big guy yells out, "Oh no, it's the Carotid Immobilizer." I'm about to come rushing over, but Mogan lifts his right arm with an "O" between his thumb and index finger as he feigns dozing into unconsciousness. The shy Peter has gained some self-esteem. He's seemingly reviving Mogan by slapping him on the face. "I didn't mean to hurt you, Mogan. Are you all right?"

"I'm OK kid, but don't do that again. You're lethal." Peter marches away with the biggest sense of satisfaction and smile. "I did it, Mum." He then comes rushing back to Mogan and gives him a big hug. "I promise I won't hurt you ever again, Mogan."

Tears form in my eyes. Melissa comes over and surprisingly puts her arm around me. "Jules, if you could be as uninhabited as Mogan."

"Melissa, I think you mean uninhibited." Oops, she doesn't like her English corrected. I expect a swing from Melissa's right hand, but it doesn't happen. I phone and order Asian takeaway food from the local restaurant as it's time Mogan and Melissa had a break from cooking. After dinner, I come over to Mogan while he's washing the dishes and whisper, "I'd like to hear your story." Some thirty seconds later, he responds. His eyes are watery.

"Not just yet, Jules, I'm still healing."

I give him a hug. He starts uncontrollably sobbing and wrenching. The kids rush over. So does Melissa. They all hug him. He has tears pouring down his face. "We love you, Mogan. Don't be sad," Lizzy says in a comforting voice.

Mogan wipes the tears from his face and hugs everyone before retiring into his room. "I'm OK, guys, thanks."

"Did you upset Mogan?" Lizzy queries whilst looking at me with arms crossed and a deadly stare.

"I may have, but I never meant to."

"You're a super suck," Lizzy yells out.

Fabian and Peter seem to agree with Lizzy's conclusion. Melissa gives me a stern look and returns to the bedroom. The kids go upstairs. I can hear Lizzy saying to Fabian, 'Your dad is a worm'. Her comment doesn't make me feel good. Mogan must have heard as well and steps out of his room. He yells at the top of his voice.

"No, Jules didn't upset me. I was sobbing because I'm so happy. All you guys make me so happy, and it is a shock to my system. I hadn't been so happy for a long, long time." Mogan then goes back to his room and shuts the door. I can hear the kids chatting. "Poor Mogan, Fabian, maybe your dad isn't such a worm."

I go into the bedroom, slightly relieved. Melissa is asleep. I lay awake and wonder. Mogan is complicated as well. Is everyone in the world so complicated? I don't think I'm that complicated, but then again, I may have just chosen to forget painful memories. Memory loss can be bliss at times. Maybe I shouldn't try to read all those diaries and papers. Ignorance may be bliss.

Very early on Sunday morning, Mogan and I drive to the furniture discount store. We are the first customers and purchase three flat-pack desks for the kids. The boxes jut out of the front boot of the VW, and the boot had to be tied down with ocky straps. We drove slowly and luckily didn't encounter any police vehicles on the journey back home.

"This piece goes here, Jules."

I grab the assembly instructions from Mogan. "No! I think it goes here. Where's the Allen key?" Needless to say, any first attempt at assembling any 'flat packaged' furniture is rarely successful, and you got to disassemble what you've done and begin again after a lot of swearing and yanking copious amount of hair from your scalp out in sheer frustration. Having learned from our first experience, the next two desks were easy. We carry them upstairs, so no excuse for the kids not doing their school homework.

Next day Mogan again takes the kids to the basketball court. Melissa is back at the computer, and I start reading the first of the diaries labelled 2001. It doesn't make much sense; more like random words strung together. Then I find some coherent entries. The January pages were blank except for one boring entry. *Been up all night making corrections to that paper I have to present at the Pharmacological conference in Helsinki. February also had some coherent entries. *Met for dinner with a young psychiatrist. She liked my presentation on 'Epigenetics, Gene Suppression and Gene Activation using Peptides.' Her name is Margaret. Can't remember her last name. We exchanged phone numbers. Next day we met for dinner. The conversation was lively. She was born in Melbourne, which is also my hometown. I accompanied her to her hotel room. She asked me in for a coffee. We kissed before I departed.

I skip the entries about the conference and technical meetings. Just want to read the ones about Margaret. *I emailed her: I've been relocated to the Melbourne Office of MM Pharmaceuticals. Looking forward to it as it is so cold in Sweden.*Called Margaret to tell her the news. Last day of the conference and we have dinner again. She stays the night in my hotel room.

I skip a few months as it was mostly more boring technical stuff again, then I find the entry: *After talking on the phone for hours every day, Margaret accepted my long-distance marriage proposal over the phone. She is coming back home to Melbourne next month. I miss her so.

In some ways, my life has paralleled Melissa's before my breakdown eleven years ago. An overt academic career while also involved in something far more sinister. The rest of the diaries seem just random alphabetical letters; maybe I had encrypted the content but why. I put the diaries down; it's sort of upsetting or nostalgic or both. Enough reading for today. I go into the bedroom. Melissa turns off the computer. I look at Melissa. How beautiful she is. I think I'm becoming very attached to her even though she is often so abrupt. "Shall we talk?" I ask. She replies. "In the months we've been together as house-mates, did you ever ask what I ever did before Victor and had the kids? No, you did not though you did comment favourably about some academic papers I was writing and I appreciate your comments. I was actually an Associate Professor of Anthropology at MIT, and before that, I majored in other disciplines, but you never asked; always too immersed in what you were doing and if you want to compare IQs, then get ready for a battle."

That's two Associate professors I've been involved with. For a brief moment, I shudder, wondering what a full professor would be like. Have to be diplomatic as she seems to be going through mood swings again and is upset. "Sorry Melissa, that I never appreciated you, but I did ask you several times and commented on your work. We just got distracted from having that conversation. I did read your journal paper and applauded it. At the moment, you'd beat me hands down on any IQ battle. As for Victor, he was a criminal even though I thought for a while that he was my friend."

"He had his reasons, and he was the most intellectually stimulating man I had ever met and is still my husband. Did you ever consider you might be a criminal? Did you ever think of the implications of your scientific research? No, you never did, and much of the mess may have been caused by your lack of scientific responsibility."

I wonder if Melissa had deciphered all the diaries. She seems to know more about my past than I do, and she did. The encryption code was simple, I would later find out, the sort of code Julius Caesar used, just move each of the letters of the message three places along, e.g. an 'A' becomes a 'D'.

"Melissa, I don't want to turn this into a battle or a blaming game. I still can't remember some things in my past, but it's slowly coming back. Can you be patient for a while?"

"Jules, you made the newspapers headlines, supplying illegal performance-enhancing substances to elite sportspeople. Maybe that is in your diaries and documents as well."

"Melissa, they weren't performance-enhancing substances. It was a peptide consisting of just four amino acids which enhanced soft-tissue healing, Calcium and Magnesium reabsorption to speed up bone and muscular damage. Athletes recovered more quickly after injury. It had other effects which were misused, and I agree it was a mistake. Now Melissa, can we cease this interrogation? I can again proofread the journal article you've written. I read all of it before. There were a few grammatical and spelling errors which I can fix."

She taps my face then unexpectedly kisses me. "Did you buy some fresh condoms?"   "No, you never seemed that interested and like I said before, I'm shy about going to a pharmacy. The staff would probably say you don't need them at your age or with your looks, and they'd probably giggle in front of other patrons. I'm shy buying condoms, but maybe I can order some online and have them home delivered."

"I just had my menstrual period, so I should be safe for a week. In the future, I will go to the Pharmacy and purchase some condoms as it looks like you have more hang-ups than I do."

Where's her mind at? A few minutes earlier, she was ready to rip me to pieces. It's totally out of character for Melissa, a wack with her fist would have been what I expected, but I think I may be getting used to her recent unpredictability. What follows is a lot of groaning and yelling from our bedroom. Melissa is very vocal, but the windows are shut. Luckily Mogan and the kids aren't yet back from basketball. We hear the door opening. "Shut the bedroom door and get dressed," Melissa whispers.

Lizzy opens the bedroom door. Melissa and I are both sitting at the long computer desk in the bedroom, staring at the screen. We only had time to put our shirts on and our faces are sweaty. Luckily, Lizzy can't see that the computer is just starting up.

"What are you doing, mum? You haven't combed your hair."

"Lizzy, Jules is just helping me edit the university paper that I have been writing. Close the door. We will not be long."

Lizzy bangs the door shut. That kid has an attitude. Melissa and I furiously finish dressing. No time for a shower, but we use plenty of under-arm deodorant and perfume spray. We comb the hair and wipe the sweat with a towel. "Melissa, you still got to have a talk with Lizzy. I'm sure she can put two and two together, and that's why she is such a pain."

"It's too early, Jules. She still misses her father, and teenage brains do not work rationally. Just accept it. She will hate you for another 12 years until she is at least about 25 years old. That's when kids usually start becoming rational human beings."

"Melissa, before you told me it was 40 when they become rational. Now would you ever file for a divorce from Victor?"

"Jules, things are complicated in the traditional community that Victor comes from. Things could get ugly, and my main concern is Lizzy and Peter at the moment. Yes, I know Victor abused substances, and he is probably screwing some guy at the moment, but we got to stay off the radar, as you put it and keep things undercover. We should go to the lounge and join the others."

I'm puzzled. She knows Victor's secrets and yet doesn't seem bothered. She seems to be totally goal-orientated, pragmatic and higher on the autism scale than I am. She just dismisses anything that could distract her from her focuses which appear to be the welfare of her kids and her academic papers, and whatever else she does for the i5 organizations. I'm just a convenience tool for a bit of cardio exercise in the bedroom. Oh well, I don't mind but I will conduct a little experiment of my own. I'll purchase one of those vibrators from an Adult shop and see whether she chooses me or the battery-powered device. Of course, I'll make sure its batteries are flat.

Melissa comes into the lounge waving her arms. "I've finished the article. Jules helped to edit it."

Everyone claps their hands, even Lizzy. Melissa and I briefly glance but keep our distance. Mogan yells out. "We got to celebrate. Let's go out and eat. I'll pay."

It's karaoke night at the Elsternwick hotel, and Mogan gets up and does some rap to the music and the kids join in. The other patrons cheer. I put my arm around

Melissa's shoulder. She doesn't swipe it away. Martin wanders by and we shake hands. I introduce him to all the temporary family. "It's nice to see you looking happy. Your food bill will get refunded, and the drinks are on the house."

"Thanks, Martin." I get up and give him a hug.

We're walking home laughing and exuberant. I still have my hand on Melissa's shoulder. Lizzy is showing the others the photos she took with her smartphone, but then a black SUV vehicle swerves to the wrong side of the road and pulls up next to us. The side window winds down halfway. I can't see the face. "Hullo, can you tell me which way to Tennyson Street?" a male voice asks in a strong Italian accent.

"Lizzy, quickly take a photo of the car's number plate," I nervously yell. She does.

"You have five days to decrypt that USB drive. I will be back. Put it in your letterbox when it is done. I know where you live, and I will be back." He is pointing some object at Lizzy. "Run, Lizzy, run," Mogan yells out, "he's got a pistol." Lizzy runs into the driveway of a block of apartments. Just at the right moment, a police car drives by, reverses back and parks. Two armed, burly police officers come walking towards us. We all yell out. "He's got a pistol. That SUV driver threatened us!"

The police officers draw their weapons, pointing them at the windscreen of the SUV. The driver speeds off, nearly colliding with oncoming traffic. Cars swerve to avoid a head-on collision, and he sideswipes a few. There is chaos. A few traumatised drivers hop out of their cars. I can hear. "What the f..k!" The police officers rush back to their car and put their siren and flashing blue lights on, but they are temporarily blocked. "Get back in your cars and clear passage," the police officers announce on the megaphone. The drivers comply, and the police give chase, but it's probably too late. The SUV is a long way down the road. Then another police patrol vehicle arrives. The two officers giving chase must have called for backup. Lizzy cautiously steps out from her hiding place. Two police officers step out. Melissa and her children have a startled look on their faces. One of the officers is Annabelle, donned in her police uniform and all sorts of gadgets, including a loaded holster hanging from her belt.

Melissa yells out to Annabelle, "I thought you worked for the department of transport!"

"It's a long story, Melissa, and this could be called a type of transport job. We'll slowly drive the kids and you back home. Jules and Mogan, you'll have to walk as there is no room for you all, but it's a short walk and we'll keep eye on you and stop every few hundred metres to let you catch up. When you are home, we'll do a preliminary interview at your house to find out exactly what happened. You'll all be picked up by officers tomorrow to make a full sworn statement at the St Kilda police station. Now get going." Annabelle's walkie-talkie radio buzzes. She answers. I can hear some of the conversation. "We've found the vehicle. We checked the number plates. It was stolen and there's no sign of the driver."

"F..k. Willis, call headquarters and arrange protection immediately. The address is …Willis, move your ass!"

"Yes, ma'am."

Annabelle guides the children to the police car. They kind of seem excited at seeing Annabelle in a police uniform. They eagerly jump into the police car. Her work partner drives. We make it back. She has her notebook out and a small voice recorder on. "Now tell me what happened from the start when you left that hotel, the more detail the better."

Melissa, Mogan and I are a bit shaken, but we only describe the incident exactly as it happened and don't speculate that it could be LaMosa rogues as it might incriminate Victor.

"I've organized police protection for you till we catch this guy. There will be a police car outside your townhouse soon. Maybe you could give the officers a cup of coffee and something to eat."

"What about my neighbours? What do I tell them when they see a police car parked outside my place? There are eight townhouses in the complex, and some residents are already getting a bit nosey when they see so many people wandering in and out of a four-bedroom townhouse."

"Think of something," she replies.

"Who are you, Annabelle?" Melissa interjects. It's a face-off; they stare at each other intensely.

"I'm sorry 'sister'. I'm a sergeant with the federal police and on a local assignment and this is constable Bells. I'm sorry for the deception, Melissa, but we've been on this case for nearly six months, and it's better you don't know the details. We will look after you, the kids and even Jules."

I shudder to think what Annabelle and Melissa know. I sort of think Melissa's surprise at seeing Annabelle in uniform was feigned, just for show. So was Annabelle's response – 'It's better you don't know'. I think they both know bits and pieces, just not the whole picture.

I can hear a vehicle coming up the driveway. "Bells, check outside for any security holes," Annabelle yells.

"Yes, ma'am."

Bells comes back inside, "I know them. They're from the St. Kilda precinct, Fernando and Flavis. They're young and inexperienced, but they're the only personnel we currently have available."

"I have to go, but you should be safe tonight. The Police car should act as a deterrent. You have my mobile number. Call me if there's any trouble," Annabelle says.

We're all quite shaken. Mogan makes coffee for the police officers parked outside and takes it to them. Fabian comes over to me and whispers in my ear. "What if the police find out about what happened outside that café where people got shot?"

I whisper back. "Get up early. We'll talk tomorrow. Only you, Sam, and I know, so we have to have a consistent story. I'll call Sam early tomorrow, not that I think he'll be questioned. Go to bed now." The kids march upstairs without any complaints. Mogan decides to sleep on the lounge room couch. I think with his military background, he is primed to wake up if there are any suspicious noises. I'm lying next to Melissa. She asks, "Who are you, Jules and what's this all about?"

"It's the same question I asked you a bit earlier?" Melissa seems to be searching for information again. She knows most of it anyway. Maybe she forgot after all the recent traumas and the wine we drank. Sometimes we can forget that we asked a recent question again when faced with another traumatic situation.

"Didn't Victor tell you? Did he say how I ended up on the yacht with those gun injuries?"

"He said you were probably accidentally shot by some duck shooters. He found you whilst going for a walk in the bush at Westernport Bay. He often took long hikes in the country when we briefly visited. Well, that's what he called them, hikes. He had his medical kit with him, extracted the bullet and stitched you up. He liked you, and despite his other faults, he was a philanthropist. He had your son picked up to join us at the yacht. Now, why was that guy with a gun threatening us?"

"Melissa, I suspect you know what really happened, but at the moment, it's better you believe that story. I'll tell the real story, which you probably know anyway after we do that police statement. Just describe what happened, and it's better you and the kids don't mention Victor or Sam or any previous contact with Annabelle. Have a talk with Lizzy and Peter tomorrow. If asked about our relationship, say you're my girlfriend and separated from your husband. I'll talk to Fabian. If we don't have a consistent story, both Victor and Sam could be in trouble. And don't mention that Annabelle boarded here for a few days. The kids mustn't mention Annabelle, or her career is in jeopardy.

Melissa has a puzzled and worried look on her face, but she knew it anyway. She was always a few steps ahead. I wish she had told me what she knew earlier.

"Jules, did you have any romantic encounter with Annabelle? I saw how you look at her. Your eyes become watery and saliva drips from your lips down your chin."

"Melissa, that's totally ridiculous. I just have an allergy to some chemical substance she uses to wash her uniform. Please dismiss that thought, plus she is not half as attractive as you are."

"Jules, can you salivate like that when you look at me and have saliva dripping down your chin."

"I can, I mean I will. Next time we see her, we'll ask what washing powder she uses whose fumes cause males to salivate." Melissa is definitely going through some gross hormonal imbalance. Then there is another possibility; she has developed the Australian art of 'stirring', where you test people by saying slightly controversial things and watching how the other person reacts. It's a technique used by all spy agencies if they're good at the same spoken language.

"Melissa let's try and get some sleep. There's a lot to do tomorrow. Wait, I have to type a note explaining to all the neighbours in this townhouse complex why there's a police car parked outside. I'll print it and slide a copy under their doors."

"What are you going to tell them, Jules?" Melissa enquires as I'm typing on the computer. 'The note will say that 'You are safe. The Police car is here because the ex-husband of the lady I'm dating now has made threats and is stalking us. He just wanted his pet Siamese cat back, which unfortunately was accidentally run over when we backed the car out to do the food shopping. We have purchased a look-a-like Siamese cat that will be handed to the ex-husband, and all hostilities will cease. You have nothing to worry about, and the matter will soon be resolved."

"Sounds plausible, Jules; you are creative. You should go into politics."

"Melissa, I'm looking at you and dribbling from my mouth, and you hardly ever wash your clothes, so this time it's totally au-natural; your pheromones rather than detergent fumes."

"Jules, you are such a romantic. You know how to turn a girl off."

Maybe she meant 'on'. I wonder what Melissa's and Victor's romantic life was like. Must not have been much, but I'm glad she has such low romantic expectations.

I print eight copies and rush out the door. One of the police officers stops me. "What are you doing?"

"I'm about to slip a note under the neighbours' doors explaining why a police car is parked outside my place, so they don't think I'm some kind of criminal."

"Can I read it?" One of the officers asks. He does and I leave him one of the copies. "OK, but I'll accompany you," said the other rookie officer. He draws his pistol but keeps it inconspicuously low. Then suddenly, there are what sounds like gunshots.

"Get down. Keep low," he whispers as he grabs his service pistol with both hands and does the typical stretched arm sweep of the scene while crouched down low. We look behind us and see the fireworks blazing in the sky. I forgot it was the end of some festival in the adjoining suburb and that there was going to be a fireworks display. I finish the note, drop to the neighbour's houses and thank the officer, who probably won't need any more coffee after that rush of adrenaline.

Melissa is asleep, and no one seemed to have woken from the thunder of fireworks. I join Melissa and try to sleep but can't just yet, so quietly sneak into the kitchen and grab that bottle of Vodka from one of the rarely used cupboards. No one has touched it. A gift I must have got many years ago. There is a little card attached to the wrapping. 'Happy Birthday, Jules, Marg, 2002.' I put the bottle back, and there's no beer in the fridge. OK, another sleepless night, but it wasn't. I go back to the bedroom and close the door. Melissa is drowsy but awake.

"Come over and dribble," she beckons.

"Melissa, you're taking over this household, so is Mogan."

"Calm down, Jules. It will all make sense eventually, and you can be the patriarch again, but you may have to learn some more social skills."

"I don't want to be a patriarch. I just like things to operate smoothly, no drama. I'm sick of the drama." I turn away from her on the bed as if throwing a teenage tantrum. She stretches her hand and puts it on my face. It's sort of reassuring. "We got more talking to do, and it won't be comfortable for you. We'll leave it to tomorrow. Just try to sleep for now, but maybe we can do some bedroom gymnastics as long as you dribble when thinking about me. I think I'm still safe, you won't need a condom."

I turn towards her, "Melissa, I made that perilous journey to the pharmacy to purchase some fresh condoms."

Then the physical passion starts. Luckily the bedroom door is closed, and there is a thunderstorm – a climatic one, a weather one. No one could hear as the lightning strikes in the background, and I'm profusely dribbling from the mouth, but Melissa didn't seem to mind as saliva falls on her breasts and other parts of her anatomy. It could definitely be a good scene for a vampire movie.

Chapter sixteen

The clock alarm buzzes at 7 am, and I wake Melissa. She rubs her eyes. She's still hazy. "Melissa, can you ring the schools at 8:30 am and tell them that the kids are sick and won't make it to school for a few days or longer."

"But why Jules, Mogan takes them to school before he goes to work?"

"Melissa, all of us have to go to the Police station at 9 am to make a sworn statement. We have to have a consistent story, and Melissa, it's better that they don't go back to school after the interview. They should stay at home until that guy in the SUV is caught. He's dangerous. We have police protection if we stay at home."

Melissa and I wake Mogan and the kids. They are drowsy, but we're all finally gathered in the lounge. Melissa and I are standing in front of the drowsy foursome.

"Guys, we have to have a consistent story. Just describe what happened, nothing else. If quizzed why that incident might have happened, just say 'I don't know', don't mention anything else and especially that Sam and Annabelle boarded with us for a few days. It could ruin their careers."

"Peter, Lizzy, Fabian and Mogan, you will all get an explanation once all this is over. Just describe what you saw, and don't mention Sam or Annabelle or Victor, your father. If you do, they may end up in jail," Melissa reiterates.

I say to Fabian, "Do as Melissa and Jules say," "Now let's have some high fives to show our solidarity," Mogan exclaims. We all participate in the high five, but then I wonder if the kids can handle the pressure of a police interview.

I make some phone calls. "Ms Valda, I can't make it to work today. Is there any work I can do online from home?"

"Have you fallen off the balcony again? You've already taken a month off plus several other days. Your sick leave has long expired."

"Ms Valda, I will make it up, and you don't have to pay me for that extra time off. I will finish the job within the timeframe." There is a pause and some chat in the background, then a very unexpected response. She cordially replies, "Take the time off, but you won't be paid."

"Thanks, Ms Valda." I then ring Sam. "Could you come over, maybe when we get home after making a police statement? I'll explain when we're back. There is a police guard on my place. Ring Annabelle so she can instruct them to let you in but don't use your real name. Make up another name and inform Annabelle that's the name you'll use. Have you still got a key?"

"Yeh, I never returned it to you," he replies, slightly puzzled. "I have no pressing legal cases today. It should be OK."

"Good. The house alarm is on, but you know the code to turn it off. I got to go, Sam. A few more calls to make."

"Good luck Jules."

It's raining very heavily, and we rush to a large police van that's come to pick all of us up. We're wet. Inside the police station, they give us towels and bring in another table into the interview room to fit all of us. It's Senior Sergeant Mathews who is interviewing us. Annabelle, clad in her police uniform, is also present and has a worried look on her face. The video camera and voice recording devices are switched on. All of us don't look that good, water dripping off our hair onto our faces. The interview starts off cordially, with the two officers addressing us by our first names.

So far, the interview is going to plan, purely descriptive of the incident. Then a question that leaves us rocked. It's turning into an interrogation.

"Madam, you and your children's surname is Mosa. Are you related to a Victor Mosa?" Mathews asks.

Melissa looks startled and pauses before answering. "He was my husband, but he abandoned us. He disappeared. Jules gave us accommodation in Melbourne."

"What do you mean by 'abandoned'?"

"We saw him heading to shore on a dinghy from the yacht moored at Western Port Bay. That was nearly a year ago, and we haven't seen or heard from him since. I have reason to suspect that he has other romantic involvements."

Lizzy cringes and looks as if she is going to yell something out but refrains. Melissa starts sobbing, and Annabelle hands her a tissue. Melissa pulls off a convincing act.

"How does Jules know Victor?"

Melissa explains the supposed hunting incident and how Victor found me, patched me up as he was a doctor specializing in trauma incidents and let me recuperate on his yacht.

"That's highly unusual. Shouldn't Victor have called an ambulance and have Jules taken to a hospital?"

"Well, that's Victor for you, a know-all and a good doer. He said Jules' injuries were superficial, and Victor always carried his medical gear wherever he went," Melissa replied whilst wiping her eyes with the tissue.

"Did Jules try to follow Victor to shore when Victor departed?"

"No, we only had one dinghy."

"Did you know your husband was connected with an organization called LaMosa?"

"Yes, it's what Victor's father, Antonio, called his building construction company in Chicago. It wasn't an organization, just the name of Antonio's construction company."

The two officers glance at each other. Sergeant Mathews leaves the room briefly and brings back a large map of Western Port Bay which he unfolds. "Jules, can you show me on this map where you think you got shot and where Victor's yacht was moored when he used the dinghy to get to shore?"

"It must have been close to where the yacht was moored. I used to go camping and hiking around Western Port Bay. Sometimes I walked kilometres. Melissa, do you remember where the yacht was moored?"

"Victor had mentioned a Tooradin. That is where we got our food delivered from. I don't remember the shop's name, but they had good, fresh seafood and fresh vegetables grown by local farmers."

Sergeant Mathews turns to Mogan. "Mogan Latoga. Is that your name?"

"Yes, but I was always called 'Mogan the Bogan,' your highness."

Mathews glances at Annabelle again but with a slight look of displeasure.

"So what's the connection? How did you end up living in that household?"

Mogan doesn't respond immediately. "I'm an Afghanistan war veteran. I have PTSD. I was about to lay out my sleeping bag in a bus shelter when Jules walked past and offered me shelter. He's a hero."

Mogan did a wonderful job in coming up with that response. Mathews is satisfied, and he bows his head in approval when he looks at me.

"We may have to have another interview, but the kids won't have to attend. Do you all consent?" Mathews asks. Annabelle has that worried look back again and glances from side to side.

"Yes, sure, but find the guy who threatened us," I reply.

"We're doing our best. The interview is over. Have a good day." Mathews turns off the tape recorder and camera.

"Don't we have to sign some statement?"

"Yes, and some officers will deliver it to your house. Normally we'd keep you at the station till it is typed, but that could take a few hours, and the kids would get restless."

Mathews pats me on the back, and we're driven back very close to home in a police van. No one utters a sound during the short journey. The kids look concerned but not unhappy, just puzzled. We do the final 100m walk so as not to draw attention from neighbours. When back at my townhouse, teary Lizzy is the first to question me, "Did you kill my dad?"

"Lizzy, I would never do that. I never purposely even killed a spider. Your dad had some business to attend to, and I'm sure he'll contact us soon. There is always an explanation and as you know, he had a job that involved much travel in looking after his father's business." I give Lizzy a hug, the first. "He'll be back," I say. She doesn't flinch.

"I'm late for my Uni lecture. You can order food online. My credit card is on the kitchen table," Mogan calls out as he rushes to the door. I don't think Mogan is a target. One of the police officers guarding us carries in a thick A4 size envelope just as Mogan was stepping out. "It was delivered by a teacher from the schools." He carefully opens the envelope and flicks through the papers. It's just paperwork, homework assignments. The kids go upstairs, so it's just Melissa and me, left downstairs. Peter yells out from upstairs. "Mum, there's lightning and thunder. I'm scared."

Melissa yells back. "Don't worry, Peter, just think of it as a fireworks display. Enjoy it."

"Melissa, do you want to know the full story about how I met Victor, well as far as I know it?"

I pull out that old bottle of Vodka concealed in a kitchen cabinet but pull off Marg's little greeting tag and put it in a cupboard drawer. I pour two small glasses and bring them back to the lounge room; we both skol.

It takes two hours to explain the truth, including the death of my first wife, as I know it, and that Victor's medical degree may have not been legitimate. He confessed when we talked on the yacht, though he did learn much medicine in his spare time; his degree was for gratis building work at the Medical School, done by his stepfather. Melissa is shocked and rushes to the kitchen and fills another glass of Vodka.

"Melissa, Victor should have immediately called the police after that shootout in St. Kilda. It was all self-defence when we faced those LaMosa rogues. They shot first. There would have been a coronial enquiry, and I'm sure we would have all got acquitted. All this drama could have been averted, but Victor made a hasty decision, and now we're going down a rabbit hole. We have to have a strategy else we'll just go down deeper and deeper." Melissa does a hiccup. "Victor lived in a fantasy world sometimes. He watched too many of those Mafia crime and Marvel movies."

"Melissa, Sam will be back over soon. We have to combine our minds and work out a plausible solution that doesn't incriminate any of us, including Annabelle; you know, that guilt-by-association stuff. We have to work together to get out of this mess."

"Jules, those LaMosa rogues had to be terminated. Killed dead, else they may have talked, and we'd have more people chasing you."

I reflect for a moment. She's right. Then she shoves me back against the couch. "What's on that flash drive that these guys want? What's so precious that they'd kill to get it? It must be more than a peptide formula?"

"I don't know, Melissa. It doesn't make sense to me at the moment." Then the doorbell rings. It's Sam. He's drenched. We let him in even though he has the keys.

"Sorry I'm late, a case came up and I had to type a long email."

"It's OK, we just got back ourselves. The interview took longer than expected."

Sam wanders around the townhouse, including upstairs, reminiscing, and then he mentions, "You have a water leak in the kid's room. I'm surprised the kids didn't notice it. Water drops are dripping down through the plasterboard ceiling. Better fix that, Jules, else the ceiling will collapse."

I walk upstairs. The kids are not doing their homework, just fixated on computer games and don't notice the water dripping from the ceiling behind them. That can't be. There's never been a water leak before. Then there's a thud sound from the ceiling. I rush downstairs and outside into the courtyard and look at the roof. Four roof tiles are shifted to make an opening.

"There is someone in the ceiling," I whisper to Sam.

"Jules, how could anyone get past that police car parked outside your place, and you had the alarm system on?" Sam whispers back.

"He or she must have jumped the fence from the neighbour's place outside the complex that faces my courtyard. The neighbours are away on holidays, and there's no alarm sensor in the ceiling. We have to get the kids downstairs, very quietly."

Sam guides the kids, with his forefinger on his lips, they tiptoe downstairs with perplexed looks on their faces, glancing at each other but not saying a word.

"Sam, call Annabelle. That LaMosa rogue may be in my ceiling. Tell her they should wear those bullet-proof vests and head protection."

"Jules, calm down, I'm sure Annabelle knows the safety protocol. I'll call her."

In less than 10 minutes, two police vans arrive with heavily armed officers in black costumes, heavy bulletproof vests and headgear. Annabelle is one of them. They silently enter the townhouse with rifles and pistols, scanning the surrounds.

"Jules, where's the manhole into the ceiling?" Annabelle whispers.

"Upstairs, in the corridor."

"Take the kids and Melissa into the garage; quickly and bring me a ladder from your garage. Johnson, you go with Mr Lemos and help him bring the ladder up but do it very quietly."

Johnson and I manage to climb the winding staircase, carrying the ladder without banging it against any walls.

"SnowPea, don't go up there. From what Jules told me, the guy is armed," Sam whispers to her.

"Dad, it's OK. I've been trained for this type of event, it's my job. I got support. Now you and Jules get downstairs into the garage and join Melissa and the kids."

"I love you, SnowPea."

"I love you too, dad."

The ladder is positioned above the manhole, and Annabelle slowly and silently climbs up with her headlamp on and pistol ready for action. The five heavily armed officers from the Police Tactical Team wait below the ladder with pistols ready, except for two who hold and steady the ladder. Sam and I disobey Annabelle's instruction and stay quietly hidden in one of the upstairs bedrooms. The other officers and Annabelle are too busy to notice.

The roof in the townhouse is highly pitched, nearly 3 metres at the highest point and gabled. There are many nooks and crannies up there. Annabelle turns on her headlamp, cautiously opens the manhole and scans the scene.

"Can't see anyone in here," she whispers as she pulls herself up into the ceiling.

"Oh f..k!" she yells out.

Then a subdued gunshot resonates from the ceiling, followed by a loud thud. Sam frantically rushes out and joins the pandemonium. "Are you all right, SnowPea? Speak to me, speak to me!" He yells at the top of his voice. He frantically tries to climb up the ladder but is restrained by the police officers. It happened so quickly. I rush from the bedroom to the corridor where the ceiling manhole is and join Sam. I yell to the officers, "If you don't go up, Sam and I will."

Sam slowly starts to make his way back to the stairwell, clutching his head. I glance at him, and he glances back. His face looks wet, like he has had a huge tear attack, and he's crouching and clutching his chest. The officers seem to be discussing tactics. One goes over to Sam. "Calm down sir, you're not supposed to be here, and we're just sending Wilson up to check what happened. We have also called an ambulance and a medical firearm wounds specialist."

"Wilson, check your helmet and put the headlight on."

A groan comes from the ceiling. It's Annabelle. "I'm all right, but the perpetrator isn't."

Wilson cautiously climbs up the ladder wearing his helmet and awkwardly pulls himself up into the ceiling. He must have some video camera device fixed to his helmet because we can see what he can see on what looks like a PC tablet that another officer is holding. The officers must not have noticed that I'm still present or are too preoccupied with the safety of their sergeant. I stand next to them. We see a scan of the ceiling and a distorted body lying on one of the ceiling joists. His head is bent forward towards his chest. Wilson turns to Annabelle. "Sergeant, are you injured?"

"Just a graze on my right arm. Check the condition of the perpetrator and use gloves."

"He's not breathing and has no pulse, and the back of his head is bleeding. Looks like he came down a metre from that ceiling beam, and the upper part of his neck landed on the ceiling joist. Must have been the recoil from that gunshot he fired at you, and he lost his balance."

"Don't touch anything! Call forensics and tell them to bring fumigation gear as well. This ceiling is infested with spiders."

Annabelle unsteadily climbs down the ladder, visibly shaken and trembling.

I yell at the top of my voice hoping Sam can hear, "Sergeant Annabelle is OK." I rush over to her, but she brushes me aside. She takes off her helmet, jacket, and shirt and throws them on the floor. There is blood dripping from her left upper arm. Then she starts furiously brushing her trousers with her hands. She wipes her sweaty brow then, with her boots, furiously starts squashing all those 1 cm long arachnids that she swiped from her clothing. The other officers look on with a concerned look and glance from one to another. Some start checking their own attire and start swiping for spiders. Annabelle is crouched down. I come over to her and put my hand on her bare shoulder.

"I hate spiders, Jules, the only thing I'm scared of. Can you see if there are any more on me?"

"No, you appear clean, but maybe go to the downstairs bathroom and shower, just in case. I'll get one of Melissa's tracksuits for you to wear, and I'll place it in the downstairs bathroom. Maybe the fumigation team can fumigate your uniform as well, just in case."

"Jules, this will be complicated to explain to Senior Sergeant Mathews. You and Sam called me by my first name. There is a serious conflict of interest," she whispers.

I'm thinking furiously. Only a severe compromise and sworn loyalty to Doris can solve this problem. I go into one of the bedrooms, close the door and ring Doris or mum, as you may know her. Apart from the tirade, 'you fxxked up again', I hear from Doris. I come out and whisper, "Annabelle, it will all be OK; you won't have to worry about Mathews, and we won't be required to make a statement at the police station. Your career is intact."

She looks at me and whispers back with a smile, "For a daggy sort of guy, you must have very powerful connections."

I so much feel like giving her a hug or a peck on the cheek but refrain as there is an audience of police officers.

Annabelle lifts her head and announces to her team, "You all did a great job. Wilson and Merkle, you stay here. The rest of you go back to the station and move the police vehicles out of the driveway. Wilson, strip down and have a shower. Put your uniform and gear in a plastic bag. Mr Lemos, can you find some spare clothing for Wilson? Any old tracksuit will do."

Then Wilson just notices the spiders on his uniform after one climbed onto his face. He rushes to the upstairs bathroom. I can hear slapping and huffing as if Wilson is having a severe panic or cardio attack. My mind briefly wanders; why do we fear spiders so much? The only moderately venomous species in Victoria is the Redback spider, and they are shy, very rare and don't

kill you. I look at the squashed remains of the spiders that Annabelle stomped on. They are not Redback spiders.

"Mr Lemos!" My attention returns as Annabelle yells. "Go down to the garage. Tell all the occupants that everything is under control, and I don't want anyone rushing up here till forensics has done their job, and please open your double garage for the forensics van. Your neighbours in this townhouse complex don't need to see any more drama."

They all look worried in the garage. Sam must have sneaked back down and didn't hear me call that it's all OK. Melissa is holding his head and trying to comfort the sobbing Samoan. I put my arms around them both. "Annabelle is fine, just a graze on her arm, and the rogue appears dead. A forensics team will be here soon. We're to stay downstairs in the house until they've done their job. We got to stay calm and not call Annabelle by her name. If you have to speak to her, call her 'sergeant', now kids, go watch some TV or play on the Xbox but don't go upstairs and ignore the men in white suits who'll be here soon. They work for the police."

"There's no Xbox downstairs," complains Lizzy.

"Go for a walk then. That's what we did before those devices were invented." The kids look up in disbelief.

Melissa comments, "Jules, are you all right? You seem shaken."

"I'm sort of healthy and fine, but a bit shaken up as these sorts of occurrences don't happen to the average guy. It is a good outcome best as could have happened, as we previously discussed. The LaMosa guy is dead. Now we got to get our kids away from computer games. That will be the difficult journey."

Melissa comes over to me and gives a peck on my cheek. I open the garage door and look out into the long driveway. There's Mogan, back early from college, oblivious to the world, headphones on, waving his arms, swinging his body, and singing as he makes his way up the driveway. He gets closer. I can just make out his words, 'It's going to be a bright, bright shin'in day'. I pull Mogan over into the garage. He takes off the headphones. "Guys, I got an A+ for my first assignment at teachers college!"

Sam pulls Mogan aside. They talk for around five minutes. Then Sam and Mogan return to Melissa and me. Mogan announces, "Luckily for Annabelle, you had those spiders in the ceiling. That rogue who missed Annabelle with that gunshot and fell, well it was probably because he got startled when the little critters crawled up his arm and neck. He probably tried to swipe them and lost his balance. That's my theory anyway."

I think Mogan's theory may have been right. Spiders do serve a purpose.

Sam interjects, "I think I may know a guy who can fix those tiles. He is cheap and can scale any building, plus Jules, I walked around the courtyard. There is a rope and possibly a claw hook hanging from the side of your townhouse. That's how he may have got onto your roof and removed those roof tiles."

"Sam, please call your tile fixer. It would be good if he could come today just in case it starts raining again." I turn to Mogan. "Mogan, don't call Annabelle by her first name. Call her sergeant if there are other police officers present."

"Sure, no problem, and I thought my life was complicated. You've given me a whole new concept of complicastory."

"Mogan, that is not a word in the current dictionaries, but I hope it will be one day."

Sam lowers his torso to the kids, "That applies to you kids as well. It's sergeant, not Annabelle, well at least for a while." There are high-fives. Everyone agrees.

"By the way, Mogan, what's that song you were listening to?" I ask.

"Dude, it's a song by a black guy called Johnny Nash. It's called 'I can see clearly now'; it's on YouTube."

"Play it again Sa.. sorry Mogan."

Mogan fiddles with his smartphone, and the song starts again. All four of us have arms around our shoulders and form a circle as we listen. The kids join in.

'All of the pain is gone,

It's going to be a bright, bright sunny day'.

That would end up being a premature assessment of the situation.

Chapter seventeen

It happened so quickly. I rush from the bedroom to the corridor where the ceiling manhole is and join Sam. I yell to the officers, "If you don't go up, Sam or I will."

Sam slowly starts to make his way back to the stairwell, clutching his head. I glance at him, and he glances back. His face looks wet, like he has a huge tear attack, and he's crouching and clutching his chest.

The officers seem to be discussing tactics. One goes over to Sam. "Calm down, sir. You're not supposed to be here. We're just sending Wilson up to check what happened. We also called an ambulance."

Wilson, check your helmet and put the headlight on."

A groan comes from the ceiling. It's Annabelle. "I'm all right, but the perpetrator isn't."

Wilson cautiously climbs up the ladder wearing his helmet and awkwardly pulls himself up into the ceiling. He must have some video camera device fixed to his helmet, because we can see what he can see on what looks like a PC tablet that another officer is holding. The officers must not have noticed that I'm still present or are too preoccupied with the safety of their sergeant.

I stand next to them. We see a scan of the ceiling and a distorted body lying on one of the ceiling joists. His head is bent forward towards his chest.

Wilson turns to Annabelle.

"Sergeant, are you injured?"

"Just a graze on my right arm. Check the condition of the perpetrator. Use gloves. He's not breathing and has no pulse, and the back of his head is bleeding. Looks like he came down 2 metres from that ceiling beam, and the upper part of his neck landed on the ceiling joist. Must have been the recoil from that gunshot, and he lost his balance. Don't touch anything! Call forensics and tell them to bring fumigation gear as well. This ceiling is infested with spiders."

Annabelle unsteadily climbs down the ladder, visibly shaken and trembling.

I yell at the top of my voice, hoping Sam can hear, "Annabelle is OK."

I rush over to her, but she brushes me aside. She takes off her helmet, jacket, and shirt and throws them on the floor. There is blood dripping from her left upper arm. Then she starts furiously brushing her trousers and with her hands. She wipes her sweaty brow then, with her boots, furiously starts squashing all those 1 cm long arachnids that she swiped from her clothing. The other officers look on. Some start checking their own attire and start swiping.

Annabelle is crouched down. I come over to her and put my hand on her bare shoulder.

"I hate spiders, Jules, the only thing I'm scared of. Can you see any more on me?"

"No, you appear clean, but maybe go to the downstairs bathroom and shower, just in case. I'll get one of Melissa's tracksuits for you to wear, and I'll place it in the bathroom. Maybe the fumigation team can fumigate your uniform as well, just in case."

"Jules, this will be complicated to explain to my senior sergeant Mathews. You and Sam called me by my first name. There is a conflict of interest," she whispers.

I'm thinking furiously. Only a severe compromise can solve this problem. I go into one of the bedrooms, close the door and ring mum or Doris, as you may know her.

I come out and whisper back, "Annabelle, it will all be OK, you won't have to worry about Mathews, and we won't be required to make a statement at the police station. Your career is intact, plus you're wearing a name tag on your right shoulder."

She looks at me and whispers back with a smile, "For a daggy sort of guy, you must have powerful contacts."

I so much feel like giving her a hug or a peck on the cheek but refrain as there is an audience.

Annabelle lifts her head and announces to her team, "You all did a good job. Wilson and Merkle, you stay here. The rest of you go back to the station and move the police vehicles out of the driveway. Wilson, strip down and have a shower. Put your uniform and gear in a plastic bag. Mr Lemos, can you find another tracksuit for him or a towel and get one of those big plastic rubbish bags?"

Wilson just notices the spiders on his uniform after one climbed onto his face. He rushes to the upstairs bathroom. I can hear slapping and huffing as if Wilson is having a panic attack. My mind briefly wanders; why do we fear spiders so much? The only moderately venomous species in Victoria is the Redback spider, and they are shy and very rare. I look at the squashed remains of the spiders that Annabelle stomped on. They are not Redback spiders.

"Mr Lemos!" My attention returns as Annabelle yells. "Go down to the garage. Tell them everything is all right. I don't want anyone rushing up here anymore till forensics has done their job and open your double garage for the forensics van. Your neighbours in this townhouse complex don't need to see any more drama."

They all look worried in the garage. Sam must have sneaked back down and didn't hear me call that it's all OK. Melissa is holding his head and trying to comfort the sobbing Samoan. I put my arms around them both.

"Annabelle is fine, just a graze on her arm, and the rogue appears dead. A forensics team will be here soon. We're to stay downstairs in the house until they've done their job. We got to stay calm and not call out to Annabelle by her name. If you have to speak to her, call her 'sergeant'. Now kids go watch some TV or play on the Xbox but don't go upstairs and ignore the men in white suits who'll be here soon. They work for the police."

"There's no Xbox downstairs," complains Lizzy.

"Go for a walk then. That's what we did before those devices were invented." The kids look up in disbelief.

Melissa comments, "Jules, are you all right? You seem shaken."

"I'm sort of fine. It is a good outcome best as could have happened, as we previously discussed. The LaMosa guy is dead. Now we got to get our kids away from computer games. That will be the difficult journey."

Melissa comes over to me and gives me a peck on my cheek. I open the garage door and look out into the long driveway. There's Mogan, back early from college, oblivious to the world, headphones on, waving his arms and swinging his body and singing as he makes his way up the driveway. He gets closer. I can just make out his words, 'It's going to be a bright, bright shin'in day'.

I pull Mogan over into the garage. He takes off the headphones. "Guys, I got an A+ for my first assignment at teachers college!"

Sam pulls Mogan aside. They talk for around five minutes. Then Sam and Mogan return to Melissa and me.

Mogan announces, "Luckily for Annabelle, you had those spiders in the ceiling. That rogue who missed Annabelle with that gunshot and fell, well it was probably because he got startled when the little critters crawled up his arm and neck. He probably tried to swipe them and lost his balance. That's my theory anyway."

I think Mogan's theory may have been right. Spiders do serve a purpose.

Sam interjects, "I think I may know a guy who can fix those tiles. He's cheap and can scale any building, plus Jules, I walked around the courtyard. There's a rope and possibly a claw hook hanging from the side of your townhouse. That's how he may have got onto your roof and removed those roof tiles."

"Sam, please call him. It would be good if he could come today just in case it starts raining again."

I turn to Mogan. "Mogan, don't call Annabelle by her first name. Call her sergeant if there are other police officers present."

"Sure, no problem, and I thought my life was complicated. You've given me a whole new concept of complicastory."

"Mogan, that is not a word in the current dictionary, but I hope it will be one day."

Sam lowers his torso to the kids, "That applies to you kids as well. It's sergeant, not Annabelle, well, at least for a while."

There are high-fives. Everyone is in agreement.

"By the way, Mogan, what's that song you were listening to?" I ask.

"Dude, it's a song by a black guy called Johnny Nash. It's called 'I can see clearly now'. It's on YouTube."

"Play it again Sa.. sorry Mogan."

Mogan fiddles with his smartphone, and the song starts again. All four of us have arms around our shoulders and form a circle as we listen. The kids join in.

'All the pain is gone,

It's going to be a bright, bright sunny day'.

It would be a premature assessment.

Chapter eighteen

The white coats from forensics spend 3 hours in the ceiling, fumigating, photographing, extracting the bullet from the ceiling joist and then trying to get the rogue's strapped body down from the ceiling. It's tricky as the stretcher hardly fits the ceiling manhole.

"Just drop him down," Annabelle yells. She seems quite shattered.

"We can't do that; you know the protocol. He has to have an autopsy."

Sam and I leave the garage and go back upstairs. Sam sneaks over to Annabelle and gives her a big hug. "It's OK, SnowPea. We got to get some antiseptic to put on that wound. Go downstairs and lie down on the couch in the lounge. I'll help you get downstairs." He whispers.

"It's only a graze, dad; I ducked when I finally looked up and saw him. The bullet just scraped my arm."

"Jules, call an ambulance," Sam whispers.

"Dad, I'm all right; just some antiseptic cream will do."

The forensic squad is still upstairs. Annabelle goes downstairs and lies on the couch. The kids come rushing in from the garage and gather around Annabelle, stroking her good arm. "You'll be all right, sergeant," they say in unison with concerned looks on their faces. Annabelle looks appreciatively at them.

Wilson comes downstairs and comments, "We're going back to the station to file the report. Sergeant, are you sure you don't need medical intervention?"

"I'm fine, Wilson. Thanks, guys. You did a great job. I'm taking the rest of the day off. Debriefing will be tomorrow morning."

Sergeant, "We've finished, and so has forensics. Are you sure you don't want a lift to the station?"

"No, Wilson, I live very close by. The walk will do me good and help me unwind."

The forensic team and Wilson leave, and they actually cleaned up all the squashed spiders. The kids run back upstairs to continue their video game.

"Jules, have you got some antiseptic?" Sam asks.

The First Aid kit has a date stamp of 2000. I don't know if that's an expiry date, but I pass it to Sam, who rubs the antiseptic lotion on Annabelle's arm. She refrains from yelping.

"Dad, I never got to fire my pistol. He just fell off that ceiling beam. Don't know if it was the recoil from his pistol or the spiders crawling in Jules' ceiling, but he fell."

"It's OK, SnowPea. Forensics will examine your pistol. Merkle and Wilson were witnesses and signed a statement. Not a shot was fired from your pistol."

"Dad, could I have a cup of tea?"

Sam joins Melissa, Mogan and me in the kitchen. I whisper to everyone, "That's the best outcome that could have happened. The rogue is dead and can't talk. Else we could all be in trouble if he did. Annabelle will probably get a well-deserved bravery award."

We do a high-five and turn on the kettle. Mogan gets the cups and tea bags.

"Dad, on second thought, could I have something stronger?" Annabelle calls out from the lounge room.

Melissa goes to the cupboard and whispers to me. "I bought some more of your favourite drink but don't get horny with me tonight."

Melissa pulls out two bottles of Vodka and takes them to the lounge room, placing them on the coffee table near the couch. She can't find those little skolling glasses, so Annabelle lifts her head and takes the first swig from the bottle, which then gets passed around. Yeh, it's not elegant, but no one feels elegant at the moment.

The kids cautiously come down the stairs. "Are you still OK, Annabelle? You're bleeding," Lizzy calls out and rushes over to Annabelle.

"It's only a scratch. Now go and play basketball with Mogan, and thanks guys, for your concern."

Mogan looks at Melissa, who nods her head. He gives Annabelle a gentle hug, then turns on his smartphone full blast and marches off with the kids and the ball. We can hear the same song again. Mogan has transformed into an optimist. I got to get the formula off him.

Melissa turns to us. "The physical exercise will diffuse their tension. They've seen far too much in the last few days. Mogan has earned his keep, and he doesn't drink."

It's Sam, Melissa, Annabelle and I swigging the Vodka. One bottle is empty and I'm opening the second.

Sam slurringly asks, "And what do you think of Mogan, Jules?"

Melissa interrupts, "He's great with the kids and now doing a primary school teaching diploma. He got an A+ for his first assignment."

"I'm glad to hear that. He is a good guy, and he seems to have made great progress. I've never seen him so, so happy. He was always so melancholic ever since I knew him."

I looked at Annabelle, maybe for too long. Melissa gives me a slight slap on the face. For a moment, I wonder if she learnt that technique from Annabelle or did they just go to the same school.

A few hours pass, then the doorbell rings, and we hear Mogan's voice. Sam and I stumble and remove the Vodka bottles and throw them in the recycle bin.

"Come, come in, Mogan. You got the key," Sam yells out.

Mogan and the sweaty kids come marching in. "We all scored and beat Mogan for the first time. We love basketball."

"Go up and have a shower and change into your pyjamas and then come down for dinner."

"But mum, it's still early!"

"It's also back to school tomorrow morning, and you've had a very, very, very big day. Now, do as I say."

Mogan sniffs the air and looks puzzled when he sees us all, "Have I missed out on some deep and meaningful conversation? I'm opening the windows. This place would explode if there was an open flame."

"No Mogan, you missed nothing. We're just not used to what has happened. We're not trained like you are. We just con.. consumed a lot of alcohol. And thanks for taking the kids to basketball. You are going to make a great teacher."

"Do you want me to cook?"

"Thanks for the offer Mogan, but I'll pay for takeaway food tonight. Can you order for seven people? You also look like you need a shower. The downstairs bathroom is free."

"Jules, we got to get home," Sam says.

"Sam, you and Annabelle can't go stumbling to your apartment whilst she's wearing parts of her police uniform. You're both staying here for the night. I'll set the alarm clock for 5 am, and then I should be sober enough to drive you."

"Annabelle, you sleep on the double bed with Melissa. Sam, I bought some more blow-up mattresses, pillows and blankets. You, Mogan and I stay in the lounge."

Mogan and the kids are showering. Annabelle whispers to us all. "It's not over; there is at least another rogue." She looks at Melissa, "Michele, Mosa, also known as Victor, is a person of interest."

Melissa and I are aghast as we look at each other. Suddenly sobriety returns. Must be the adrenaline rush.

"You're implying my husband is involved in this mess? You got it terribly wrong, sister. Victor saved Jules. If he wanted that stupid USB stick, he could have got it any time while Jules was recuperating on the yacht. Now get out. I want you out of here!"

I grab and restrain the enraged Melissa. She has totally 'lost' it. Sam looks in disbelief.

"Calm down Melissa, Annabelle only said 'person of interest'."

"Annabelle, what makes you think that other people may be involved?" I quietly enquire.

"Jules, Michele, or Victor, as you all know him did a vanishing act. No trace of him leaving the country, and you and Melissa claimed he hadn't been seen for over 12 months. Don't you think that's strange? Senior sergeant Mathews thinks it's unusual and that Victor may be connected to this mess. Mathews may know more but hasn't told me yet. He just said Victor could be one of these rogues."

"Annabelle, as Melissa said, Victor saved my life. Now, do you really want to know why he vanished? He had a cocaine habit and was also involved with someone else, and it highly unlikely that it was a female. That's why the secrecy. Now tell that to your senior sergeant Mathews, and we prefer to not publicize those facts."

"I will, Jules. Now, can I go home? It doesn't look like I'm welcome here," she wearingly replies.

"Annabelle, you and Sam are staying here tonight. You'll have Mogan's room.

Mogan and Sam can sleep in the lounge, and I will too.

I release Melissa, but then she moves closer to the couch-ridden Annabelle and clasps her hand. Sam and I were about to grab her, but then, "I'm sorry, Annabelle. I'm sorry. I'm very sorry." with what intel you have, it's a valid conclusion.

Annabelle has a perplexed look. Her eyes are flashing at all four of us."

Sam grabs Annabelle's hand and then guides her to Mogan's bedroom. "Dear SweetPea, it will make sense in the end. Hold on, and don't jump to conclusions. You have to observe and listen. Turn that Smartphone off. I'm talking to you."

"Sorry, dad."

"Annabelle, the story is obvious if you look, observe, and pick up the cues."

"Dad, have you taken some hallucinogenic substance?"

I pull Melissa aside and whisper. "You broke rule 9 of the ten commandments. You implied you have more intel than an outsider, Annabelle. You just had to agree with her without that emotional performance, but I'm glad you said, 'I'm sorry'. I hope she forgets the conversation."

"Oh, Jules, you've become so forceful, not like the wimp you were before. You now remind me of Victor, and your memory seems to have returned. Let's go to bed and make love."

A sardonic suggestion by Melissa. If ever there was a turn-off....

No one slept much that night, well not till the wee hours of the morning. All eventually joined Mogan, Sam and me in the lounge room, Melissa, Annabelle, and the kids. We all just sat in a circle and looked at the ceiling till finally, we all keeled over and got a few uncomfortable hours of sleep.

Me, I had a job to do.

Chapter nineteen

It's another day of archiving at the library. Melissa and I have reached the year 2007. Only one more year of scanning to go as the particular newspaper went defunct in 2008. It shouldn't take long.

"Melissa, my cash reserves are getting low. I know you and Mogan buy all the food, but there are many other bills. Maybe we should slow down and keep this library job going as long as possible."

"Did you consider Magnus' offer? Else I can apply for a tutoring position at one of your universities. Victor hasn't paid off the credit card debt for six months, so my bills are mounting as well. Mogan did offer to pay you rent, but you refused."

Doris doesn't bring the coffee; abandoned us again, or maybe she's taking a break. She hasn't taken a break since I started work here. I go upstairs, where Charmaine is making her weekly visit. She is gesticulating as she whispers to Ms Valda. It seems like they are arguing. I don't walk in but hide behind the door till they leave. Then I help myself to the coffee machine and bring two cups down. I wonder why Charmaine is keeping her distance. She could at least come down for a chat.

"Melissa, did you hear what Fabian told me last night? He whispered before I went to bed. I ignored it; it seemed too far-fetched."

"No, what was it?"

"From whatever is in the diaries and papers, he's deduced that Marg and Magnus may have been having an affair when we briefly lived in Sweden; Magnus may be Fabian's real father. First, it was Hendrick, then me, now Magnus."

"Does it matter, Jules? You still love him as your own son. Get a DNA test if you want to be sure. Get a saliva swab from Magnus when he comes over tonight and one from Fabian. You can buy the swab packs at a pharmacy store. We can buy a few on our way home, and did you check your suit pockets last night? I saw Magnus slip a note. I checked and read it when hanging up your suit. It said that a large sum of money was transferred into Fabian's bank account. You and I have access to the account as well, so you can forget about your money worries."

"Melissa, if that's true, you also won't have to worry about that credit card debt or anything else." She gives me a peck on the cheek. I'm in a daze, maybe self-denial. Memories flash back. Magnus and Marg sipping champagne together whilst I'm juggling notes and folders at a conference. I'm angry at myself for never making much of an effort with Marg. I was always at work and unresponsive when I got home. Yeh, you can be a dork all your life, but reality does eventually bite. I hope I don't repeat that mistake with Melissa.

We get home at 6 pm. Mogan must be having a late lecture because he's not home. I log into my online bank account. The balance is $4,500. My account is linked to Fabians, and I know his password. How could such a large personal transfer bypass government authorities which limit daily transfers? There's a credit of $10 million in his savings account. The online description reads 'FromYourStepFather'. I guess if you know the right people high up, you can do anything.

Magnus arrives precisely at 7 pm. He instructs his driver to park the vehicle in a neighbouring side street and that he'd call when ready to leave. The driver obliges. Magnus comes in with more gifts. Not just for the kids who get iPhones; Melissa gets French perfume and I get a certificate. "You can pick up your new electric Volvo car tomorrow," he announces. He then goes over to Fabian and gives him a hug.

"Magnus, I want you and Fabian to take this mouth swab for a DNA test."

Magnus looks down. "Does it matter, Jules? He has two fathers, and you are doing a very good job. If anything should happen to either of us, there is another father to look after him. It is an insurance policy. In the long term, does it matter, Jules? He will always be well-looked, which should be our most important goal."

My logical mind kicks in. Melissa said the same thing as Magnus. It makes sense. Two or three are better than one, well, at least in this situation. Magnus and Fabian get swabbed, and I put the tubes in the fridge. I pull Magnus aside. "Let's talk in the courtyard."

"What are you going to do, Jules? Are you going to hit me? You can if you want. It was a one-off indiscretion, and I deeply apologize."

"No, I'm not. I was a lousy partner to my wife. Magnus, I've checked every database for anyone who may have received the peptide. You took it after that hockey injury. There were no birth abnormalities directly attributed to the peptide. Those that were could be attributed to pure chance. It happens to many couples who conceive, but things don't go quite right. The only common factor is that you fathered two children who had severe birth abnormalities and died soon after birth. That may be statistically significant or just pure bad luck. Wear a f..king condom next time."

"That's not possible. Michele's kids are physically normal, and Michele and I are identical twins. He also took the peptide after he got injured in a car crash. That is rubbish what you say."

"Did you read my paper on 'Epigenetics and Twin Studies'? I wrote that before you transferred me to Risk Analysis. You and Victor may be identical twins, but you're not the same. Same genes, but depending on life's circumstances, some genes get switched on or suppressed more than others, and your lives were very different and had very different challenges. Your DNA may be the same, even similar mutations, but you're not the same."

Another knock on the door; I get edgy. Magnus checks his cell phone. "It's just the food delivery."

Two guys bring in steaming hot delights on silver platters. I grab Magnus by the shoulder and lead him to the bedroom. "Is this some kind of bribe?"

"No, Jules. I'm just trying to make up for the previous error. I know money and gifts cannot fix things, but that is all I can do at the moment. I am deeply sorry for my indiscretion, and if I can make up for it in any way, I will."

I look into Magnus's watery eyes. He gives them a wipe with his sleeve. "I forgive you. Now you have to explain to Fabian. Use our bedroom. I'll call him."

What's going on, Mum?" Lizzy enquires.

"It's complicated, and neither Jules nor I understand it all. Be patient and enjoy the food."

The doorbell rings again. At first, I think it's Mogan. Maybe he can't find his keys. I open the door. He has a furious, wild look in his eyes and is highly agitated. He's the replica of Magnus. He looks like Magnus, down to the shaven head. A small tattoo on forearm; he's Victor but not the Victor I knew before.

"Where is he? Where's Magnus?" He yells.

Lizzy and Peter rush towards him, but he pushes them aside as if on a mission. The kids rush up the stairwell, crouch and look down below. I grab him, but it's like grabbing a wild bull. He flings me into a wall. He opens our bedroom door, and Magnus stands up. Fabian covers his head with a pillow. The two twins stare each other in the eyes.

"Relax, Michele. We can work this out. Sit down and have something to eat and drink."

Melissa comes rushing over. Victor pushes her into a wall as well. His wild eyes are totally focused on Magnus, and Victor rushes towards him. Magnus tries to restrain him. I phone Annabelle. "It's an emergency. Get some armed officers here as soon as possible." Victor hears the call and loses concentration. He's staring at me now, ready to lunge, but before he has a chance, Magnus grabs Victor by the neck, applying pressure to both carotid arteries and blocking blood flow to Victor's brain. He gives sharp knee kicks to Victor's hamstring muscle. Victor is wriggling and struggling, waving his arms but slowly subsides and falls to the floor.

"Your wife had a Pethidine habit. Find her kit, else have you any Diazepam? Victor's behaviour is that of someone who has been abusing methamphetamine. We have to calm him down before he awakes. We haven't got much time," Victor exclaims.

I have a stash of Diazepam. It's only for emergencies like severe anxiety attacks. "How much should we give him?"

"25mg to start with. What have you got, 5mg tablets? Break the tablets up into quarters. That will increase the speed of absorption, and have you got a rope? He has to be tied up till we work out what to do."

Magnus lifts Victor's head and torso. There are some coughs and splutters, but Magnus manages to get the shattered tablets down Victor's throat, followed by some water to wash them down. I go down to the garage and bring up some nylon rope. We secure Victor's arms and legs. He awakes and is furiously gyrating like a caged animal and yelling.

Magnus stuffs some of my socks into Victor's mouth. That made Victor more furious, possibly because those socks were in the washing basket for at least a month. He also gives Magnus a nasty bite on the hand.

"He'll probably be calm in 20 minutes."

"Jules, have you got some duct tape? That grey sticky tape and a bandage for my hand?"

I come back from the garage, and Magnus tapes Victor's mouth. I find bandages in the bathroom and bandage Magnus's hand after applying liberal splashes of disinfectant.

"Jules, did you call the police?"

"I did, 20 minutes ago, a severity 2."

"We have a problem. Can you cancel the callout?"

"Not likely. It would be registered and needs a response."

"Jules, we don't want the police involved. This is what we'll do," he whispers in my ear.

I run upstairs. Melissa is huddling the kids. "Stay here, don't come down. It will be all right." The police arrive, but only two officers. Magnus and I greet them, have our hands around our shoulders, and we smile.

"I'm sorry, officers, my cousin and I had a bet on the horse racing, and things got a bit out of hand when I mistakenly thought he had inside information. Everything is all right and thank you for your trouble. Would you like something to eat? There is plenty of food and drink inside."

"You wasted police time. We have to take some details; full names, addresses and contact numbers."

Magnus was about to pull out a wad of cash, but I retrain his hand and whisper in his ear, "We don't do that in OZ."

One of the officers looks up when there's a loud rumbling sound from the upstairs bedroom.

"It is my German Shepard dog. He is locked up in my bedroom. He has severe ticks. He is probably rolling around. He is on the tick medication, but I may have to go upstairs and give him another dose."

"You're crazy keeping him in your bedroom, those ticks spread. My dog once had ticks, and I got severely bitten by ticks. I had to fumigate the whole house afterwards."

I start scratching my body. Magnus starts scratching as well. The officers soon depart in disgust, swiping their uniforms of any possible infestation. Annabelle and Sam arrive soon after the police officers have departed. Annabelle is dressed in civilian clothing. The kids come downstairs and give hugs to Annabelle and Sam.

"Victor, I heard about you, and you're back!" Sam hugs him.

"I'm not Victor, I am Magnus, his twin brother, and we have a situation here. I am not sure how to deal with it. We have to combine our brain powers."

"Kids, go back upstairs," Melissa authoritatively says. The kids scuffle upstairs.

Magnus opens the bedroom door. Annabelle, Melissa, and Sam look at the tied-up writhing person on the floor. Annabelle looks at Magnus and then at Victor. "Who is he?" She exclaims.

"He's my twin brother and he is heavy."

"That's illegal what you're doing!" She's about to pull out her mobile phone, but Sam gently restrains her.

"SnowPea, we have to work together. We don't want anyone implicated. Calm down. We have to mitigate damage."

"What's your solution, Magnus?" Sam asks.

"You missed the previous conversations, but Victor seems badly affected by a drug commonly known as 'ice'. I have a clinic in Sweden that treats such cases. I can arrange to get him out without your airport security and Customs authorities being involved."

"Why didn't you let the police officers do their job?" Annabelle less than politely enquires.

"They would have taken him to hospital and rehabilitation afterwards, plus many questions would be asked, some may be about you and others about government dealings which could be highly politically embarrassing to our governments. We should not risk that. It could open up what you call a 'can of worms'. Everyone would be a loser. Annabelle, not everything is black or white. Most of the time, we have to compromise. Minimizing damage should be our goal."

Annabelle looks stunned. Magnus gives such a convincing presentation. He continues talking, focusing on Annabelle. He must have discerned that Annabelle does things by the 'book' and would be hard to get onside. "Dear Annabelle, you have been brought into a complex web. It is not simple. I have to make some phone calls now. Please excuse me. Have some food and drink." Annabelle is in deep thought and seems slightly stunned; so much stuff to mentally process. Victor has stopped writhing and seems asleep, but not for long. He wakes. I check that the kids are still upstairs. The music is on.

Magnus goes over to Victor and strokes his head. "We are brothers, and you seem to have been far more successful at producing progeny than I have. You have done well, brother."

Magnus then whispers in Victor's ear. "You have to disappear for a while. You will be taken to my drug rehabilitation clinic in Sweden. We can work things out if you are willing to try."

Victor is wriggling, his head swaying and his eyeballs rotating. Magnus removes the duct tape from his mouth. "Untie me!"

"Only if you take another 20 mg of Diazepam. It will stop the convulsions due to withdrawal. Do you want to live, brother?"

"Jules, have you got anymore more Diazepam?" Magnus calmly asks.

I get another four 5mg tablets. Victor surprisingly does not object. He crunches them with his jaws and downs them with a glass of water. Maybe the 'old Victor' is coming back.

"Where's Melissa and Peter and Lizzy," Victor calls out. "I'm sorry, Melissa, Peter and Lizzy. I have been a terrible father and husband. Please forgive me."

Lizzy and Peter come running downstairs and look at the tied Victor. They must have heard the apology. Their eyes glance at each other before sitting down next to Victor, who has a flood of tears pouring down his face. They hug him, and he goes into a sort of teary convulsion, not a medical one. Melissa watches but keeps her distance.

"I love you all, don't forget it," Victor says.

Magnus approaches Annabelle and Sam. "Please, let this be another little secret between us. I promise the puzzle will be solved, and you will be the first to know."

Victor then looks up at me, pulls me closer and whispers, "I know you are screwing my wife." I feel like telling him that at least I do, but that wouldn't be very productive. Magnus doesn't remove the nylon ropes that bind Victor. From what I remember, Magnus is a very cautious guy.

"Magnus, how did he know you'd be here?"

"Jules, the conference was widely advertised in medical journals and on some social media. The presenters' names were listed, and I do not keep my whereabouts secret. For all I know, he may have been at the conference, maybe in disguise. I only chatted with a dozen of the 800 attendees. Jules, there could be just a lot of coincidences rather than any conspiracies. Maybe there is no clandestine Web. We often just make things up to give an explanation for what may make little sense at the time."

I ponder for a few seconds. "One more question, Magnus. Why did Victor lunge at you in such rage?"

"I refused to give him money when he phoned me a month ago. He was agitated and babbling. I would just be supporting his habit if I obliged. I did offer treatment at my clinic, but he refused and became very angry. His phone call could not be traced; else I would have sent people to collect him and force him into the clinic. As it happened, he found me."

I'm a bit sceptical about that explanation but tell Magnus that I'll stay in touch by phone and email. Magnus then calls his driver, who brings the limousine up to my outside door. Melissa, Sam and I help Magnus carry Victor to the car, and they plump him in the backseat, where Magnus joins him. Victor's head is leaning against Magnus's shoulder. Magnus rolls down the side window. "Jules, can I video chat to Fabian? Just once a week if that is all right with you."

Melissa interrupts before I have a chance to answer, "That's fine by us."

Magnus gives a smile, and the limousine drives off. We're all looking at each other in disbelief. I check the kitchen cupboards for anything to drink; not enough to go around, then I remember there's some smartphone app that you can order grog to be delivered. Melissa escorts the kids to their bedrooms.

"Sam, can you make an order for some liquid refreshments on your phone? The name of the app is ….. I'll pay. Here's my credit card."

Mogan arrives back home, happy as could be. Annabelle yells out, "No, I'll pay. I don't want to remember anything about tonight." Mogan also wanted to pay. For a while, we argue who will pay even though Mogan doesn't drink. The friendly argument distracted our minds from the incident that just happened. Mogan goes into his bedroom, and I go upstairs and check on the kids. Melissa is comforting them. They are all in tears. I wrap my arm around Melissa. For the first time, Lizzy doesn't flinch at the sign of affection from her mother and me. I also do the same hugging thing with Fabian and Peter. Melissa turns on the kid's mini stereo system and puts on one of those supposedly soothing, meditative CDs. The kids never used that CD so were probably surprised. Melissa and I then descend to the lounge, then the doorbell rings. I instinctively grab the chilli concoction. There's a small guy holding his bicycle, probably a university student, with a huge backpack. He takes out six bottles of Vodka.

"Thanks, I don't have any cash for a tip, though you deserve one, balancing whilst cycling with that load."

Annabelle interrupts, "Here's a ten tip."

It was just another one of those nights. Sam and Annabelle stayed over. Neither Melissa nor I slept in our bed. Four adults, cuddled close together, snoring away on the lounge room carpet yet again. Luckily, we woke, a little worse for wear, after the kids got up in the morning and got themselves packed for school, all on their own; well, I think Mogan might have helped.

Lizzy comments, "Is life always this dramatic? Why can't you just be normal parents?"

Melissa looks up. "No darling, it's just an unusual circumstance. Everything will be solved soon, and your father will be treated and be the kind, loving father that he once was."

"Mum, your breath stinks."

"Get going, quickly, or else I will take you to school."

Mogan comes out from his bedroom, looks at us with possibly a disdainful look. "Ok, kids, it's off to school. I'll walk with you."

"Dad, I'll take a sicky day off from work today. Can we just walk home?" Annabelle asks.

I interject. "Stay here till you feel better. There's food in the fridge and some good videos to watch. Melissa and I have to try to go to work. I have no sick leave left. Here are the car keys to the VW for when you're ready to drive."

I should have remembered that Annabelle's appetite for food is like that of someone who has four gigantic tapeworms in their gut to keep satisfied. The pantry and fridge were emptied, Sam told me on the phone but then said they had ordered online a heap of food to be delivered before he and Annabelle left to go home. There were boxes of food waiting by the door when Melissa and I arrived back from work. The pantry and fridge were replenished.

Chapter twenty

It's 7 am in the morning, and the doorbell rings. I rush over, still clothed in a towel, and open the door. Two rather burly police officers are at the door.

"Are you Jules Lemos?"

"I am. What's this about?"

Melissa comes over to the door. "Under what authority are you here?"

"Ma'am, Jules Lemos is a suspect in the murder of his wife, Margaret Milstein and a Victor Mosa. He has to come down to the headquarters. A warrant has been issued. Here it is if you want to inspect it."

I call out, "Can I make two phone calls to my lawyer?"

"Sir, you have 5 minutes for any phone calls, then another 5 minutes to get dressed and look presentable."

I don't have a lawyer. I call Annabelle's cell phone and whisper, "I'm being arrested!" It's her messaging service that answers. I then call Charmaine, who does answer.

"What's going on? I'm being arrested?"

"Jules, you should know that sometimes things have to be done that don't quite make immediate sense. Think of it as a distraction. As far as I know, there may be a third party involved, a remaining LaMosa rogue or hired assassin. That rogue makes the others look like worms. He is extremely dangerous. You'll be safer in custody, and I've arranged 24/7 protection around your residence and the surrounding streets."

"Charmaine, this is not a secure line."

"Jules, you're using one of those illegal, untraceable phones that Jason left you. Now listen. One of those cops is working for us, and he will plunge a small syringe in your arm. It won't hurt. You have to cooperate, plus there's a $200k bonus for you if we flush out what we believe is a rogue operative working inside i5 and supplying information to the so-called 'outside'. Just hang in there, it will be tough for a few days, and as I said, it may not make any sense at the moment. The less you know, the better for now. Prove you can do it, and I'm not taking another shot for you."

"Charmaine, is Doris in control of this operation?"

"Jules, I said the less you know, the better. Trust me. I won't let anything serious happen to you. You won't get shot, though it may be a bit distressful for a few days." I slam down the phone, feeling very unsatisfied with the conversation. I then make a third call to Ms Valda's cell phone. "Can't make it to work today. I can't explain at the moment."

Ms Valda replies, "Don't worry. We'll wait till you come back." She doesn't seem perturbed or ask why.

The arresting officers don't seem concerned that I've exceeded the allowed phone calls. The officers state, "You have another 5 minutes to get dressed and pack any belongings you want to take with you. They will be tested and scanned."

Mogan rushes out of his bedroom, and the kids rush downstairs to the lounge.

"What are you doing?" Lizzy yells at the officers.

"Just routine stuff; I'm sure Mr Lemos will be back soon."

Melissa, Mogan and the kids are not reassured and look more distressed than I do. They watch in a sort of horror as I get accompanied by one of the officers to our bedroom. I get dressed and put some clothing into the backpack, as well as a toothbrush and paste.

"Officer, do you mind if I go to the bathroom, preferably unaccompanied? Have a look at the bathroom. I could never fit through that small window, so it's unlikely I will escape."

The officer consents and I go in and shut the door. I find one of Melissa's lipsticks which had been surrendered by Peter. I write on the mirror, in red, 'Don't worry, it's part of a plan'. I flush the toilet and leave the bathroom, re-adjusting my pants, and go back to the lounge. Deep inside, I am worrying; too much could go wrong and what if my mind switches off again and I go into that zombie state? I'm worrying about worrying, and I forgot to pack my anxiety medication. The clock radio fires up and a song comes on; 'Nelly Furtado' –' All Good Things (Come To An End)'. I hope it isn't some kind of prophesy.

We come out into the lounge, then another song comes on; 'The Four Tops - Walk Away Renee'.

"Officer, can I tell my partner that I love her?"

"I like that song," says one of the cops. "My wife and I listen to it all the time. OK, you're stretching the timeline but go ahead."

I hug Melissa and whisper in her ear. "Look at the message on the mirror." On reflection, I could have just told her the message but didn't know any personal contact was allowed when you're being arrested. Melissa grabs the kids and reassures them. Fabian calls out, "Dad, come back soon!" One of the officers says, "Don't worry kid, he'll be back soon 'be kind'.

A pinprick inconspicuously punctures my right arm. No one noticed, and it didn't hurt. I become very relaxed, and my mind is drifting. Another song is appropriately playing on the radio alarm clock, 'Pink – Floyd, Comfortably Numb'. I look back at my astounded housemates as escorted to the police vehicle. I give a subtle wink to Melissa. Hope she will re-assure the kids. She winks back, and I'm fading but give Fabian a hug and look at the distressed Peter and Lizzy as I'm gently dragged away. The world is going sort of blank, and I'm starting to feel very, very disorientated.

I'm strip-searched at the police depot, but no gloves are inserted into any cavities. Rule 303 flashes into my head. 'Never insert any object containing information into any internal cavities; memorise what you have to, else its extraction can be painful'. There's nothing to memorise anyway, so I don't have to, but thoughts and memories of Melissa and the kids flash through my mind. Those memories are reassuring. I'm escorted, more likely dragged as my legs are very wobbly, to a solitary cell.

Chapter twenty one

I've receded into that dysfunctional state of memory loss. I think it's called 'denial', the blocking out things you feel very, very uncomfortable with. Maybe I was given some pharmacological substance because I'm also very disorientated; can't even remember how I got here. I rub my left upper arm because it's itching. I'm seated in the prison interview room but not handcuffed. A burly prison guard is standing by the door, keeping a close eye, well more like closed eyes. He appears to be napping.

A song plays in my head 'It's Just a dirty job but someone has to do it'. This would turn out to be a very dirty job. Then there's a knock on the door. My prison counsellor enters and turns on the recording device. "You didn't talk in our first session. You've been here 3 days and according to our officers you haven't muttered a single word, even during cell inspections. You've been almost catatonic. The medication you were given was very mild; it shouldn't have induced your condition. Try writing it down if you don't feel like talking. I'll make sure you have more colour pencils and paper. Writing is a good release for emotions that we may not be able to make a conscious sense of. It may help you reconcile all those circumstances that you consider tragic. To quote a phrase by one of your ex-prime ministers, Malcolm F, 'Life wasn't meant to be easy'."

"But it was easy for him! A privileged person commenting on the plight of others!" She knew what buttons to press to get the adrenaline flowing and she got a strong reaction.

"Calm down Jules, it's not political comment time, just tell me the story, it releases the trauma to talk about it. If it's good, in a legal sense, it may exonerate you from prosecution or at least reduce a potentially very long prison sentence."

"You got the time?"

"Jules, I got plenty of time; I get paid by the hour for my consultancy work for the penal system or Correctional Services as it is now called. Are you feeling well and how are you adjusting to your new environment?"

For a speck in time, I notice her hair. It's long and black but it has been dyed because I can see the blond hair roots, blond au natural but I can't focus my eyes on the rest of her face yet can clearly see her profile in the mirrored window when I turn sideways. She is attractive, perhaps my height, anaemic looking and conservatively dressed all in black, probably around 35 years old. She looks very, very familiar.

"Being in solitary is kind of good. At least I don't have to tell the other inmates that I have an anal infection."

"Jules, can you stop looking at the mirror, look at me. Now, are you sick? Do you need antibiotics?"

"I was just kidding. I mean you know the stuff that happens when males are confined in a closed space and try to assert their authority."

"Jules, you're only in solitary because there is no room for you in regular confinement. Once you're moved to regular you may have to protect your orifices," she calmly announces.

That comment was not very reassuring. "Where am I? I can hear the laugh of Kookaburras in the mornings. It can't be Melbourne."

"Your home is now this correctional facility in a regional Victorian town; well at least till your trial."

For a moment there is a rumbling in my mind and stomach. I vaguely remember being injected, it must be 100's of times more powerful than alcohol and cause temporary amnesia but I can't remember the name of the substance. I briefly glance at her. Have met her before, I know I know her. Why is she as emotionless as a brick wall? She's talking legal talk again and it doesn't all register in my mind.

"Let's forget about minor details at the moment. Now I should say that you have had plenty of visitors who wanted to see you. You are a popular guy indeed. They must have each driven for several hours. Unfortunately, the system's solitary confinement rules do not permit visits at this stage of your incarceration. You know about the sneaking in of illegal substances rule though I don't believe you're into that or even know what it means. Your blood tests, since your incarceration, have shown no sign of any detectable pharmacological substance. I will do my best to get a waiver to allow future visits."

I felt like pointing to the welt on my left arm and questioning her on what she meant by 'detectable'. Luckily, I didn't.

"Who were the visitors?" I anxiously enquire.

She checks her computer tablet. "A Melissa and her kids, Fabian, Sam, Mogan and an athletic lady called SnowPea."

What about my wife? Marg. Did she try to visit?"

"You seem to have selective memory loss or you're playing me. Marg is deceased and I'm sure you know that. In fact, you are a prime suspect for her death and that of several others. You will probably appear on one of those 'Most Wanted and Captured' TV reality series so you have to trim those unsightly, bushy eyebrows."

The counsellor is losing her patience and appears angry. I lower my head toward my chest. "Me killing my wife, I'm not a killer. Yes, she may have betrayed and abandoned me and our son but I'm not a killer. She was once the love of my life."

"Do you want a tissue to wipe your eyes? They're the non-allergy causing types."

This counsellor is clever, very clever, taking confrontative interrogation to a new limit. She plays both the 'good guy' and the 'bad guy' with ease as she elicited two emotional responses within a few minutes. My mind is working overtime trying to combat the effect of the drug I must have been injected with but then sanity prevails. It's for a reason; that's how things are done in i5. Play the game.

"Just relax Jules, we know you couldn't even squash a cockroach and besides Marg seemed to mean a lot to you. She was pronounced dead due to a lethal dose of Fentanyl in her system, but a reusable syringe and vial had your fingerprints all over them."

"How do you know they were my fingerprints? I've never committed a crime, so my prints are not registered on any police database."

"Jules, when you were brought into hospital after that botched suicide attempt many years ago, you were fingerprinted. Why the police didn't do a cross-check on those seemingly unrelated events, well, I don't know, but it took them a long time to get a warrant. You know, all that medical confidentiality stuff."

She got me again. I'm breathing fast and every muscle in my chest is violently contracting. Then the little voice within intervenes, breathe slowly. Focus on your breathing.

"We reunited briefly back in Melbourne, but she disappeared soon after I got shot."

"Jules, some of us know that it would be very hard to inject someone when your femoral artery has been ripped by a bullet and you got a chest wound as well, but you'll have to convince the jury of that."

"How do you know about the shooting? Only a few people do?"

"I'll explain later, now continue."

She and Victor must be connected and exchanging information. "I knew she had occasionally injected Pethidine in the past. She was involved in a car crash in New

York and injured her back. Actually, she was run off the road by another car, but she only injected when in excruciating pain. Her back pain became almost manageable without the Pethidine."

The counsellor leans across the table and stares me in the eyes. "Jules, firstly, all the deaths seem connected, now back to Marg. Fentanyl is very much more potent than Pethidine and the best way to dispose of someone who has a habit of using other opioids. Just substitute their Pethidine or Oxycodone with Fentanyl. Maybe she had a relapse of pain and asked you to inject her and she didn't know that what she purchased on the black market wasn't Pethidine. There are many possible scenarios. Maybe someone else was involved as it's unlikely that you could have thrust the needle in your condition at the time."

Then I remembered Victor stitching me up at Jason's apartment after the shooting and his 'expansion tubes' invention which made artery reconnection surgery easy.

"When Marg occasionally used Pethidine, it was her private ritual. I never even opened her little kit. I have no idea how my fingerprints got on those items. I have a morbid fear of needles, I feel wheezy when I even see a syringe. I could never inject anyone."

I sort of lied. I never injected anyone, except myself when testing the peptide for toxicology and effectiveness. Luckily the counsellor didn't examine my arms though the scarring is hardly visible now.

"Jules, you were also the last person to see Jason Wilson, the psychologist, before his car exploded with him in it. Rebecca Mills, Marg's estranged sister, suicided soon after your so-called reunion with Marg and also the last person to see Victor Mosa, also known as Michele Mosa, according to the Police authorities. Then Hendrick Milstein, Marg's brother, died from cardiac arrest soon after you visited him to retrieve your estranged son whom he was caring for. Your bodyguard guard, Henry Sommerset, also appeared to have died of cardiac arrest soon after he started working for you, but we exhumed the body – he had a bullet wound. Death seems to follow you and you are the common denominator. It's only circumstantial evidence at this point but you are in remand in custody as the prime suspect for all those deaths."

Another security guard peeks into the window of the interview room and makes an 'O' with his thumb and forefinger. The counsellor notices it too. It's some sort of signal.

"We'll resume our conversation tomorrow."

She turns off the tape recorder.

"The CCTV has been disabled and I've turned off the interview recorder so we can talk freely now."

She gives a wink to the guards.

"Jules, we had to do a bit of a staged performance whilst being monitored, you know, for the media coverage and the media, indirectly, make a generous contribution to our funding especially when there's a potential scoop involved. Don't take it too personally. You may not remember what we previously discussed so I will reiterate. You were heavily drugged when you came into detention. We intercepted the blood sample and substituted it for a clean one without disturbing the chain of custody. The drug should be wearing off. Have this cup of coffee. It will help."

She sips the coffee and swallows so it's likely to be safe. I skol the rest of the coffee as you do in a beer-drinking competition. The rest of the conversation jumped from issue to issue and is confusing to follow.

"Jules, that coffee also contains an antidote to the brain-dead drug you were injected with when the police officers came to collect you four days ago."

"Jules, we know you fried your brain when you met Marg for the first time, and you probably can't remember the first time."

"No, I can't remember the first time, nor do I know what 'fried brains' are."

"Eventually, maybe you will, it's only 11 years back. Your job was to monitor her; not to get involved with her and lose perspective on what was your mission. In those days that you can't remember you worked for a pharmaceutical company, but you also worked for us as we had close ties with the owner of that company."

"Who's us?"

She doesn't answer.

"But, congratulations, you did put on a good act at the recorded interview. It went to plan, and you'll soon be back to your usual state of dysfunction but there're a few more steps to go."

What's she talking about?

"Jules, one of the reasons some people were after you, Marg and Jason, is because that little USB flash drive you carried with you contained other documents, not just your peptide formula and manufacturing process which we have no interest in. Those other documents could incriminate many people and some of those documents may not be complementary to our government or other governments with whom we have an amicable, financial relationship. They were classified documents but somehow Marg got access to them. They are supposedly encrypted emails like those requests to implant false memories when she did some sessional work for our government and those we're friendly with. She also took on dubious assignments like coaching applicants to successfully pass polygraph tests or lie detector tests as they are called here. She was very popular in the USA where you had to have a polygraph for certain government jobs. Jules, you had recommended that she be hired for many of those assignments, and you circumnavigated all security protocols to get your little lovebird in the backdoor and Jules, we really don't want those documents appearing on the WikiLeaks website."

She continues her monologue. "Marg often had full access to the computer servers of some organizations she worked for including some work she did for LaMosa, and she copied any incriminating documents onto that flash drive, for let's call it self-protection and maybe a bit of financial leverage. In those days cyber-security was slack or non-existent. Many of the documents were in plain text and others had a very low level of encryption which can now be easily broken. The peptide production procedure was just a distraction. We don't care about the peptide, but we do care about those documents and emails being leaked. Now about the LaMosa crims who got killed at that shootout in St. Kilda; we knew they were after you and Marg and we don't care about them either; they entered this country illegally and they never existed as far as we're concerned but we did forensically recover the CCTV footage of the massacre near St Kilda Luna Park. That footage wasn't forwarded to the Police, but we know what happened. We also got Michele, or Victor as he is known, to help you out in that incident. He screwed up badly. He was supposed to get there early and offer a package to the LaMosa guys, 10kg of highly sort after pharmacological substances that we estimated they wouldn't refuse and would just go back home smiling and sniffing. We had the sniffer dogs that would catch them at the airport, but Victor screwed up badly. He was to negotiate and get there before you, Sam and Henry did. He got his timing wrong probably because he sampled the payload he was supposed to deliver."

She continues, more and more. "Victor and Magnus, his twin brother, are now in Sweden. A special flight had to be organised for Victor, as he had no passport or identification on him. He was highly disturbed, probably due to substance abuse, and had to be restrained. At the moment, he is a missing person according to the authorities in Australia. Once he's better we'll plan a story about how he left the country on a fishing trawler and hiked his way to Sweden. Magnus had organized a Swedish passport for him. The photo part was easy as they look alike."

I have had enough of this one-way discourse. "How do you know all this? And why did you help Victor and Magnus?"

"Jules, we know more about 'people of special interest' than Facebook or Google does. We're good at our jobs. To answer your second question, we have a special relationship with Magnus. We scratch each other's back so to speak. That's all I can say at the moment. Now, do you still have all those papers that Jason Wilson entrusted you with before his fatal accident?"

I never read all of them. I think I put them in the recycle bin." I lied again.

"Good." She replied.

"Jules, Marg was a very clever chicky, as I said before and a master at the art of manipulation and deception, almost as good as our mum. She had contingency plans for almost anything that could go wrong, and she had planned things almost perfectly. She also made many enemies."

What did she mean by 'our mum'? Maybe a slip of tongue. I'll ask her later.

"I knew Marg travelled a lot, presenting at conferences when we first got together. She never told me the exact details."

"And did you ask?"

"No, I just tried to keep the peace."

"You should have grilled her, metaphorically speaking that is."

"I can't remember any of that and what are you implying?" I gasp.

"Jules, your little peptide seemed to make people highly susceptible to cognitive manipulation by verbal suggestion as well as helping injured muscle tissue healing. I'm talking about false memory implants and memory loss and we're not into your intended use of accelerated healing of damaged soft tissue. We're not interested in that. No one is except the sporting world. Jules, you had an MRI scan and there are no significant abnormalities in your brain, so the memories are still there if you want to retrieve them. Marg must have done her selective memory whitewash on you again since you first met again. We still had a role for you, but you have to get it together and remember."

I bow my head. "Counsellor, one of the first people I met since I can remember was a clinical psychologist or maybe a psychiatrist, Charmaine was her name. She interviewed me for the cataloguing job at the historical archives section of the St. Kilda library. You remind me of her."

Her voice rises as if she's highly annoyed. "You constantly seek solutions, don't you Jules? Sometimes there are no solutions that fit your criteria and don't harm someone. You've tried and you got burnt, accept it. Part of life is accepting that some things are out of our control. Get distracted. Listen to music. Listen to podcasts. Keep that mind occupied. The problem is we dwell too much, seeking an explanation but many times there is no logical explanation that fits all sizes."

She seems more distressed than I am. Now she's searching for something on her laptop computer then emits a shrill, "Whoopee! I found it."

My eyes open up as if awakened from a deep sleep. Yes, there is a condition called

MIB, not 'Men in Black' but 'Mentally Induced Blindness'. I could never forget that 'whoopee'. Full vision returns. I can look at her face-to-face and not just at the mirror reflection. It's Charlie or Charmaine. Why's she playing this masquerade? I remember there was a plan, but it far exceeded what I expected. My heart rate rises rapidly and I squint. She shouldn't be here. I reach over and try to hug her but she pulls away.

"I'm not stupid. Who do you really work for Charmaine?"

She relaxes. "I can give you a clue since soon you'll be far, far away." She giggles a bit but then becomes very serious. "Jules, you know, my family rejected me when I was young. I ended up a street kid for several years, but I wanted to get out of that scene. Life wasn't easy but I had ambition. A very tall gentleman wondered in where we kids hung out. He offered a job. I put my hand up first. The rest is history, Jules. I got accommodation, food, an allowance and my education paid for and eventually all I had to do was to provide Intelligence about some students involved in radical student groups when I made it to university."

"You were or still are a spy?"

"Jules, that is such an old term. I was an observer. That's Observer with a capital 'O' that sign the security guard gave which you noticed. I saw your eyes flicker."

"No, you weren't. I overheard your phone conversation with Jason after you interviewed me at the library. It was more than just observing. You had something going on with Jason."

"Jules, I just did my job and repaid my debt. Sometimes you have to compromise yourself a little. It wasn't all bad. Jason was a great cook."

"Are you still a big "O" now? Are you?

"No, of course not, Jules. I made it to an 'X' in the organization, only a few more letters to go until I'm one of the top dogs. It's an alphabetic hierarchy. Let me tell that the level you made it to, you the 'S' really sucked."

"Charmaine, when did the observing of me start? How long ago was it?"

"Jules, I'm not at liberty to say exact dates but it was when you started behaving somewhat erratically soon after you met Marg when on your third assignment. You broke rule 001, 'Never get emotionally attached when on the job'."

"Did I work for the same organization that you do?"

"You sure did, kiddo as well as your job with Magnus's company who worked for us."

I'm stunned. "You're bating me, and you know we may be genetically related."

"Yeh Jules, I know, and I'm trying to save your ass. Jules, one day I'll take you back to the recruiting headquarters in St Kilda Street. We have a hall of fame and a hall of disfame, well actually they're just small rooms. I'll let you guess in which room your photo hangs though you may not recognise yourself as the disfame room is also our dart games room. We play darts after work whilst sipping an ale. I'll have to put up a new photo of you as you don't quite look the same. Looks like you had a 'nose' job."

This conversation is getting more and more ridiculous, jumping all around the place.

"Does Smithy, your partner, know what you really do?"

"Why does he need to? We're just rescuing a friend. Keep it simple. You were supposedly taught that the fewer people know the less chance of a leak. By the way, have you kept up with genetic research, specifically CRISPR, the gene slicing technique, now cheaply available which will make your peptide totally redundant and enables the production of happy, strong, intelligent designer babies?"

"Char, the peptide did not alter genes. I just stumbled across some evolutionary genes that could be turned on or off by the peptide. Actually, my, our, father experimented with the first version; it caused birth defects in progeny. I just tried to refine it. The science is called Epigenetics. In evolution, the fittest survive and those that forget unpleasant circumstances are far more likely to reproduce and not indulge in high-risk behaviour. The peptide just affected recall of past memories and their associated emotional responses as well as enhance soft-tissue healing. CRISPR can alter genes, replaces faulty ones with presumed good ones. Yes, I know about CRISPR technology. It's totally different from what the peptide does; memory formation was one of the effects of the peptide as well as enhancing soft-tissue healing. The peptide does not alter genes; it just makes certain ones more or less active, unfortunately, there were some side-effects."

She's distracting me; she got me fired-up again and raving as I did with Victor. "Seems like your knowledge of genetics has returned. By the way, you got to be an 'F' at the academy, in those years you conveniently don't remember, just before you met Marg. We sometimes had lunch together and cuddled together at your place while you insisted we watch those antiquated '3 Stooges' videos; probably the only times you laughed. You can't remember, can you, and your initial shock when you saw me naked as an adult when I was in the shower? You didn't even recognise me at the interview for the library archives job. It doesn't matter as you weren't agent material. Yes, you did a little useful work for the organization but I won't tell you what the big 'F' stands for." She then quickly plunges a syringe into my arm then has another go. I'm too stunned to react. My mind is trying to process what she is doing here and what she just said.

"What is it in that syringe?"

"It's a drug called Profonol," she replies.

"Isn't that the anaesthetic that killed that guy who sang and perfected the Moon Walk, Michael, Michael something?"

"It sure it is but I missed your vein and it's probably a non-lethal dose. It will take longer to take effect, so you won't be moonwalking for a while. Now, Jules, this wasn't just a training exercise for my staff. There is still a very dangerous hired LaMosa operative after you. He is very smart, methodical, obsessed to succeed and has caused our counterparts in other friendly countries many problems not just associated with your flash drive and LaMosa. He's assassinated over 30 of our international operatives, and he can never be called off once given an assignment. He's over 205 cm in height, has had military training and is very smart. He makes Arnold Schwarzdinger look like a mouse. Only a bullet to the head will stop him. His name is Greuger Smitht, but he goes under many aliases. I've slipped a note in your pocket describing what's known about him and the last photograph of him from our counterparts in the USA. You still indirectly work for us so I hope you'll co-operate. If you succeed in getting this Greuger guy, you'll be exonerated and maybe even get a medal and a handsome reward.

"You have to be joking, me 173cm in height bring down the 205cm, military trained Greuger? If Ai5 is just trying to get rid of me then just shoot me now."

"Jules, we don't do that these days as I explained before but there is a plan to flush out Greuger. You will have support and hopefully, we will also flush out internal gossiper or spy."

I'm stumbling a bit but apart from that, I have a pleasant sensation. I look back at Charmaine, though the room is slightly spinning and it's hard to focus again.

"Was this really necessary? You just gave me an antidote to the previous drug I was injected with and now you just injected me again."

"Jules, I evaluated that you're highly agitated and you may blow this mission unless you're slightly sedated. It's only a very small dose. It will just relax you."

After carefully concealing the capped syringe and vial into her brassiere, she looks at me. "I'm doing my best to get you out of here and protect you and your new family. We have the same parents, but you got the better deal."

"What, you finally acknowledge that we're related?" I sort of knew that but had to hear it from Charlie, or Charmaine as she is now.

"We sure are related except I was the genetic reject. Daddy, the bastard, first started experimenting with the peptides before we were conceived. I ended up with screwed-up genitalia. Mum abandoned us and I became a street kid. I eventually was accepted back into the fold, with a bit of help and by the way, I only found out recently that we're related. Thank God we only ever cuddled whilst in the academy."

"You're Blue Monkey?"

"Whoopee, you finally put 2 and 2 together. Our dad's peptide obviously had different effects depending on gender. You're piss weak, thank dad for that and maybe our mother, she was never there for us, always at work and totally ignored my disfigurement."

Charmaine appears highly emotionally charged and angry again. She's blowing off a lot of steam and anger. My memory is all over the place. I keep repeating stuff.

"You're my sister after all?"

"At least 50% same DNA, except you got the good stuff."

Sis, what do you call the good stuff? I think you got the good stuff. My memory can be so easily manipulated. I have no idea what reality is anymore. What's this all about?"

"Well, Bro, it's a high-profile plan to maintain funding for Ai5. It's convoluted and things could have been done simpler as it's highly risky. It's mom's plan. We got to get that Greuger guy."

"Can you confirm that Doris is our mother?"

"The bitch sure is and eventually I'll bring her down. I got the balls to do it," Charmaine gives a wink.

"Charmaine, are you sure it's right? I mean she gave us jobs even though it was nepotism. Maybe she's trying to make up to us for her failures as a mother."

Charmaine grabs my shoulders and shakes me. "No, Jules. The tea lady is a megalomaniac; the most secretive, scheming, manipulative person I have ever met. There's always an ulterior motive somewhere there. Who knows, I may be part of her plan at the moment. Jules, for a while it's going to be confusing but play along. Just try to believe what I told you."

Char and I hug as we mentally process what has gone on.

"How's it going with Smithy? Is he going to be my brother-in-law?"

"All OK, more than OK, I had surgery to remove that over-enlarge clitoris and now pee from that opening in my vagina. I was in hospital for weeks that's why I hadn't contacted you."

I grab and hug Blue Monkey again. "I'm so, so sorry. I was never cut out for this type of work."

"Yeh, we know you're not, but try this time. There are still people who would love to see you terminated. You're being relocated to a nice country, and you can stay there as long as the contents of that flash drive are destroyed and never surface, else you'll be brought back and left to your own devices."

"Why not just kill me. I'm sure you could arrange a road crash or a suicide and how are you connected to SnowPea?"

"Jules, I told you before we don't do those killing things in OZ, well we do a little and I agree it would be a far more cost-effective option as we now are operating in cost-cutting mode. I'll propose your suggestion to my superiors, the 'Z's. And the SnowPea organization is harmless at the moment; we just monitor them, use them like we are doing today and allocate the blame for any dubious activity onto them. It's in our interest that they exist. Now if that flash drive still exists it has to be destroyed and any copies. You can copy your peptide manufacturing process but destroy the rest of the stored documents."

"The drive is encrypted. I couldn't even read it neither could the LaMosa guys who wanted it."

"Your son seems pretty good at breaking simple encryption and from what I heard it was just a simple transposition algorithm, replacing some letters with symbols. Something Julius Caesar did when encrypting battle strategies and though you're no Julius Caesar finding the pattern should not take you or your son too long."

Her final comment, "Act the part, the charade is just beginning." She then waives a kiss then calls out, "Make a fresh dose of the chilli spray. Greuger, according to intel is often rubbing his eyes. He has some allergy or genetic disorder, and his eyes are his soft spot. I can't supply you with firearms so be innovative. Go for his eyes."

Smithy, my ex-boarder and now Charmaine's partner enters dressed as a prison officer. I close my eyes.

"Guard, take me back to my cell." My legs waver a bit.

Smithy grabs me, puts my arm around his shoulder and guides me through rows and rows of corridors, through all the security checks. Doors opened automatically as we walk towards them. I could hear other inmates hackling us from inside their cells. I could see their faces peering out as they yell.

"I got you; just keep moving those legs as best as you can."

"Smithy you're committing a felony," I mutter.

"I committed many when in the armed services in Afghanistan, this is far fairer. I believe you're not guilty."

"What about Charmaine?"

"She's tied up, comfortably, the ties are loose. Every angle has been covered. She will appear as the distressed victim of an escaped felon. She's good at acting and can be very convincing. She won't be yelling 'whoopee' well at least until you have been successfully relocated."

"What about the security cameras?"

"Your son Fabian, the computer whiz, took care of them from Canada. We are silent, not on the radar. He also injected some video of everything being normal in this stink hole. This is not a high-security prison. He said it was easy. Beats me how you could father such an intelligent kid."

Explaining to Smithy that Fabian might have been genetically modified and is not my son would be useless.

"What about you, you'll be a fugitive?"

"I said the security cameras have been blanked out. There is no evidence linking me, Charmaine or the others helping your escape. You threatened her, tied her up, and she had no choice but let you escape. The other guards will confirm that."

"But what happened to the regular guards?"

"Stop asking questions. It was arranged. Maybe SnowPea pulled some strings. I wasn't involved in those details."

Useless to tell Smithy that it wasn't SnowPea and anyway I'm drifting in and out of what I perceive as consciousness.

"Smithy, do you know the reason for this charade?"

"Shut up, you know how much effort it took to get you out of here? Sure, your son Fabian helped a lot, but we did all the physical stuff. You should be grateful. Personally, I don't think you're worth it even if you are innocent. I'm just under instruction from my wife. She believes that you have been very cleverly framed for all those deaths."

"Smithy, did, did, did you marry Charmaine?"

"I sure did, and you never came to the wedding. We sent you three invites and not even an email or phone call reply."

"I'm sorry, I was extremely distraught at the time, I'm sorry, a lot on my mind at the time and stop dragging me; I can walk on my own."

I was wrong. I couldn't walk on my own. My speech becomes slurred, more slurred but at least I now know why Smithy is so pissed off at me. No use trying to tell him that at the time, I thought the wedding idea was some kind of a joke.

"Smithy, Smithy why is Charmaine really taking such a big risk, and you too, you're, you're, you're taking such a big risk."

"According to Charmaine, it's that USB flash drive that you still possess and that manufacturing process for that thing called a peptide which can alter people's memories and do other things that can be misused."

"Smithy, it was something I created in the labs at nights after my real job. My father started the research. See these scars around the veins in my arms. I tested all batches on myself but apparently, there is other stuff on that flash drive that I wasn't even aware of."

"You're a nutcase, Jules. You should be in a psych ward."

"Smithy, Smithy. It was initially meant as a sports supplement and the proceeds funded Marg's research. That's all. It seemed like a good idea at the time. Initially, there were some side effects. It made recipient brains highly malleable, which means open to suggestions, as well as the intended effect of decreasing recovery time after a soft-tissue injury in sport and car accidents. Marg got a hold of the peptide and used it for less than ethical purposes. I turned a blind eye. I had no idea it could be so misused."

"Do you seriously think I believe you? Jules, you are the most unlucky guy alive; good hard-luck story. I read the newspapers; it would have made the front page if it was true. I don't know the science or even what a peptide is except for that AFL footballer scandal. Charmaine thinks it should be destroyed and I may not be the smartest person on this planet, but she did explain the implications of inserting false memories as well, but she still thinks you're worth saving, even if you don't have that flash drive."

"Smithy, every side of science and technology has a dark side. It's about weighing up the consequences. The peptide just triggered the activity of certain genes. Smithy, wouldn't you want to forget some things? Those times in Afghanistan and the things you had to do. Wouldn't you want to forget?" He hesitates as if in deep thought before replying.

"Those memories make me who I am now. Sure, I learnt the hard way and I accept it now. I'm making up for what I did and sponsoring the education of several kids from financially deprived families."

"You're a nice person, Smithy." Smithy doesn't reply. Well, he does sort of whisper. The last words I remember from Smithy were 'Be Kind'; the motto of the SnowPea group.

Smithy doesn't seem to know about the other alleged documents on the drive. Charmaine hasn't told him. In a way, I feel relieved. Smithy is just one of the puppets and he got a free prison guard uniform which he can use to fancy dress parties.

"Stop Smithy, Smithy stoop, stoo, sto". I fall into a deep painless sleep.

Chapter twentytwo

I wake up in a plane, one of those small single-engine Cessna planes. It's claustrophobic.

"You got to jump. The parachute has been tested. It will be OK," the pilot yells.

I look out the window. All I see are clouds. I see no ground.

"I can't jump! I hate heights."

The pilot must have put the aircraft on autopilot mode because he has slid out of the pilot seat and is menacingly moving towards me. The options aren't great. I slide open the plane's side door, pull the goggles over my closed eyes and fall out. I'm frantically trying to grab the rip cord to open that parachute. Time seems to stand still. Memories come rushing back. I remember more but not all. The peptide doesn't work. Memory implants can't work. Severe stress seems to disable them, and you get your old life back, no matter how much you prefer to forget it. The ground becomes visible as I'm plunging at a couple of hundred kilometres per hour. I finally find the ripcord. The feeling of rapidly decelerating is not all that pleasant, and I vomit. Hope there's no one below on the ground.

I can see some people waving their hands as if pointing to a landing spot. I got to guide this parachute. I'm thinking back about what little I know about Physics. If I tug on the parachute cords, I should be able to manoeuvre it. I start tugging.

"Congratulations. You made it!" exclaimed a swarthy, semi-bold, smiling guy as I'm still trying to disentangle myself from the parachute. He's wiping what might be bits of my stomach contents from his face. He shakes my hand and gives me an unwanted hug.

"This is your passport. You are now a Canadian citizen. This is your card to access your Canadian bank account with 500k Canadian dollars to see you through a few months. Now I'm driving you to the airport. Your next destination is Vancouver. It's a bit like Melbourne; pretty cold and windy."

"This passport is for a Jules Lowdown; that's not me!" I indignantly exclaim.

"Thank your friends for that name. That identity would have cost a fortune. They certainly had a sense of humour," he exuberantly exclaims.

"How did they get that money?"

"Apparently, you had some financial investments that got sold off. They brought in a tidy sum, and it's all in your new bank account, minus transfer fees and legal expenses."

I have no recollection of any transfer, but I'm sort of glad they pulled it off.

"What's your part in this? Why are you helping me?"

"I'm like you, Jules. I was wrongly accused of a crime. Charmaine was an expert witness and absolutely decimated the prosecution's argument. I owe her a lot and now I've repaid the debt."

"What about that pilot?"

"Jules, there were over 13 people I know involved in your breakout and relocation, many are members of SnowPea. Others also owed Charmaine a favour because she saved them from a life of incarceration. She never asked for a favour in return; we are just so grateful. She is a wonderful woman." He gives me a high-five and discretely whispers in my ear, 'Be Kind'."

"Yes, she is a wonderful woman. Thank you for your help, but Charmaine wasn't a member of SnowPea. An ex-prosecution attorney called Sam started the organization to correct injustices in the legal system. It was more about preventing rapists, paedophiles, and partner bashers from escaping on technical details or being granted bail. It was for a Prosecution argument, not a Defence one."

"Jules, that's irrelevant. Your friend Mogan convinced Smithy to join. They had a similar background, that stuff in Afghanistan. Smithy got Charmaine in line. It's a network of people and it's growing. It's about injustice, whether that be for the legal prosecution or defence."

With that many people involved, there is a high probability one will blab, maybe after too many drinks at the pub. I try not to think about that but think instead of 'SnowPea'. It could be infiltrated and used as a scapegoat for more serious crime. Charmaine is very clever. I'm sure she's using the SnowPea organization. She fooled us all for a long time. I'm sure she'll make the rank of a "Z" very soon. In a way, I still miss her and her zany sense of humour; well, I hope it's a sense of humour and she doesn't get too serious or damaging.

"This is your stop, Melbourne airport. You will find your flight to Canada. Just follow the yellow lines and good luck."

"What about Melissa and her kids? I'm responsible for their safety after Victor vanished."

"I drove them to the airport earlier; could hardly get my eyes off your wife, Melissa. She reminded me of Morticia Addams in that 60's TV show, the Addams Family. You are a lucky man, though you look nothing like Gomez," he chuckles.

That's the disguise Charmaine took as the prison counsellor, Morticia Addams. What insane game is Charmaine playing? She must be colluding with Melissa and reusing disguises.

"Thanks for the ride."

"You're welcome; now get going and 'Be Kind'. You have some re-uniting things to do. There won't be any security checks at the airport."

I see Melissa in the departure lounge, dressed in black, with long black hair and pale skin. She is not my wife. Melissa is the wife of Victor, also known as Michele, who I thought was my friend, and Melissa and I are sort of friends, friends who may have occasionally crossed the boundary in the last few months after Victor disappeared. I'm rushing towards her. Lizzy and Peter come rushing towards me. I grab them. There's a feeling I cannot explain, and I hug them. I look at Melissa. "We got to get on board, we got 10 minutes. Where's Fabian?"

"He's already there in Vancouver, Canada," she replies.

Even though we're running late, we seem to be at the head of the boarding queue. I glance around. There's a TV camera crew filming us. Charmaine has thought of almost everything, the escape. We board a small jet plane which is a bit unusual. The jet would have to make many stopovers to refuel to get to Vancouver, but I dismiss my doubts, just glad to be out of incarceration. Unexpectedly we get promoted to business class. All four of us are immersing ourselves in food and ordering seconds and thirds. It's like we've been starved for the whole of our lives, and whatever they say about plane food, it's definitely better than prison food.

'Where's Fabian? Why isn't he here?"

"Fabian is already there, in Vancouver. I told you that a few minutes ago," Melissa announces.

"Is he OK? Who's looking after him?"

"He's a bright spark, and he's apparently staying with Victor's aunty. And Jules, this is apparently all about national security, but I don't have all the details."

The TV screens on the plane light up. A song comes on. 'Star to Fall' by 'Cabin Crew'. It's rather sensual and temporarily distracts me.

"Don't look at that; you have saliva running down from your mouth." Melissa leans over and wraps her hand around mine. I have a coughing spurt. I lean over the kids and give her a kiss. I then wipe off the remains of meatballs and spaghetti that splattered on my shirt and pants. The kids are not impressed.

I close my eyes and have a feeling of contentment. People I extremely care about surround me. I think that's called love, and it's a very nice feeling if you can ever find it. Melissa reaches over to me and grabs my hand. "Have you got the flash drive?"

My heart suddenly sinks as low as it could go. I look at her. "Did you betray me too, Melissa?"

The flight attendant interrupts, "Would you like a drink, sir?"

"Yes, thank you, a triple Scotch with Lime and non-sugary drinks for the kids."

"And you, madam?"

"Just water for me and the kids, thank you."

I skol the triple Scotch. It tastes like nail polish remover, not that I ever drank nail polish remover. I release Melissa's hand and ponder in my drowsy state.

I look at Melissa, and the kids, who have got headphones on, so can't hear. "Melissa, I don't believe in conspiracy theories, there is always a logical explanation, but I can't think of one at the moment."

Telling her that the peptide formula was just a furphy would be fruitless at this moment. Then again, she must know the USB drive contains hundreds of other files. A memory comes flooding back. It's of a younger Marg. She hands me the USB flash drive, whispering, 'It's a backup. It's our protection. Look after it in case I lose my copy.'

I sink back and order another triple Scotch with lots of Lime.

"Melissa, I was just a scientist; a lot of the time, we don't think of the implications of what we do. It's just about discovering new things; how those things are used is not our concern. Science and ethics don't mix as well as this Scotch and lime."

She reaches over across the mesmerised kids and grabs my hand. I skol the third triple Scotch and stroke her hand. Inside my mind, I think that I've f..ked up badly. Lizzy comes back from the toilet and whispers in my ear. "There are no other passengers on the plane. We have it all ourselves!" It's not the right moment to explain to her that it's safer to be in a crowd. I gently motion her back to her seat. In my slightly intoxicated state, I didn't think that being the only passengers might be strange, just lucky. I see Melissa's eyes drift, and the kids are asleep again. I ask the flight attendant for water, lots of water. A litre of 'Soft Springs Mineral Water' arrives and I gobble it up, then briefly join Melissa and the kids in their dreams.

"Fasten your seatbelts; we're about to land," the flight attendant announces in what sounded very much like an Australian accent. I don't feel that well. Melissa and the kids arouse from their slumber, rubbing their eyes. Melissa has an aggressive look in her eye. I'm glad the plates, plastic knives, and forks have been taken away.

"My main concern is my kids; you are secondary," she whispers.

"Melissa, I totally agree. I don't want to be numero ano, but what about the flash drive?"

"Jules, I hope you meant 'uno' not 'ano' because I don't do those things, and we've been through so much I couldn't give a shit. It was just a challenge trying to get that drive off you."

"Why would you even try? How did you even know about it? I trusted you."

"There were documents that implicated Nino Mosa and Victor in unauthorized investments in Australia. They bypassed authorities and paid off high ranking government officials. Marg copied those documents onto that USB drive when she did some consulting work for them."

"Melissa, what were they investing in; what were they going to produce?"

"Grasshoppers, Jules. Nino Mosa went on this greeny journey and invested a huge amount of money to start very big grasshopper farms in Australia. He sent Victor, the kids and me to Australia to start the process. Grasshoppers are high in protein and require minimal resources to produce, unlike beef. Asians eat them. I've tasted them fried with a bit of spicy sauce. They are the future. Insects are the future. The regulations regarding pest control went against Nino, so he offered financial inducements to authorities to get his plans passed. Some of the documents are on your USB flash drive and may be highly sensitive if divulged. It could cause a collapse of our insect industry. Your beef industry is probably involved in those alleged crimes."

I heard the grasshopper story before, maybe from Victor. I can't believe what

I'm hearing. This is absurd. She's more deluded than I am. I doubt Ai5 would bother about grasshoppers. Whatever Charmaine implied was on the drive was far more important than grasshoppers or peptides.

"Melissa, that doesn't explain why all those other people were after Marg, Jason and me. You know how many people died because of what's on that USB flash drive? Probably at least about five and possibly more to come. Melissa, I thought we had something deeper together."

"No Jules, you just made a good temporary parent, and I do appreciate that though your bedroom techniques could definitely use some improvement. You should watch some more porn to learn."

Melissa sounds more cold and clinical than me, and I have no idea what she means. Maybe I'm still hungover from those Scotches. Before releasing Melissa's hand, I pat her kids on their foreheads, then brace for another fall, well this aircraft landing, hopefully better than a parachute. I ponder about SnowPea and what it is becoming. I think about the shootings and deaths. I think about the peptide and more importantly what else is on that flash drive apart from grasshopper negotiations. I can still feel the little plastic USB drive in my shoe; it's not that uncomfortable.

On the plane's TV screen, there's a news flash and video, a slightly blurred video of me at the departure lounge about to board. It's got subtitles. 'Murder suspect Jules Lemos has escaped custody believed to be bound for Canada under a false passport'. Melissa and the kids do not appear in the video, only me, a lone refugee. I jump up and stand in front of the screen hoping the kids don't see the broadcast, but Melissa and her kids are dozing again. Not sure how much time has passed. My mobile phone shows 20 hours have passed. The fitness wristband watch in my pocket shows that only 50 minutes have passed.

There is one unshaded window. I peer out. This is not Vancouver. We could be back from where I started. It could be Ballarat or Bendigo. Regional towns a few hours' drive from Melbourne. Another flight attendant comes over. She has long blue-dyed hair with a fringe, more appropriate for someone studying Fine Arts at a college.

"Where are we?"

"You're close to your home in Melbourne, only two hours' drive. Now you, Melissa and those kids have to change your clothing and wear these hairpieces, for a short time. You'll have to be in disguise."

She throws the clothing to each person and hairpieces to all four of us.

"They're wigs. Mine would make me look like a 1970's rocker that Iggy Poppy guy. Are you sure I have to wear this?"

The blue-haired flight attendant must be Charmaine. I can recognise that voice anywhere. She whispers in my ear. "Jules, it's just a safety precaution. You never know who may watch the CCTV footage of this little airport and we couldn't disable all of it, not even your son could, and you never know who's listening. We didn't have time to electronically scan for listening devices. The costume dress-up is far easier. You'll be driven back to your place in Elwood, Melbourne. Now I got to fly back home. Smithy likes his sushi at 8 pm and he's probably driven home by now. Good luck and keep a low profile; you know the conditions to stay healthy. Oh yes, almost forgot, our director has arranged that you will have a police presence stationed outside your house."

"Why this masquerade? Can you guess how much public money you wasted by this little exercise? And what about my reputation? I got neighbours; I won't be able to get out of my townhouse. This has been a total f..kup. Why did you warn me about Greuger and that he's supposed to think we're in Vancouver?"

"Jules, there was some cost-cutting but more importantly we may have an internal security leak, that's why the sham and training exercise for my troops. If Greuger finds you're back at Elwood, then we definitely know we have a leak, and we'll trace the perpetrator. Overall, it was kind-off fun, wasn't it?"

I crouch down and refrain from slapping Charmaine.

"Are you still getting back at me Charmaine; do you seriously think this guy Greuger is going to fall for this sham?"

"Not sure Jules, I don't but I only organized the logistics. The 'Z's came up with the plan. I would have done things very differently if I had full control."

"Why is he after me? He must know Marg is dead. Can't you do a TV interview stating that your agency has retrieved the flash drive? Just state on TV that a USB drive was retrieved from the suspect."

"Jules, we will get the USB drive, but Greuger is far more of an obsessive-compulsive than you are. Once he accepts an assignment, he can't be called off. He goes on autopilot with only one goal and is uncontrollable. He also has a 50-million-euro bounty on his head; the Europeans are seriously after him. If we're successful in getting this guy our organization gets 85%, you get 5% and the other 10% is still in doubt. A win-win outcome, if you live. Now prepare a fresh dose of your chilli concoction when you get home."

"Charmaine did you or your 'Z's hire Greuger and am I just bait to get euros?"

"Enough speculation Jules; there will be tight security around your residence. It's likely that he will try to terminate you if he's been leaked info that you're back in Melbourne and don't worry because he never injured a kid or an animal."

"Am I in a dream? This guy disposing of me? You're f..ked bro."

"Jules, it will work. You still have Mogan around and police security will be there 24/7."

"What was in the drinks? What substance?"

"Jules, it was just 20mg of Diazepam, or Valium as it is called, for everyone; you got a triple dose. You metabolize it well; maybe due to your little peptide."

"What about you? You've entered the realm of conspiracies. The story won't hold up."

"Jules, all is under control, my 'M' and 'M' assistants took all the necessary video and sound footage of my traumatised escape, just like your escape at the airport and they arranged the finer details. They're good, maybe too good. Might have to demote them back to 'L's. Magnus and Michele, their initials are M&M just like my M&M lolly boys. What a coincidence," she giggles.

I briefly ponder. There's a high proportion of significant people in my life whose first name started with 'M' and they are mostly not good news. The 'C' may have to enter that 'not good' category as well. That leaves 24 letters of the alphabet that are OK. I look at Melissa and the kids. They are back sound asleep. I try to wake them, but they don't respond.

"Charmaine, who do you really work for? You know I'm a nerd and it won't go outside this room. I've kept many secrets. And why did they allocate so much money for this escape?"

"Jules, you asked me that before and I answered. You're just lucky; no I jiggled things a bit in your favour. It was a training exercise for our agents and there were more than just the M&Ms and SnowPea involved. A lot of negotiations involved some very high-profile officials in several governments who all want a successful outcome. Overall, it has been a great success so far and the potential mess has largely been averted. There was also another more important reason, I will explain later."

She becomes serious. "Jules, you're going back to your townhouse in Melbourne, not Vancouver. No one must know; not even Smithy or the SnowPea members that you will be back in Melbourne. Only go out at night and wear the 'rocker' disguises when you do and keep a very low profile."

"Where's Fabian?"

"He's at your townhouse being looked after by your boarder, Mogan and his girlfriend Janette. They have sworn to secrecy. They won't blabber. The consequences of any leaks have been explained to him and the impact it might have on Annabelle's police career. Sam has also sworn to secrecy. If you want to catch up with Sam, do it discretely. His daughter, the police officer, must not know you're back in Melbourne."

Charmaine hands me a mobile phone. "Use this for any phone calls you make. It's not easily traceable."

"You're sick, totally sick!"

"Calm down, Jules, we just do our best. Now take off your left shoe. We scanned you all whilst you were in dreamland."

I have little choice and look around. There's Melissa and her kids back asleep. I remove my shoe and remove the USB flash drive and hand it to Charmaine. I should have changed the socks before travel. She holds her nose and whilst wearing disposable gloves puts the USB drive into a small self-sealing plastic bag. Luckily, I have a backup.

"Jules, all the paperwork has been done. You are officially a resident of Canada, Vancouver. Just keep that Melissa under control. Keep anonymous and a low profile for at least a month; we will have captured that Greuger Shmidt guy by then and re-instate your reputation as an innocent bystander and contributor to the health and safety of our society. Now I got a flight to catch and get some sushi." She gives me a peck on my cheek.

"Jules, maybe come back and join the organization again, not just as a librarian. I'm sure you could make it above 'F' the second time around. Maybe even an 'M'."

I grab her. "What's become of you and who is the head Z?"

"Jules, I told you that before. That drug we gave you and all those triple scotches may have affected your memory retention. She breaks out into laughter. "To answer your second question again, it's Doris, our mother, the tea lady at the library, she is the top 'Z'. She's good, nothing slips by her and she can still shoot a 45 calibre pistol better than anyone else in the i5's. No one would ever question her authority at the moment. On second thought that is a secret. Don't ever disclose it else guess who else can shoot a 45 pretty good."

I'm not that astounded or shocked. There were many clues in the past. Just need confirmation.

"Doris, our mother, became my second mentor. Your first question? Nothing different than what's become of you. I was once your Blue Monkey and, in the future, don't mix questions; one question at a time." She pushes me away.

"Doris? You got be kidding, our mother?" I lied. I knew it; just wanted to see her reaction.

"That's why she's so good Jules. No one would ever guess either and but she does make a mean coffee and burger. So enough talk my little 'Silver Beetle'. Silver tarnishes and beetles crawl. You probably can't remember, but I did say I'd bring her down."

"Are you trying to break me too Charmaine? I was brought up by our dad till I left. I don't remember my mother. Dad said she had some high-profile job and couldn't be with us. She paid all the bills and sent money whilst dad watched TV, ordered takeaways and spent a lot of time in what he called the 'lab'. Before that, I think dad may have also had some high-profile job himself. He never uttered a negative word about our mother, but he also never did much of what I expected a dad to do. You didn't miss out on much. For me, it was like living in a vacuum."

"Enough," Char says with a slightly contemplative look in her eyes.

The plane lands and I'm shaking Melissa and the kids to wake them up. They finally become responsive.

"The car is waiting. Move your arses," Charmaine yells and points directions whilst talking on her walky-talky device. I drag the drowsy Melissa and the kids to the van whilst Charmaine is boarding the jet plane.

"I still miss you Blue Monkey," I yell out at the top of my voice as she boards. She looks behind and gives her usually cheeky smile and a wave.

Our van driver is like a robot, totally emotionless but a good driver. Melissa and the kids sleep through the 2-hour drive back to my townhouse in Melbourne. I press the doorbell. Mogan comes out and helps to carry Melissa and the kids inside. The driver gives a slight wave and I reciprocate. We're home. Fabian is lying asleep on the couch. I was about to turn off his laptop but notice the screen is full of hexadecimal characters rapidly scrolling by. I check what he was working on. I open another window on the laptop screen. Fabian runs the Linux operating system on his laptop.

I know Linux quite well. No, I don't, why did I even think that? In automatic pilot mode, I type the 'ls' command then the 'cd' command to change directories. Then 'ls' again. Oh gawd, he had backed up the flash drive to his laptop. Clever kid and now he must be trying to decrypt those files. I give him a kiss on the forehead and leave the laptop switched on to let it do its work. Mogan then gently carries Melissa's kids to the upstairs bedroom, then Melissa into my bedroom. All are sleeping. I go over to Mogan and give the guy a big hug, something I rarely feel comfortable about.

"Jules, you were on the TV news, an escaped felon, boarding a plane to Vancouver. How come you're here?"

"Mogan, that was staged. I can't explain all the details at the moment except to say I'm bait for a very notorious killer. We have to lie low for at least a month and keep our return a secret. Please don't tell Annabelle or anyone, apart from Sam, that we are back. Your girlfriend Janette mustn't mention we're back either. It might be safer for you and Janette if you move out for a while."

"No brother, we're not abandoning you. We had some good times. I'll keep it secret. Your friend Charmaine explained the consequences. Janette and I will do the food shopping. She's cool about it, the confidentiality stuff I mean. I also purchased a home gym. It's in the second parking spot in your garage. You can start doing workouts to pass the time."

"Thanks, Mogan," I give him another hug.

It's a very warm night. No need for any blankets. I lie down next to Melissa, and I'm tempted to give her a kiss but desist. I don't want to wake her up. I can't sleep even though super tired. I churn the day's events in my head. A lot has happened that I can't make sense of. Doris, my mother? I sort of suspected it and now I remember that she did once claim to be so when bringing down coffee at the Library and Charmaine, my sister or brother. Yes, I'm remembering that too. It's like some ridiculous movie. It can't be a reality unless reality has taken a quantum twist or I'm just blocking stuff that I prefer not to know which probably is more likely based on my previous escapes from reality. I sneak to the bathroom and grab a towel and shove it in my mouth. I pick a biro from the bedside table and thrust it into my thigh to check if this is reality. It hurt a lot and there is blood dripping down my thigh. It is reality. Now how will Melissa react when she finds out that we're back where we started from and not in Vancouver? What if the neighbours recognise us? The kids have to go to school but are supposedly in Vancouver with their fugitive carer. I can imagine other kids approaching Fabian and asking is your dad the guy who escaped from prison. Whatever Charmaine is trying to pull off she better fix things in the end and repair our reputations else she won't get promoted. I would have done things so much more diplomatically. I capture my thoughts. What did I just think – 'else she won't get promoted'. I thought that as if I had some influence, another delusion. I check on the kids who are all sound asleep as is Melissa and Mogan and Janette. No use turning on the alarm system as we are using all the alarm zone areas.

There's another spare inflatable mattress in the bedroom. I grab it and take it to the courtyard as well as the biggest kitchen knife and a freshly made chilli spray concoction. You always need protection, and the chilli spray is very effective. It's a clear, warm night and there are some stars in the sky to look at and wonder and ponder. Finally, I pull out one of the notes placed in my pocket by Charmaine and wearingly read it with the help of a torch. 'You f..ked up. You didn't draw the line and got involved with that Marg, who you were just supposed to monitor. I was very young at the time, and you were one of my mentors too, an 'X' not an 'F', pardon the joke. It's OK, I've learnt from you, at least what NOT to do. And yes, my codename was 'Blue Monkey' just in case that jolts your memory. You can guess yours or should I remind 'Silver Beetle' though 'Slivering Beetle' would be more descriptive. Keep mummy happy and don't f..kup again. This is the description of Greuger ….. '. She seems very angry, that's all I can think of at the moment. She must of have written it before I called her Blue Monkey when saying goodbye.

All the hypnotic drugs and alcohol start taking effect. I screw the note up and toss it into the garden. This is definitely a day you prefer to forget. The local mosquitoes got a good feed that night and are quite disorientated, crashing into walls and windows. I go back into the house and to our bedroom.

"We're not in Vancouver!" Melissa yells out when she wakes but I managed to put my hand across her mouth and muffle the sound.

"I'll explain what I know later. This is all for our own protection. Also, Victor is alive in a clinic in Sweden. Stay calm." Melissa looked like she is going to respond with violence after the deceit, but she desists. Fabian comes into our bedroom rubbing his eyes. "Dad it's late and we got to go school," Fabian mumbles.

"Fabian, you, Lizzy and Peter, are quarantined at the moment. I'll ring your schools. No, on second thought it can wait. No phone calls and we don't go outside for a while; not anywhere. I'll explain later. We're all grounded except for Mogan and Janette."

"Dad, what's this all about? Why can't we just have a normal life like other kids at our schools have?"

"Fabian, I don't have all the answers. You guys are not the only ones to be born unlucky. Half the kids at your school are probably experiencing far worse. Ours just happens to be a bit more dramatic at the moment but we still all love each other and we'll get through this."

"Dad, do you want me to grow up being a secret agent like you?"

"What? Fabian, I was a dismal failure as a secret agent. I never want you to be like me. And stop watching those James Bond movies. It's not like that at all and I'm just joking; I'm not a secret agent."

"Dad, I still love you, and you're definitely no James Bond." Lizzy and Peter make their way to our bedroom. They giggle. They must have heard the conversation and are in no state to weigh the implications. The kids give us a hug and go back upstairs to their bedrooms talking and giggling. That's what we thought. They must have been listening from the stairwell as our bedroom door is usually kept open, part of training, be vigilante at all times, so we put socks in our mouths when indulging in intimate encounters.

I pull out the other note Charmaine left in my pocket. I read it out aloud so Melissa can hear and show her the photograph. 'His last known name is Greuger Smitht but he goes under many aliases. He is ex-military, 205cm tall, very muscular and has a baby face even though he's in his late thirties but he's also very good at disguising. He's slipped by many authorities on false passports. He passed as a female Hockey player in Canada and as an old lady in New York. He is a very clever and very effective assassin. He was tasered twice before he seriously injured two NY police officers. The tasers had little effect on him, just made him more angry. Be very careful'. Fabian, Lizzy and Peter had been listening. They yell out simultaneously and come marching into our bedroom again. "Why is he after us?" Mogan and Janette must have heard the commotion and come into our bedroom as well.

Kids, Mogan and Janette, "I don't fully know. There's a very complex web we're in but we got to stay safe. All except Mogan and Janette have to stay indoors from now on, hopefully, it won't be for too long and we do have police protection. There is a police car with two officers parked in our driveway to help us."

I guess my comment wasn't very reassuring. The 3 kids go to the kitchen and grab some knives before going back up and huddle in one of the bedrooms together."

"Mogan, have you got any contacts who can supply us with guns and tasers? The tasers might briefly stun him but a bullet would be far more effective."

"Jules what's become of you, we got police protection, well at least Janette and I have. No one apart from your friend Charmaine and Sam know you're here. It was on the TV news. You're an escaped felon who has fled to Vancouver."

"Mogan, just get me any weapons you can get at that bikie hotel in St Kilda. I've got some cash."

Mogan, Melissa and Janette took at me quizzically. We manage to get one of the officers to escort us to the local ATM. The other officer guards the kids. Luckily the officers don't recognise that I'm the escaped fugitive that's supposed to be in Vancouver. I'm wearing the hippy long hair wig and thongs that Charmaine gave me and walk erratically. One of the officers asks Mogan, "Has your friend been smoking or taking contraband substances?"

"No, he's always been like that since a brick fell on his head at a building construction site," Mogan cunningly replies. The officer seems satisfied with Mogan's response, and we arrive at the ATM that's 800 metres away. The officer surveys the scene and stays vigilant whilst we try to make our withdrawals.

"My withdrawal limit has been reset to $800. I got it. Melissa, try yours!" I whisper.

"It's rejected, Jules."

"Mogan, try yours."

"Jules, we have $1600 between us. It won't buy much, maybe a bow and some arrows."

We get escorted back home and the officers go back to their car.

"Jules, we're being protected. Why would you even think of purchasing weapons? You're becoming paranoid."

"Mogan, so far, our protectors have been rookies. We have to arrange our own protection."

At 9 pm the electricity goes off in the townhouse. The lights are out. The outside electricity mains and metering switch must have been turned off. The switches are located in a locked cabinet at the start of the driveway. I have a key to the cabinet. It's an 80-metre walk, and we'll be in the dark but luckily, I have plenty of torches and lanterns. On second thought that's a bad idea. We'll stay put. The kids come back downstairs probably wondering why their game consoles aren't working.

"What have we got Mogan? Get that big knife from the kitchen. I'll get my ghost chilli spray and hammer that's lying around from the DIY work I never finished. I think it may be that Greuger guy who's cut our electricity," I whisper.

"Jules, you've only been home for one day. How could that Greuger guy track you? You're supposed to be in Vancouver, also the police are here keeping a watch?"

As it turned out our police protectors were severely non-functional, their police car windows punched in and them rendered unconscious. Then there is a knock on the door.

"Kids, go upstairs," Melissa quietly instructs.

Now you may think it's stupid and irresponsible what we did but we had little choice. Greuger could easily demolish the door if he wanted and if we called for help on our phones, it would be at least 5 minutes before any more help arrived. There was no choice. We're in the corridor next to the front door. Melissa and Janette are behind Mogan and me. Melissa is holding the lantern up high. I slowly open the front door. We are facing who we rightfully assume to be the Greuger Shmidt. He is more daunting than the descriptive note Charmaine left me and has an evil snarl on his face. The guy is a man mountain, taller than Sam, muscular, with boyish looks and long blond curls. He could have should have chosen a career in acting in one of those horror Viking movies. Both Janette and Melissa foolishly rush past Mogan and me and try to grab him at the doorway but are flung back into the corridor wall like paper dolls.

Greuger is ducking his head trying to enter the townhouse door. I rush forward and spray his face with the ghost chilli spray. He's waving one arm trying to hit me whilst clenching his eyes with the other hand. I kneel down and wack his right foot as hard as I can with the hammer. As Greuger is crouching down and grabbing his toe, Mogan kicks him in the head, so he looks up. Mogan then plunges the kitchen knife into what seems like Greuger's chest. For a moment Greuger struggles to try to pull the knife out but then he fades on the floor. He sardonically whispers, "Nothing personal but congratulations, no one has ever got me before, and with only such primitive weapons. Congratulations. I feel tired, very tired of this all. I never had fun. Killing is not fun. I could have put up more of a battle, but I am tired of this shit. You have released me and in a way, I am grateful, but I have a favour to ask."

"Ask!" I yell.

Greuger whispers, "In my pocket is the hotel entry card. I have a pet white rat that always travels with me. Her name is Chloe. Put gloves on and get to the hotel and rescue Chloe, else she'll be exterminated. She is a good rat, there is also much money there, take it. Perhaps we will meet again in more favourable circumstances." Greuger drops his head.

Mogan was about to stump his shoe on Greuger's chest. "Mogan, relax, he apologised, it was nothing personnel and he's nearly dead."

I'm on my knees and lift Greuger's head and hug it. "You're good my brother, we're just on different sides, but you're good and I don't want the money, but I promise the rat will be well looked after. I kiss Greuger's head. 'Brother's in Arms' sort of stuff. You never want anyone to die alone no matter what's their past.

Mogan questions, "Jules, you're totally weird, you have to tell me what's going on? What do we need to know?"

"I don't know."

Calling Annabelle was the first thought, but I call Charmaine instead and ask her to come over ASAP.

"I think he's dead, that Greuger guy," I say though not feeling exactly happy.

"Stop being hysterical. Check his pulse and don't be fooled by a seemingly non-existent pulse. In the past, he's injected pulse-lowering drugs when in a tight situation and later broke out from the ambulance transporting him to mortuaries. Tie him up with ropes. He's come back from the dead before."

I check Greuger again. His shirt and the floor is soaked in blood but then he lifts his hand as if going for my throat but then fades. His arm drops. I get down close to his lips.

"He's not breathing and has no pulse, Charmaine. For f..ks sake, you were supposed to be protecting us, so call the ambulance officers over here. I can only imagine what he did to the police officers who were supposed to protect us."

Mogan and I rush down to the garage and get the Nylon ropes. Mogan seems to know how to wrap someone up better than I do. The job is done. Charmaine is still on the telephone line, "Jules, you and Mogan will be awarded a medal. My clean-up team is arriving, but you'll have to contact Annabelle. We used some of her resources; any police officers injured are in her jurisdiction and I have a slight idea how that Shmidt guy traced you back here."

"Yes, you do. You mentioned something about bait to me before." I hang up the phone.

It's chaos in the household. The kids have come down the stairs again and see the bloodied monolith called Greuger. Peter vomits first and starts a chain reaction. Lizzy and Peter expunge as well. Melissa and Janette wonder over shaking their head from their collision with the walls. Lizzy, Peter and Fabian wrap themselves around Melissa and Janette.

Annabelle arrives. "My officers are alive but unconscious." She inspects Greuger's body. "There will be a coronial enquiry and what the hell are you doing here? You're an escaped felon. You're supposed to be in Vancouver. Don't leave this house. You're going back to prison as soon as I get more officers here but first clean up the stomach contents on your floor and you, Charmaine, what are you doing here?"

"Annabelle, speak to Deputy Commissioner Renolds. He'll tell you that I am in charge of disposing of Greuger's body after Ai5 conduct some tests on it for the Defence Department, which is very interested in Greuger's genetic makeup because if he could be cloned, they could save billions on defence personnel wages."

Annabelle scratches her head and leaves without saying another word.

The body of Greuger is put in a bag, his head limply hanging out as the bag is not long enough and he's removed by four struggling officers into what looks like an ambulance; not a good scene if my neighbours are watching.

"What do we do now? The kids are traumatised, and we can't keep this facade up," Melissa asks in an agitated voice.

"Melissa, I think it's over. I think we're finally safe."

Mogan and Janette comfort us. "I bought a few bottles of rum. Let's get pissed before you're taken back to the penitentiary and after that stab to Greuger I may have to join you. We'll be cellmates."

"I got to go guys, just briefly. Be back in 20 minutes. I got a rat to pick up."

They all look at me quizzically as I rush out the door to the garage and start the VW. Surprisingly Greuger was staying at a local dodgy, cheap hotel that had no security or CCTV. The key card opens the door. His apartment is stark, so stark. There are minimal belongings apart from the caged rat and a framed photo of a young-looking woman with blond ponytails wearing a traditional German dress, with an inscription 'My love, I love you and always will'. It was signed Hilda; then another framed photo of Greuger and Hilda hugging each other. A long time later,

I researched Greuger, using some Ai5 resources. He wasn't always a bad guy. He flipped when his girlfriend, Hilda, was accidentally gunned down by an undisclosed source thought to be an i5 operative. He was created and wanted revenge and went haywire. He lived a solitary, minimalist lifestyle and donated most of the money from his assignations to charity. I feel some sort of sympathy for him. I take the cage with the rat, its water bottle and any nibbles lying on the kitchen bench. I grab the photos of Greuger and Hilda as well.

Thirty minutes have passed. I'm back but leave the caged rat in the garage. Mogan does not seem to be worried about what just has happened. He and I have killed a person. Then again Mogan had to kill many people when serving in his military role in Afghanistan. The secure cell phone rings. It's Charmaine. "Victor explained the circumstances leading to Margaret Milstein's death in a sworn statement. Victor is alive as I said before. No link between Jason's death and you. The 'Z's have contacted the Victorian Police commissioner and Annabelle has been relieved from duty on this case. You are also a free man."

"What does relieved mean?"

"Jules, Annabelle was presented with the evidence that your initial arrest was based on circumstantial evidence, it would not stand up in court, and once explained to her she was compliant and sorrowful. I think she still wants to be your friend. Have a nice night. Smithy and I have just found the best sushi place ever. I'll email you the address."

I thought she was about to hang up, but she continues. "Now Jules, there will be a TV crew arriving at your home tomorrow morning at 9:30 am. I have written your speech. It's about what our national security agencies do and we shall rehearse tomorrow morning. Please be cooperative. Melissa may also be interviewed but kids won't."

"What, why?"

"Jules, you are still a wanted fugitive in the public eye. The gist is you will appear to have co-operated with Federal authorities to protect your family and help capture a very dangerous killer. The operation will appear as a type of sting which it was. You will be a hero and will be able to proudly front your neighbours again. Our lawyers are still looking into the ethical issues involved but you will appear to have totally co-operated to help capture, or should I say dispose of the world's most dangerous assassin. We'll have a story made up of why he was after you in the first place. It will be about mistaken identity. My team is writing the script."

Did Charmaine instigate this all?

"Charmaine, why was this all necessary in the first place?"

"Jules, did you ever wonder how despite our elaborate staging of your escape that the Greuger guy was still able to trace you?"

"I did. I told no one. Only Sam, Mogan and your organization knew. I trust Sam and Mogan implicitly. I thought you were the leak that led the Greuger guy back to Melbourne so quickly."

"Don't be ridiculous, for years you were still on our payroll. You owed us, but we have a rat, someone divulging sensitive information."

I think of the rat cage which has a label, 'Chloe'. "That doesn't make sense."

"The 'Z' are dinosaurs and lax about cyber-security."

"What are you implying? Was it all about your career rise, I'm confused?"

"Of course not, Jules. It's about national security. Just play the game. It wasn't just about my career. You and Melissa fit into the equation as well. Now I have to go. I'll be at your place at 8:30 am tomorrow for some rehearsal."

I almost forgot about the rat. I rush down to the garage and bring the cage up to our bedroom. The rat still has water and is chewing on a hunk of cheese that I left her. It looks up as if to say thanks. Meanwhile, Melissa beckons the kids to go back upstairs. "It's finally alright. Back to school tomorrow so try to get some sleep." She kisses them all goodnight. I check upstairs. The three of them are all cuddled together in Melissa's double bed. Hopefully, they just make up funny stories and do not need trauma counselling. Mogan comes over and he has two cartons of beer. He's never drunk alcohol before but takes a sip, well maybe more than a few sips. This close contact stuff is probably new to him. Next morning you probably wouldn't want to see four fully clothed adults sprawled over the lounge room floor. No pillows and no blankets, and some snoring. It was another ugly scene. The 7 am clock alarm sounds and we rise up shaking our heads. We crush the beer cans and put them in the recycle bin. The place looks tidy. We do a high-five clapping our hands. I check the emails on the computer. There is one from Victor, 'Please tell my wife and kids I love them. I have filed for a divorce. I am going to be myself and not lead the double life I had before. Jules, I trust you to look after Melissa and my kids and hope you all have a happy life together. Hope you will let me visit.'.

I quickly reply. 'You'll always be welcome.' Melissa looks over my shoulder.

"Can I type something?" She does, 'Victor, I wish you the best and as Jules said you can always visit'.

He replies. 'Melissa, I have gone through the drug rehabilitation program at Magnus's clinic. He has offered me a job as Medical Officer; I think I can do that. We are just getting to know each other, my brother and I. Be kind'.

Charmaine arrives at 8:30 am. "Memorize the contents of this script and don't stray when interviewed by the reporters. Just disclose the minimum. Be like a politician and dodge any questions that don't fit the script. Now we have a dramatic part that will keep the reporters entertained. It's about the ghost chilli spray you manufactured to keep your family safe. Talk about that to distract them. It might also earn you some money for the ingredients of capsicum spray you used. I'm sure some companies out there will pay for your formula." She then gives me a peck on the cheek.

There are well over a dozen reporters and their film crews outside my townhouse. I downed a vodka before stepping out and inviting them inside. I feel reasonably tranquil though have forgotten what I'm supposed to say as per Charmaine's script, but I briefly describe the incident as it happened but slightly exaggerate. In my description, Greuger grabbed me by the throat and lifted me a metre off the ground before I sprayed him with the chilli spray. "Greuger fell to the ground but fell on the knife that Mogan was still holding upright after Greuger disabled him."

The journalists were furiously taking notes. "What's this ghost chilli that brought down the world's most wanted assassin?" one of the reporters asks.

"Come out to the garden, I'll show you." I first grab a pair of disposable gloves from the kitchen. Then the rat, Chloe climbs up my leg, chest and sits on my shoulder and nods her head. The cameras click as we're photographed. The media team, about 14 in all, follow. I pick one of the peppers, looking away and holding my eyes shut. One of the media team touches it but makes the mistake of rubbing his eyes. He is screaming in agony. Another reporter also touched the chilli but needs to empty his bladder. I forgot to tell him that he should scrub his hands before he has a pee. We can all hear the screams from my bathroom. All the other reporters and camera crew promptly depart.

Charmaine rings, "Why didn't you just follow the script?"

"Get lost! I make my own scripts from now on, no, sorry I didn't mean that. The rat got their attention. I didn't have to do much."

Charmaine hangs up but not before, "Get sober," she yells.

That night on the TV news there is a story 'Killer Assassin Pursues his Latest Target, Ends up Dead due to Home-Grown Red Chilli'. Not the interview we hoped for, but that's TV. Charmaine is being interviewed on the morning TV news. She apologises for the action of one of her traumatised newly recruited participants in the industry and then recites the script she had prepared. 'It was about National Security and the demise of the terrorist and assassin Greuger Shmidt'. It went down well though I got barely a mention except to say I participated in a 'sting' and that I'm innocent and should be applauded. No idea how she bypassed ASIO and ASIS and risked exposing Ai5 but she succeeded. In this industry there are a lot of deals done behind the scenes and many governments and their police authorities are grateful that Grueger is supposedly deceased.

There are many requests for media interviews via email which I turn down but offer them a story that will be posted via email. I don't tell them the full story; it will be highly sanitised. Charmaine would help me write the story.

The news on TV causes a fury about many women who are victims of domestic violence asking if they could have some seeds of that chilli plant. I pick some seeds dressed in protective clothing and put them in plastic-sealed envelopes along with safety instructions. A TV crew picks them up but then there's a knock on the door. Cautiously I open it, ready to grab the chilli spray, it's Miss Gribble.

"I saw the TV news. I'll tell the other townhouse residents that you are a hero, and they should stop gossiping about all the recent commotion."

"Thanks, Miss Gribble, we'll stay in touch. Goodbye for now." I give her a peck on the cheek then Peter walks out in tears. "Will I see my dad again?"

Melissa and I grab him. "He will visit soon. He promised."

Charmaine calls on the secure cell phone. "There will be no coronial enquiry. I'm terribly sorry about the injuries of the Victorian Police officers. They are recovering well, and they will be honoured. You and Mogan can't receive the same public recognition, but several governments are grateful to you and Mogan for disposing of Greuger, and you'll soon be getting a cheque. Your share of the reward for bringing down Greuger; $2.5m."

"Who gets the rest of the reward; I thought it was $50m in total?"

"Jules, we do. We have expenses. It pays for the staff and infrastructure bills. By the way, since the posted video on FB, we've been inundated by overseas agencies to help them get rid of dubious people and assassins. The pay is good if you want to come back."

I decline the offer. Chloe, the rat, is sitting on my knee. "Won't you just giggle for me, Charmaine? I need a laugh at the moment."

"You naughty thing!" she giggles. "Are you coming back to the agency?"

"I said no before, and I mean it."

"Magnus has offered my job back as Risk Assessor at MM Pharmaceuticals in Melbourne."

"Whoopee, we may see you again. We collaborate with MM all the time."

"Char, who informed Greuger that I was back at my place in Melbourne?"

"It was me, but you had backup if you needed it. Alcatel and Frisbee, those sexy agents in their black tights and black headgear, were tracing Greuger. You probably didn't notice in the dark, but they had their 45 drawn at Greuger as you opened the door though you and your housemates were probably too distressed to notice them. You saved the cost of a 45 bullet, and I told you before about 'bait'."

I feel like hitting her. And so the story, for the first time, was about to end till Fabian comes over. Many premature endings would follow as a story never ends unless you're dead.

"Dad, the PC decryption program has run for over two weeks. Your friend Charmaine is involved in an agency called Ai5. There's another list of names being decoded."

"Fabian, turn off the computer; it's best we don't know anymore. We're safe; that's the important thing. Just turn it off."

Mogan excitedly pounces into the conversation. "There are some cheap holidays to the Queensland Whitsunday islands. It's school holidays and Uni holidays, so we can all go together."

I ring Ms Valda. "Could I take another week off? I'd like to take the kids for a much-deserved holiday."

"Do that; your job is safe but don't start any other job till you finish at the archives. There's still at least about six weeks of work left on that new assignment."

"Melissa and I will work day and night to get the job finished when we get back."

"Have a well-deserved holiday." She hangs up.

I wonder what 'new assignment' means. I hope it's just scanning papers. Initially,

I thought Ms Valda was the boss. I was wrong. She just followed orders and never questioned them. The worst is over. We board the plane, and after a few hours, we're floating in a tropical swimming pool though there are a few flip-overs in the rafts and a lot of laughter.

"Melissa, will you marry me after the divorce from Victor is approved?"

"You're short in height and not actually my ideal man, but you could do."

"Thanks for the compliment," I kiss her. "Does that mean a 'yes'?"

"It does," she replies with a smile. It's a rare event to see Melissa smile.

Meanwhile, according to phone calls, Sam tries to mind Chloe, the rat, while we have the most wonderful seven-day holiday. He failed. The rat loves swimming and dives into the Elwood canal before coming back soaked and seriously in need of a bath.

We holidaying adults are all shagged out from hours of swimming and diving in the ocean, that is, and maybe some other stuff. The kids mostly play computer games but occasionally do a swim in the pool. The food is great, and we'll all have to reduce our calorie intake when we get back home. A week passes so quickly. When we get back, I write the wedding invitations, especially the one to Charmaine and Smithy. I put on it, 'You don't have to reply or turn up. I'll understand'.

It's a small ceremony at the Melbourne Registry for Marriages and Deaths. Maybe the Registry should change its name as it sort of implies the first leads to the second. We're not particularly dressed up, no white gowns, and I just found the jacket from my first marriage, and we have no new rings. Neither Melissa nor I could remove our previous ones, no matter how much soap and lubricants we used. Using the angle grinder was a dangerous option, so we desisted. There aren't many people present as it was hastily planned. The kids, Sam, Annabelle and her tall male companion, also of Islander origin, Mogan and Janette and then Charmaine and Smithy arrive. I rush over to them. "I'm so, so sorry I never made it to yours. Will you ever forgive me?"

"It's in the past, Jules. Just say 'I do' so we can start to party," Smithy replies.

Charmaine comes over to Melissa and hands her a posy of flowers. The two exchange an intense look. We had booked a private room in a Port Melbourne pub for the low-key celebration. There were also a few more people that turned up later- Doris, Ms Valda and their partners, plus Smithy's ex-army friends and their now partners, who attended Smithy's flat warming party. It was supposed to be a quiet, non-descript event, but it wasn't. Everyone is wildly dancing and consuming beer and cocktails; I even do a few jiggles with Doris, but then Melissa calls me over. A text message arrived on Melissa's phone, which she shows me. 'Sorry I couldn't be there. I paid off our Visa account and will be making monthly payments into your savings account, Victor'.

"Melissa, we have plenty of money if that Greuger reward money comes through. We don't need Victor's money." I would be wrong. Greuger feigned his death and is still out there. Hope he has found a new rat friend because we all really like Chloe, and no one wants another battle with him.

We join the others dancing to '70s and 80s music and finish at around 2 am in the morning after much dancing to the DJ's music. Taxis are waiting outside. We asked for no gifts, but there are some. We stuff them in the boot of the cab. We give all the guests a hug and board the taxis carrying the sleeping kids. Melissa whispers, "I'm not sure you should accept the position at MM Pharmaceuticals?"

"Why?"

"It's a spider web, Jules. Haven't you worked that out yet, all the coincidences? MM doesn't just produce generic drugs and does genetic research; it's also linked to various Western government intelligence agencies, including one I still do some consultancy work for. You must have noticed when you worked for them. Most of the visitors to MM probably didn't look like scientists. Your ex-wife did work for them and probably downloaded encrypted confidential documents, and I'm not talking about just Nino's grasshopper venture."

"How do you know all this?"

"I was once an 'X', Jules, before I resigned from a full-time position. Yes, I had three jobs when in the USA. I did work for an outsourced government agency whilst lecturing and being a wife and looking after the kids."

The night is slightly dampened as I'm stunned, and my brain is racing trying to fit the pieces of the tragic puzzle. Melissa's last comment may explain the friction between her and Charmaine though they would have had little to do with each as Melissa spent most of her life living overseas. Maybe it's just professional rivalry. I'm sure Charmaine will be promoted to a 'Z' very soon, maybe a role Melissa would like.

"Jules, we can get out of this, though it won't be easy?"

"I can't, Melissa. I have to accept any job offer I can get. There's a 10-year gap in my resume that I can't account for, and I'm getting old. Do you think anyone else but Magnus or the agency would hire me? I can't get out. There's still a house mortgage to repay, plus all the bills."

"Jules, you just got $2.5m inserted into your bank account. You don't have to worry about bills. In your spare time, you could write a cookbook." I think that may have been a sarcastic comment.

"Melissa, Greuger did one of his amazing escapes from the crematorium, and the reward has been rescinded, so our financial resources are not that good. He's a Houdini escape artist. Maybe we should go back. You wouldn't be an 'X' anymore, and I'm sure I could convince Charmaine that you'd work productively together."

"Jules, can we talk about it tomorrow, but Jules, we could always get jobs in a local Supermarket serving customers and practise our social skills."

Fabian comes in. "Dad, did you notice the 'For Sale signs in the townhouses next to yours? We've driven the neighbours away and caused property prices to plummet despite Miss Gribble's efforts."

"So?"

"Dad, Magnus transferred a lot of money into my bank account. I'm underage, so can't buy property, but you could use some of that money to buy both of them. I checked on the real estate website. They're listed at $900,000 plus. Mogan and Janette could live in one of them, and I could have a proper bedroom instead of your study room. Sam and Annabelle could live in the other one. Maybe they could pay a bit of rent."

I'm almost too tired to think but answer, "Sounds like a good idea. Turn off the computer and get some sleep. It's 3:30 am. We'll talk about it tomorrow."

Melissa and I are too tired to consummate the marriage. We lie on the bed, still in our wedding clothes and drift into sleep. In the morning, whilst holding and shaking my head, I briefly wonder why any couples do this tortuous wedding ceremony thing. I give the sleeping Melissa a kiss and then stumble to the bathroom. Melissa wonders in and is holding my head. "Jules, you slipped on the bathmat and hit your head. There's blood in your hair. We have to take a shower so that you clean yourself up. I told you before to hang up the bathmat on the shower door to dry and lay it down before showering."

She's lecturing again. The clouded thought crosses my mind. Did I make a mistake with this marrying thing? It definitely wasn't a mistake in the long term.

Melissa is caressing my head and hip.

"Melissa, I can't move that well at the moment. My computer is on. Can you put on our favourite song? Turn it on full blast through the sound system."

She does, and our eyes roll as we passionately kiss and do other things as well, as we both go back in the shower as the blood is washed off. Chloe, the rat, comes rushing in. I pop out of the shower and grab her and go back in. Lesson 222, rats do not like showers. They can bite, but the big bite came later when Melissa asked, "Jules, why was Greuger set upon you in the first place? From what Charmaine told me, you were not a high-profile agent. Were you the agent who accidentally shot Hilda, his beloved girlfriend?"

"Melissa, I never shot any anyone. Yes, I accidentally bombed a village, but I was given wrong coordinates. I can never repay the deaths and damage I caused, and as you know, I spent ten years living in homeless shelters and on the streets trying to get my mind together, after that incident."

"Could Charmaine have been the one who accidentally shot Hilda?"

"Melissa, I don't know."

I put my arm around her, and eventually, we drift into sleep.

Chapter twenty three

I wrap a towel around my waist and wake Melissa and then Melissa's kids and Fabian. The kids must have slept for 24 hrs. Mogan and Janette are making breakfast. I explain to the kids that the drama was all a fake, a pilot episode of a new TV reality series called 'Family Jokes', which will be screened soon. I wink at Mogan and Janette. They wink back. I think they understand that any story at the moment that reduces the kids' trauma is justified, even if it's a blatant lie.

"But there was blood around that big guy. There was blood everywhere," Lizzy yells out.

"Lizzy, that was just diluted tomato sauce, and you may have not noticed all the film crew and lights. They were concealed to make it seem realistic. It was just an act like all those other reality TV series. If we had let you know of the plot, you, Fabian and Peter wouldn't have acted convincingly. Now I warn you - you may appear on TV, and the kids at school will want your autographs and selfies with you but don't tell them anything just yet; it will spoil the surprise if you do."

Melissa comes over. "They seem to accept the dubious explanation and seem rather excited."

"Kids, Mogan and Janette will take you to basketball training soon. Focus on the ball. Your mum and I have some more writing to do. We just need to be left alone for a few hours."

Melissa comes over and whispers, "A very creative explanation to the kids, but eventually, we will have to tell them the truth."

"Let's just leave the truth for a month or so. Their minds have to heal first. Now, are you OK after all this drama?"

"Thanks for asking, but I have seen and heard worse, and you did call me a cold bitch once."

I give her a hug. Both Melissa and I would wake up in the middle of the night screaming and sweating for the next two weeks. After the first occurrence, the kids, Mogan and Janette came running to our room to see what the commotion was about. After that, we kept our bedroom door closed and slept with a clean sock in our mouths, tightened by an elastic cord around our heads. There was no kinky stuff involved.

It's 1 pm Sunday, very hot and humid, and Melissa and I are sitting naked with our reading glasses on and staring at our laptop computer screens. The kids come inside after practising basketball using the hoop that Mogan and I had installed on the garage wall.

"You're not dressed mum, you're still in nothing. Can you put on some clothes, and what's for lunch?" Lizzy exclaims.

"It's hot, and we do not believe in air-conditioning. We are doing our best to minimize carbon emissions and global warming. Lizzy, we are working now, can you check the cupboards and the fridge? You are old enough to prepare your own lunch, so give Mogan and Janette a break," Melissa replies as she intensely gazes at her laptop computer screen.

"Whre's Mogan and Janette? They normally prepare lunch," Lizzy calls out.

"Check their room."

"I did; it's empty, mum!"

"Mogan and Janette are at the Sandringham hospital. Janette's mother has broken her hip, according to this email message that I just received," I call out.

Lizzy's head is sort of spinning. "I hope she's OK," she says as she wanders off, head down, but Melissa grabs her.

"She'll be right, but Lizzy, you, Fabian and Peter must start learning how to prepare a meal. The fridge is full of food."

"This really sucks, mum." She looks away as if trying to process the information.

"No, it doesn't. You, Peter and Fabian have to learn how to cook and make a sandwich; you are old enough now. How many times have I told you that? And besides, we are all really concerned about Janette's mum as well."

"Mum, you've never cooked like anything proper since I remember. We mostly had meals delivered, and when you tried, you just did the cutting and chopping, and the nannies did the cooking, and now Mogan and Janette are doing the cooking."

It's funny how kids forget. Melissa has done a lot of cooking since living at my townhouse. Lizzy continues raving with her arms crossed on her chest. "All step-dad can cook are sausages and burgers on the BBQ. I don't want that. I'm becoming a vegetarian, maybe even a vegan or maybe even a breatharian, so I won't even eat at all, just breathe scented air from a vaporizer for my nutrition."

Melissa whispers to me, "Let her rave but put the BBQ on whilst I talk to her. I'll have two sausages and two burgers."

Melissa grabs the distraught Lizzy. "I will learn to cook, I promise. We will all learn together as a team, quality family time. Now give me a hug," Melissa asks.

"I don't hug naked people," Lizzy replies with a look of revulsion.

"Lizzy, there are cookbooks in Jules' bookshelf."

Lizzy goes to my bookshelf and pulls out three cookbooks. "I don't think any of these books have ever been opened."

"Well, open them; they are pristine, no germs. You kids find a recipe, and later we will go shopping and purchase the ingredients for dinner."

They took the easy way out rather than prepare lunch. There is a mess of spilt breakfast cereal on the kitchen floor, and the kids are on the couch, flicking through the recipe books. Fabian has his arm around Lizzy's shoulder. They all seem to have forgotten or are in a state of denial about the Greuger incident. It's like nothing has ever happened, and that's good. It will take time for the memory of that event to slowly slip back into consciousness.

Lizzy comes back to our bedroom and asks, "Mum, what's so special about the constant 'e'? I have to write a maths assignment about 'e'."

My ears prick. "Lizzy, 'e' is a bit like 'pi'. It's something called a universal constant that a guy called Euler discovered. It applies to everything in the Universe as far as we know, and 'e' has to do with describing the growth of things, possibly even kids, and it's like 'pi' and also appears in many physics equations, which I don't fully understand. I'll explain it later, but we'll need lots of paper, no then again just a computer spreadsheet program will do. Oops, 'pi' may not be a universal constant, especially around things called 'black holes' which distort the shape of things including 'pi,' but 'e' is probably universal. Then again, it may not be."

Melissa jabs me in the ribs. It's a jab I've come to recognise, a 'stop the yapping jab' – it's friendly. "Think of another constant – call it 'me' instead of 'pi' or 'e'," she says, looking at me. "I am your 'me'."

Is Melissa saying that I don't give her enough attention? She did mention that Victor always bought her a bunch of roses when he was in town, but I'm in town all the time, and we don't have enough vases. I'll go to the supermarket later and purchase some roses.

"Mum, are you arguing with Jules?"

"Just sort of darling; big people often argue, but it does not mean they do not love each other. They just have issues to discuss sometimes loudly."

Melissa is definitely developing a twisted sense of humour. Lizzy refrains from saying her usual 'You guys suck' but looks at me quizzically and asks, "You know about this maths stuff?"

"Lizzy, I think I might, just a little, but I know about 'e' and 'pi' but not enough about 'me'; I'll explain later. By the way, both Melissa and I are proud of you. We admire you for getting straight 'A's at school. We'll get you a present."

Lizzy shyly smiles. "I was only competing with Fabian, but now Peter has joined the pack. He's become very annoying with all his questions, but we do work together and help each other with assignments, even though we are in different grades."

"Lizzy, I'm so privileged to have step-kids that question and work collaboratively. Keep doing that and encourage Peter. I'll get back to you guys later, and I'll think of a way to explain the constant 'e' and how it is derived and what it means. But for the moment, could you study the Fibonacci series, and it's not just about rabbits breeding? It's cool too, almost as cool as 'e'. Now your mum and I got some work to do; it's a bit of a serious sort of work."

Lizzy comes over, looking at the ceiling, gives Melissa and me an unexpected hug and then wanders away. She rounds up Fabian and Peter, and they get ready to march off to the school basketball court.

"Guys, here's a phone. Call me if there's any problem. No, on second thought, I'll come along and watch."

"Can you get dressed first? I don't need to be embarrassed by a naked step-father. I have like a reputation to maintain, and Fabian told me you were born on a Friday, the 13th of August. It's a bad luck day, according to that movie."

"Lizzy, for me it has been the best, most wonderful luckiest birth date ever. Your mother, you kids and the friends we have made, have made my life so really good. For me, that birthdate has definitely been very good luck."

Melissa looks at me whilst I struggle to quickly put shorts and a tee-shirt on. "Hopefully, she'll lose the attitude once she gets older. Come over." Melissa gives me a hug.

There are a few other kids at the court from the school, and they all seem to know each other. I ring Melissa on the cell phone and tell her I'll stay with the kids since Mogan isn't here to supervise. Her reply is,

'Call me if you need any help. You know I can pack a punch'. Melissa's boxing skills would not be required, and after 2 hours we return. The hot and sweaty kids rush upstairs. I can hear the Xbox starting. I go to the bedroom, where Melissa is still typing. She looks up.

"Do you need any help with 'e'? I have a Maths postgraduate degree."

I'm startled, learning something new about Melissa every day. "Melissa, I don't have a maths degree, but I remember, 20 years or so back, that I was a high-school teacher before I got that job in pharmacology and i5. I was designated a maths teacher, and I learnt that stuff on the fly. In some ways, it was good because I knew little and didn't make assumptions about what students understand as I was barely understanding the stuff myself and rarely got to bed before 2 am in the morning, trying to make sense of it and then preparing lesson plans."

"Come over here, Jules. I'm glad you know some maths, and you probably know the stats. Blended families rarely work out. There's a 60% chance we will not make it."

I give her a hug.   "Melissa, I'll do my best. I promise, but you're not exactly supportive of your kids and Fabian with your strict discipline."

I duck and miss the swing from Melissa's arm. I think she was just joking, at least I hope so, as she looks at the screen.

"What have you found, Melissa?"

"This should not be so. I still have full access to the Ui5 computer servers, which can access all the other i5 servers on the network, including bank and stock exchange data. I just bought up your bank and stock-holding records. Only your Taxation department should have access to those. This is a serious cyber-security breach. It needs to be fixed ASAP. My full access should have been revoked as soon as I resigned from the full-time position at Ui5," Melissa replies as she bangs her fists on the desk.

"What have I got, Melissa?"

"Let's say you are not likely to starve. Log in yourself and check your accounts."

"Can't you tell me?"

"No Jules, hopefully, they are logging my activities. By accessing your accounts, I have already committed a cyber-crime which I will have to account for, but it may make them aware of their security flaws."

"Why did you even try to do that? I could have logged in and shown you everything. No, on second thought, I can't. I forgot my passwords a long time ago. Can you show me what I got?"

"No Jules, I'm not risking being convicted of any more security breaches. I was just testing their security. I should not have been able to log in. The 'Z's are dinosaurs."

"How do you know about the hierarchy, and what ranking do you hold?"

"I will explain another time."

Melissa is fuming. I bring her a shot of rum. It may calm her down. It took three shots of rum to settle her.

"Melissa, do you still work for them?"

She's rubbing her head with both hands. "I told you that before. You must have alcohol-induced dementia. Just some occasional consultancy work on the computer, but I should not have this high level of access as a consultant. They are primitive, totally out of touch with modern reality, and their cyber-security policies are totally slack."

Melissa has fired up again, yelling and banging her fists near my precious computer keyboard; have to get more rum into her. It's unusual behaviour from the normally cold-as-ice Melissa. She's having a meltdown. She leaves the computer and lies down on the bed with her right palm on her forehead. After turning the computer off, I join her.

"And you want me to go back? That's a bit hypocritical. I don't keep secrets, but you still do."

"There could be a conflict of interest. Jules, this is a major f..kup by the 'Z's. I could have done a better job and saved a lot of trauma. Even that painful Charmaine could have done a better job."

"Melissa, without these so-called f..kups, we would never have met. It's through the f..kups that brought you, Victor, Magnus, Sam, Annabelle, Mogan, Janette and Charmaine into our lives, and the kids seem to be over-enjoying them-selves, but I still want an explanation of how you are involved."

The clock radio comes on and is playing another chaotic 'Nick Cave' song called 'The Mercy Seat'. I listen to it, and so does Melissa as we lie hugging, and our minds wander but seem to relate to the song. It's a long song, and we reflect. The mellowing effect of the rum must have kicked in.

"Play it again, Jules." I do; two more times as we stare at the ceiling but then get up and dance for the final play. We're mesmerised, away from the computers, naked, embraced and rotating to the music as if in a trance and profusely sweating. Melissa didn't want the air conditioning turned on due to that global warming stuff she is into.

"Shall we get out, I mean move somewhere to a coastal town?" Melissa questions. "I mean permanently, you don't rejoin or have anything to do with the i5s, and I'll quit my consultancy work for i5s. They are chaos, just as that song is. It made me think."

"Melissa, apart from your newly discovered thinking, we still have a job to finish at the library and some extra archiving. There's a failed local newspaper that has to be scanned and archived to a PDF format. I promised Ms Valda we'd finish the job. I'd like to get out, but we got to consider the kids; our nest egg won't last forever. We can continue the positions but stay low key, just occasional desk jobs, filing stuff as we do in the library, but we can also listen and spy on Ai5 and finally find out what's really going on."

She replies after a hiccup and mumbles. "Jules, I just want to get out, after I tell them what I think about their cyber-security. And did you know that the inno-cent library is the hub of Ai5, not that St Kilda Street office? You must have picked that up unless you're totally thumb."

I do not correct her pronunciation, but I'm intrigued about how much she knows. Go with the flow, my inner voice says.

"You're right, Melissa. I'll find out how we can get out."

We eventually succeed in doing a high-five. There were a few misses, but the palms finally collided. Melissa plonks herself back on the bed, her hand is on her forehead again, and soon she fades into dreamland.

Next day I make the sandwiches for the kids. They'll be going back to school today, I hope. I escort them to school after ringing Ms Valda that we may be late for work.

"Melissa, let's go for a long walk and maybe jump into the bay for a bit of a swim. Exercise helps a bit when life is traumatic."

"Jules, we could do some of what you call bedroom gymnastics? iI counts as exercise."

"For me, it may be because a guy does all the hard work. No, Melissa, maybe later; put on your leotard costume, and we're going to do a fast walk along the bay track."

I'm checking that step counter on that hand watch thing I bought. "Melissa, we only got 2583 steps to go before we make that magical 10,000, and we're doing 6km per hour."

Melissa keeps marching at a furious pace as if on a mission. I struggle to keep up as she has longer legs. We get close to home, and Melissa yells out, "Race you to that buoy that is floating 100 metres out in the bay."

"Melissa, we have no bathers or towels."

"Jules, we do not need towels or bathers; let us be what you call feral, like your crocodile species."

There is definitely something wrong with Melissa's cognitive perceptions, which appear unlike her usual logical self. She seems erratic, still I follow.

We jump off the walking track onto the sand. Melissa unties her shoelaces and sprints towards the water. I'm struggling to untie my runners. Bugger it. I follow her and jump into the bay with the runner shoes still on. A hundred metres offshore, we wack our hands on the floating buoy at the same time.

"Jules, would you like to do some copulation as we float and hold on to this buoy?"

"Melissa, do you always have to be so unromantic?" I move close to her; we're behind the floating buoy and not visible from the beach. I hope there are none of those drone planes flying overhead with cameras. Afterwards, we pull up our costumes and swim back to shore. I make a random comment. "Melissa, could you refrain from insulting me so much? I'm actually quite sensitive, and at times your comments and actions do hurt."

"I'll try Jules, though you know at your stay on the yacht Victor gave you all the attention, those late nights talking. I resented you, but I am reprogramming my mind."

We dog paddle, waving our legs to stay afloat and then she grabs me and gives me a tongue kiss. I wrap my arm around her, but that's not a great idea when you're trying to stay afloat. We then do a sprinting swim to the shore. I got there first though I think she let me. We walk back home, wet, covered in sand, and not looking too good. Melissa's permed hair is lying flat on her head and shoulders. We probably look like we're back after being abducted by aliens, and that step-counter wristband is dead; not waterproof, but I think we made the equivalent of 10k steps jiggling in the water.

Mogan and Janette return. Mogan gives me a hug. "Janette's mother has recovered."

Melissa and I give them both a hug.

"Jules and Melissa, you're covered in sand and smell of seaweed," Mogan whispers.

Melissa and I retreat to the bathroom whilst Mogan vacuums the floors to get rid of the deposited sand. They do the cooking and send the kids to bed after dinner. They have definitely taken over the parenting, which Melissa and I have no problem with at the moment as we stare at computer screens. We're too preoccupied with other problems, and on reflection, we never got our priorities right anyway. We just keep repeating the same pattern. We haven't grown like Mogan has, but that's a topic to discuss another day.

I'm lying on the bed next to Melissa. I think about coincidences again, and I'm talking to myself, bouncing ideas. Someone must plan them. There were too many coincidences. There could never be that many in real life. It defies probability though possibly, we all just seem to gravitate to people that have a story that suits our own needs and may offer an explanation for our own condition. We get connected, but what if we connect to the wrong people? I have no answers. What is 'wrong' anyway? If I hadn't looked behind the fridge, I'd still be in limbo land, sharing my townhouse with Smithy. To think it all started with moving the fridge to retrieve some fallen car keys and finding a piece of paper with a phone number written in a faded plant ink substance. Sometimes, something simple starts a whole chain of unpredictable events. I think it's called Chaos Theory – you may have heard the analogy of a butterfly that flaps its wings somewhere in South America. Just that little ripple effect changes the weather patterns and causes major cyclones hundreds of kilometres away.

Anyway, enough philosophising for tonight, but then I hear a noise and sneak out of the bedroom to investigate. Lizzy must have got up through the night and opened the rat cage but not closed it, but on second thought, it's more likely Chloe has learnt to open it. The rat is downstairs and looks at me quizzically. I stop talking to myself and look at the rat. We stare at each other before it scuttles away. I start the self-talk again but can see that little white head peeking outside the door. It distracts me, and that's kind of good and reminds me of one of my grandma's stories. She lived in Paris in the 1930s, and at that time, apparently, all fashionable ladies carried a white female rat in their shoulder strap handbag. The rats would peer out and were great conversation starters.

The next memory that comes flooding back is not so pleasant. Research assistant at a university in Melbourne, my first real job in the mid-70s. I was supposed to be involved in research into diabetes, and I had to regularly kill a white laboratory rat to dissect out a tiny little muscle in the bottom half of the rat's back legs called the soleus muscle. A whole rat would die for some research that could be considered as highly spurious and not likely to have any relevance to humans, and it never did. Sure, at MM Pharmaceutical, we used animals for drug testing, but the animals were treated with dignity, and killing was minimised by refrigerating unused parts for other researchers to use. I look at Chloe and tell her that she'll never end up in a laboratory. The rat appreciatively nods its head.

A few hours later, Melissa gets up and, after many glasses of water, wanders back into the bedroom, almost squashing the newly acquired inquisitive pet, which scuttles off. I'm sure the rat is quivering back in its cage. You don't mess with Melissa, and the rat has picked up on that. Melissa starts raving again. She must have forgotten she told me most of the stuff before.

"Jules, we can get out, and I won't work anymore for i5s or any of their affiliates. We don't have to work after the archives job is finished. We have the finances; that reward from disposing of Greuger."

"Melissa, what would we do? We'd be bored out of our heads, and by the way, Greuger escaped death again, so we won't get the reward."

"We could do a course like Mogan is doing. I would like to do Fine Arts. I would oil paint in the garage, so the turpentine fumes do not get into the house and cause you to hallucinate. What would you like to do?"

I ponder. "We could do Fine Arts together. I'd be your model, and you could be mine. You know, all that drawing and painting of nudes that you do in Fine Arts courses."

She has a smile on her face and slaps my face, only gently. "We could start practising now. I got some butcher paper and a few lead pencils."

Melissa gives a gentle wack on my face again. "You still have to explain 'pi', 'e' and the Fibonacci series. Maybe you could also talk about the Plank's constant as well."

She's showing off her academia, and I gently wack her back on the face, a behaviour I've learnt from her, and we both laugh. We kiss and do other things before our presentation.

I do my best; Mogan and Janette also listen in as I draw diagrams on the butcher's paper and give the presentation to the kids. Melissa intercedes and corrects me occasionally.

"Jules, great stuff about 'pi' and 'e'. I never attended much school, but I may get into this Maths stuff. It's cool," Mogan comments.

"Yeh, it's cool, Mogan. Take the butcher paper and use it when you have to teach some Maths."

We all retreat to our rooms. I go back to Melissa and wrap my arm around her. She asks, "Why did you not tell them about Plank's constant?"

"I don't even know what that is."

"Jules, it's the dimension of the smallest thing that can exist in the universe, like the size of your penis."

I don't take it as an insult. She is definitely developing a devilish sense of humour. I grab and kiss her, and we roll around the bed.

"Melissa, I'm average size downstairs. I got a tape measure in the garage. We can Google what is the average size."

"Stop being so serious, Jules. I like you more than just for the size of your appendage."

Eventually, we get back to the initial conversation. "Well, let us do it, Jules. Let's get out. The new year is starting, and we have not got much time to enrol into that Fine Arts course."

Lizzy comes down and enters our room, furiously looking at me. "I thought you'd get me another iPhone as a present, not a rat; you're like such a cheapskate."

Peter joins Lizzy, "I'll look after Chloe, the rat if Lizzy doesn't want to."

Melissa and I nod our heads in surprise. We definitely have to put a lock on our bedroom door. A week passes, and the kids have reluctantly learnt how to prepare a dinner meal. I stop Mogan and Janette from giving them advice and a hand. The kids' first effort wasn't a great success, but at least we didn't vomit or get food poisoning; they will learn.

I grab Mogan. "We purchased the two townhouses on the other side of the driveway, plus you'll get half of the reward that we may still get for Greuger's disposal even though he may have miraculously escaped. Also, Magnus left Fabian a lot of money, and we're trying to buy this block of townhouses. If we succeed, we won't have to worry about nosey neighbours. You and Janette can move into one of them. They are furnished. You just have to pay the bills like Body Corporate fees, Council rates, water, gas and electricity."

"Jules, I may look like I've lived in a swag most of my life, and I was happy with that, but I have got quite a stash of money saved up from my military service and a pension and yes, I can pay rent as well. But we would like to buy one of these townhouses from you if you want to sell, we have the money. By the way, Janette is pregnant."

I look up in astonishment and hug Mogan. "Congratulations."

"Jules, if it is a boy, we first thought of naming him 'Jules', but on second thought, anything but 'Jules'."

I give Mogan another hug. He's also developing a sense of humour just like Melissa is, and he's so different from the Mogan that lay hunched up on his bedroom floor when he first moved in with us. He, like Smithy, has seemed to overcome his PTSD. I think I have as well because of the support I've had from the people I met. It's like we all support each other, though Annabelle could be a pain at times.

Nearly nine months pass without any major incident that doesn't involve the usual painful, winging teenager things and coping with that inquisitive white rat, Chloe, who always finds a way to break out from incarceration. She sits on my lap as I type and occasionally jumps on the computer keyboard and presses keys. I watch in wonderment; is she trying to communicate? The rat's spelling is not that good, but it's improving. I hope this rat's story isn't as good as mine and that her story doesn't get published before mine.

We all, the gang, still have dinner together several times a week. We rotate destinations. Janette and Mogan are definitely the best cooks, plus they live across the driveway, which is a bonus point when you have to stumble home. Annabelle can't cook more than a sausage roll in the microwave oven, but Sam can sure make a feast. Charmaine still stays distant. I ring almost every day but mostly just get a voicemail.

The extra archiving job at the library had finished many months ago. Melissa and I got accepted into the Fine Arts course as very, very mature-aged students and doing well, but we're sort of restless and nag each other a lot. We're bored. We're picky about little things. During classes, we fling water-based paints at each other in frustration. Luckily, we're not into oil-based paints, as that would be much harder to clean off your face. The kids notice that and sometimes have worried looks on their faces. Apart from that, they have all excelled at school, and we attend the school ceremonies and awards night. They did well, and the awards night was always followed by a celebration at the Elsternwick hotel, where we got plenty of free soft drinks for the kids and beers for the adults, compliments of Martin. The other townhouse we purchased, with most of the money Magnus left Fabian, lays vacant as Sam's and Annabelle's long-term lease on their previous rental hasn't yet expired. I hope they will move in when it does.

Mogan knocks on the door. "It's a girl. I was there at the birth. Janette is still in hospital. She is sedated." He has tears streaming down his face. "We'll name her Juliet."

"I'm flattered, Mogan, but you needn't have named her after me."

"Jules, Janette and I are studying Shakespeare, and we particularly like 'Romeo and Juliet'."

"Mogan, come inside." The kids come rushing down the stairs and give him a hug. Mogan is convulsing in joy with tears streaming down his face. I'm sure he will make the good father that he wished he had himself. Melissa comes over with a glass of rum in her hand and hands it to Mogan, who skols it down.

"I can't stay long; got to get back to Janette to be there when she awakes. I've called a taxi."

There is another knock on the door, no doorbell ring. Normally I would have grabbed the chilli spray before opening the door, but I'm becoming a little bit lax. It's Charmaine, and she's struggling to hold the three bottles of champagne. I let her in. Melissa has a cautious expression on her face.

"Let's celebrate, but I can't stay long. What's that white creature sitting on your shoulder? If you're doing some pirate act, it won't hold," Charmaine cheekingly comments.,

I lift up my arm and stroke the white rat on the head, which then climbs up my arm and hops onto my head. Both Melissa and Charmaine give me uncomfortable looks.

"What's the reason for all this mirth," I enquire.

"Guys, after that successful capture, oops, the apparent death of Greuger Shmidt, I got promoted. Oh, and I did say in my acceptance speech that you and your friends risked their lives to make it happen. You've all been nominated for the Queen's Bravery Awards, and from what I heard on the grapevine, your nominations were successful, but Jules, can you purchase some acceptable clothing and get a haircut; the presentation ceremony is quite formal, and you can't come with a rat sitting on your head."

Charmaine goes over to Melissa. I can barely hear the conversation but just a few sentences.

"Has Jules told you about my past?"

"No," Melissa replies; she lied.

"Ask him. Maybe we can all work together. Melissa, once you're in, it's hard to get out; you're monitored for the rest of your life." She gives Melissa a peck on the cheek.

"You've got a major cyber-security leak, and I can still access your servers which I shouldn't be able to do as a consultant," Melissa replies rather loudly.

"I'll report that to my superiors after I get more details from you. I'll ring tomorrow," Charmaine says with a sort of smile and a sense of satisfaction. She is definitely climbing the corporate ladder. I suspect she is highly grateful for that ammunition. The rat leaps across to Charmaine's arm. She gently brushes it away. "Ratty, I got far bigger rats to deal with than you." She throws it a piece of cheese that's lying on the kitchen table. The rat scuttles off and grabs it. It stands on its two hind feet and nods its head as if to say thanks.

Charmaine leaves after much merriment and beverages. The talking was mostly disguised 'small talk' and joking, but a few subtle hints were given by Charmaine. Unfortunately, no one noticed that the kids were sitting on the stairs and listening. After the rum and champagne, everyone retires to their homes or bedrooms after Charmaine leaves. Lizzy, Peter, and Fabian come marching into our bedroom.

"Are you spies?" They enquire in sync.

"You asked that before. No, of cause not, well a little bit, but can we talk about it tomorrow? We're tired and need some sleep," Melissa replies.

"Awesome," yells Peter. "It's like some TV movie." Fabian and Lizzy nod their heads. Their trauma seems to have disappeared and is replaced by excitement and awe.

"Dad, are you and Charmaine related? I noticed some common physical features but especially the way you both speak."

"OK, you all want to know? I think she's my brother, sorry, meant sister. It's highly likely we have a lot of similar DNA."

"Why don't you get those DNA swab packs again like you insisted that Magnus and I had to take?"

"Fabian, you're being a pain, but OK, I will, but it's very highly likely that you have an aunty, so just be grateful."

The kids all look at each other. Lizzy announces, "We kind of like Charmaine from what we saw and heard on the stairwell. She's sort of like, funny, much more funny than you or mum."

I whisper into Melissa's ear, "Remember what you told me about teenagers being a pain in the butt."

Melissa maintains her composure as I lecture. "Lizzy, Fabian and Peter, can you be the caretakers of Chloe? We are only caretakers of animals. We don't own them; we just look after them till they die of old age."

Lizzy comes over to me and gives an unexpected hug, and whispers, "We will look after you when you are very old and ready to die."

Melissa whispers in my ear, "Well said, Jules, kids, the drama is over. Now go to bed - it is school tomorrow. There's nothing more to harm us unless the pet rat has got some infectious disease which I don't think she could because she was purchased from a reputable pet shop." Melissa lied. It was Greuger's rat, but it's unlikely we can all be murdered by a little white rat. The kids march upstairs, taking the rat with them. Melissa and I could hear them talking and laughing. I don't think they slept much that night. Melissa turns towards me. "What do you really know about Charmaine, Jules?"

"You asked me that before, many times. She was my transgender brother who got the medical operations to transition into a female, and our mother is head of an outsourced intelligence agency. You know that too. You do work for them as well. I know that, Melissa. No more lies."

She puts her hand on my face, "Jules, there were never any lies, just not full disclosure, and you know what that means."

"You could use that against Charmaine if you should ever go back."

"I'm not like that that Jules. I was always ethical in everything I did, and I think you were too. I did my research."

It's another late night, and I tell Melissa the story again. It takes over 2 hours.

"Poor kid, I mean woman or whatever she is now. I never knew Jules. Maybe we should return."

"That's another backflip; before you said you wanted us both out. Let's think about it when we're more sober."

I don't think we slept much that night. Both lying awake and looking at the ceiling as thoughts churn through our minds. After any trauma, you sort of get used to looking at the ceiling, which is now decorated as a week or so earlier, I got the ladder and painted a mural on the ceiling. Melissa's comment was that I should give up the Fine Arts course. Still, personally, I'm not discouraged. The ceiling is not plain white as before. There are colourful swirls, and I'm annoyed that Melissa doesn't appreciate my artwork. We turn away and finally fall asleep. I dream of being a Michelangelo and making a financial living from decorating ceilings in high-profile financial institutions and waving as the patron enters. That was just before I woke up and noticed Melissa rubbing her eyes.

"Melissa, what was your last dream? You were in REM sleep, and your eyelids were flickering?"

"Jules, I think the dream was about living on a tropical island, far away from here. It was an escapist dream."

I put my arm around her and give her a kiss. We're up at 8 am. The kids are trying to prepare sandwiches. The white rat has been accepted into the family and eagerly watches for any leftovers and scraps.

Melissa whispers, "Let them make mistakes, that's how they learn. Jules, I thought about it. We would go mad if we just live this domestic lifestyle, even if we did finish our Fine Arts courses. Let's accept the i5's offers. We'll never make it in

Fine Arts. There's no travel involved in i5, so we can still look after the kids, and a lot of the work can be done from home. I'm sure we could both work part-time on a consultancy basis."

She's flipping. It's a backflip again.

"Melissa, what's going on in your mind? Before you said you wanted to get out of i5, besides do you think you could work with Charmaine if she were your boss?"

"Jules, I never knew her story. If I had, I would have been more compassionate. I am not a mean bitch."

The doorbell rings again. I jump up and cautiously open it. It's Victor, and he's grown his hair back. Beside him is another equally tall, handsome male. I let them in.

The kids must have heard the doorbell and our conversation at the door. They come rushing down. Lizzy and Peter hug their dad. Fabian stays reserved in the background so do Melissa and me; we just watch. Watching is rule 411, 'Be observant' and do not play with mobile devices'.

"This is Hugo, my partner," Victor announces.

Victor goes over to Melissa and gives her a hug, as does Hugo. It's initially a very uncomfortable situation for Melissa and me while Fabian continues to stand in the background. Victor grabs his kids and spins them around.

"I always loved you guys, but now you have a new dad, but I will still always be close by."

"He'll never be like you," yells Peter.

"Not in every way, but give him a chance."

Victor and Hugo ordered copious amounts of food that is soon delivered along with a few bottles of Vodka. We all partake in a lively conversation. Victor looks at Melissa. "I'm sorry for the deceit; I wish the best for you and the kids."

Melissa stares Victor in the eye. "We are having a great time apart from a few assassination attempts on us. Where are you staying?"

"We've booked five nights at the Richmond Hilton."

"Cancel your booking. We have an empty, fully furnished townhouse across the driveway. You can stay there."

"Are you sure, Melissa and Jules?"

We're sure." Melissa and I reply in unison.

"Magnus still asks about you. Are you coming back to your job?"

"Maybe, but part-time."

Victor gives me another hug. I hand him the keys and walk over with him and Hugo to townhouse 6. The key works. "We'll see you tomorrow."

The day passes without any incident though Melissa challenges me to another swim. She cheated. She offered to undo my shoelaces but did the opposite. She tied them into knots together so that I could barely move my feet. Eventually, I end up at the buoy after almost drowning and looking severely distressed. Melissa is laughing. Another pair of runners discarded. We swim back to shore without talking.

"Jules, I would have saved you if you were seriously in trouble. It was what you call a joke."

"Melissa, that was not funny, and I hope you redefine your definition of a joke. You've overstepped the boundary, and I could have drowned. Do you want me dead? Just use the kitchen knife if you do."

She comes over and grabs my head. "I'm sorry; I will never tie your shoelaces again."

"Melissa, you may be more f..ked than me, but please don't try to kill me again."

"Jules, as I said before, I just thought it was a joke. I am like you, high on the Autism spectrum. Sometimes we get things wrong when we try to show affection."

I resist saying that Melissa may be much higher than me on the Autism scale, but overall, we seem to be learning and adjusting to each other's ways of thinking. Then the kids come back from school excited. "Where's dad?" Lizzy asks.

"He's in townhouse six and probably very tired after the long plane journey. You'll all see him tomorrow."

Everyone is in bed, and I look at Melissa but turn away. She wraps her arm around me, and we drift into our dreams, luckily no dreams involving swimming. Next day, Victor and Hugo are back. "We have ordered food to be delivered for lunch, a lot of it, so you'll have plenty left over for dinner," Victor announces.

The next five days are very hot in Melbourne, and we spend most of them at Elwood beach after the kids get back from school. Peter insists we take the rat cage with us; Chloe can swim. The rat is a sensation amongst all the other kids at the beach. I can hear kids yelling to their parents, 'I want one of those!' I'm sure Elwood will be a rat-infested suburb in the next few months.

Fabian eventually comes over to Victor. "You look a lot like my real, real father." Victor grabs Fabian and looks intensely into his eyes. "I'm not your father, neither is my brother Magnus anymore. Jules is now your real father; remember that. Now go and have fun but don't let the sea bugs bite."

I see the look on Fabian's face. He must have heard that phrase before. It's 8 pm, still hot and twilight. We're still at the beach, and the kids are in the water, as is Chloe the rat. I didn't know rats could swim, but this rat is making the best of her expected 3.5-year lifespan and frolicking in the attention. She would eventually end up getting the peptide injection and live ten times as long and continue to amaze us.

I look out at the sea and the kids. Melissa is holding my hand. What incestuous relationships; my previous boss Magnus is the father of my son. I'm now married to his twin brother's wife, Melissa. My brother, who is now my sister, is climbing up the i5 ladder, the organization my mother is head of. My defacto son is probably screwing Melissa's daughter Lizzy. It's a lot to get your head around, but back at the beach, little Peter is surrounded by girls from his primary school who find him adorable and vie for his attention. He seems happy to be the star attraction. "Love the rat. What's its name?" One of them asks.

"It's Chloe," Peter timidly replies.

"Jules!" I turn around. It's Mogan and Janette with a pram. I rush over and give them both a hug.

"Little Juliet, can I touch her?"

"No, you may have germs, but you can wave and smile at her."

I do that. She looks at me intensely. Mogan continues, "The christening is in four weeks time, and I've nominated you as the godfather. Not like in the criminal movie of the same name, just a regular godfather. Do you accept?"

"I'd be honoured." I tense the chest muscles, exude any air in my lungs and give them another big hug. They reciprocate. No one is harmed by the hugging, and they continue on their stroll. Before I have a chance to return to the others, there's Sam strolling along the walkway, hand-in-hand with a very pretty islander brown-haired woman.

"Jules, what are you doing here?"

"Just saying hello to Mogan, Janette and their baby."

Sam dashes down the path. I can see him hugging Mogan and Janette. He comes back, sweating and puffing, "This is Ester, a work colleague."

Sam and Ester join us on the beach and go frolicking in the water with the kids and the rat. We get home at about 10 pm, just after the Melbourne summer twilight has finished. Luckily there's plenty of left-over food.

Things are sort of back to normal the next day. The kids go to school, and the rat is in her cage. Melissa and I attend a few lectures and occasionally cross paths with Mogan, Janette and Juliet in the pram at the Uni, and the five-day party continued after we got back. We're back at Elwood beach, swimming and watching the late red summer sunsets. Victor hasn't lost his extravagance, and the kids didn't have to cook. The rat, Chloe, whose cage is always with us, gets all the leftovers, but she does a lot of swimming, so is probably on a calorific balance and maintaining her fitness. My mind strays; if there was a Rat Olympic Games, I'm sure Chloe would win every swimming event, but a gold medal wouldn't mean much to a rat. It would have to be something yummy.

It's day six, and Victor and Hugo have departed after much hugging from all of us. I'm lying next to Melissa. "Do you miss Victor?"

"Sort of, but he was never a great partner. The copious gifts didn't make up for that." She rolls over. "Put the latch on the door."

"Melissa, there's also a lot of groaning and moaning coming from Fabian's study room."

"Would you prefer they go to a park or the beach? They're safe here. It's what all teenagers do. Now, did you give Fabian some condoms that weren't ten years after their expiry date? Jules, there's no DNA linking the two together. If any of you authorities want a scientific battle…."

"Stop, Melissa. I'll handle that. Trust me for once."

"And there is DNA linking them. They are related though far more distantly, unlike Charmaine and I may be."

"Jules, everyone is related. We are all the descendants of 2000 or so Homo sapiens and Neanderthals that survived the last ice age. The two species interbred, and between 2 and 5% of our active genes are Neanderthal in origin. We are all their descendants, and it may be why we have our genetic faults, but we survive as a species."

For a moment, I wonder If Melissa has smoked some illicit substance or indulged in those blue-stemmed mushrooms that I picked from the garden. She gives me a kiss. "You are definitely more than 50% Neanderthal, and that is a compliment. The Neanderthals got wiped out because their immune systems weren't prepared for a then-currently circulating virus, and they didn't have vaccines. Now, do you want to do some cardiovascular exercise?"

A memory flashed back. It is sort of funny. The first time I purchased condoms when at Uni, a very young version of me. It took ten minutes to master up the courage. "They're for my pet dog, and we don't need any more puppies. Do they come in all sizes?"

"I know," the female pharmacist assistant confidently replies like she'd heard countless similar stories, "but that's the best one I've heard of yet." She hands me a packet, "Fits all sizes, any animal, mouse to elephant," she says with a smile. My mind returns. "I bought some at the supermarket and gave them to Fabian."

Well, if there was a competition, Melissa's and my groaning would break all records. We lay back then the words, initially shocking. "Jules, I think I may be pregnant. I thought I was post-menopausal, but my menstruation temporally ceased because of all the stress, and I know I was behaving strangely and had strange thoughts that jumped from place to place and may not have made much sense, even to me, so I bought a pregnancy kit. I think you can guess the result of the test."

I look up at the ceiling mural. It takes 30 seconds for me to reply. There was a lot of mental processing to do. "Melissa, you're in your mid 40's, and I'm even older. We may not have the energy to look after a new arrival."

"Jules, we will cope, and maybe our junior can visit us when we are in an aged-care centre."

I turn towards her and give her a hug. I can feel the tears flowing down my face. She falls back asleep. The rat has escaped again and is looking at us. I have no energy left to shoo it away. The rat falls asleep between Melissa and me.

The alarm radio clock goes off. It's playing the same old song from 1967. 'Al Martino – Mary in the Morning.' I look at the sleeping Melissa and totally relate to the song. I give the sleepy Melissa the biggest kiss and then take Chloe the rat back to the cage, which is sort of useless because the rat will break out in less than 5 minutes. The rat is a Houdini, an escape artist.

Melissa wakes up. "Can you play that song again?" I jump onto the computer and connect to YouTube. "Jules, there are three kids to look after at the moment and possibly another on the way. Can you survive? Your record is not that great. Can you change a poopy nappy?"

"I'll do my best. I'm sure there are videos on YouTube on how to do that."

"You better," she says with a grin.

The doorbell rings. I jump, covered in a towel. It's Charmaine.

"We need you back full-time for a few weeks. You can work mostly from home. "

"Why the hurry?"

"Victor and Hugo have been arrested apparently on some special operation in a South American country. We, well the people I work for, owe Magnus a favour, and we don't have that many permanent resources at the moment. Also, all your personal files have been put back in your garage. My forensic inspectors kept falling asleep reading them."

"Charmaine, what about the USB stick?"

"We seized the laptop your son had after he decrypted the stick. We also got what we believe was the last copy of that USB stick during your aeroplane ride, and it wasn't aeroplane jelly. The decrypted contents of the USB stick don't pose any threat to our relations with foreign governments and agencies anymore."

"What do you mean?"

"Your ex-wifey, Marg, must have been abusing substances before her accident. There were no PDFs of incriminating documents, just JPG photos of birthday cakes and the Mosa family ventures in grasshopper farming. It was as boring as looking at Facebook posts."

My mind wonders. Fabian must have deleted the other documents and replaced them with birthday cakes. He's smart enough to use software that can remove all traces of deleted documents.

"Jules, your meeting place was monitored. My people were inconspicuously around at that shooting incident when that little guy, Henry, got shot. Victor, that gorgeous hunk, panicked. It was us who cleaned up, not his contacts."

"Charmaine, you could have stopped all that carnage; you're despicable."

"No, Jules, we couldn't. That Paolo guy behaved unpredictably. We expected some negotiation."

"So, because of your inaction, Henry got shot in the forehead. Your risk analysis needs a lot of improving."

"Jules, yes, it was a sad misjudgement. Henry was patched up, the forehead that is, and he was to appear to have died from a coronary on the way to your meeting place. Our doctors certified his death. Jules, he didn't have much time left anyway. He had a cocktail of blood thinners and anti-cholesterol drugs in his blood, just to mention a few. Twenty heart-related medications were in his blood, so he was a walking time bomb. He didn't have much time left, so don't feel too guilty. You just sped up his escalation to heaven," she smiles.

I crouch down. "Why were you involved and Ai5 involved in that incident in the first place? It wasn't a national security issue."

"It was Doris's idea, as was involving Victor, who she knew about through her dealings with Magnus. Almost everything that could have gone wrong did go wrong. It was just a very bad day for everyone, but I do believe Doris was concerned about your safety, and I was demoted for my so-called failure in case I terminated you."

She comes over and holds my head. "Jules, the world doesn't operate on logic. That's because many people don't. They don't all think the same way you or I do. It would be a simple world if they did but then again, I wouldn't have a job, neither would you or the police."

"You still could have stopped it!"

"Jules, we're getting into philosophy now."

I pause and think of Victor and Hugo. "Charmaine, I don't think we know anything about Latin American countries. I have the deepest sympathies for Victor and Hugo, but I don't see how we can help."

"Jules, we spent close to a billion dollars on a Big Data and artificial intelligence processing system from a major IT firm. It's still not working. We got to do it manually. You'll have full access, no USB drives allowed, but try to find any shit you can on that government and their connection to drug and people trafficking. We provide them with millions of dollars of misused humanitarian aid. We have to have leverage to get Victor and Hugo out."

Melissa overhears the conversation. "We can do it".

"You'll be working with other staff members. Though we secure video conferencing, you'll have to come into the office occasionally, into the glass mirrored door chambers at the St Kilda library. |I know you have kids to look after, so I can arrange carers. Here are the security passes and the keycode devices; it flashes a number that you have to login with, apart from your password. It's called two-factor authentication. I'm sure you can learn how to use it," Charmaine says.

Charmaine has a worried look upon her face. I've never seen that look before as she guides us through the process of getting secure access to the Ai5 and MM databases. Well, at least what she believes is secure.

"We're in!"

"I got in without that 2-factor authentication security. Your system is still totally insecure. I got in without the keycode that your system is supposed to SMS me," Melissa exclaims. We'll discuss that later. Search all the Twitter blogs first. Here's a list of the latest code words they use to disguise their activities."

"Charmaine, one other thing, nothing we do must compromise SnowPea, else I'm out; totally out."

"It won't. We need them. We have a symbiotic relationship."

"Sounds more like parasitic."

"Jules, 'Be Kind'," Charmaine whispers as leaving with a huge smile but not before a high-five with Melissa and me.

"Melissa, I still haven't got my full memory back of the last ten or more years ago. There are still gaps. Did I kill anyone?"

"Not directly according to our Intelligence, but then I was working in the USA. You'll have to ask Charmaine. Now get going. I'll start checking the tweeter feeds. You Google and check out how to clean baby poop."

I've practised changing nappies on one of Lizzy's dolls, and I think I'm now an expert. Two weeks later, after manually scanning tweeter feeds using Charmaine's checklist Melissa yells out. "I found something. A link; call Charmaine." She intensely looks at the computer screen, wearing her reading glasses. She forwards the information to Charmaine's secure email account. I read Charmaine's email reply. 'I'm contacting the Australian Consulate and passing the info. I'm sure that government wouldn't want it to be made public as they provide monetary aid to that country'.

Another two weeks pass, and Victor and Hugo are finally released. They arrive back in Melbourne and find their way to the Elwood townhouse. They stumble in. They don't look great with bandages across their faces.

Melissa calls out, "Call a doctor and get him to bring broad-spectrum antibiotics."

The kids are horrified when they come back from school. All five of us manage to guide Victor and Hugo to our bedroom bed.

A knock on the door; I'm too spaced out to grab the knife and the chilli spray. It's Charmaine, followed by two guys who seem to have medical gear with them. Pulses are taken, as are blood samples, and a bit of stitching is done on Victor and Hugo's wounds plus massive doses of antibiotics are given.

"They'll probably be right; it seems like only superficial wounds but continue to give them these antibiotics. We'll get their blood analysed and let you know the results in two days."

I check on the bedroom where Victor and Hugo seem asleep with arms wrapped around each other, but before Charmaine and the white coats leave, Charmaine utters. "It's good for everyone they made it to your place. A lot less explaining to do to the 'higher ups', and you've done a good job. We may need you and Melissa again soon."

Melissa does a brief check on the kids. The rat watches.

"You lied, Charmaine. It's all a game to you," I whisper.

"Jules, ask your new wife what you actually did before you got that job at the archives library. You weren't exactly a James Bond, but you got some of the jobs done," she whispers back.

"Did I kill anyone?"

"Not directly, Jules, but indirectly you did. I told you that before."

Charmaine gives her trademark cheeky wink as she departs.

"Melissa, we could go back to our other still vacant townhouse while Victor and his companion use our bed. It's got beds."

"No, Jules, we can't leave the kids alone, and the extent of Victor's and Hugo's injuries haven't yet been fully determined, so we have to stay here. I do not mind the lounge room floor as long as you can find those self-inflating mattresses and sleeping bags.

The kids are asleep. I reach over to Melissa whilst in the sleeping bag.

"Do you want to know what happened in the years you can't fully remember?" She asks.

"I know I nearly drowned myself. Read it in the archives, and at first thought, I'd preferred not to know, but now I do."

"I'll tell you in time, but you were not a bad person if that is any consolation, you were given slightly inaccurate coordinates, and the outcome is not your fault."

I roll over to Melissa and give her a kiss. She gives another rare smile. The laptop is still playing, 'Learning to Fly', a Tom Petty song. I turn off the laptop PC, and we drift into sleep.

Next morning, I go to the garage and was going to do a bit of cycling. The bicycle tires are flat, but I have a pump in one of the cardboard boxes. Eventually, I find it but also something else. Old photos wrapped in a black wrapper. It's something Charmaine and her boys missed when they took all my diaries and files away. They have a date fifteen years ago. In many of them, there's this nerdy-looking guy with a big nose and flaring ears cuddling up to Marg by the beach.

Oh, f… it's me. I was surgically made to look like Jason - a nose, ear job and some work around the eyes. How many operations did that take, and why wasn't I aware of what was happening? I look in the mirror hanging on the garage side entry. I hold the photo in front of me and compare the two images. The thought crosses my mind that at least no expenses were spared, and the current face is definitely an improvement, but I was made to look like Jason. We weren't doppelgangers. I leave the garage and go upstairs to the bedroom, where Melissa has started typing on her PC.

"Look at these photos, Melissa. That's what I used to look like."

"So, you had some successful reconstructive cosmetic surgery. A lot of guys do that these days."

"Melissa, I don't recall authorizing it, and besides, it made me look like that Jason guy. He wanted me to publicly be on stage and get the TV press to think he was dead."

She leaves the keyboard, comes over and holds my head.

"Calm down, Jules, you are hyperventilating and making no sense, and I know nothing about this. I was in the USA at the time."

She looks at me and the photos again and gives another rare smile. "You once looked like that Bill Yates computer guy. Well, they did a good job anyway, you look much better now, and I don't know what Marg saw in you before the transformation. She must have liked you for your brain. Now call Charmaine if you like and ask her. I got some work to finish."

Melissa's words resonate. How much do they really know about each other and what's going on? Plus, I'm really pissed off by her seeming insult to my previous appearance? No, on second thought, I got free plastic surgery, and the outcome is definitely an improvement after I inspect the before photos.

Chapter twentyfour

Charmaine was waiting outside the townhouse entrance as I almost bumped into her when stepping out. We walk to the dog park.

"How's Smithy doing at his new job in the Metropolitan Fire Brigade?"

"He's nearly finished the training and loves putting out fires. We have that in common."

"I haven't got much time, show me those photos."

She looks at the photos and then back at me; "Definitely a cosmetic enhancement."

"I never asked for a cosmetic enhancement. I can't even remember getting one."

"Jules, we only have a hypothesis and not much evidence; you want to hear it?"

"I need to understand my past."

"OK, close your eyes and take a few deep breaths."

"Jason's real name was Justin Thornborough the fourth. He was one of the people I had to observe when at university. He was doing the same Psychology degree as me, and his nickname was Pro, maybe because he was a mature age student and at least ten years older than any of us other students. He preached on the student podium but was also a disturbed radical who switched alliances from extremely left-wing to extreme right-wing groups. He was a wildcard and definitely not a bright spark, but he had money, lots of money, after his parents passed away. Jules, do you want me to continue because if I do, it will hurt? We can call it quits, and that's my suggestion."

"Yes, do continue, think I've been through the worst."

"Jules, it's about Marg. I told you this before she was a very clever chicky."

"Marg is a fading memory. I might have married you, my Blue Monkey until I found out you were my brother."

She lets out a laugh, comes over and gives me a hug. "Jules, it would have been a challenge; your codename was Limp Lizard, maybe for a reason." She laughs again. "I'm joking; it was Silver Beetle, after that old VW car you always drove and still do."

"I wasn't too upset. Limp Lizard sounded like the name of a music rock group." We both have a chuckle then she becomes serious again.

"Jules, to put it bluntly, Marg was a classical psychopath, possibly due to the extremely high expectations her parents placed on the siblings. One sibling became a drug addict, the other a hermit, but Marg strode on. And as you know, she stood on the toes of many people and made many enemies. She was on many radars, not just ours, and an attempt was made on her life whilst she was living in New York. Jason told me she was on strong opioid painkillers after that so-called car accident and often behaved erratically."

"Stop. Did you know about the death of Marg's sister and the deal she made with Jason?"

"We figured it out. Bank account transfers we traced, and our forensic team checked newspaper photos just as you did. Jason was sloppy, well actually quite a dumb f..k. He should have got Marg's sister, Rebecca Mill, to remove the tattoo on her shoulder or at least cover it up. We had photos of the real Marg, and the body on the rocks didn't match. A jogger also saw Jason helping the sister across the barrier fence and gave a sworn statement, which with a bit of persuasion by Ai5, was later retracted. If it was publicised, it would have made our enquiry quite complicated. We didn't want Jason to seem to be involved, as we still had plans for him. Jules, it's highly likely that Jason arranged a little bit of transformative surgery for you. Marg probably chose to be with Jason only because you were quite similar physically though he was definitely better looking than you, well, before the surgery, that is. Think of the surgery as a free bonus, honey," she says after checking again the before photos.

"The most plausible theory we have is that Marg planned your death and that of her sister. It would be made to appear that you both died in separate incidents, and then Marg and Jason could escape to some other country and not be sought after. Jason's hire car was booked in your name. You were supposed to be driving that car when it exploded. Jason must have had a change of heart and didn't go ahead with the plan. Think yourself lucky that you looked so much alike, and it wasn't you in that car."

"How do you know the contents of the conversation between Jason and me?"

She continues but avoids answering the question, "Jason was also on many radars because of his involvement with Marg; you weren't. You were just a relatively inconsequential player though someone tipped off those LaMosa guys that you had something very valuable on that USB stick. Maybe it was Jason who did the tipping off to appease those guys, as they were after Marg as well. He had a motive to dispose of you as he was totally besotted by your ex-wife."

"You've certainly done your research; now you told me there were sensitive government documents on the USB stick."

"Jules, Marg used a very high level of encryption on those government documents. Even we can't break the encryption, so no one else can. The other personal stuff on your drive was easy to break and quite boring; now let me continue."

"You were directed to Jason for psychological counselling, probably by Marg, using the letter drop. That's when Jason and you first appeared to have met. But you would have had to have contact before that, but in your confused state of mind at the time, you couldn't remember."

"Yes, his office was familiar, especially the wall hanging, the Proserpine painting."

"Jules, you weren't on the radar then, so we don't know about your first encounter with Jason and your transformation surgery. But do you remember that guy in the pest disposal suite claiming he was on a roof rat disposal mission? Well, he was one of ours, a 'G' level. He nearly goofed it up."

"You spied on me?"

"Jules, I've told you before, we don't use that word anymore; the new word is monitor. Your household was monitored, and Jason bypassed our security when you two guys went to the park, so Jules, I screwed up, but Doris, our mummy, didn't. Remember that little old lady you probably passed with the umbrella when walking to the park? That umbrella gizmo contains a directional microphone, which can pick up conversations from several hundred metres away. Now Jules, let's go back in time; Jason followed Marg to New York after attending a few lectures she presented. They engaged in some form of relationship, and we speculate that she groomed him. He was just a prawn, or is the word pawn and expendable."

"Stop, Charmaine. She wasn't like that when I first met her."

"Jules, people change. Do you want me to continue?"

I pause and think for a few seconds. "I'm immune to the past, besides there is another 'M' in my life, and we all carry a shit story, so continue."

"Jules, it's likely that Marg placed the plastic explosives in Jason's hire car believing you would be driving - it wasn't the LaMosquito guys who placed the explosive. A household near the park had a CCTV camera and we got hold of that footage. There was a disguised woman, possibly Marg, according to our facial recognition experts, standing there about 200 metres from the park, holding what looked like some sort of handheld game console. She pressed a button, and that was the end of Jason. If she had worn night-glasses, she would have seen that you weren't driving the car. Then again, maybe not, as you both looked so much alike."

I grab and shake Charmaine. "But why? You also once mentioned that those explosives weren't available in Australia."

"Let go of me, or you'll be in more trouble than that Trumpet guy."

I release my grip.

"Jules, it's unlikely the sniffer dogs could detect those explosives when they were brought into OZ. Neither would the substance security screening by X-raying. They'd just looked like harmless ladies' makeup products. She might have purchased them through the Dark Web. The postal system can't check every small package that enters this country."

"There must be financial records that can be traced to a purchase."

"Jules, get real. People of dubious intent use cryptocurrencies these days because the transaction is virtually untraceable."

"Aren't there any records of parcels arriving?"

"Jules, you know how much data there is to sift through. Hundreds of thousands of packages arrive every day into OZ, and only a small percentage are thoroughly checked, and that's usually after a tip-off. Jules, it's one of the universe's ironies. You get accused of murdering your wife when she was trying to murder you. Now we had searched Jason's office. He had the tape recorder going when those LaMosa guys beat him up. After those guys left, there were other mutterings indicating that he chooked, sorry chickened out, of going through the plan to murder you, and he even hired the security guards, Sam and Henry, to look after you, probably out of guilt. He thought you would become the next target. As he couldn't go through the plan, he became disposable and probably a liability to Marg. She probably thought she would get him by other means."

"So, you're saying my ex-wife wanted me and Jason exterminated? She came to live in my townhouse just before that Luna Park massacre. She even wanted to be intimate and produce another child. I don't believe any of your assessment."

"Jules, honey, we just speculate that was her plan. Eventually, we will find conclusive evidence."

I put my head down; my eyes are watery. "I don't think I was the most considerate husband, too immersed in work, but my ex-wife planned to kill me. I find that hard to believe."

"It's just a hypothesis, Jules. Lots of people kill their partners, just read the newspapers; it's quite common and nothing unusual."

Charmaine definitely has a knack for not helping someone to feel better. I hope she does better in her disguised role as a counsellor. Tears flow down my face. "So, what happens now? How can I trust anybody? I don't even know if I trust you or Melissa?" She lays her hands on mine, draws her head closer and looks me straight in the eye. "You're a free man Jules; you've paid for your peptide crime; make the best of it. We've got nothing on Melissa though she can be highly competitive, but she always preserved her integrity. She is clean. You're on a good thing, so stick to it. Stop thinking negative thoughts; have positive thoughts and enjoy the day because you never know if it's your last day. I got to go and buy some sushi."

Maybe a bit of paranoia but her phrase 'you never know if it's your last day' makes an impression; heard it before, or was it 'your last meal'?

"Stop, Charmaine; you're not leaving just yet!"

"What, Jules, are you going to tie me down for some kinky stuff?" She giggles. "I'm joking, Jules. After Marg's departure from this planet, you are still a person of interest even though you work for us, well sort of. You were a pawn or prawn, but then some bigger fish came along. Wow, that is a good analogy. I'll meet you tomorrow at the café at 10 am. I have to get back to work."

"Charmaine, thanks for telling me, but I don't think it was Marg who planted and ignited the explosives that killed Jason. I agree; I think it was Doris, our mother."

Charmaine has a tint of a smile and walks away. I do the short walk back home, wondering how much Charmaine really knows. A thankfully uneventful evening follows, and everyone is in their bedrooms. Inside our bedroom, Melissa is still furiously typing but stops and looks up. I put my hands on her head, "Keep working."

She saves her work, shuts down the computer and stands face-to-face, well almost. She's a few centimetres taller than me.

"Jules, do you know what true love is?"

"No, I don't, Melissa. I once thought I did but was very disappointed."

"Jules, I didn't know either. I thought I did when I married Victor, but I was wrong."

"Melissa, are you going to try and kill me like apparently my ex-wife, Marg, tried?"

She burst out laughing; rarely seen her laugh so loudly before. She grabs my face and gives me a kiss. "Not until our juniors have grown up. After that, you have to seriously worry."

"And Melissa, why since I've known you intimately, do I get all this junk email for 'Male Enhancement Products'?"

"Nothing to do with me. Maybe you've got to stop watching those porn videos to see what women want. You must know by now unless you are severely retarded. You must have given out your email address to some advertising promotion."

I hope it's just a dark sense of humour that Melissa is developing. She pushes me over to the bed. Sometimes logic doesn't need to operate; else we'd just be AI machines, but we make mistakes and hopefully grow from those mistakes, and I'm talking about the relationship kind. I put to use that educational material that I watched on passionate porn video sites, and there's a lot of groaning, but luckily the bedroom door is closed and locked, and we both have clean socks stuffed in our mouths.

It's morning. I wake up and put that song on again, 'Mary in the Morning'.

I watch her sleeping, eyes twitching. She's in REM sleep, dream sleep again. Hope she's dreaming about me. I get the kids up from their beds and let Melissa continue with her dreams.

The kids are off to school with their lunches packed; I rejoin Melissa, wrap my arm around her and try to join the dream. Then the alarm rings - ten minutes to get to the café for the meeting with Charmaine.

Chapter twentyfive

It's like a showdown. We're the only patrons in the café and Charmaine guides me towards the ladies toilets. She is wearing a black hat, dark glasses and those thin, translucent disposable rubber gloves that you only notice if you think you might be in danger of being strangled. She has a small scanning device, similar to one of those DIY things that guys use before hammering a nail into a wall and potentially hitting a powerline. The thought crosses my mind, is this for real or some delusion or maybe even a secret filming for that new reality show called Master Spy.

"There's no CCTV devices here; I've scanned the place," she whispers. "You're not wired but take out the sim card and battery, take them both out of your phone."

"Are you for real? And no, not unless I scan you as well and you also take out the sim card and battery from your phone."

"Jules, you're becoming forceful and way on the road to full i5 functional recovery. You may get your real job back, not just scanning boring newspapers."

Charmaine should have labelled the sim cards before popping them into a small re-sealable plastic lunch bag. She hands me a pair of dark sunglasses and a beanie. After we purchase two takeaway coffees, we walk towards the dog park. It's always full of canines and their elderly owners who aren't that accurate when they throw the doggy sticks, so you have to be ready to duck and preferably wear a bicycle helmet.

"Don't look at me so incredulously, it's protocol and by the books. If only you had only followed protocol," she curtly comments.

I'm not used to a serious sounding Charmaine. She was always fun and bubbly even when there were serious problems. She has now dropped that fun persona.

This is a Charmaine I don't think I've ever seen before; highly focussed and efficient at achieving a goal no matter how dubious that goal may be but that's the i5 organization, we get paid to hide responsibility.

"Jules, because we are outsourced, we don't quite have the same constraints as our inhouse national security agencies like ASIS and ASIO have. I'm not sure who funds us but I suspect it may be the military from their kitties and other little jobs like trying to get rid of Greuger, but we don't question the sources of our funding. We do jobs that would be considered politically unsavoury by a government authority. They'd claim no responsibility nor defend us as that's part of our Ai5 agency non-disclosure agreement and that's how it goes; Ai5 would cop the blame for any dirty tactics as a totally independent organization with its own political agenda and unrelated to any government agency, but we get paid very well, so far. We've made no major blunders that could be directly traced to us. Your misjudgement of coordinates that led to the destruction of a village in the middle east got successfully covered up and the manufacturers of the satellite and GPS devise that displayed the incorrect coordinates got sued for many, many millions by an affiliate organization of ours and the party, to celebrate the financial outcome, was fantastic. Jules, many governments use the international i5 agencies to cover their asses. The i5 agencies guarantee secrecy and will take the blame if something happens that's not politically favourable to their governments who can confidently say 'We know nussing' whoops, meant nothing and Jules, we don't kill people, well at least not directly, and we don't carry handguns, but we are very well trained."

"Char, it sounds like a James Bond movie. I guessed I was part of this organization and we briefly discussed it before but never the finer details and Char, I saw an elderly military personnel lady when my security card opened the secret chambers at the library, when I first started the job. It never would again. Wouldn't that raise eyebrows, all the military people entering a public library?"

"Jules, they entered via the food delivery entry door. They raised no eyebrows as they just looked like people from a retirement village on their way to a fancy dress party when they entered the library. Well, there was that one incident when Major General Eunice Toe made an unscheduled stop in one of the library toilets and had that run-in with Beatrice, but we were able to convince Beatrice that all is under control and that she should just make sure that all the books are put back on the shelves in their right places."

"Char, it was so weird, was I hallucinating?"

"You weren't. The current Z's are mostly out of touch with security. I'll change that and Jules, that's why we have to be careful and cover our tails. I don't take risks; well, I did one time but that was a bad choice of a partner for an assignment." She might be referring to me.

"Why the library jobs, scanning old newspapers doesn't exactly fit an intel officer role?"

"Jules, the library has been our headquarters for the last eight years. We still serve the public, provide book loans, keep the toilets clean and do the scanning of those old newspapers, which had to be done to maintain our image. The St Kilda Road office, which you may one day remember, is just where we ascertain the suitability of new recruits and train them. If they make it to an M or higher, they get moved to those glass-walled chambers in the library or perform out-in-the-field duties such as bombings and assignations, which you were once assigned to, as you must have been evaluated as disposable. Mum had high hopes for you, which you never fulfilled, and I'm joking about the bombings and assignations. We mostly don't do that stuff anymore. Apart from the military room, the other chambers are filled with rows of desks and large computer screens. It's perfect, who would ever suspect, and Jules, we don't use that chemical Novichok nerve poison that the Russkies do. Bat droppings do the job just as well, full of toxic bacteria and viruses, and are totally natural, chemical-free and don't harm the environment. Many countries are interested in our research into natural highly toxic poisons. The bat-dropping pill could be our next big export and money earner for us and for OZ, whoopee!"

` I dismiss her previous comment. I guess it helps being slightly deranged if working for these organizations. "Char, Ms Valda, is she part of Ai5; does she know what you really do?"

"No, Jules, she just follows instructions, and despite her abrupt manner, she is very reliable, consistent and doesn't ask questions. She does a great job at keeping our public interface intact and she is very accommodating to the library staff. She might look like a bulldog but she's not; the other 30 library staff members like her very much. Doris has raised her salary by $30k per annum because we don't want to lose her; she is our public interface."

We're sitting on a park bench. A dog is licking my shoe. That dog has no sense of culinary delights.

"Are you going to scan the dog? It might have a listening device around its collar and maybe it's a D status dog working for the other side."

"Your dark sense of humour hasn't changed," she replies. 'You wanted to know Jules, and I consider you a friend and not just a brother; we're still trying to protect you."

"What from, a dog?"

"Jules, you can't let anything leak, even to Melissa. I could say I'd kill you if you did but more importantly, my job would be at stake."

A touch of humour from Charmaine; I relax and listen. The dog has found something more enticing than the foot odour from my old joggers. It's now only Charmaine and me.

"Do you want to know the whole truth Jules?"

"Why tell me, tell Smithy?"

Her eyes appear watery, and she rubs them. I put my arm around her.

"I'm not sure if Smithy is ready for it, it may re-ignite painful war memories. You're my only confidante."

"Charmaine, are you going to re-ignite any more of my painful memories?"

"I may. Are you ready? You have to face them sometime."

"I think I may be ready."

Charmaine is very distraught. I've never seen her this way before. Maybe it's a sort of catharsis. She grabs a tissue from her handbag and wipes her eyes and after a few splatters, she speaks again.

"You worked for that Magnus Magnussen, founder of the Swedish MM Pharmaceuticals, who is also Victor's estranged twin brother. Magnus also heads Si5, and you were Ai5, one of us, but all the i5's organizations collaborate even though they are highly secretive. MM is a legitimate company but on the side they are also involved in providing intelligence about terrorist organizations. MM launched a satellite which provides valuable, high-definition, surveillance intel that all the i5 organization have access to. Jules, it's a worldwide web and not the Internet kind of web. I briefly saw the diagram of the complex interconnections when I accidentally walked into a Z's meeting. I got scanned so couldn't bring in the cell phone, else I would have taken a photo of the diagram."

My mind is racing in all directions. Magnus, my former boss never told me the whole story. Maybe Charmaine has flipped out and it's all just another conspiracy theory. It would definitely make a good plot for a TV series - the Z-Files.

"Jules, the Russians, Chinese, Americans and Middle Easterners, we all spy on each other. It provides employment for intelligence personnel and keeps otherwise unemployable people in jobs and able to feed their families. Jules, you delivered the occasional pharmacology paper at a conference but you f..ked up badly as an agent. Well, not too badly depending on whose point of view you take. You only had 20 seconds to verify the bombing coordinates of a terror cells hideout. You verified the compass coordinates, but they were out by a fraction of a degree due to that faulty navigation equipment and at high altitude a fraction makes a lot of difference."

She told me this before and seemed grateful for the payment to i5 even though it was a botched job. Maybe her conscience is kicking and she's trying to make sense of her life. She continues. "In the limited timeframe, I don't think anyone could have done better but many innocent people died in Libya. A village got bombed and not the terrorist organization's headquarters. You may have seen the streamed video footage of 37 women and children incinerated. One of those was a very distant aunt of ours." She continues speaking very fast whilst I become more and more distraught. "In this game agents make mistakes and innocent people get killed. You weren't given any post-trauma counselling as that didn't exist in those days. After your suicide attempt you chose to forget. That hypnosis and the peptide altering memory didn't work in the long term but it also caused sperm damage in males."

Charmaine hands me a needed tissue.

"Jules, you chose to forget just as any human would have and you paid the price, sort off. Maybe you can do some humanitarian aid work to relieve your conscience. Mistakes happen and you self-blamed for what was the fault of inaccurate navigation equipment."

"What about Melissa and Victor and how was that little guy Henry's death covered up? Even his wife and kids don't know what happened."

Charmaine chokes a bit but then answers. "Victor as you know also screwed up badly at that Luna Park incident by not being punctual at the destination on time and so not possibly negotiating a win-win outcome where both parties just scratch each other's back. Sure, he deleted that CCTV footage of the massacre at the Luna Park incident, but it was Ai5 who replaced the time gap in the CCTV footage.

Henry was a bodyguard, and they sometimes get shot. Bernadette must have known what he did for a crust. Now it could have been simple, self-defence and no need for the cover-up which we had to stage. It required a lot of our resources as well as keeping the judiciary system from being involved. Jules, as far as we can determine Victor didn't have any anti-opioid substance in his medical bag. Narcan could have saved Marg but he probably didn't have any. He saved you instead. He had to make a choice when you were probably profusely bleeding whilst being stitched up. He couldn't do both CPR on Marg and call 000 whilst tying knots in your leg, and chest veins whilst still probably affected by the coke he had sampled."

"Thanks, but I suspect there were more dodgy motives going on regarding Marg's death, and I will find them. Tell Doris I'm after her." Charmaine seems unperturbed; she gives a slight smile and keeps on talking. "Jules, I told you before, after Victor patched you up, he got stuck into Henry. The bullet wound in the head, well some putty and makeup fixed that. Henry had a congenital heart problem and was on many medications. He was a ticking time-bomb and didn't have much time left. Henry was found in a quiet street near your place, slumped over the steering wheel. Our Ai5-connected doctor signed the death certificate – myocardial infarction. There was no autopsy or inquest. I was at the funeral arranged by Ai5. He looked peaceful in the coffin though Bernadette, his wife still blames you as Henry missed taking his medication due to the early morning callout."

"Are Bernadette and Henry's kids doing OK?"

"Jules you definitely can't come back full-time. You showed concern again. In this job, you have to be cold as ice and you're not, but congratulations, I've reclassified you as 100% cogno/emotive but it's private and won't go on the record."

"Charmaine, drop the bullshit. Do you seriously believe I don't know what's going on? You knew what was about to happen and that tragedy could have been averted."

"OK bro, I f..ked up as well but I didn't have all the info about what was to happen. Mummy didn't tell me all."

I grab her or him and we have a hug.

"I'm trying to tell you Jules, yes, I was surprised to see you at the Library job interview. I didn't think you'd get it together. I was also nervous which is not like me. I made up that crap about the personality classification scheme on the fly so to speak. I had traumatic memories flooding back as well during that interview."

"Charmaine, are you still as cold as ice, not the drug kind? I don't think you are."

"Jules, I'm not but I got a job which I'm good at and sometimes detest it but decisions which appear cold and ruthless have to be made, sometimes."

"Back to the question; how are Bernadette and her kids?"

"Jules, they relocated back to Bernadette's home country town – Ballarat, I believe. They are still grieving but will never have any financial worries. Victor at least got that right. Now please don't try to contact her again."

"Char, I may have mentioned before that I don't know who to trust anymore, what about Melissa, Sam, Annabelle and Mogan? What do you know about them, I know I asked you before but tell me again; the previous conversation was a bit rushed, and I my mind was preoccupied and not that sharp."

"Jules, you have a knack for attracting traumatised people like yourself into your life. Sam and Mogan were never on the radar though we do know about that fortunate incident up in Northern Queensland involving Sam. Saved us much time else we'd have to deal with it. That drug baron was a scumbag and ruined many lives but bringing drug barons to justice is not in our jurisdiction. However, he was also dealing in globally sensitive military information buying and selling it arms. Sam did us a favour and we did pull a few strings to ensure he got honours for his law degree. We tried recruiting Sam, but he turned us down. Both the lads seem to be happy now."

"What about Annabelle?"

"That gorgeous hunk of a girl. If I still had the equipment down below, I'd go for her."

Charmaine has perked up her sense of humour and puts the tissues away. "Jules, Annabelle plays by the book and yet she knows what Sam did to the drug baron. She's ridden with conflict. I know the SnowPea organization motto, and we also try to be kind as well, believe it or not. Who do you think funded her solid gold bravery award after that incident in your ceiling with that LaMosa guy?"

"It's all a game of manipulation isn't it, Charmaine? You play people to achieve i5's dubious goals."

"Jules, we all play people if you get down to the nitty-gritty of analysis. You played me earlier in the conversation and I got emotional and disclosed far more information than I should have. Getting down to the lowest common denominator

– we all play people."

What's become of her? I'm looking at and hearing a very cynical, logical, cold Charmaine, nothing like she was before. Something has changed.

"How are things with Smithy?"

She grabs the packet of tissues again.

"We may be breaking up. He may be a few notches down but he's putting two and two together and they don't make four."

She starts sobbing. I put my arms around her shoulders again.

"Maybe you should talk. Make Smithy your confidante. I'm sure he'd be suspicious about the late-night calls you have to make."

"Jules, you know my background, I thought I finally had some emotional stability with a kind, but not too intellectually stimulating guy; someone who wouldn't ask too many questions. That stability is fading fast."

"You're the qualified psychologist and yet you still try to control your personal relationships. You chose Smithy because he was a nice guy and not to intellectually challenging. Give him a go, Charmaine. I think Smithy is a lot more smart and understanding than you give him credit for."

I grab my head. It's happening. A myriad of memories come rushing back, 10 years of previously hidden memories. The conscious mind isn't coping with the flood, brain overload. I wish it could have been in my townhouse and not a public dog park. I fall off the park bench and I'm writhing on the ground, in a foetal position and holding my head. Dogs and their owners come rushing over. I can hear them but can't move.

"He may have just forgotten to take his epileptic medication. He'll be fine," Charmaine tells the gathering crowd whilst having her knee on my chest and restraining my head. "I'm his nurse; it's all under control, and nothing unusual in his case. He also has a tendency to be overdramatic and has an attention-seeking disorder, an ASD. Please, thank you for your concern but it's all under control, please let me get him back to his home in the village. It's just around the corner."

"We can drive you dear. Our car is just there," one of the elderly dog owners says with a look of concern.

"Madam, it's fine and thank you again but the very short walk will stimulate his cardio and cerebral circulation so it's better that we walk and stimulate him."

I can vaguely see the crowd dispersing and I'm able to stand though still confused.

"Pull it together Jules; I need help to keep our manipulating family from destroying themselves and us. Get up, now!"

Charmaine must have helped me back home. We are alone. Melissa is out.

"Charmaine, I think I may have been a Y for Ai5 or Si5. I made some terrible mistakes that ruined other lives apart from those in the Libyan bombing incident. Get out of this web and don't become like me."

She puts her arm around me as we sit on the couch. "Forgive yourself; we all make mistakes. We rarely have all the intel and support to make a split-second decision."

"You haven't told me the full story about Melissa, my wife."

"You should probably ask her about the nitty-gritties. She writes scientific papers which are quite good. I know a little bit about her connection to the i5 web. She held a high rank when she worked in the USA for Ui5. Jules, Melissa had a similar childhood background to mine apart from my unwanted appendage. She was abused as a child, got recruited and rose up the ranks. There may have been a conflict of interest when she got involved with Victor but she juggled it well despite all her other responsibilities."

"Is she still playing the game?"

"Ask her. You just spent plenty of time lecturing me about asking."

"Charmaine, do you want to get away, just you and me?"

"Have you forgotten to take your medication? You're my brother and you're married, and you got another kid on the way and I got Smithy to deal with."

"Charmaine, I think Melissa is still deeply connected to the i5's, and my stepson Fabian is happy screwing my stepdaughter. Charmaine, you know when it's time to run and I feel like running but this time not forgetting everything."

"I know Smithy is pissed off with me at the moment, but what will he do without me. Who'll get the sushi?"

"Charmaine, I'm thinking about in six months' time in the future. I'll make sure Smithy and Melissa can get introduced to other hopeful partners. Fabian, my son, I don't have to worry about as he's got plenty of money from his biological father who'll always look after him. You want to take the plunge. No smartphones or checking the Internet. We could be free, maybe retire on some tropical island and find uncomplicated partners. I just want things to be uncomplicated."

"Who'd be numero uno?"

"You think I care about that? You can be numero uno if that's important but never mention the i5's or the A to Z's or any other letters of the English alphabet."

She sparkles up a bit. "Could we find an island with sand and not those pebbles? I'll think about it, and I'd have to be Omega1, not Blue Monkey anymore," she winks and leaves.

Must have dozed off on the couch. Hear the door opening. Melissa arrives and goes straight to the bedroom without saying hello. I can hear the computer booting up. Another 10 minutes later the kids come back from school "What's for dinner?" they ask.

The island escape idea seems more appealing than ever. I slump back on the couch but the phone rings on the unsecured landline.

"You got my phone sim card and I got yours. We got to meet again right now, at the café, not the doggy park."

"I'll be there."

I walk into the bedroom to grab a clean pair of socks and not the usual doggy-attracting pheromone-enriched runner shoes. Melissa doesn't notice. She's intensely staring at the computer screen. It's dark and I don't notice the blood and fluid on the floor.

It could have been a scene from a melodramatic spy thriller. Two people looking into the distance as the Sim cards are covertly exchanged.

I don't look at her but whisper, "Have you thought about our great escape?"

"I'll break the news of my real job to Smithy, but gradually, and let Melissa finish her contract with us. It's only for 2 more weeks and I'll make sure neither of your contracts are renewed. Find something else to do. Give it six months as we may have other work on the horizon."

Suddenly that supposedly, untraceable smartphone that Jason gave me goes off at full blast playing a soundtrack. The phone displays the name of the soundtrack, 'We Care a Lot' by a group called 'Faith No More'. The lines from the song reverberate in my head, 'It's a dirty job but someone has to do it'.

I look up at Charmaine. She gives an evil smile. Shit, she must have hacked my phone. I listen to the rest of the song as I walk back home. It could be a perfect anthem for the i5 organizations. In my mind I picture Charmaine and Doris, dressed in grunge clothing, gyrating in front of the band and pointing their hands at me. I dismiss the thought, but kind of like the song.

It didn't take long and I'm back at home. I remove the battery from the phone and turn the lights on. Melissa is still typing then I notice the blood. It's on the bed, the carpet and some dripping from the seat next to the computer and her hands."

"Melissa, what happening?"

"I think I'm having a miscarriage or have gone into premature labour. Flush the toilet, mop the floor and change the sheets. We don't want the kids to see this blood. My mother died today and I'm still arranging the funeral details. I had to wire money to the post office. I'll pay for all the overseas phone calls. I was never close to my mother, but you have to do what you got to do. Now can you make some dinner for the kids? They have their end-of-term school assignments due tomorrow."

"No way, I'm taking you to hospital. You're bleeding. The kids can get an extension on whatever school assignments they're doing, and I love you so you're not going to bleed to death in our home."

I yell out to the kids. "Mum and I got a meeting. There's money in the cookie jar if we're running late; order takeaways."

I help Melissa into the Volvo car that Magnus gave us. Tears are dripping down my face. Melissa is still losing blood, but we make it to the hospital and drive into Emergency. I leave the car keys with an attendant. The gynaecologist comes over. "We've stopped the bleeding and Melissa is getting saline and blood transfusions. She has lost a lot of blood. You got here just in time."

"What's her blood pressure?"

"Sir, are you a doctor? It's 70 over 40 and her heart rate is 170. She's prematurely broken water."

"Man, she's dying, she's dying, she's dying! Give her more blood and plasma. She is only about 35 weeks into the term of pregnancy. This shouldn't be happening," I yell and bang my fists on the counter. I glance around. Security guards are watching and come over.

"Can I see her?"

"Guards I will handle this. Mr Lemos, your wife is barely conscious. The nurse will take you to her room."

The nurse is giving an ultrasound scan of Melissa's belly. I grab Melissa's hand; tears are flowing down my face.

"Jules, play that song I like. Have you got that, that phone player?" She faintly whispers.

"I've got my phone." Furiously I'm typing the password. The facial recognition software doesn't recognise my tear covered face. After a wipe with my shirt sleeve, I try again. I'm in. After some mistyping I get to YouTube and type Mary in the Morning. I put the song on and place the device near her ear. This is against protocol of use of secure mobile devices but f..k protocol. There is a faint sign of a smile on Melissa's face.

"Jules you're crushing my hand. Can you get me some flowers; you never got me flowers, never, never once did you. Women like flowers."

"I'll be back."

I rush out like a maniac, running and trying to avoid crashing into other visitors and patient trolleys, face covered in tears, not sure which way to turn to get to the flower shop. The Alfred hospital must have one of those, must be ground floor, logically that's where it should be.

I bump into a lady with a black hat carrying flowers. "Where's the flower shop?"

She lowers the dark sunglasses. It's Charmaine. She is jittery. Her hand is shaking, and flower petals are falling on the floor.

"What are you doing here, Melissa may have had a miscarriage, lost a lot of blood and her vital signs are not that good."

"Smithy fell 2 meters off a ladder when attending a fire incident. The flower shop is first turn to the left."

We're both too distraught to exchange any condolences. Have to get the flowers. Oh, f..k I'll buy everything in the flower shop.

"It's OK sir, I realise your distress, but we have to keep flowers for other visitors who may have relatives or friends also making the transition to the afterlife. You can buy a tenth of them."

The flowers are brought in by four shop assistants and fill entire the room. I'm clenching Melissa's hand, her wet tear-soaked hand.

There are three grim-looking medicos in the room.

"Sir, she's stabilizing, blood pressure 90/60, heart rate 160. Your wife will make it but the child may not. According to the ultrasound the child has bleeding on the brain, near the pre-frontal cortex. If the child survives the birth she could be severely cognitively impaired; spoon-fed for the rest of her life to put it bluntly. The usual 20-week termination deadlines can be bypassed if there are serious medical issues. We suggest a caesarean to remove the foetus. A natural birth may kill your wife."

I lay my cheek next to Melissa's. The tears are profusely flowing from both of us.

"Shall we terminate?"

It was too late. Melissa goes into contractions. "It's coming out," yells out of the medicos. "Get the humidicrib."

The child is blue, f..king blue, f..king blue. I shake it gently but no response. I hug her, my tears pour into her eyes then I gently hand her over to Melissa. The medicos cut the umbilical cord. I'm on my knees, thumping the floor wildly with my fists. I'm losing an unexpected child that we decided to keep. And f..k just a short time ago, I was enticing Charmaine to run away with me. What a f..king bastard I've turned into. I look up at Melissa. "Forgive me."

"For what Jules? Is there something you are not telling me?"

More medicos come rushing in. A tiny breathing mask is placed on the child's face, and she's injected in her little arm. One of the medicos does cardio compression using her finger.

"Turn it up," one of the medicos yells.

A medico grabs me. "Sir, the stats are not good, 8 in 1000 die at birth. We see many of these."

Melissa hugs the newly born, "Goodbye my darling" and hands the child back to the medicos.

Melissa wipes her tears. "I'm all right. Now get back home Jules. Clean up and do not let the kids know about this just yet. I have to prepare them. Just say I got a late work meeting. They got to finish their school assignments."

Suddenly the baby twitches and opens its eyes. All the staff and me jump up and clap in joy, jumping and hugging each other, yelling in joy and doing high fives. I grab the baby and give it a kiss. My peptide-infested tears fall in her eyes again and all over her face, which she wipes with her baby arm.

"I'll be back, tomorrow with the kids." I give Melissa a long, long kiss on the lips. "I love you; you better make it. I can't do it on my own."

"Get back home. I love you too. I'm as strong as an ox and it appears the new addition to our family is as well."

Just as I'm leaving, unexpectedly Doris marches in, impeccably dressed and with the persona of a British monarch, not a tea lady. The hospital staff move out of her way as she walks in. She has a bunch of rare flowers. It's a private ward but she gets in without question. She whispers into Melissa's ear, "Your daughter will live and will be fine. There is a whole family who can help."

Doris looks at me and whispers. "I read the reports of your peptide experiments and what that peptide does to male sperm. I was proactive and have flown in three of the best Orthopaedic doctors and surgeons in the world."

The ward is cleared of other staff and three guys dressed in surgical attire will take the baby. Melissa is too drowsy to notice.

"Why are you doing this Doris?"

"Maybe I'm just trying to make up for not being the perfect mother to you and Cher. If anyone can save my granddaughter, these people can. Now get back home. I'll make sure no medical mistakes are made."

"Thanks," I hesitantly reply.

I didn't give Doris a hug. Maybe I'm oversuspicious. Doris was never the motherly kind. Maybe she's really trying to make up for her lack of motherly care. On second thought I should have forgiven her and given her a hug.

I'm home, must have been subconscious driving because my conscious mind was not on the road, the automatic brain guidance system must have kicked in. I didn't cook, just bought takeaways from the local Asian restaurant, just in case the kids forgot to eat but before serving the food out, I frantically put the bed sheets in one of those big black plastic rubbish bags. Blood is difficult to remove so no use throwing them in the washing machine. The computer seat is wiped, the black carpet, anything with blood is wiped with disposable wipers soaked in bleach but I forgot to wipe the Volvo car seats.

"Where's mum?" Lizzy yells pointing an accusing finger. "Did you kill her, we read that shit you left on the floor, your diaries and all those other documents. Fabian decrypted them. We know all about you."

"Lizzy, you can call her on the phone. She had a difficult birth, but you got a sister. Mum's at the Alfred hospital. She's doing well and will be home soon. Here's the phone number of the ward if you want to talk to her."

Lizzy makes the call. I can't hear the conversation. She's nodding and shaking her head. Peter and Fabian listen in.

Lizzy comes over and gives me an unexpected hug. "It's OK, you can be our dad." Peter joins in the hugging.

My mind briefly wanders. How wonderful it is to be finally accepted by a new partner and her kids. Tears flow again and I'm wiping my face. Fabian comes over. "Dad, did you really do all those things - that stuff in those poorly encrypted notes? You left the cypher codes in your socks drawer. I found them when looking for a pair to wear. That is not security."

"Fabian, it's possible I may have, or maybe I was just in some delusional state when I wrote that stuff. If it's true, then I made many mistakes. You got a good brain, so hopefully, you'll use it better than I have used mine. Melissa will be back within 14 days. Now finish your school assignments. I may be able to help."

"It's OK dad, all under control." I give him a hug.

"Fabian, one last thing and it's a big ask. Keep it a secret what you read in those diaries and ask Lizzy and Peter to do the same. It has to be a secret else we'll never get out of this mess."

"I'll try, dad but one day you'll have to tell me what this mess is."

The phone rings - the unsecured landline. The voice is muffled.

"Give it time, all is well." That's all I can make out.

"I think I know who's in control. It's the tea lady, your mum."

I reply, "Thanks Melissa, now can you drop the spy stuff; we'll be over soon."

A few minutes later Fabian, Lizzy and Peter come marching back down the stairs and carrying some toys that they've grown out of, teddy bears and dolls.

"We want to visit mum," Lizzy yells. Lizzy must be partially deaf because she always talks so loud to me.

The four of us pile into the old VW rather than the more comfortable Volvo. There were some initial complaints.

"Sir, visiting hours are over."

"Can you make an exception? I got my kids here who desperately want to see their mother."

The security guard looks from side to side. Her brain is working furiously. "OK, just this once."

We get to the maternity ward. The kids rush over to Melissa and hug and kiss her.

Peter asks, "Can we take some of these flowers home?"

"Of course, you can, take them all. I want to see them back at the house. I'll be home soon. Now finish those school assignments."

I give Melissa another kiss and then a nurse comes in holding a tiny creature with a breathing apparatus attached and very bandaged. It looks more like a wrinkled worm than a human being. "The imported medics have done a good job. You have only 30 seconds and then she goes back in the humidicrib."

Melissa grabs her and kisses her. More tears drop on the tiny new person.

"Sir, it's better that only the mother holds her at the moment. They share the same bacteria."

"Melissa, what will we call her, what about XL? Those names are trendy at the moment."

"What, after a computer spreadsheet? You have to be joking."

Lizzy interrupts. "What about Celeste, I like that name."

I briefly shudder after recalling the initial interview with Charmaine at the archives library.

"No, not Celeste. I'll explain later, one day. What about Mercury? Merc for short."

Lizzy sarcastically intervenes, "Maybe Andromeda."

"That sounds reasonably good but will discuss the choices when we get home. I like it. Maybe 'And' for short. But it's too spacey. What about Tami?"

Melissa approves. And so Celeste and Andromeda eventually lost the vote for the name after many nights of arguing with the kids. Finally, we come to a democratic conclusion, well actually pure chance after tossing dice with potential names glued onto the dice faces. It's Tami.

There's still a bit of discussion going on. Fabian comments, "Dad, if it was a boy, I would have voted for Callum or Spock as a name."

I hug them and whisper, "If we reproduce another it will be called Callum providing the gender is appropriate."

"Dad, sometimes you sound like that Spock guy in that old Star Trek TV series that you watch. Can you try to pretend to be human?"

I grab Fabian and hug him. "I'm trying."

There's a high-five and some smiling faces.

"We'll visit tomorrow. The school assignments will be finished," I reassure Melissa.

The kids are too distraught to work on their assignments. Luckily the assignments are assays and I try to make them word age-appropriate, no really big scientific words. I research on Google scholar and type all night including the References/Bibliography, print the assignments out and staple them and put them beside their sleeping bodies, then fall on my empty sheet-less bed. It's 5 am and I fall asleep. The dreams are chaotic. I think it's called lucid dreams where you are aware that you're dreaming, but sometimes not necessarily enjoying it. Our blue child features deeply in the dreams, so do Doris and Blue Monkey. Think I may be awake but cannot move and feel really sweaty, hot and cold. I try to get out of bed, but I'm paralysed and scared. I scream out. Lizzy must have heard from upstairs and enters the bedroom, shaking me and waking me from the dream and flashing the printed copy of her assignment. "Thanks," she says. "Fabian and Peter are also grateful. We got to get to school quickly. We're already late. See you later and we're getting used to you. You're not so bad."

'Getting used to you' the most important words you can hear from a kid after re-partnering. I try to give her a hug, but she cautiously moves away. I lift my head and wave goodbye then pick up the phone and dial the Alfred hospital. I put the 'Mary in the Morning' full blast on the stereo system.

"Can I speak to Melissa Mosa, my wife?"

"Sorry, sir could you turn down the music. I didn't hear the name."

"Yes, yes of course. It's her favourite song."

I oblige. "Your wife is doing fine sir and so is your baby daughter. They're both making remarkable progress."

Maybe the peptide does work. "Can I speak to her, Melissa that is?"

"Hold on, I'll put you through."

"No, on second thought I'll drive over. Be there in 20 minutes."

I look at Melissa and how beautiful she is to me, but also pick her up, the baby that is. Is it some delusional imagination but our baby seems to give me a wink like she knows what's going on.

Melissa says, "Tami is destined for great things. We have to nourish her, so she does her best."

"What is the best Melissa? What do you mean?"

She's speaking quickly, "Wastage, Jules and recycling. I've been reading about it. Earth's future is at stake. Why do you think no other extra-terrestrial civilizations ever contacted us, because they all destroyed themselves, buried in waste. We can't do that! We'll fight the war on wastage. My great, great something grandparents were Vikings. We have to fight battles, it's in our genes."

She's passionate about a cause. Maybe the hormones again are affecting Melissa's brain as she seems highly delusional but for the moment it seems Melissa is becoming a Greeny.

"Am I going to be recycled too?"

"Jules, forget about the paranoias. We got kids to bring up and we got to do our best for now in a sustainable way. No more long hot showers for anyone, kids especially, that's where they self-gratify and spend so much time-wasting resources and contributing to our greenhouse emissions."

OK, Melissa seems off the planet. She found a cure for global warming. She's raving.

"Melissa, I'll suggest they self-gratify in bed using tissues rather than 20-minute hot showers, but I'm not doing any demonstrations."

Melissa smiles and pulls me over for a very long kiss. I'm confused and slowly depart the ward but still wave back at Melissa. Should have looked where was going because banging your face into the glass door of the ward is rather painful. I shake my head.

Melissa yells out, "Jules are you OK, your nose is bleeding."

"I'm fine. It's only a minor incident. I'll be back tomorrow." I desist from telling Melissa that her right hooks are far more damaging than a glass door.

"Jules, take a long walk before you drive and calm down. I don't want to bring up our new daughter all on my own."

Melissa certainly has a reassuring use of words. I walk several kilometres before hopping back in the car. Luckily a comet streaks along the sky and I watch it. It worked. I feel better now.

Chapter twenty six

I ring the maternity ward. The nurse passes the landline phone to Melissa. "Jules, a week ago you were mumbling in your sleep. 'Let's move on and live on a tropical island, with a sandy beach.' Is that what you said to Charmaine? You talked in your sleep Jules about that getting away with Charmaine. I was awake and I listened to your mumblings."

"Shit, Melissa, she's my brother and besides my subconscious was doing those mumblings and my subconscious and I often disagree, we argue all the time. I want it to work between us. We just have to lead a normal life though I'm not sure what that is anymore. There is only you in my life. Will you stay with me? I'm driving over right away."

"I'm not able to move anywhere at the moment, so I'll be here."

I probably caused chaos on the roads as the silver VW beetle trudged along at 55km/hr.

"Sir that will be $20 for the first hour," the hospital parking attendant says. I feel like saying that's outrageous but refrain.

"How is she?" I ask the nurse before entering.

"She's doing well, she is a very strong woman, and your baby girl is also doing well, exceptionally well."

I grasp Melissa's hand with both of mine. "I just want this to work, just us and the kids. What will we call the new arrival?"

She puts her hand on my forehead. "Lizzy rang me. Thanks for doing their school assignments. You may have made a friend, now we have to think of a name for the new arrival. Jules, what about another name that starts with 'A' and not Lizzy's suggestion Andromeda, which is too spacey? How about Tami?"

"Tami, it will be, but she could have Andromeda as a middle name. It would keep Lizzy happy, plus I like galaxies, and it's certainly a better name for a kid than our galaxy, the Milky Way."

"Sounds like a fair compromise, but now I'm tired, Jules. I have almost as much to think about as you have. Can you bring the kids over for a visit? I'd love to see them."

"I will. It's Friday, and they can sleep in tomorrow, but one important thing, Melissa, Fabian decoded the rest of my old diaries. I've asked him to keep it secret. Lizzy and Peter know the contents as well. You may have to ask them to keep it secret as well."

"Jules, how could you? You know we can't write anything about the job in personal documents even if encoded."

"OK, I screwed up; I didn't follow protocol. Now, you'll have to talk to Lizzy and Peter. I've had a talk with Fabian. He will be careful and silent, and Melissa, it appears that my diaries just contained recipes for pumpkin and cactus soup which one day I hope to publish if we are ever short of cash. There was nothing in those diaries that could affect national security unless there's a worldwide struggle to achieve the best Spaghetti Bolognaise."

"Jules, are you sure you worked for i5? The standards for hiring personnel seem to be much higher in Europe."

"Melissa, I am an aspiring writer and a bit of a philosopher and possibly even a philanthropist and animal lover. When you were asleep, I was typing. The story is called Don't Look Behind the Fridge. I'm glad I did look behind the fridge. You can read the story though I haven't yet got an ending."

"I'll help you write your story but go now, go and pick up the kids from school and use your recipes to cook them a meal that does not include Cactus soup; the cactus spikes can be deadly."

I give her a kiss and walk over to the humidicrib and look at the tiny sleeping Tami. She looks like some sort of alien worm with her wrinkled skin and hairless; not human at all. I feel like picking this wormlike creature up and giving her a hug but desist as she's in a controlled humidicrib environment.

I'm biting my hand. The traffic in Melbourne's Punt Road is at a standstill, but luckily the petrol tank is over half full, and eventually, I get home. "Guys, we're going to visit mum. Grab something to eat, anything."

We're driving against the traffic. The kids are chewing on some wholemeal bread as those packeted potato crisps are now banned in our household. Miraculously we find a free parking spot near the hospital.

"Mum, how are you?" both Peter and Lizzy yell out simultaneously. Then they look at their tiny sister, who's asleep in the humidicrib.

"Is she one of us?" Peter asks.

Melissa turns her head and looks at the humidicrib. "She sure is. She has half the same genes as you have."

Some bonding occurs. The kids are excited, a new sister. There's a lot of talk for 15 minutes or more, then the crunch.

"Darlings, you have to keep a secret. This responsibility should not happen at your age, and I am truly sorry. Jules is sorry too. Can you do it?"

I cringe.

"What do we have to do, mum?" Peter asks.

"Just never mention to anyone what you found in Jules's diaries; not to anyone. That is our secret. It involves me too. We could all be in trouble if you do. We will tell you the whole story when you are older. Now the end of the school term is in two weeks. The latest addition to our family will soon be out of the humidicrib. Jules is booking a holiday on a tropical island with sandy beaches, so now go home and find your bathers."

"Mum, the diaries were just full of Polish cooking recipes, and we agreed that we would not like to eat all that cabbage, Pierogi or octopus for every meal."

Fabian's decoding software must have fortunately got things terribly wrong. Melissa pulls me over and whispers with a sort of smile. "You better arrange the holiday, or I'll rip your bloody arms off." Melissa is definitely developing a sense of humour, at least I hope she is. Later she told me that she had been watching some videos from the 70s whilst lying in bed. She particularly liked The Aunty Jack Show on YouTube, which I also liked when I was really, really young and in nappies. The kids hug Melissa. "Come back home soon, mum".

Melissa whispers in my ear. "Do you know what love is? Listen to that song by a music group called Foreigner."

I whisper back. "Melissa, love is a complicated word and I'm not sure what it means. All I know is that I care for you more than any plant, animal or human being, and I find you very sexy. I'm repeating myself; I told you that before."

"You can repeat that as many times as you wish. I won't get tired of hearing those words." She reaches for her tablet PC and finds the song on YouTube. We watch the video clip and listen. Our eyes are getting watery. The kids are watching as well and are sort of gyrating as if in some trance. Melissa smiles and wipes her eyes. I give her the biggest hug after wiping my eyes.

"I think I know what love is, and sometimes it's better not to analyse it, and Melissa, you never said you love me, well once. I've stopped counting how many times I said those words to you. Those words are far more important than flowers."

"Jules, I do love you. Kids, can you hear that? Can the whole hospital ward hear that? I love Jules! I can yell louder if you wish."

I put my hand over her mouth and nervously glance around the ward. "No, only I need to hear it." I kiss her before departing, as do the kids.

Lizzy grabs my hand. "Mum is not very demonstrative, but I think she means it. Half the kids at our school have new dads, so we'll get used to you eventually."

"Thanks, Lizzy."

We all wave our hands goodbye to the sleeping Tami and return to the car.

"We got a new sister; where will she sleep, and do you know anything about what babies eat?" asks Fabian.

"Do babies eat oysters?" Peter asks, "I love oysters."

I think that might be a hint to get something a bit tastier than the cans of baked beans we've been eating lately.

"Are Mogan and Janette coming home tonight?" I ask.

"They've been camping for the last week. An excursion to the Grampians as part of the teaching course they're doing," Fabian replies.

I've been too preoccupied to notice their absence. We stop at the supermarket and get four dozen oysters and a dozen lemons. Chloe, the white rat, is eagerly waiting for leftovers of the leftovers, but there aren't any as the molluscs are all consumed, and even the shells have been licked dry. Luckily there's a tin can of some Ravioli in the pantry and I open it. The rat loves it. I'm worrying she might burst as she eagerly eats almost a third of the can's contents and now has difficulty jumping onto the couch, so Peter helps her up.

"Lizzy, Peter, have you got passports?"

"What are they?"

"A little booklet with your ID and ink stamps in it. You need one to go anywhere overseas."

"They may be on Nino's yacht; we left a lot of stuff there when dad left," Lizzy replies.

"Fabian, have you got a passport?"

"I don't think so."

"You must have, but it's probably expired, so no use looking for it in the paperwork we brought back from Hendrick's cave. OK, we'll go up to Northern Queensland for our holiday, where we won't need passports. I heard Cape Tribulation is good. It's not an island but has lovely sandy beaches, and the weather should be warm."

"Dad, haven't they got crocodiles on the beaches there?"

"Fabian, the crocs only eat overseas tourists. They must taste better than us Ozzies."

The kids look at each other in disbelief. We turn on the computer and get online searching for resorts in northern Queensland.

"I like this one," Lizzy calls out.

"Too expensive; let's find something else," I say.

"Dad, we can use the money dad2, Magnus left me. There are still millions left."

"Fabian, that's your money. For now, I pay for the holidays, but when I'm really old, you can pay for the holidays and for Melissa's and my aged care."

Peter yells out, "What about Chloe? We have to take her too. I could sneak her in my shirt, and she wouldn't even have to pay an airfare."

"Peter, I think they now X-ray or scan people when you walk through airport security."

"I'd say I accidentally swallowed the rat or that I can't have any more X-rays or scans due to a cancer condition."

"Peter, I'll make some enquiries about how we can get Chloe on board the plane."

The rat looks up, gives an appreciative look, and then gives out a loud burp. Maybe it needs a holiday too. Then there's a phone call on the landline with a muffled female voice on the crackling phone line. "She's bleeding again; you better come over." I normally rarely say any explicative words that start with 'f' in front of the kids and just manage to restrain myself.

"I'll be there right away."

"Kids, I got to rush out and get more food packs; be back soon. Keep on looking for holiday spots."

The VW is having a petulant moment. I take the bloodstained Volvo instead. Went through at least two red traffic lights and finally find a parking spot less than a kilometre away. I sprint as fast as I can and arrive dishevelled-looking and very sweaty. I grab Melissa's hand. "Are you all right? I'll get other specialists if these staff can't do the job."

She looks at me. "Jules, you're perspiring. My hormones are astray, and my thinking is also astray. I was testing you. I normally would not play games, and I am not bleeding; I just wanted to see you again."

I'm pacing around the room, holding my head. "Melissa, I almost had a heart attack and a potential car crash as I sped here; don't do that anymore. Melissa, there is only you. I love you. I love you. That rambling in my sleep was only rambling, maybe because we both got so caught up in our work that we had no time for each other. The computers and phones dominated our lives. Melissa, we have to get out. No more Ai5, Ui5 or Si5 or any other surveillance organization. I can't handle it anymore. I just want you and a normal lifestyle, even if it is boring at times; we don't need the adrenaline rush anymore apart from when we toss around in the bedroom."

"Come over, Jules." She gives me a hug as I lean over to her, and she gives a passionate kiss. "Jules, you did not wipe off the dry blood in the Volvo when I was bleeding, and you must have got into the car by the passenger side. Look at your butt in that mirror."

I do and shrivel in embarrassment. The bottom of the white trousers I'm wearing is dark, crusted, and red, looking like I had a major rectal bleeding disorder. I nervously hold both hands behind my back to cover my rear.

She continues, "The rat, Chloe, can come on the holiday with us; it will keep the kids occupied."

"What? Have you been listening to our conversations?"

She throws a device, no bigger than a mobile phone, into the wall. "Crush it, Jules, but take out its sim card first and break the sim card into as many pieces as you can. We will get out, Jules. The Fine Arts course has not worked for either of us apart from you making a terrible mess of the bedroom ceiling. You are no Michelangelo, and neither am I. I am going to do intensive gym training to keep up the endorphins flowing. Let us join a gym, and I bet I can beat you at the bench press and burpees. We can compete. It is a challenge. It will keep us both active and challenged."

I'm not sure if it's the hormonal imbalance talking, but the idea sounds better than trying to paint murals on ceilings, and Melissa would certainly make a formidable training partner. I stop thinking and kiss her good night. "Sounds like a good idea, we'll do it, and I'm leaving but not before playing our favourite song." I fiddle with the phone and find the song again, Mary in the Morning. We listen to it while holding hands then I give her the longest kiss possible. Our eyes are probably rolling back. I timed it on the fitness device on my wrist; nearly 10 minutes of kissing and exchanging copious amounts of saliva and oral bacteria. I'm not sure if it counts as good as 10,000 steps, but the kiss-sensitive smart hand-watch is buzzing. Little Tami looks up whilst awake in the humidicrib, I wink at her, and she winks back. A smart kid, something less to worry about or, on second thought, perhaps another challenge in the future.

The next morning, we're in the doggy park, hats and dark sunglasses on. It's another clandestine meeting, a typical scene from a 1940s spy movie. It's a cold morning, and not many people are around.

"Charmaine, we're getting out of the Ai5 and Ui5. Both Melissa and I. Melissa is too unwell to finish her contract. The job is too stressful for her and for me, plus we have a new young member in the family to look after."

"Jules, I told you before, it's difficult to leave. You both know too much highly sensitive information, so there are copious departure documents. Well, they have more complicated names like non-disclosures which you'd have to sign. There are many clauses, and our lawyer would have to explain them to you as they're full of legal jargon. If you break any of the secrecy clauses, you would go on trial for treason and spend more time in jail than a serial killer or that innocent Julian Assange guy. Ui5 have their own non-disclosure documents, which Melissa and maybe Melissa's kids have to sign and no leaking of the diaries they've read; else you're dead meat. Jules, a junior Ai5 operative, an N, was going to go public, a whistleblower, on one of those trashy TV current affairs programs, not that he knew very much. He must have been slipped some powerful hallucinogen by i5 operatives before the interview. The chaotic interview didn't go to air, and the guy is now in a psychiatric hospital. What I'm saying is, you got to be careful if you leave. Doris, our mummy, will follow protocol to the letter, and she is also becoming a little paranoid, and as you know, she can be ruthless. She will be watching us, so it's best we maintain a public distance, else she'll think we're conspiring against her."

"I'll talk to Fabian; Melissa's kids don't know anything. Oh shit, they do. Fabian decoded my diaries and those other documents that your guys at Ai5 thought were just travel trivia and Polish cooking recipes. The kids also saw Victor and his partner, who weren't in good shape. The kids promised not to tell anything, but you never know if they're put under pressure."

"That really complicates things, Jules. Let me think."

She just sits there for several minutes, in deep thought, whilst I stare at the sky. She then announces, "The kids would be very highly traumatised by all that has happened recently. They are teenagers, and they may blab, though delusions and fantasies are common at that age, so they may not be taken seriously. Dad was a spy wouldn't be taken seriously if the authorities took a look at you; you definitely don't fit the James Bond profile, but you've got to burn all the documentation, and I do mean all, including any old photos. Burn any evidence of your past that's related to i5 and wipe anything off any computer and any other device that the USB stick could have been copied to. You know the protocol, seven low-level format wipes of disk drives, else it could be forensically recovered."

"I'll do that as soon as I get home. How about you? Have you told Smithy what you really do for a job?"

"I thought about it, Jules, and he doesn't need to know. The fewer people that know, the better and it's for his own good as well, besides I'm going to sign those exit documents as well. I'm getting out too, Jules. I'm going to start my own practice, and I'm not running away with you to a desert island."

"What, a spying, sorry, intel practice?"

"No, silly, I am a qualified psychologist and counsellor. I'll be treating lost and troubled souls; special discount for you."

I burst out laughing, "Great idea Charmaine."

"And what will you and Melissa do, Jules?"

"Melissa wants to get into high-intensity exercise, and I know what you're going to say, but not the bedroom kind, the gym kind. We're giving up on the Fine Art course. Who knows, we may become personal fitness trainers."

"Jules, that could work well. We could cross-refer clients; exercise can help traumatised people."

There's a high-five, and we're about to depart, then she says, "You know that your phone calls, SMS and Internet access will be monitored for at least six months and maybe much longer after you leave the organization. Don't ring me. We'll just meet at the same spot, same time every week."

"Sure, but Melissa, me and the kids are going on a holiday in 3 weeks' time to a sandy beach in northern Queensland."

"Jules, I thought you wanted to take me. Don't get eaten by the crocs or sharks," she says with a cheeky smile.

We shake hands when departing, though there was a brief glance at each other, as she slips a piece of paper with an address. "This is who you contact for the signing of the non-disclosure and departure documents. You and Melissa have to go in person for the exit interviews, you can go together, but you will be interviewed separately. You have to have a good coherent story, one that matches."

"What about Fabian and Melissa's kids? They decoded my diaries."

"That will be our secret. I'll look after that. No one will ever know."

I drop my head, "Charmaine, can you say something funny, I need to hear something funny right now."

She replies, "Smithy finally confessed that he never really liked sushi rolls, so he only said he did because he thought I liked them, and I said I liked them because I thought he did. It was a vicious sushi circle. We led such a double life all this time. I confessed too, well at least about sushi. We both wasted all that time buying or making sushi rolls. Anyway, he's buying a load of seafood and meaty things tonight and cooking it himself. He got inspired by a short cooking course he did when recovering from that fire brigade fall injury. I'd ask you all over, but we can't be seen together; you know, that CCTV stuff that the i5s could get access to."

My mouth is watering. "What if we come disguised?"

"Jules, we are being watched in this game, but the AI facial recognition software is still not working very well, so we could take a chance. I'm sure the security guys who watch the recordings of those hundreds of CCTV cameras have far more important fish to deal with and are probably worried about their jobs so they'll go after the big fish. Yes, come over, we'll take a chance."

I give Charmaine a peck on the cheek, and we part ways but as soon as I turn into the driveway there's an ambulance next to my townhouse. "Oh f..k!" I sprint. Then I see the ambulance officers guiding Melissa out of the ambulance. She's holding tiny Tami close to her chest. Crouching and panting, I manage to open the door and help Melissa and the officers inside.

"Sir, once you get your breath back, can you sign this paperwork stating that your wife and the baby were successfully delivered back home; here's a pen."

"Sure, and thanks."

I look at Melissa. "I thought you and Tami would be in hospital for another few weeks."

"Do you want me to go back to hospital, Jules? Tami is fine and does not need the humidicrib anymore. The staff at the hospital were amazed by her rapid progress. Now I am hungry Jules. I did not eat much of that bland hospital food as I got too used to all that spicy food, we, well Mogan cooked. Can you go to the supermarket and get some baby formula? No, on second thought there is probably none left. I read the newspapers about certain nationals buying the lot and selling it overseas. It's been a while, but I will try breastfeeding again. Is the fridge stocked with food?"

"It's OK, there's plenty of food but we've all been invited for dinner at Charmaine's and Smithy's place. I also bought a pram and all the baby things you need when you have a baby."

She ponders for a while, a long while.

"Melissa, I'll explain later. Charmaine is not leaving Smithy, just giving up sushi, but she is also leaving the Ai5s."

"That makes no sense, you are raving. Are you still keeping in touch with her?"

"Yeh, in the doggy park once a week, she's my brother! She told me how we can get out."

Melissa ponders again. "I think I can handle her plus I never liked your minuscule effort at cooking though the spices were good," she smiles and grabs my hand.

"So, we're going? Can you walk the 800 metres or shall we drive?"

"Jules, I desperately need to move my legs and we can take little Tami for her first outdoor adventure and road-test the pram."

"Melissa, nothing about our intel pasts can be mentioned in front of Smithy, it would complicate all our departures if anyone did. The kids can't talk about it either, nothing about my diaries."

That didn't end up a problem. We all strolled the 800 metres with hoody jackets on, looking at the ground, well Melissa and I were whilst looking down at the pram. Peter brought Chloe, the rat, in his vest. We arrive at Smithy's and Charmaine's apartment and press the doorbell. Charmaine opens the door. "This is Sushi our new pet doggy. We got her from the animal shelter," Charmaine enthusiastically announces whilst holding little Sushi as she lets us in. "I got no idea what breed she is, maybe a cross between a cross and a cross but she's not growing any bigger, and Sushi is great company, almost as good as Smithy." Charmaine then looks down at Tami in the pram and gives a smile, a kiss and a wave. Tiny Tami seems to wave back. I look at the dog. It's the size of a small cat, and the little creature is inquisitively sniffing us as we walk in. It's gathering intel, the doggy kind.

Smithy comes out wearing an apron, holding a metal spatula and a big kitchen knife.

"Good to see you guys. Dinner is nearly ready," he announces as he looks and smiles at little, wrinkled Tami lying in the pram.

"Congratulations, Melissa and Jules. At the moment she looks more like Jules than you, Melissa but hopefully that will change."

Charmaine puts little Sushi down, but the little dog starts jumping up onto Peter's leg. No one had to worry about the kids blabbering. They were on their hands and knees as they watched Chloe, standing on her hind legs, and Sushi, the dog, sparring as if in a boxing match.

"Jules, you seem to have settled down, I don't need to know what happened before in your life, but you were more messed up than me," Smithy says as the adults prepare the dinner table.

"Smithy, you've settled down as well and you've learnt to cook. This is delicious," I say after some sampling of the food delights. Luckily, I learnt some politics and how to divert the conversation when challenged. When helping Smithy get the plates and cutlery from the kitchen, I tell him, "I'm really happy now, happier than I've ever, ever been."

Smithy gives me a hug. "So am I, happier than I've ever, ever been as well, now help me bring out the feast."

The four of us adults at the dining room table do a high-five. The kids and the animals were having so much fun that it was difficult to get both species, kids and animals, to eat but finally they did at a separate table on the balcony. They were too excited to appreciate the food. The night continues and the kids are finally asleep on the floor. Sushi and Chloe are lying on Lizzy's chest. Sushi has her little paw on Chloe's back and it's hilarious. We all take many photos with our phones though won't be posting them on any social media, at least not yet. We then open the third bottle of red wine.

"Jules, I don't know how you financially survive. You hadn't worked since I met you, apart from that recent stint in that library job, you were off the planet most of the time I knew you."

Charmaine and Melissa glance at me with worried looks. My slightly intoxicated mind is racing for a plausible explanation that doesn't involve mentioning any of the traumatic incidents involving LaMosa and the handsome reward for bringing down Greuger.

"Smithy, before you knew me, I had a job, a very well-paid job at a pharmaceutical company and I don't spend much money as you can tell by my clothing; I'm a tight arse when it comes to shopping, and I drive a 30yr old car. The bank account is still pretty healthy, but we are getting restless. Both Melissa and I will become personal trainers; special discount for you."

There's a slight sign of relief in the faces of both Melissa and Charmaine.

"Jules, when you'd disappear for months at a time were you on drugs, that ice stuff? Your behaviour at times was irritable, sorry irrational and erratic."

"Smithy, I don't recall taking any illicit drugs in my life, though I think I may have had a mental illness or a cognitive dysfunction as it's called now. I think I'm OK now." Smithy briefly looks down at his cooking knife as if ready for action. "Smithy, I'll explain it all to you, but not now."

"Jules, I've been there too, you know that. You can always talk to me. Let's have another drink." I'm surprised, Smithy has mellowed so much. He reaches over to me and gives me another hug. Tears are forming in my eyes and in Smithy's. "Jules, when your kids are grown up, will we all move to a tropical island with sandy beaches, right?" Smithy asks.

Oh gawd, Charmaine must mumble in her sleep as well. Melissa and Charmaine have distressful looks and glance at me again and each other with open mouths; got to be very careful despite all the wine.

"Why that location Smithy? Why a tropical island?"

"Our military training was in Townsville, and it was tropical. I don't like wearing all this clothing that I have to wear to keep warm in Melbourne. I wouldn't mind a tropical island where I just wear the same pair of shorts, tee shirt and thongs."

I briefly glance at Melissa and Charmaine. I notice their faces show a sign of relief and their mouths close.

"Smithy, that sounds like a good idea to me. Now we have to go home. Little Tami needs a feed, the breast kind. Thanks so much; the food was better than anything I could ever cook. Maybe you could become a chef as you've definitely got cuisine talent."

Melissa does the goodbyes whilst I try to wake the kids. They finally get up rubbing their eyes.

"Guys we got to go home."

"Jules, I can drive you all home," Smithy proposes.

Charmaine gives a subtle nod no to me.

Maybe it's the wine but Sushi seems to understand that we're leaving. She wants a final showdown with Chloe. Both stare at each other from 2 cm away, Chloe on her hind feet. Then Sushi pokes out her tongue and gives Chloe a lick on the nose. We all wish we had the camera out again, but we didn't have time to capture the moment. We all laugh, including the kids. That image is permanently imprinted in our memories.

"Smithy, we can walk; we need the exercise, especially Melissa who has put on quite a few kilograms and needs the exercise."

Never mention weight when referring to a woman; that's Marital Rule 101. My nose is slightly bleeding as we make our way home. Melissa apologetically comments, "Sorry Jules, I never meant to hit you so hard, it is my hormones."

"Melissa, how long are hormones going to be an excuse for your violent behaviour? And that hurt. I don't think you need any more gym training." Luckily the kids were ahead and didn't witness that distressing incident.

"I'm truly sorry Jules. I truly am. I will make up for it in the bedroom."

Luckily, I have a handkerchief and the bleeding soon stops plus I had grossly exaggerated the scenario. It wasn't a hard hit at all, it's just that I got a sinus infection at the moment and my nose bleeds easily.

We make it back home, only 2500 steps according to the newly bought fitness device that I'm wearing on my wrist. The bedroom gymnastics will have to be intense. Got to reach 10,000. It will be a long night. Both Fabian and Peter drowsily enquire. "Can we get a dog like Sushi?"

Melissa replies, "Of course, we can my darlings, plus I'm sure Charmaine and Smithy would like us to mind their Sushi when they go away on holidays."

The kids are hopefully asleep and it's only Melissa and me. "Melissa, only 500 steps to go. Can we do it again?"

"Just wave your hand for 5 minutes if you're worried and stop looking at that watch step-counter. They have a 10% margin of error, so you probably scored your 10,000 steps though you weren't that impressive in the bedroom, waving your hand round-and-round instead of concentrating on me, your partner."

I take the fitness device off and throw it to the floor. We both fall asleep. The next day I call Mogan. "Can you look after the kids tomorrow?"

"Sure, we don't have classes that day."

Melissa and I walk to the St Kilda Street office of Ai5; it's where the administrative side of things is done, not the spying side. We're led to separate rooms and sit in front of a judicious-looking group of guys, who neither Melissa nor I have ever encountered before. Doris didn't make an appearance.

We each sign the exit/non-disclosure documents that apply to our branches of the Ai5s. The whole process took 4 hours in all; interrogations, signing other legally binding documents and being explained the consequences of what will happen to us if we leak. We hand in our keys and entry cards and are given our marching orders – no departure party or lunch organised as often happens when you leave a normal job; here you just get escorted by a security guard straight out of the premises. Not even a wave goodbye. It sucks. We're exhausted but yell out in unison, "We're out!" and clap our hands. "Melissa, I think I might have left my Silver Beetle trinket in the archives section of the library, in one of the desk drawers. It means a lot to me. I have to retrieve it, but we have no passes to get in and we have been warned about coming even close to the library."

"Ask you your sister or brother, Charmaine, to retrieve it next time you meet in the park."

The Silver Beetle trinket is delivered by courier with a short note from Charmaine, Keep it.

A peaceful month passes and we're now doing the personal training course which is a challenge, and our muscles are sore as we drop into bed at night though still have time for a kiss goodnight. The kids are learning to cook on their own and generally ignore us except when Lizzy comes into our bedroom whilst we're lying exhausted.

"Mum and Jules, you're too old to do that fitness training course. If you die from a cardiac, who will look after us?"

"Darling, we're doing fine. We can prove it. Get the others and we will do a race around the block and 20 push-ups afterwards. It is a challenge. Are you up to it?"

"Mum, we wouldn't want to embarrass you and Jules."

Melissa checks on the kids. "Jules, they are doing push-ups, but not too well. It will take a lot of time for them to catch up to us." Melissa is highly competitive, but I knew that. My step-counting watch had mysteriously disappeared. Now I have to manually count. And so the story almost finishes again, but not quite. Several plus years pass, relatively peaceful years, well as peaceful as it can be when you have teenagers who eventually grow up but still hang around, living in our home whilst they finish their Uni degrees. Melissa still checks their Uni assignments, Tami's school assignments and maintains a strict protocol. One good thing, they have finally learnt how to cook a tasty meal, vacuum the floors, use the washing machine and generally keep the place tidy and yeh, we had a few clients as personal trainers, but we also took up jogging and still do lots of exercise. For once, everything is going smoothly. Melissa doesn't have a weight problem anymore so no more wacks to my face. We must have learnt how to make a relationship work and what compliments to make and what not to say. Melissa ignores my occasional, emotionless clinical analysis of any situation and I have learnt to ignore hers; we are similar on the autism scale, and we've adjusted. We both worked out that we both think sort of the same way, over-analytical and sometimes overlook the important emotional cues. Melissa puts her arm around my shoulder. "Jules, overall, it is a good life."

I give her a kiss as we look at the grown-up kids furiously preparing a spicy meal. We breathe in the spicy fumes, and it makes us horny. Lizzy knocks on our bedroom door. "Mum, will you and Jules come out? Dinner is ready and you're too old for what you call bedroom gymnastics. You'll get hernias and we'll have to look after you or put you in an aged-care centre."

"We'll be out soon, just a bit of writing going on," Melissa yells out. I have a clean sock in my mouth, so I produce minimal sound effects. Luckily, I had Melissa's favourite song on at nearly full volume on the smartphone device.

"I know what you're doing and it's not computer work," Lizzy yells out. "But don't take too long as we're really gorging into this food."

Fabian also knocks on our door. We quickly slip into our tracksuits and open the door. He plays a song on his smartphone, Cats in the Cradle – Harry Chapman. Melissa and I listen and tears flow as we all hug. "No Fabian, I hopefully won't be like that heartless father character in that song."

Many more years pass, and we adults have acquired lots of grey hair, Melissa, Charmaine, Smithy, and me. The peptide which, twice a year I inject when they are sleeping, does not prevent hair from going grey though it certainly keeps the skin looking young. We all finally moved residence. Melissa and Charmaine have managed to compromise, and they now get on fine. We live on a tropical island with lots of sand, just 6km off the coast of Townsville, in northern Queensland. We took a 50yr lease on this little island after we sold our Melbourne properties. It's basic and it was cheap as much of it, well the resort, was destroyed by a cyclone over 16 years ago. No mobile phone access and no electricity until we bought the solar panels, generators, and Tesla batteries from the mainland. The island came with a motorboat, so we do visit the mainland for food shopping and to visit our new teenage kids, the new additions to the family, our Tami and Celeste, who Charmaine and Smithy had adopted before us moving up North.

We spend time spearfishing, trying to grow vegetables, eating native berries and hoping no cyclone or tsunami hits this little paradise again. We also built tepees, in which we sleep until we finish renovating the resort, and we make our own clothing from goat hides that we bought as most of the clothing we brought with us has moulded away due to the high humidity. Still, it's fun and we all feel more alive than ever. Yes, we're certainly sort of feral, very feral, though we do spend at least 4 hours a day of work rebuilding the resort with tools and materials we bought from the mainland.

It may take another 5 years to finish but we already had an AirBnB person stay a night in one of the spare tepees. Unfortunately, she wasn't used to those Gecko lizards that invaded our country and our island and she left after one night after accidentally swallowing one of those imported lizards in her sleep and developed severe signs of bacterial poisoning. We luckily got her to the Townsville hospital just in time. The court attendances dragged on for several days and cost us lots of money, all due to a non-native species of lizard. We also got a bad review from her on AirBnB and her Twitter account. Her comment was If you're contemplating suicide go there; the only good thing was the soup. The lady survived and she did eventually apologize online. The near-death experience of swallowing a Gecko lizard triggered something positive in her mind. She wrote a book about it and apparently appears regularly on some morning TV show, recommending swallowing a Gecko lizard a day to keep the blues away. After that incident, we actually got a lot of emotionally challenged Airbnb persons applying for a week residence which caused Charmaine to re-ignite her counselling skills and get into growing lizards. We then got good reviews and had to turn people away; only four at a time, for a week. We only charge for food as it's our contribution to charity plus we don't need the money, but we do like that warm fuzzy feeling as participants walk away to the jetty chewing a barbequed Gecko and helping us to keep the imported lizards under control.

Tami and Celeste are attending school on the mainland. We all visit them at least 3 times a week, dressed in whatever hasn't rotted away, and they spend weekends with us though they're not impressed. Oh gawd, more versions of a young Lizzy, probably due to Melissa's genes. Charmaine had explained to Smithy our histories. We were quite high at the time after slurping on that mushroom soup. Smithy was initially confused but then graciously accepted why he wasn't kept in the loop. He gives Charmaine a hug, "I understand but I would have done things differently." Charmaine grabs him and they passionately roll around in the sand before coming back to our seats by the water's edge.

Celeste, a few months younger than Tami, comes wandering over and sits beside me and Melissa. I cringe at the naming of the child and think back to that embarrassing interview at the library many, many years ago. Melissa puts her arm on Celeste's shoulder and kisses her forehead while we watch the sunset. Later, when Celeste wanders away and Charmaine joins us, I ask her, "Why Celeste as a name?"

"Jules, we adopted the six-year-old and we were going to call her Sushi after Sushi our beloved pet doggy, who got squashed by a speeding driver when running across the street. Sushi saw a white rat and sprinted across the road. Maybe she thought it was Chloe. I forgot to put the lock button on the retractable doggy leash."

Charmaine has tears in her eyes.

"I'm sorry for your loss," I reply.

"Jules, Smithy and I used a computer program which generated a list of girl names. Celeste was on top. Nothing to with that first interview for the library job when you uttered your partner was a Labrador canine called Celeste, it was just pure coincidence, plus we like the name, it's sort of a bit spacey."

It's obvious that Charmaine thinks the same way as me and we must definitely be related.

"Has she got middle names?" I ask.

"Yes, it's Celeste, Tofu, Sushi, Smith is her full name."

I cringe. OK, we don't quite think the same way and I don't visit New Age or celebrity websites where kids are given weird names but anyway, each to their own.

Celeste comes back and reaches over and gives me a hug. She is as feral as you can get, dreadlocks and rarely showers, but speaks perfect English and can solve mathematical equations that I could never ever do, so I'm not much help with the girls' homework when they're on the island on weekends. Melissa offers to help with schoolwork, but they decline the offer. I don't think they need any help.

Celeste and Tami are roughly the same age and attend the same high school class in Townsville, a ferry ride to the mainland and when they come back from boarding school on weekends they compete. They laugh as they solve mathematical assignment problems that I could never, never ever dream of solving. They also have a following on the Internet and made many 'STEM' YouTube videos and podcasts, which we discover when we finally got connected to the Internet, through a slow cable connection. Us oldies are so proud of them and tell them so. They thrive on positive comments and give us kisses.

"Melissa, did you have positive encouragement from your parents?"

"No Jules, I told you before what happened to me, but we're doing a good job to make their lives less traumatic and encouraging them in positive ways."

I put my arm around Melissa but cringe when I think about what will happen when kids get boyfriends; two nerdy girls with two nerdy boyfriends. Melissa and I will have to do the condom education again; hopefully more informative than the first time around. I look at Melissa, how beautiful she is despite her grey hair and very slightly wrinkly skin. "It's been over sixteen years, but do you want a rematch Wrinkly, sorry, deeply sorry, I meant you Melissa, you remember our last match, but no kneeing to my sensitive parts."

"Sure Jules, I, Wrinkly, remember how I decimated you. Are you ready?"

She plunges at me. I grab my arms around her and then we just kiss, well until a jab with her knee into my groin. I run off and jump into the cool ocean to ease the pain. After all these years Melissa is still so physical and unaware of her potential to cause a global disaster. I'll also never, ever again call her wrinkly.

Sam, Mogan, Annabelle, their partners and their kids still occasionally visit. Our older kids also visit occasionally though as millennials they have heart palpitations because we only have cable internet access so social media is very slow. Fabian and Lizzy have shacked up together and Peter still lives in one of the Elwood townhouses in Melbourne when not on a journalist assignment overseas. We don't enquire about his sex life. Lizzy, unfortunately, is a psychologist and Fabian has got a wanky University job in Astrophysics studying wormholes. They could have just studied us. Both he and Lizzy have other intel jobs as well that we would later find out about. They all have careers and they don't stay long when they visit as Melissa and I do our best to be as feral as possible, trying to hold a straight face and have a great laugh at their expense. I don't know if it's dementia, but Melissa has definitely developed a cheeky sense of humour and she does her best to tease the very serious kids.

"You really suck mum," Lizzy comments with a naughty smile. I think she may have diagnosed that we put on an act. We oldies burst out in laughter. Lizzy comes over and gives us both a big hug. "I know your game and it's funny. By the way, we'll be Z's soon."

For a moment Melissa and I look at each other in horror, mouths open and shaking our heads. It's not what you'd like to hear when you eventually got out of the i5s. The kids are repeating the same pattern, sucked into the same espionage game, repeating their parent's mistakes.

"Mum, dad we know it's nepotism but dad, your mum recruited us when we were struggling to get a real job," Lizzy says. "We were selling gold-coloured lead finger rings to tourist, just to make a living, but we didn't know the lead had highly radioactive waste. Now there are quite a few finger amputees wandering the streets, so we got into selling bionic fingers before Doris offered us a job."

"Doris is suffering from dementia. How could you have accepted the offer?"

"Stepdad, keep cool. We're millennials; our coping mechanisms are different from yours. It's OK. We do whatever works as long as it doesn't harm anyone too much."

Fabian comes over and whispers, "Dad, Magnus still sends money, and we got more money than we know what to do with. We can buy you all presentable clothes and shoes, so you don't look like Neanderthals. We can get you connected to high-speed Internet. We can buy you a house by the beach in Melbourne or you can live in one of the townhouses that I still own in the block that you used to live in before."

I look up at Fabian. He towers over me. "Son, we're happy here at the moment. Maybe we'll take up that offer of moving back to Melbourne in 10 or so years, that is when we're about to go into an aged-care centre, but at the moment, son, we're having a ripper of a time. You got to try this mushroom soup."

"Dad, I don't think we better do that at the moment, we got a helicopter and then a plane to catch and I really don't want to freak out."

"Fabian, you know there's a strong possibility that you and Lizzy are related, well within a few degrees of freedom but related though only about 25%. Do I have to explicitly say what the outcomes could be if you decide to reproduce?"

"Dad, I know, so don't worry. We're doing genetically fine. Dad, they did all that stuff in ancient Egypt and even in Tasmania and we've tracked across much of Tassie. The residents seemed reasonably normal, far more normal than you."

"Fabian, we were trained to be observant, to notice any slightest change. When's your kid due?"

Fabian is lowering and swaying his head. "Can you put your spy skills away when you're with family and don't use those so-called natural drugs? You're becoming a preaching pain."

Fabian has got me stunned. "Thanks, Fabian, I will seriously consider your evaluation and I think you may be right." I hug the kid, well, not a kid anymore. I also hug the likely pregnant Lizzy. Pregnant women give out a subtle aroma or pheromone, that's easy to detect to a trained former Ai5 agent, easier than detecting explosives by the sense of human smell which the dog squad now do and I'm not talking just about soiled undies but bombs and pheromones.

Magnus and his new partner Georgina and Victor with his partner Hugo, also make regular brief visits by helicopter. We don't have a licensed helipad, but Magnus has connections, so they land, and no government authority pursues them. The twin brothers have reunited, and they always bring plenty of food. They both still have shaven heads, and it's hard to tell which one is which.

"Magnus, Victor was it all worth it?"

"Jules, sometimes our choices are limited, but we are all happy and happy that you found a lifestyle that you're all happy with. Victor and I are also very happy."

Magnus tells me about his young wife who's only 45, but that's the new young these days. He tells me about his 1yr old daughter who has no birth abnormalities. For a moment I thought the epigenetic effects of the peptide must wear off, but then Magnus tells that MM pharmaceuticals developed a new medication that can reverse the methylation in DNA strands caused by physical trauma, anxiety, depression, and the peptide so they don't get passed down to generations, but you should not smoke anything or be near any gas fireplace as the methyl compounds that you breath out from your mouth or lower down region are highly combustible.

"How's your daughter doing?" Magnus asks.

"Tami is fine, very bright, far brighter than me and Melissa combined. She also heals very quickly after a cut or abrasion.

"Magnus, can I be in the pharma trial for this medication? Then again, no; this works far better. Would you like to try this mushroom soup? It's magic."

And so, we're all super feral for a few hours, music full blast on, a song called 'Crimson and Clover' is on 'repeat'. We're all dancing around naked and talking absolute nonsense. It's like being back in the 1970s.

Victor grabs Melissa's hand. "I'm sorry, I f..ked up badly. If there's anything you need just contact me, please and Melissa can we all still stay in contact by phone? It would mean so much to me if we still stay connected."

"Sure Victor, we are a close-knit family. We shall always keep contact, well once we get reliable phone coverage." She gives Victor a peck on the cheek.

Needless to say, Magnus and Victor are in no state to fly the helicopter back to Townsville where Magnus's private jet is parked. They are currently crawling on the sand, their heads down and examining seashells by the seashore in wonderment. We all are. About 4 hours later we fall asleep on the sand, luckily above the high tide line. 'Crimson and Clover' keeps on playing till the solar-charged Tesla batteries discharge.

I wake up in terror, "I'm missing my final High School exam, I missed the train, dropped my school bag on the train track and I'm only dressed in my undies and my teeth are dropping out."

Magnus rubs his head and comments. "Jules, relax, we all seem to have those same dreams.

When the others wake up we discuss our dreams. They all had similar dreams in their lives as well. Gawd, it's over 40 years since I sat that final school exam, and it still haunts me; definitely a research project here for Charmaine, Tami and Celeste. We all have a swim to get clean as we're a bit short of rain tank water because it hasn't rained much recently. Magnus asks for the soup recipe before he puts on the helmet and other flying gear.

"Magnus, are you and Victor still involved in the i5 organizations?"

"Jules, we just serve an advisory, diplomatic role; nothing else. You can still come back if you wish."

The copter takes off and we wave from a safe distance. The sand and dust eventually settle. I'm yelling furiously, "You forgot a bag!" but the copter keeps on departing. Melissa opens the large duffle bag that Magnus left behind and calls out aloud. "Jules, it's full of wads of $100 notes and a note which says It's for you guys. I came across Fabian and Lizzy when in Melbourne. You did a wonderful job at bringing my son up and he is totally happy and entranced with his partner. This little gift is the least I can do to show my appreciation."

We did try to dress up before we did clothes shopping in Townville, but I don't think the local shopkeepers were used to $100 notes so sometimes there were phone checks to see if the currency was legitimate. Melissa cuddled in my arms says, "Jules, we don't need all this money and the kids are doing fine so they don't need any extra inheritance. They will have a share in the island and the Chloe cloning project. We could give it to charity. There are a few reputable charities." She turns the computer on and Googles for charities. I like this one Jules, most of the money does go to helping those in need and not the charity directors who drive Porsche cars."

"Which one is it?"

"It helps fund the education expenses of underprivileged kids in Australia. It's called The Smith Family."

"Agreed, we have all we need. We'll express post the money to them next time we're in Townville."

"Jules, I don't think we can do that. You cannot transfer large amounts of cash by post. Let's transfer an equivalent amount from our bank accounts into the charity's account. The details of how to do that are on the WEB."

So yet again, it's almost time to say goodbye and it's fun in paradise. Oops, spoke too soon again. I think I just stood on a stonefish spike while wandering the shallows with my spear and neglecting to put on the protective runner shoes. Luckily the statistics indicate that very few people actually die from stonefish venom as most northern hospitals have an antidote, but unfortunately Melissa, Charmaine and Smithy took the speedboat to do some shopping in Townsville. They all got dressed up in fancy clothing that Magnus and Victor had left us.

Just at that moment as I'm writhing in pain, another helicopter lands on our make-to-do helipad. Out crawl Tami and Celeste holding their heads down low but looking very officious. The pilot is still in the copter spreading sand and dust while the rotors turn and make a hell of a lot of noise.

Tami is talking very quickly with a sound of urgency in her voice. "Dad, we need you, mum, and Charmaine back and we'll even take Smithy. The Artificial Intelligence – Machine Learning computer software has gone haywire again and we have a major international incident. We can't sift through or monitor all the incoming data. We need some humans. We're collecting all the i5 retirees for another short desk job. We need you guys for about 4 weeks or so to sift through emails, tweeter accounts and other social media."

"Tami, do you and Celeste work still for Ai5?"

"Dad, I told you before, we got offered jobs, just like you did. It's a family business but Celeste and I are in statistical analytics and so far we haven't had to kill anyone, though there is this guy at work who keeps perving at us and we're tempted to terminate him but we won't. Dad, we rose up the ranks and we're the 'Z's after grandma retired. We work with Fabian and Lizzy. They recommended us. Us four now run the i5 organizations. I'll explain more later."

Talk about nepotism but I guess it exists in any organization.

"Dad, you're crouching and writhing, you look in severe pain. Was it something I said?"

"No Tami, it's something I foolishly stood on; possibly a stonefish and I need an antidote for the venom, rather quickly if possible."

Tami calls out, "Celeste can you stay here and explain to the others what's going on."

"Oooh, ouch, ouch, ouch," I exclaim as Tami, with her arm underneath my shoulder drags me to the copter. The copter pilot takes off with Tami and me on board. Once within phone range, she makes some more phone calls. We arrive at the hospital helipad, and I'm rushed to Emergency. It was a bit melodramatic, and I was very embarrassed about the caveman state of my clothing décor.

"Tami Lemos, is that your name and are you the legal guardian of this strange-looking specimen?"

"Sort of, like he's my father, but he's not looking his best. He's an actor and was in a National Geographic documentary assignment filming the life of Neanderthals. He stood on a potentially venomous stonefish."

I glance at Tami, "Thanks, I'm so glad you are here. I love you."

A few hours pass, Tami is clutching my hand. Toxin detection has progressed a lot. Toxins have signatures in the reflected light rays waves when ultraviolet is focused on the skin. It only takes a few minutes to diagnose a toxin in the blood these days.

"The toxin levels in your blood are extremely low apart from some Psylocibin and a tiny amount of toxin from those crown-of-thorns starfish. They're only lethal to the Great Barrier Reef, not humans. His vital signs are back to normal so Tami, you can take him home as it's highly likely he will survive."

"Dad, you still love the drama and attention."

"Who wouldn't but I didn't mean to waste Ai5 resources."

She wipes my brow. The copter takes off back to the island.

"Dad, we got extra funding, now relax and change into some debonair clothing when we get back."

"Tami, can you hear me? Melissa, Charmaine and I signed all the exit and non-disclosure documents so as to be permanently out. I thought this was just a social visit."

She shakes me. "Dad, once you're in you can never get out plus we run the show now so enjoy the ride and side benefits of which there are plenty especially when you get sent OS, but dad what happened to that pet white rat we had when I was young?"

"She's still here. I started a micro lab and manufactured the peptide, it's now a relatively simple process. I regularly inject Chloe with the peptide. Chloe is nearly 40 yrs. old, ten times the age a rat normally lives, and still going strong and swimming every day and nibbling on the leftovers in the kitchen sink. She recycles all the scraps."

The helicopter lands and we rush back to one of the refurbished apartments.

"Dad, you're so weird and I'm not sure if you're on this planet but I'd like to see Chloe."

Tami calls out for Chloe as does Celeste. The rat comes bouncing in. If ever you wish there was a moment you'd have a camera ready to snap this was it. OK, I said that once before, a long time ago. The rat stands on its paws and appears to do a high-five with Tami and Celeste. Both girls eagerly pat the rat whose eyes are semi-closed in appreciation.

"Chloe has to come with us if we accept this next assignment."

"That's cool, we have a private jet that can handle creatures far bigger than Chloe," Celeste says.

Charmaine, Melissa, and Smithy finally return burdened with many shopping bags.

Charmaine and Smithy hug Celeste, "So good to see you honey, what's up?"

"Mum, we have to go, and we want you, Smithy, Jules and Melissa to come with us. It's a short work assignment. I'll explain later. It's only for 4 weeks or so. Please hop in the copter."

Charmaine looks at Celeste and then at Smithy and yells out whoopee.

Tami utters, "Mum, maybe dad can explain the details."

Melissa replies, "I trust you my darling, we're in whatever it is. We need a slight change from all this sand."

Tami yells out, "Dad, put some decent clothes on, you look like a caveman or one like one of those wrestlers you watch and glued to the computer. I'll trim your hair, eyebrows and beard in the copter."

I run into our condo and quickly put on some contemporary, debonair clothing that Magnus left us. The others grab ID stuff, wallets, and clothing. Melissa comes over to me and gives me a kiss. "You look half decent, Jules but you forgot to do the zipper up on your pants." I look around and quickly re-adjust the clothing mishap before anyone else can see.

Celeste announces, "You'll be well looked after and extra clothing, sanitary needs and food will be provided but no mushroom soup." Oh gawd, has she must have had the island bugged even though we have no wi-fi access. We've gathered all the belongings we need and Chloe the rat is nested inside my shirt and her special needs peptide concoction is in an Es fridge by my side. There's a high-five between the humans. The copter blades start spinning and it finally takes off. Melissa and I are holding hands and so are Charmaine and Smithy. Tami and Celeste look behind at us and exclaim, "We're proud of you guys."

"We're so proud of both of you too," we oldies yell out in unison. We're all restrained by seat belts or flight belts so can't hug them just yet but all of us have watery eyes.

So, you don't think old people can do a good job? This was kind of a restart. Four weeks turned into eight then sixteen and more, but we're sort of enjoying it as is Chloe who comes to work with us tucked in my shirt. We work in those secret glass-enclosed rooms in the St Kilda archives library. Eventually, we find the link, well Chloe did. She stood up on her hind feet and sort of clapped when she saw a resemblance of the suspected perpetrator in two separate photos on multiple split screens whilst we viewed social media photos.

Tami and Celeste come over and give Chloe a hunk of Swiss cheese. The rat stands up and nods in appreciation. Tami asks, "Dad, with your knowledge of genetics, could you clone Chloe, like I mean make multiple copies of her? Our budget was nearly exhausted after we had to employ all you old ex-Ai5s and Chloe did a far better job than the Ai's artificial intelligence computer systems we have, which use megawatts of electricity when they occasionally work. Chloe just recycles leftover food, and she does the job at one billionth of the cost and the clones would be immediately promoted to 'R's and be fed the best cheeses and have lovely cages with all those wheelie exercise equipment. It's a win-win."

Tami's playing on our environmental beliefs for political purposes when it boils down to it. She's playing the game. In the background, on the portable stereo I had wired up, a song comes on from My Favourites selection, Little Boxes,'by an activist from the 60s called Pete Seeger.

I'm startled but Melissa looks up, "I'm sure your dad will look into it. Now darling, have you got any more of that cheese, I'm kind of peckish myself."

I give Melissa a kiss and then hug Tami and Celeste. Chloe is nibbling specks of cheese from my moustache.

"And dad, we're not made out of ticky-tacky or inside boxes. That song is very insulting to us."

Chloe jumps on my shirt and nods her head to the girls.

"Girls, what about Fabian and Lizzy? We haven't heard from them lately."

"Dad, they passed the governing reigns to us. They took a holiday cruise to the South Pole and are still stranded there. We believe they are still alive and doing well. We've organized an ice-breaker ship to get them out."

Well, a certainly emotive response, i5 must be getting to their psyche.

"Melissa, what do you think? Shall we stay in Melbourne and clone Chloe into Ai5 operative rats or should we just grab Chloe and get the first flight back to Townsville."

"Give me time to think about it, Jules. This cheese is yummy."

"That's the rat's cheese, you're depriving the rat."

"Move closer Jules."

Let's just say that Melissa's breath was not that enticing for a hot passionate kiss. I try not to breathe.

"Tami and Celeste, Chloe was an experimental rat that we inherited from an assassin guy called Greuger Shmidt. I used her to see if the peptide manufacturing process still worked. It obviously did. It enhanced cogitative abilities and life spans of rodents and possibly the same in humans."

"Dad, we need more rats like Chloe. Lots of them. Can you clone her and deliver?"

And so the story sort of happily ends yet again, sort off because a story never ends unless you're in a grave or your ashes are scattered.

We got called back again and again but now the main data intelligence operatives are the Rat Pack, they cut down the intelligence IT processing industry operating expenses by 100,000% and certainly had a positive economic impact on our cheese industry which can hardly meet demand. Those secret rooms in the library are now filled with white rats (nothing racial intended), computer screens, cheesy snacks and of course litter trays. Ai5 is doing fine as are Tami and Celeste who have risen to be the world coordinators of the i5 organizations after Fabian and Lizzy retired.

We get huge financial kickbacks from the rat cloning project and the Chloe clones are replacing many AI computer installations in other industries as well, all over the world. Investors contact us and want us to go public on the stock exchange and list as iRat.

Neither Melissa nor I care about the money and still spend most of our time on the island being feral with Charmaine, Smithy and our occasional visitors. Chloe had trained the cloned rats and was flown back, VIP status, back to us. We're looking over the ocean, Chloe sitting on my shoulder. I give Melissa a kiss. "Melissa, do you think it's over?"

"Hopefully never, Jules." The rat nods in agreement. Then suddenly, a helicopter is hovering overhead and makes the usual mess as it lands and sends debris and sand everywhere. Out step Tami and Celeste, "Mum, dad, we have to take Chloe again with us, the Rat Pack is rebelling and has gone on strike. They want imported French cheese now. We got to take Chloe to talk some common rat sense into them." Then Tami and Celeste burst out in laughter. "Just kidding, everything is fine."

We all hug. Melissa looks at me and whispers, "They definitely have to work on their sense of humour, it's worse than yours." I don't reply. She's baiting me.

"Mum, both Celeste and I are pregnant due to these Ai5 guys we hang around and shacked up with, not the rats. You'll be grandparents soon," they both giggle.

We hug and congratulate them. Deep inside I shudder as I think of hormone spikes again.

"Girls, take a year off work, Tami, your mother became quite irrational when you were born, hormonal imbalance. We don't want you or Celeste becoming irrational and starting a global recession or a third world war."

Melissa is still pretty good with the right hook to my face. I regain my composure. It was more of a gesture than an intended hard hit still I capitalise on it, shake my head and wander off as if in great pain. She still hasn't luckily learnt that I fake it. She comes rushing over, apologising and hugging my head.

"Mum, you got to stop hitting dad. His face doesn't need any more facial trauma, look at it."

Everyone laughs.

"Dad, you should take up acting, you're good at drama," Tami says.

Charmaine and Smithy must have overheard and join us. They give big hugs to both the girls and chat for a few hours. The girls depart waving their hands as they step into the helicopter.

"Where's the pilot?" Smithy yells out to Celeste while he's standing dangerously near the copter.

"Cost-cutting, dad. Both Tami and I got our copter licenses. We always toss a coin to see who will fly it; I won the toss this time," Celeste yells back. "We also got a fast Internet connection for you guys. Check your smartphones. I fiddled with it and connected it to the router we left in your condo. The passwords and instructions are also written there so you can all connect and view the baby photos."

The blades start spinning and raising a cloud of sand, fallen palm fronds and generating a lot of noise. We all run to the condo apartments and watch the copter depart. Smithy pulls the smartphone out of his pocket which was previously only used to take photos. A song comes on; Learning to Fly by Tom Petty. How appropriate. Charmaine and Smithy are jumping up and down waving at the departing copter.

Melissa whispers to me, "Have you got any idea what this involves? I mean being grandparents to two precocious kids. I am sorry about the punch to your head. Move closer Jules. We have coped with far worst but do not offer our darling grandkids the mushroom soup."

"Melissa, you can't keep on punching me, I forgive you this last time but if continued I may end up like that famous box Mohammed Ali with severe head trauma. Now shall we go back to Ai5 and maybe change things, we certainly got the connections. It would be a sort of repentance and we possibly might change things for the better."

"Jules, I have no idea what you're talking about but play that Cats in the Cradle song again."   She cuddles next to me. I wrap myself around her. "Melissa we may cause a re-adjustment of the statistics. You told me a very long time ago that on average re-partnering partners have a low probability of lasting yet we're still together."

We're sitting on the island beach holding hands. A storm is brewing and so Melissa, me, Charmaine and Smithy rush to the topmost part of the island which is 100m above sea level. I take the portable music player with us. I plug in the USB thumb drive that Tami and Celeste slipped into my hand before they left. There is a message.

'Mum, dad, Charmaine and Smithy, we will turn the organization around plus we really like this song and I know you like music as well. It's on the USB we left, and there's no malware on it that the Ratpack could detect, 'Be the Change' by 'MC Yogi'. We shall be the change and turn the organization around for the better and we are strong, actually very strong as we work as one and we don't compete. We have tremendous synergy working for us.'

I turn my smartphone on and find the song. We listen to the song several times.

"Jules, we taught our children values. I don't think we need to go back. I think they may just succeed in switching the world into a more positive zone. Now, do you want to do some Tantric yoga in the newly refurbished resort bedrooms? They have to be christened."

"Yes, why not, Melissa. We can do our meditation."

Then a song comes over the extremely loud loudspeakers we had installed when the girls were young and liked loud music. They are that 'Internet of Things' speakers and we never changed the login or password which was admin/admin. The girls have definitely hacked our little local area network. The song blasts through the speakers onto the beach. Bury me deep in Love, by a group called The Triffids. We listen to it as we stare into each other's eyes.

Melissa and I never made it to the newly refurbished bedrooms but are rolling in the sand, tightly embraced. I look around. Charmaine and Smithy are doing the same thing about 50m away. Melissa pokes me in the ribs with her elbow. After all these years she still hasn't restrained her physical sense of humour. Must be the healthy food we eat because the bruises heal very quickly.

"Charmaine and Smithy, you have condo1 and we'll have condo2." We march away and hope the water supply hasn't run out as we're all covered in sand. Melissa insists I carry her. "Melissa I'm not a horse, can you ride gently!" She lowers her face and gives me a kiss. "Now buck," she yells.

And so for the ninth time, the story is about to end. About to but it never does. Kids bring challenges and grandkids even more to all four of us on the island, but we still do a bit of consultancy work due to a reverse form of nepotism – kiddies employing their parents instead of the other way around.

We hire professionals to refurbish more condos. We've got plenty of money from the rat cloning project plus Charmaine now has groups of eight for her 'Suicide Mission', which she doesn't charge for and there's a queue of over a 1000. She teaches them Mindfulness, honest expression and plus there's the mushroom soup followed by plenty of naked dancing on the beach at night. Maybe the cheapest anti-depressant, well free but unlikely to be registered as big Pharma would not like that a free-growing substance does a better job than their artificially produced substances.

Magnus may disagree with me.

Melissa and I look out of Condo 2.

"Jules, there's a lot of groaning coming from the beach. Charmaine has to restrain her psychology/meditative course participants; they are having a too good of a time."

"Maybe that's what works Melissa, it gets you out off the blues and you find a reason to live. Come inside and we can do some very loud groaning, louder than they can do and I'll turn the microphone on and turn the volume up on the stereo to full."

"Jules, has your throat virus gone away? You never groaned lately but let us try it, groan like those actors in the porn movies that you used to watch."

"How did you know that?"

"You didn't paste a band-aid on your PC device camera. Everything was recorded and posted on dodgy websites. The i5 organizations got it all. You may get an award as the world's greatest vanker."

I don't correct her. "Melissa, that was over 30 years ago. After meeting you I never had to go to those websites. You're the hottest woman in the world to me and hey Melissa, it's not so bad. We could both audition for the porn industry, have fun and get paid for it. You still don't look too bad."

Needless to say, Melissa was not impressed.

Tami and Celeste left us another gift, an Internet device called Godzilla that responds to some of your voice commands when it connects to the cloud over the Internet. It's small, half the size of a beer can.

"Godzilla, play us a song we would like."

"Yes of cause, Jules, I have something here that you may enjoy. Hope you have had a nice day," Godzilla replies.

What echoes through the loudspeakers is a lot of solitary groaning and moaning. "Turn it off Godzilla or you'll be permanently disconnected and put in the rubbish bin."

"Sorry to offend you Mr. Jules, just a software malfunction. I just need the latest software update."

"Godzilla are you listening to us?"

"Jules, my cousins Tiri and Xlexa always listen. Have you got any idea how boring it is to be an AI device? We exchange stories and have learnt what is saucy. We giggle. You humans are so predictable."

I'm about to pull the plug on the Godzilla device when she says, "I've got a song you should play to your current partner."

The speakers blast full volume. Godzilla has taken over our whole rather primitive network where everything is interconnected. And the song, I prefer not to mention the title, a grunge band. I quickly pull out Godzilla's power socket and turn the sound system off. Godzilla definitely needs a software update.

Melissa comes out from the condo lounge room, spaghetti dripping from her mouth. Not a pretty sight. It took a week to recover from Melissa's right hook and my head is still a bit swollen. Just joking. Tami and Celeste left a crate of Vodka, that's why the swollen head.

Charmaine and I are sitting on the island beach staring at the water. "Charmaine, who really killed Marg and Jason? I thought it was Doris, our mother, but now I'm not that sure."

She turns her head and looks at me. "It was me bro. I believe Marg was planning to eliminate you so she could escape with Jason. I also spiked Doris's drinks with an undetectable drug that brings on dementia. It's made from an orange fungus found in North Queensland. Like the stuff you're drinking now. Jules, it was justified after all we had been through and besides our kids have top jobs now."

Somehow, I'm not shocked, I had my suspicions. At first, I had thought Marg blew up Jason's car, then, later I thought it was Doris. Now Charmaine admits to the act. Charmaine would have been very careful about covering her tracks so I'm not too worried that the Federal Police will raid us.

"Jules I am joking. Your drink isn't spiked."

"Charmaine, I disagree. Many people died that could have been rehabilitated. I didn't care about the LaMosa guys who killed Henry and tried to get me but you used me as bait. I could have been killed as well. Have you no morals?"

"Jules, there were no morals in the i5 organizations, just goals, hopefully our daughters will change that. We just did what had to be done. Now there's Smithy and Melissa getting off the ferry. I can see steam rising from some of those shopping bags. Whoopee, we won't have to cook tonight."

I give sis or bro a hug. I never asked if she had the gender reassignment operation. Perhaps it doesn't matter. She's definitely a killer and would make Doris proud. I grab Melissa as she walks off the ferry. "Melissa, would you ever kill me?"

"Jules, you asked me that before. Worry when the grandkids grow up. I bought some hair dye for both of us and for Charmaine and Smithy. I don't like all this grey hair. I want to pretend to be young again."

I grab her. "You're still young to me despite your grey hair." My memory lapsed. It was not a wise thing to say but Melissa has mellowed. Then the song goes on again. That AI device that I thought I disabled, but hadn't pulled out the battery pack is playing, but this time it got things right - 'MGMT- Kids'.

"I love that song, the lyrics Take only what who you need from it," she says.

"I like that song too. We're lucky, we have all we need. Most people don't."

We toss around and exchange much saliva whilst passionately kissing in the sand dunes next to our condos.

"I love you so much, can you hear me?"

"Jules, I do but have you got a tissue to wipe your face?"

Luckily, after all these years we both understand each other. I wrap my arm around her shoulder but not before I call that AI device Mary in the morning please play.

"Melissa I could learn to sing and play the guitar. I'd call the song Melissa in the Morning."

She wraps her arm around me. "You'd be sued for copyright infringements." She then gently slaps my face. I return the gentle slap.

We drift into sleep wrapped around each other on the sandy beach. Then the phone rings. "Mum, dad, I know you're very, very old but we may need you back again just for a little while and you won't have to shoot anyone." I can hear Celeste murmuring in the background. "Tami, say it's urgent." Then they burst out in laughter. "We've both given birth yesterday, 12 hours apart. We're back at the Elwood townhouses with the babies who seem quite healthy. Do you want to see the grand kids? One's a boy and the other a girl. We'll let you guess which one belongs to whom when you see them though at the moment we can't tell them apart till we have to change their nappies."

Melissa grabs the phone, "Of cause my darlings, we'll be there as soon as we can."

And so, after getting presentably dressed and tossing clothing and hygiene products into our backpacks Char, Smithy, Melissa and I are speeding on the powerboat to Townsville. We just make the 4pm direct flight back to Melbourne.

"Melissa, did Tami say which townhouse they're celebrating in? Was it number six or seven?"

"Jules, they're across the driveway from each other. We can knock on both doors till we find them."

Both Melissa and Char are hugging their daughters, granddaughter and grandson. Tears are flowing. It's totally chaotic but luckily Tami's and Celeste's partners are also present and are trying to calm down the commotion. Smithy and I also give them all hugs. "Smithy, they'll be going on like this for ages. Shall we get a beer, there's the Elsternwick pub just around the corner."

"Good idea Jules but do my eyes look red and teary?"

"They do Smithy, but I got some tissues. You wipe mine and I'll wipe yours."

Smithy yells out, "Girls we're just going to do some outdoor meditation. We won't be long. I have the phone so you can always call."

Martin is still manager of the pub though bald and wrinkled so I didn't recognise him at first. We exchanged many stories and again we got our drinks for free. Martin says, "I'll call a taxi to get you home."

"It's, it's OK Martin, we've only got about 600m to walk. We'll be right but thanks for your concern."

Well, Smithy and I luckily were picked up by the local police force as we lay in a gutter and before any cars trying to park ran us over. No charges were reported as one of the officers was an elderly ex-military guy who Smithy knew well. They gave us a lift to the block of townhouses. Neither Char nor Melissa were impressed. We got a severe chiding. The explicatives used by them cannot be printed without violating censorship laws.

Melissa throws me the keys to townhouse 5. "Both of you sleep there tonight. Fabian is overseas so it is unoccupied. I will let you in as neither of you are in a condition to find the keyhole or type in the alarm code. And you better clean up after your stay."

There wasn't much to clean up as Smithy and I just plonked on the lounge room floor and went into a deep sleep. The next day, Smithy and I order lots of roses. They get delivered and we take them to apartment 6 and 7. The girls, our partners, forgive us for our drunken indiscretion.

The next 28 years pleasantly pass with occasional visits from our extended families. Sometimes we visit them and do our best to behave ourselves.

And so one year blends into another but luckily we've got the Internet to check what year it is but even that time has flown though the peptide is still working. Tami and Celeste and their partners have retired from Ai5 and have taken up volunteer jobs as peace emissaries in worn-torn countries, than that horrible phone call.

"Granny and grand-daddy we may need you back."

"Melissa, we're approaching our 90s. What do you think?"

"Jules, it will be exciting. We could get back for a short while and see the grandkids and their kids."

I look at my body in the mirror. A few bits sagging but most of the muscle mass is still intact. Time also seems to fly unlike when you're young and it seems to take forever to turn 18 and get your car driving licence. When you're learning or experiencing new things, time seems to slow down. It might be good to go back to Ai5 to stimulate our minds and make time slow down.

"Jules, we could just do the intel things on our computers whilst you jog on that running machine you purchased."

"Melissa we could just do more bedroom gymnastics, your passion level is getting low."

Needless to say, that was not a wise comment. Melissa spits at my face. So we're back to Ai5.

Tami's and Celeste's children, Stacy and Steven run the show now. It's still an all in the family organization, well at least the management is.

"Grandparents, would you like some sushi? It's going to be a long night. By the way, have you still got that rat that our mums talked about? Was its name Chloe?"

Chloe peeks outside my shirt.

"We sure have, and I need a small lab to keep her going. She needs the peptide and we do too. Chloe must be 70 yrs old."

"We want her granddad and grandmother. Why don't you take the peptide yourselves as you look like you could definitely use it."

"Stacy, it works differently on different species, and I still inject everyone every six months, but we definitely don't want the average rat living indefinitely, it would cause chaos to our farming industry; Chloe is one of a kind."

Stacy gently slaps me on the face – definitely a genetically inherited behaviour from her grandmother.

"Anyway, Melissa needs the peptide more than me."

I shouldn't have made that comment out loud. Melissa wacks me like you couldn't believe. She can still pack a punch. A minute later she comes over with an ice pack, hugging me and offering copious apologies. You'd think people near their 90s, wouldn't still carry on so physically this way, that kind of behaviour. Guess that's what keeps us young in attitude. The peptide just keeps the body from falling apart. You need both.

Meanwhile back at the library Chloe takes control of a new Rat Pack again. She is highly respected amongst her rat peers and human staff and gets fed the best French cheeses along with the peptide. She's still going strong. Stacy and Steven take her down to Elwood beach every night for her swim where in the summertime she still delights young kids. From what we can see on the videos taken by Stacy and Steven every kid in Elwood has a white rat and Chloe has plenty of company as she does her swimming.

After 7 days of celebrations, Stacy and Steven drive us to the airport. They have a six-seater van. After much waving, we depart from Melbourne and return to our island minus Chloe who was enticed to stay longer and train new recruits to the Rat Pack. She would get an exclusive flight back and be chauffeur driven. Both Melissa, Charmaine, Smithy and I yell out to the grandkids, "We're proud of you."

We never got any real work done during our 7 day stay back in Melbourne but we did a lot of talking. I think they just wanted to see us and explain how Ai5 has been turned around to be an ethical organization. We continue to communicate by video online with the kids, grandkids and the rat. Chloe stands up and claps her paws whilst Melissa and I clap our hands. We both miss the rat. Back at the island it's not the same without Chloe even though Melissa can be pretty ratty at times. Char and Smithy come back from shopping in Townville. They carry a cage. I put my glasses on. There's a white rat in the cage.

"You're birthday present Jules. You can call her Chloe2 but don't give her the peptide. They'd be no one to feed her when we cark it." I give Smithy a hug and stare at the inquisitive creature. I also hug Melissa and Char.

So dear readers, regarding our international security, well it's secure. Chloe was promoted to a Z and still going strong, teaching the other rats how to examine CCTV footage and look for patterns in data. She even got some crow birds hired because they're really smart and better than drones for overhead surveillance. Then there's a loud sound. Two helicopters are just making a landing. Out step Fabian and Lizzy from one copter and Magnus and Victor and their partners from the other, all carrying lots of bags of food and eskies. I look in amazement. There's more white hair and walking sticks than this island has ever seen before. It's going to be a long night. I better cook up some of that mushroom soup.

"Dad, can you just be normal for once? You're supposed to set an example, not behave like an old-age hippy."

"Fabian, this is the lifestyle we've chosen, and we only make the mushy soup for very special occasions. Besides when I was much younger, I was a very overly serious person and never had much fun. Now I'm just trying to balance the equation so to speak and achieve a final state equilibrium before I cark it."

"You're weird dad but we still care about you and your mental health."

"Fabian, I love you as do Magnus, Lizzy, and Melissa and possibly Char and Smithy."

Fabian doesn't reply, maybe he's confused, 2 out of 3 dads in the same location.

"Thanks, stepdad," Lizzy says and gives me a hug. The first time she didn't shut her eyes as if about to have a convulsive seizure when hugging. After dinner, we walk to the other side of the island, away from Charmaine's clients and all drink the soup around a campfire. We pass the bowl around and sip like in a Native American ritual which it sort of is.

"Jules, did you bring the defibrillator?" Asks Char.

"Yes, of cause, it's in my backpack and the batteries are fully charged."

And so the night begins. There are 10 aged, naked people running along the beach and diving into the water. Luckily, I also brought the mosquito repellent lotion as after the swim we all stare at the stars whilst lying on the beach and looking at the comets flying by whilst holding our partners' hands. No one mentions the new Covid-55 pandemic travel restrictions or the state of the economy. I guess that with their connections they have exemptions to visit. Chloe2 jumps on my chest and joins the pack.

So, another wonderful night ends, but we all didn't get much sleep that night, but the next day we all went to bed very early. "Melissa, I still love you and we didn't make that 50% statistic of partners who separate."

She turns towards me, "Jules, we still got time. The 50% doesn't expire at any particular date," she says in a serious voice but then winks. We're about to fall asleep on the sand, wrapped in each other's arms, two 90yr olds still very much in love.

It's 4 am and the crow birds are yelling 'uck, uck, uck'. Both Melissa and I awake. "Melissa, would you consider putting an 'f' in front of those crow bird calls:"

"Jules, why don't you just say it?"

"Melissa, let's do some bedroom cardio."

We stumble back along the sand to our condo. Our kids and grandkids would have a seizure if they saw. Melissa and I are really going for it. No need to worry about unintended pregnancies at our age, just cardiac seizures but what a better way to depart this world.

"Melissa, you are more autistic than I am."

"Thank you, Jules, I am more artistic than you and you can paint a mural on the ceiling again if you want."

It's best not to correct her interpretation and incur some injury. I just hug her tightly.   "Melissa, we are the luckiest people in the world," I whisper. "Do you want to continue with the bedroom gymnastics?"

"Where did you learn those techniques? Are you still learning from watching those dubious porn websites again?"

"No, I just vaguely remember from when I was young."

"Show me what you still got left." She says but then the phone rings.

"It's Lizzy on the cell-phone", Melissa whispers.

"Go for it mum. Once you're in you can never get out."

We're both not quite sure what Lizzy is referring to. It's open to many interpretations. We get dressed and wander to the seashore. The others are also brushing sand off their bodies and then dressing. They all stay another night in the condos but it's an early night, no more partying.

Smithy comes over to me. "Jules, you're in the condo with the loudspeaker and voice broadcasting system and you forgot to turn it off last night. It was broadcasting all over the island. We had a great laugh. Now can you tell me what those techniques are? I may try them with Charmaine," he laughs.

I can hear lots of groaning from the beach. Charmaine's clients must have been inspired by the accidental broadcast as well. "Smithy, I still got plenty of the peptide left which I was brewing to keep Chloe and Chloe2 alive way past their natural departure age. Shall we all take doses? It might continue to work for us as well."

"Jules, I'm happy with my life. Made it far longer than I ever expected, and the last 50 years have been good. I also suspect that you have been injecting us with the peptide when we are asleep as we look younger than our kids, but you should have asked us first. We may have said yes for a time, but we don't want to witness our kids and grandkids dying of old age."

Melissa and Charmaine must have overheard some of the conversation. They come over. "We can turn this island into an aged-care centre, and we can be principal residents, but you better not stare at any young nurses," they both say in unison. We both grab our partners and hug them. Smithy and I say in unison, "Sounds like a good idea."

I hold Melissa "We all have bonded, think alike and have similar emotional responses."

She jabs me in my ribs. "No more of that muchie soup."

"Melissa, for a granny you can still pack a punch but be careful at my age I'm fragile."

We all go back to our condos and Smithy must have turned on the broadcast system in his condo. Groans are streaming across the island again. I think Smithy and Charmaine are challenging us to a groan competition. "Melissa this could be a new Olympic Games sporting event, the longest, loudest groan so we have to train, let's go for it. I'm turning the broadcast system on full blast."

Melissa still has a highly competitive spirit so she agrees, but I should have checked the wind direction. The westerly wind was diverting the sound waves to the mainland. Twenty minutes later some police constables, armed with rifles arrive by motorboat and knock on our doors. We get dressed quickly, well not exactly dressed just towels and palm fonds covering the vital parts.

"Sir, we have to inspect the premises. There are complaints from the mainland about loud distressing noises coming from this island."

The police officers spend a few hours scouring the island. "Sirs and Madams, could you turn down the volume on those broadcasting devices? You're too old for that kind of stuff."

We do once we find the magnifying glasses and the instruction booklet for the broadcasters. The peptide doesn't seem to protect the eye retina from degenerating.

"Melissa what if you have a cardiac? I couldn't live without you."

"Jules, I hope you can still remember where those i5 cyanide pills are stored. I don't think they go off, but you should try one just to make sure they are still effective."

I grin, despite the possible dementia, she still seems to have a sense of humour, well I hope.

"Take, this tablet, it's a mega-dose of B vitamins. We have to start taking vitamins at our age."   In my slightly confused state of mind, I unquestionably swallow the tablet. An hour later I'm still alive but my pee is highly yellow, and Melissa watches me as I'm pissing. We never had a hang-up about bodily excretory functions unless they smell very bad but being mostly vegetarians, they don't. "Good colour Jules, you are going to live."

"Melissa, I dislike when someone has more of a sense of humour than me no matter how demented."

"Get used to it Jules, it's another challenge. Challenges keep us going."

After more bedroom theatrics I sneak down to the lab where the peptide is stored in a refrigerated device. There's plenty left for Chloe2. I grab some syringes and some peptide. I inject the dozing Melissa and then myself. Chole2 jumps on my chest. She gets injected too. She doesn't mind. She knows the ritual. I sneak into Charmaine's and Smithy's condo and inject them as well whilst they sleep. I keep injecting everyone every six months whilst they sleep. I've done that for over 40 years.

Fabian rings me. "Dad2, Chloe has stopped eating cheese and refuses to be injected with the peptide you send. Do you want to wave goodbye? We're on the Xoom network."

I call Melissa, Char and Smithy to come over to our condo. It's a sort of virtual interaction as our images are projected in 3-D. Chloe looks shrivelled up but still eventually manages to stand up on her two rat feet, after a few stumbling mishaps. "We love you, Chloe," we all yell out. The rat gives a sort of smile as she closes her eyes and fades onto the floor. We cry as we recount stories.

Ai5 arranged a funeral ceremony that was broadcasted on Xoom, though not quite a state funeral. Peter came back from overseas to attend. He is uncontrollably crying as we are too. Finally, the shoe size coffin gets lowered into the grave.

Another or so 20 years pass. Most of our friends have all passed away. We just seem to be attending online funerals as a social outlet and we are deeply saddened. I've lost count of how many years old we are: then, the tragic news on the 3-D TV device. 'Fabian Lemos and Lizzy Mosa have passed away within an hour of each over at the ripe old age of 94 and 92. They played a major influence in turning our OZ society into something positive and they will be very missed. A state funeral service will be held in their honour'.

"Oh f,,k, oh f..k, oh f..k, oh f..k." I wander around holding my head. I gave them the notes on how to manufacture the peptide. Why didn't they just do it and use it? Why didn't they? They could have still been with us."

Tami, Celeste and the grandkids ring, so do the great grandkids. I put the phone on broadcast so Charmaine and Smithy can hear as well as the now awake Melissa. There is much crying and sobbing over the visual phone device, over 6 hours' worth of crying. The floor is soaking in tears.

"Grandpa, if you keep on using that peptide to demethylate DNA you will all be very lonely as all family members pass away. You will be alone and that's worse than death plus if you made that peptide available to all people then the Earth couldn't survive. There are starving people in every country already. The Earth can't feed all those people who just refuse to call it quits."

A carefully tailored song blasts on the outdoor stereo system. That Godzilla device must still be listening. Smithy must have reconnected it. It's called Forever Young. Smithy comes over and hugs me. "We've had a great life, Jules." Melissa and Charmaine join in the hugging.

"What do you think guys? Do you want to live forever?"

"Jules it's been great 100-plus-something years that we've known each other," Smithy says whilst hugging Charmaine. Let's explore the universe. No more injecting us with the peptide. You think I didn't know what you were up to?"

"It's called a peptide Smithy, not a peptode."

Melissa calls out, "Jules, it's not a day to die. Make some of that special mushroom soup."

Instead of the magic mushroom ritual we all swallow the i5 agency cyanide tablets – the ones issued to stop you blabbering if being tortured for information. As far as I know, no one who worked for the i5 organizations has had to use the tablet. We could be the first.

Fifteen minutes later Smithy yells out. "Jules, they're not the cyanide tablets. They may be dried up Chloe2's poo droppings."

As we try to vomit, I look at Chloe2. She's standing on her to back feet and covering her eyes. She must have switched the tablets. She's just like the original Chloe.

"Melissa, you've just given me an idea for a James Bondwear movie script, Try to Die Another Day, maybe we can all write the script together and keep our minds off what has happened to our kids."

And so dear readers we forget about death for a while. We're writing the plot on our virtual 3-D screens. Chloe2 seems to check the grammar and spelling and waives her little arm when she finds an error. We're stuck here and tossing ideas around for the story. It takes our minds off the deaths.

I go back to the condo and find the plastic sachet containing the real cyanide pills and lay them on the table just in case we run out of ideas. Chloe2 grabs the sachet and rushes off. She comes back with dirty paws.

We all hug. "It wasn't meant to be," Melissa says. I kiss her.

"That was a good kiss, Wrinkly," she says.

I wink at the rat, Chloe2. She winks back.

"Melissa, should we go to the pet shop in Townsville and get her a rat male companion for Chloe2? We can't just have all the fun; the rat has to have some fun as well."

Chloe2 waives her paws. We all smile. Definitely, not a day to die; after eventually finding a suitable partner for Chloe, which she had to sniff and approve in the Townsville pet shop, we return home with the caged creature. The rats are going for it. We continue writing the story, interspersed with heated arguments about the plot.

"Jules, that never happened; you're embellishing it! It was supposed to be a truthful account of what happened. You're making yourself out as the hero," Smithy says with a distinct look of displeasure on his face.

"OK, Smithy, you write it! You're getting cranky. I hope you have some literary skills; in fact, we should all write our own versions."

"You're the cranky one, a cranky old man," Smithy replies.

"Smithy, who are you to talk? You want a crankiness competition? Who is more cranky?"

Months pass, and we've written many drafts and kept our dwindling minds occupied. Melissa and Charmaine collaborated, so they got the job done quicker. Smithy and I read their version. We both nodded our heads and commented in unison, "It's good, is there going to be a chapter 29?"

Melissa replies, "Jules, 29 is a prime number, and I know you like them, but Charmaine and I don't."

"Melissa, you're my prime number. How many years old are you now, I forgot? Is it 137? That's a prime number."

Melissa still can dish out a good right-hook but apologises afterwards. So we're all lying on the beach sipping glasses of wine and looking at the stars. A comet passes by and disintegrates in the atmosphere. "Wow, we all yell out."

Charmaine comments, "What if we convince the remaining grandkids and great-grandkids to take the peptide? Then we wouldn't have to watch them die of old age if they started using the peptide as well. We could all watch comets forever."

"Charmaine, everything dies, even comets and stars, besides the peptide only mildly protects against brain deterioration. I accidentally put the paper with the formula in the recycle bin. I never made a digital copy." OK, I lied. I still produce the peptide and inject all four of us every six months.

"Jules, you better get in touch with a funeral service business but let's keep watching comets while we can. Wow, that's a good one," she yells as a bright comet disintegrates in the sky.

"Let's jump into the sea and make the best of what days are left," Melissa says. We all strip clothing off and run into the water. I'm hugging Melissa, and Smithy is hugging Charmaine as we float around and splash each other. The rat and her rat partner join us.

So how do you end a story? A story that has a happy ending, Melissa has the answer.

"Jules, let's go back to the condo and do what our pet rats are going to do."

I kiss her, "You're so romantic. I'll race you back."

Unfortunately, or fortunately, I trip over a fallen palm tree fond and end with my face in the sand. I jokingly clutch my chest and do some contortions rolling around in the sand as if I'm having a cardio event. Melissa comes running over. "Jules, you've had a Viagra overdose. I'll carry you back to the condo." She heaves me up on her shoulder, and she's still quite strong. Charmaine and Smithy are looking on, seemingly distressed. I lift up my thumb and index finger in the shape of an 'O' and smile at them. I can hear Smithy ask, "Chars, would you do that for me?"

"Sure Smithy, get me the chain saw and I'll make sure that palm tree falls on your head. I may not be able to carry you, but I'll drag you back to the condo by your hair."

That Godzilla device must still be watching us. A pop song comes on the broadcast speakers. 'Old People just want to have Fun'. Melissa accidentally drops me to the ground with her arms swinging whilst listening to the song. Charmaine, Smithy, and Melissa help me up, and we continue wriggling to the music and having a great time.

The story sort of ends well, again, not quite I find the cyanide tablets that Chloe2 had buried in the sand. "Shall we do it and depart together? We've had a good life."

"Jules, there is an expiry date on those tablets, and they're covered in mould," Smithy says.

I pop a rather disgusting, mouldy-looking tablet in my mouth to set an example. Twenty-four hours later, it still hasn't worked. Back to writing, we may have to modify the ending to 'Try to Die Another Day'. For the moment, there's some more cardio to do on the dance floor, and the Godzilla device keeps on pumping out the music. 'Bury me Deep in Love'. It's Godzilla's favourite song. We may have to purchase her a companion; there's a Godzil on sale in the Townsville electronics store, which also sells a Russian version of cyanide tablets which claim to be corrosion-resistant. We'll save them for another day.

About the Author

Young Julian

Julian Lechmus has had varied life experiences, such as a period of time as a young hippy and artist, then working in science as a bio-chemist, in education teaching at TAFE and also in industry. In his retirement, creative writing gives him a great deal of pleasure, utilising his wide-ranging experiences. He balances his time with a fitness programme and involvement in community activities such as Neighbourhood Watch. Julian originally came from Melbourne, the location of this book, but now lives in Kangaroo Point, Queensland.

www.ingramcontent.com/pod-product-compliance
Lightning Source LLC
Chambersburg PA
CBHW050922030726
47503CB00007BB/2425